The Viscount Made Me Do It

"You are the only woman I can see."

Her face softened. "You shouldn't say such things."

"And I am not dallying with you. For you to even suggest it is an insult to us both." He barely contained the anger in his voice. How dare she believe that of him? Of herself. "You are not a woman a man trifles with. You are the kind of woman a man never wants to leave."

She stared at him. "That's ridiculous."

"Why?" He stepped closer, his pulse bounding strong and hard at the base of his neck.

"Because there can be nothing real between us."

"This feels very real to me."

"I am a laboring girl. A bonesetter. The daughter of foreign merchants. You are a viscount born into privilege. We could not be further apart. Oh!"

He swept her into his arms before she could finish her sentence. "What are you doing?" she asked breathlessly.

"Unless you tell me to stop, I am going to kiss you."

Also by Diana Quincy

Clandestine Affairs series
HER NIGHT WITH THE DUKE

Rebellious Brides series
SPY FALL
A LICENSE TO WED
FROM LONDON WITH LOVE
THE DUKE WHO RAVISHED ME

Accidental Peers series
COMPROMISING WILLA
SEDUCING CHARLOTTE
TEMPTING BELLA
ENGAGING THE EARL

Atlas Catesby Mysteries series
MURDER IN MAYFAIR
MURDER IN BLOOMSBURY
MURDER AT THE OPERA

THE VISCOUNT MADE ME DO IT

A Clandestine Affairs Novel

Diana Quincy

AVONBOOKS

An Imprint of HarperCollinsPublishers

THE VISCOUNT MADE ME DO IT. Copyright © 2021 by Dora Mekouar. All rights reserved. Printed in the United States of America. No part of this book may be used or reproduced in any manner whatsoever without written permission except in the case of brief quotations embodied in critical articles and reviews. For information, address HarperCollins Publishers, 195 Broadway, New York, NY 10007.

First Avon Books mass market printing: August 2021

Print Edition ISBN: 978-0-06-298681-8
Digital Edition ISBN: 978-0-06-298683-2

Cover design by Patricia Barrow
Cover illustration by Chris Cocozza

Avon, Avon & logo, and Avon Books & logo are registered trademarks of HarperCollins Publishers in the United States of America and other countries.

HarperCollins is a registered trademark of HarperCollins Publishers in the United States of America and other countries.

FIRST EDITION

21 22 23 24 25   QGM   10 9 8 7 6 5 4 3 2 1

To my Citi Fatima,
a fierce matriarch and shrewd businesswoman
who was way ahead of her time.

Chapter One

London
1816

Thomas Ellis, Viscount Griffin, was a haunted man.

His torment colored all his actions and influenced most of his daily decisions, including this afternoon's sojourn to the ancient coffeehouse off Red Lion Square. But the musty venue and acrid brew offered little escape from his troubles.

Until *she* walked in the door.

He noticed her at once. She was the sort of woman who commanded attention. Proud posture. Midnight eyes lined in black that gleamed with keen intelligence. An aura of intrigue trailed her like the tail of a comet.

"Here comes the quack!" The voice of a young buck one table over quivered with excitement.

"That's her," one of his companions, a boy with curling ginger hair, affirmed. "That's the bonesetter."

The third man at the table, a dandy with artfully tousled sandy hair, hurriedly pulled a white protective healing sleeve over one wrist and set his arm on the table before him.

"Over here, madam," one of the bucks called out before whispering to his friends, "How much blunt to do think she'll want to fix it?"

"She's a bonesetter like her quack father," responded the tadpole in the protective sleeve. "She'll try to get as much as she can. Grasping sorts, those foreigners."

As she drew nearer, Griff's pulse beat harder. Flawless tawny skin and firmly etched features were punctuated by a wide pink mouth that could make a man forget his troubles. Even when that man was Griff. Despite what happened to his parents. And the agony blasting through his arm—a memento from the war.

The woman's astute, thick-lashed gaze assessed the palpable sense of anticipation infusing the air. She addressed the pups in a calm, almost bored, manner.

"The boy who summoned me says somebody here has put out a bone." Her deep, raspy voice sent a blast of heat through Griff. "Who would that be?"

"I am Mansfield." The patient's eyes reflected excitement rather than the pain one might expect of an injured man. "I cannot move my wrist."

"I see." She removed her deep gray cloak to reveal a violet gown, its modest neckline made even more so by the snowy lace fichu tucked into the square neck of her bodice. A long golden necklace almost reached her trim waist. "What happened, Mr. Mansfield?"

"I fell."

"Allow me to have a look." Setting her wrap aside, the woman took the seat across from the young man and gently removed the protective covering from his wrist. From his vantage point, Griff couldn't make out any obvious signs of injury. The woman held the buck's forearm in one hand while testing the range of motion of the patient's wrist with the other.

"Does this hurt?" she inquired, her attention focused on the joint in question.

"Like the devil." He grinned over her head at his two companions but then seemed to remember himself and grimaced instead. "I believe I've put out my wrist."

She moved his wrist in the opposite direction. "And this? Any pain?"

"That is even worse." Mansfield raised his eyebrows at his companions, who watched raptly with barely contained grins.

She drew her hands away. "Please move your wrist to the best of your ability so that I might assess your range of motion."

"I fear I cannot." His eyes twinkled. "It's pure agony."

She asked more questions. Then she said, "I see what the problem is."

One of Mansfield's co-conspirators hovered close. "Do you?"

"Can you repair it?" asked the patient. "What do you think?"

"I think you are wasting my time."

"Really?" He smirked. "How so?"

Something ominous glittered in her midnight eyes. Griff almost felt sorry for the tadpole. The boy was too thick to realize he was outmatched.

"There *was* nothing wrong with you," she said.

Confusion filled Mansfield's face. "*Was*?"

"Was." Taking a firm hold of the whelp's forearm, she wrenched his wrist backward with a sudden, forceful jerk. "But now there is."

The pup shrieked and yanked his wrist away. "What the devil did you do?"

"Your wrist is dislocated." She stood and reached for her cloak, swinging it around her shoulders with the air of a conquering general.

"What did you do that for?" asked Mansfield's horrified friend. "He wasn't really hurt before you showed up."

"I abandoned a patient in need to attend to Mr. Mansfield," she said. "I do not appreciate having my time wasted."

"Good lord!" Mansfield moaned, cradling his wrist, his crimson face twisted in pain. "She's a witch."

"Wait!" Ginger Hair implored, raising his panicked voice to be heard over his whimpering friend. "You cannot leave Mansfield in this condition. Look at him! He is in terrible pain."

She brushed a cursory gaze over the flushed man hunching over his injured appendage. "If Mr. Mansfield wishes to have his wrist repaired, he may come and see me this afternoon."

Without another word or a backward glance, she departed in long, unladylike strides. The gleaming pale sapphire pendant swinging from the chain around her neck glittered, catching the light like a falling star.

Griff's gaze caught on the necklace. A sharp pain stabbed his chest. He almost slipped off the coffeehouse bench. He hadn't noted the pendant at first. But seeing that oval stone again catapulted him back fourteen years to the worst night of his life.

He knew that jewel.

Intimately.

The bonesetter was wearing the necklace ripped from his mother's neck the evening of her murder.

ELLIOT TOWNSEND, THE Duke of Huntington, frowned. "Are you sure your mother was wearing the necklace"— he paused—"on the evening in question?"

"Absolutely." Griff was still shaken. He'd come directly from the coffeehouse to Hunt's palatial home on St. James Place in Mayfair. The duke was Griff's closest friend. Truth be told, he was Griff's only true friend. Everyone else was just an acquaintance. Only Hunt was steadfast in his support at Harrow after the murders. Even now, Griff mostly kept to himself. He rarely came to London. Mingling with the ton was deuced awkward when half of society believed he'd murdered his parents.

"The necklace was taken that night. Mother wore it practically every day." Griff tried to keep his hand from trembling as he accepted a glass from Hunt. "But that's not the maddest part."

Hunt settled in an upholstered chair opposite his friend. "What's crazier than your mother's necklace turning up fourteen years after her death?"

"This." Griff withdrew a gold signet ring from his pocket and presented it on the palm of his hand for Hunt's inspection. The cool metal felt fire-hot against his skin.

"What's that?"

"My mother's ring." He stared at the ornately carved band and wondered who'd twisted it off the finger of a dead woman. "She was wearing it that night. It was also taken."

Hunt's brows shot up. "Where did you get it?"

"The ring was delivered to Ashby Manor several weeks ago. Of course, I wasn't there." Griff hadn't returned to the scene of the murders since the day his parents' corpses were sealed in the family vault. "It arrived by mail wrapped in a parcel addressed to me. Just the ring. No note. Nothing."

Hunt edged forward to examine the circular band. "Where was it sent from?"

"A post office off Red Lion Square. That's why I am in London. I went to the post office hoping to learn who sent it. But no one there remembered anything."

"That's quite the coincidence."

"My thoughts exactly." Trying to settle his nerves, Griff took a large gulp of whiskey. The liquid produced a satisfying burn down his throat and into his chest. "After fourteen years, someone in the vicinity of Red Lion Square sends me my mother's ring. And then today, in the same neighborhood, I see a woman wearing Mother's necklace."

"I suppose you intend to find the woman."

"I already have." He shifted, trying to make his injured arm more comfortable.

Hunt noticed. "How's your shoulder?"

"It's fine," Griff lied. "The woman with my mother's necklace is a bonesetter. The coffeehouse owner gave me her direction."

"A bonesetter? That doesn't bode well. She's most likely a fraud."

"Possibly."

"What do you intend to do? Ask her about it outright?"

"I can hardly ask a stranger why she's wearing stolen jewelry and expect an honest answer."

"From the expression on your face, I'd venture to guess that you already have a plan."

"Most definitely." Griff swallowed the last of his whiskey. "It's time to put this damned war injury to use."

"Did you keep your finger wet?" Hanna Zaydan asked her neighbor.

"Oh yes. I wrapped it in a bag of bran just as you instructed." Claudia Lockhart was the widowed proprietor of a nearby grocery store. "Are you certain you can fix it?"

"Yes," Hanna said. "The tissues around the joint should be softened by now."

Mrs. Lockhart watched Hanna gently unwind the wrapping around her injured middle finger. "I didn't realize you are treating patients."

"I am." Even though her family disapproved. "But mostly just friends and acquaintances." Hanna had refused to completely stop seeing patients after her father's death. She continued to treat them in Baba's old examining room at the rear of the narrow town house off Red Lion Square.

It wasn't easy, given that she shared the house with a revolving set of relatives—brothers, cousins, aunts and uncles—depending on who was in London at any given time. Right now, beyond the closed door, they could hear *Citi*, Hanna's grandmother, rattling around in the parlor.

"The doctor says the joint is enlarged and that I should apply iodine to it." The widow's words were punctuated by a long, heavy cough.

Holding Mrs. Lockhart's weathered hand in her palm, Hanna assessed the injury. "He's wrong."

"How can you be so sure?"

Hanna gave the finger a sudden violent wrench. A sharp crack, similar to the sound of cracking knuckles, rent the air.

Mrs. Lockhart yelped and yanked her hand away. "What in the world—"

"That should do it."

"Do what?"

"Your joint was out of place. I put it back in."

"You did?" Straightening up, Mrs. Lockhart gingerly tested the affected finger. To her obvious surprise, it moved easily.

"Any pain?" Hanna asked.

"None." The older woman repeatedly opened and closed her veiny hand. "Although your bedside manner does leave something to be desired, young lady."

"If I had warned you, you would have tensed up." Hanna disposed of the bag of bran. "You won't be needing this any longer."

Mrs. Lockhart stared at her moving hand in wonder. "I had no idea that you could truly cure me."

The older woman's frankness didn't offend Hanna. She'd learned early on that people came to bonesetters as a last resort after traditional medical treatment failed them.

"Have you decided to become a bonesetter just like your father?" Mrs. Lockhart asked.

"I *am* a bonesetter." Her mother and grandmother would be scandalized to hear her speak so. But Hanna couldn't deny her true calling any more than she could change the color of her eyes. "My father tried to teach me everything he knew. I worked by his side every day since I was a girl."

"I thought you were just his assistant."

"Eventually I became his apprentice. Papa said I had a natural talent for bonesetting."

"I agree with your father." Mrs. Lockhart's kind words ended in another protracted cough.

"One day I will open a dispensary where patients can come to be treated." A place outside of her home, away from her family.

Mrs. Lockhart's brows went up. "You intend to become a woman of business?"

Hanna drew her shoulders back, bracing for the older woman's censure. "I wish to be able to treat patients unhindered by my family."

But Mrs. Lockhart surprised her. "It is always best for a woman to be able to look after herself. I'm a widow with no children. If my late husband hadn't left the grocery to me, I would be a pauper dependent upon the generosity of relatives and strangers."

"Mama and *Citi* do not approve of my work. They prefer that I wed."

"You cannot blame them. Marriage secures a girl's future." Mrs. Lockhart patted Hanna's hand. "But if you ever open that dispensary of yours, I shall be your first patient."

Hanna helped the older woman off the examining table. "It's just a dream." She and her friend Evan Bridges, the neighborhood physician, often talked of opening a clinic, but they lacked the funds.

She escorted her patient to the front door. "Get that cough looked after." After they said their goodbyes, Hanna headed back to Baba's office but was interrupted by a knock at the door. She returned to answer it.

"Did you forget something?" Hanna asked as she pulled the front door open.

But it wasn't Mrs. Lockhart.

Instead, she found herself staring at a well-built man of average height clad in a crisply tailored navy overcoat. He gazed down, the rim of his black beaver hat obscuring his face. He slowly lifted his chin, revealing an elegant face punctuated by a distinct nose and thin, bow-shaped lips.

Their gazes met, and Hanna found herself staring into hooded steel-blue eyes that reminded her of a cold winter morning. His was not a welcoming visage, but something inside her chest twitched.

"Are you the bonesetter?" The words were clipped.

Unaccountably, Hanna flushed. "I am."

"I am Griffin. I require your services."

Chapter Two

$\mathscr{H}$anna's new patient was in tremendous pain.

She couldn't send him away. Even though she usually only treated people that she knew or were referred by a trusted source. Inviting strangers into one's home came with risks, the most daunting being her grandmother's death stare.

"Please have a seat," Hanna said when they reached Baba's office. "I am Mrs. Zaydan."

Presenting herself as a *Mrs.* invited respectability. People tended to make scurrilous assumptions about a female who put her hands on male patients. Her family would not abide any impropriety. At the first hint of scandal, Mama and *Citi* would forbid her from seeing any patients at all.

Settling behind Baba's desk, she reached for her wood-cased pencil. "Your name, please. I believe you said *Griffin*? Mr. Griffin?"

He paused. "Erm . . . Mr. Thomas. My name is Griffin Thomas." He spoke in frosty, polished tones. Definitely a toff.

She recorded his name in Baba's old ledger. It was

a familiar, even comforting, task. She'd always taken down her father's medical notes. "How long have you been in pain?"

"Why do you assume I am in pain?" He asked the question as though she'd insulted him.

"I am a healer. It is obvious." There were clues he could not hide: fine lines at the corner of his hooded, elongated eyes and the dark smudges beneath them. The pinched lips and grooves bracketing his mouth spoke of strain and lack of sleep.

"Too many patients hide their discomfort," she continued. "I cannot help a patient who will not truthfully reveal what ails him."

He bristled, a muscle spasming high on his right cheek. He wore a day-old beard that prickled over a precise jaw that could have been shaped by a glass cutter. "I see no point in bothering other people with my discomfort."

"How long has your arm been paining you?"

"For two years. Since I fell from my mount. Or, rather, since the animal was shot out from under me."

She looked up from Baba's ledger. "You are a soldier?"

"I was. Briefly. I was injured during my very first battlefield engagement, so I can hardly say that I saw combat."

"Your injured shoulder suggests otherwise."

He ignored her remark. "I returned home after the accident. I am of little use in battle with my arm as it is. I can no longer ride the way I used to."

"That must be difficult."

"I survived." His cool tone discouraged empathy. Yet Hanna detected a tinge of sadness in his guarded gaze. "Many men . . . and others . . . who should be alive are no longer with us. Can you cure me?"

It was obvious from the way he asked the question—with an arrogant condescension that he barely bothered to hide—that her new patient doubted Hanna's abilities.

"I shall try my best." Mr. Thomas was not Hanna's first skeptical patient and would not be her last. "Please remove your tailcoat, waistcoat and shirt."

Surprise stamped his angular face. "I beg your pardon?"

Hanna stood. "I will need to examine you to determine the extent of your injury." She crossed over to the porcelain bowl containing fresh water and bathed her hands. Out of the corner of her eye she saw him stand and remove his cravat. She busied herself with drying her hands until Mr. Thomas was bare from the waist up.

Hanna faced her patient. Despite any physical limitations, he possessed an athletic physique. His wiry body was powerfully cut, as though someone had taken a knife to it, carving generous shoulders, a sculpted abdomen and streamlined hips. His only physical imperfection was his slightly withered left arm, and an odd bend at the elbow that made the limb appear deformed.

Her gaze dipped to the smattering of hair that dusted Mr. Thomas's ridged stomach before disappearing into the waistband of his trousers. Divested of half of his clothing, it was easy to discern the muscular curve of Mr. Thomas's buttocks and the bulge at the apex of his strong thighs.

"Should I sit or remain standing?" he asked coldly.

Heat rose on Hanna's cheeks. Had she been staring? "Yes, certainly."

"Certainly stand or certainly sit?"

"Remain standing for now. And then I will ask you to sit upon the examining table." She used her most authoritative voice, shoving aside her very inappropriate interest in Mr. Thomas's half-naked body.

She silently admonished herself. Why was she being a *habla*? Only an idiot would behave as Hanna was at the moment. It wasn't as though she'd never seen a man in dishabille before. She'd lost count of how many partially disrobed male patients she'd treated while working alongside Baba.

Granted, none of them were blessed with Mr. Thomas's extraordinary physique. Still, his haughty manner certainly did not invite familiarity. Besides, she was a healer, and he her patient. Hanna was accustomed to quashing her feminine longings. Such urges had no place in the life of a bonesetter who could never marry.

"Now"—she issued her usual advance warning—"I am going to put my hands on you as part of my examination."

"Do your worst."

She gently handled the affected wrist, testing mobility, probing it with as light a touch as she could. His skin was warm, the dusting of hair along his arm

springy and gently abrasive under her gliding fingers. His scent, of shaving soap and freshly bathed male skin, filled the air. The office felt uncomfortably warm.

"Well," he asked tersely, "what is your assessment?"

"Your wrist is terribly affected."

"Yes, I am aware." Again that barely veiled skepticism.

She ignored it. "A callus has formed in your elbow."

"How does that signify?"

Her hands slid up his arm. "Your elbow is out of joint. This sort of injury frequently occurs when you land on an outstretched hand during a fall, which I suspect occurred when you fell from your mount. Please sit on the examining table."

When he complied, she inched closer to inspect his shoulder. With him seated on the table, they were almost of a height. Their heads were bowed in proximity, in the way of intimates sharing a secret. He smelled far more pleasant than most of her male patients, who were primarily stevedores, laborers and others who did not bathe regularly.

"Your shoulder has been driven forward," she said. "When the elbow joint is out of place, it can cause damage to other parts of the arm."

"That does not sound promising."

It was not. Mr. Thomas's arm was a mess. "If I may speak plainly?"

He lifted his chin so that he was peering down his distinct nose at her. "Please do."

"The major joints in your arm are out of place."

Hanna could not even begin to imagine how Mr. Thomas had borne the pain for so long. Each of his injuries alone was significant; the pain from all three must be almost unbearable. "That lack of proper alignment is the source of your considerable discomfort."

"Can you make me better?"

She straightened her spine. "I would not be much of a bonesetter if I could not."

As THE BONESETTER slid soft hands along Griff's sensitized skin, it crossed his mind that she might actually be a whore. A damned good one, too, given the way his body reacted.

She almost made him forget his purpose for seeking her out. He certainly didn't believe she could cure him. Her performance at the coffeehouse demonstrated she knew enough about joints to dislocate them at will. But when it came to his own injury, Griff doubted she would succeed where London's finest physicians had failed.

The bonesetter resided in a modest but comfortable house off Red Lion Square, a long narrow park best known for the stone watchhouses at each corner. Once a rubbish-filled dumping ground that attracted thieves and other criminals, the renovated square was on its way to becoming fashionable. The bonesetter's terraced home, situated on a lane off the square, was increasingly surrounded by respectable neighbors such as doctors, shopkeepers, solicitors and watchmakers.

But no respectable woman of Griff's acquaintance would ever be caught alone with a bare-chested stranger in a closed-door chamber. Women of a certain class did not touch a man the way the bonesetter's confident fingers explored his skin. He could not imagine her husband, whoever he was, standing idly by while his very attractive wife ran her hands all over strange men.

"How did you hear about me?" she inquired as her warm fingers roamed his chest.

"From the proprietor of the coffeehouse at the end of the lane."

She pressed a point in his elbow. "Does this hurt?"

He clenched his jaw. "Yes."

Her fingers shifted. "And this?"

He willed himself not to flinch. "That is even worse."

Griff surreptitiously studied the bonesetter's face. Smooth olive skin, wide-angled cheeks and a generous mouth. She'd pulled her hair into a tight bun at the nape of her neck. The style emphasized the V-shaped point in her hairline at the center of her forehead. Beneath her white apron was a simple, long-sleeved deep burgundy gown. A fichu tucked into the square neckline preserved her modesty. She wore no jewelry.

Perhaps she was trying to play down her substantial sexual appeal. It wasn't working. Her touch had an alarmingly arousing effect on him.

To blunt the unwelcome bodily stirrings, Griff tore his attention away from the bonesetter to survey her examining room: the desk, one comfortably deep chair tucked by one of two sashed windows, and two hardback chairs opposite the desk. The lone embellishment on the wall was a rather macabre sketch of a skeleton. There was no sign of his mother's necklace.

"Can you raise your arm?" she inquired.

"Only a little."

"Could you show me? I wish to observe what range of motion you do have, however limited it might be." Griff did as she asked. He raised his arm a few inches and froze when the pain became too much to bear. She shifted around to run her fingers along the back of his shoulder.

Maybe she'd fooled her own family into believing she was some sort of doctoress. Griff had to admit it was a clever setup. If she was a whore, Mrs. Zaydan could service clients under the guise of semirespectability. Bonesetters might be quacks, but society still viewed them more favorably than prostitutes.

"You may lower your arm." She stood so close, just inches away. Her feminine scent, something lemony, wafted under his nose.

Maybe there was no husband. Perhaps this was part of her technique, pretending to examine a man while purposely exciting him. Her straightforward, almost stern, demeanor might very well be part of her performance. It definitely had an impact. Griff braced for her to ask for a small fortune to fix his arm. He was tempted to pay her asking price to have those clever hands continue their exploration.

Regrettably, her hands fell away. "You may dress now." She returned to her desk to scribble in her ledger.

Pulling on his shirt, Griff watched the bonesetter

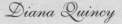

from the corner of his eye. He didn't know what to make of her. She certainly acted as if she knew what she was about. If this was a performance, Mrs. Zaydan ought to take her talents to Covent Garden.

Once dressed, Griff took a seat opposite her desk. "Can you do anything about my injury?"

She didn't look up from her writing. "Yes."

"How can you be certain?"

"I am a bonesetter." She regarded him with serious, kohl-rimmed eyes. "I fix broken bones and dislocations. And I am quite good at it."

She radiated such confidence that Griff almost took the woman at her word. Even though he knew she was a swindler. All bonesetters were. "Over the past two years, I have visited the first physicians and surgeons of the day. None of them have been able to mend my arm."

"They are not bonesetters. It takes a particular skill and years of training to treat injuries such as yours." She was hardly ancient. The bonesetter couldn't be more than five-and-twenty, although her brisk, humorless manner made her seem older.

"What do you propose?"

"Treatment that will take anywhere from a fortnight to one month."

"What will that involve?"

"A great deal of pulling, twisting and stretching. And, of course, a potent oil."

Of course. She'd arrived at the heart of her scheme. "I suppose you sell this oil."

"No, indeed. You may purchase neatsfoot oil at the

druggist, but the embrocation will cost half as much if you go to a tripe shop on Tottenham Court Road."

His lip curled. "Neatsfoot oil?"

"It is an oil extracted from the shinbones and feet of cattle," she explained patiently.

"I know what it is. Am I meant to imbibe this oil?"

She laughed as if he were the ridiculous party. "No, indeed. It is an ointment that must be rubbed into the shoulder daily to soften the tissues in preparation for my manipulation. Morning and night. Use hard friction, rub as vigorously as you can tolerate."

"What will you charge for this . . . treatment?"

He expected her to demand an outlandish price, four pounds, maybe five.

"I will require two guineas."

"Per session?"

"In totality." She came to her feet. "Our appointment is at an end. I have another patient to see."

Griff blinked. She hadn't asked for a fortune. Perhaps this was all part of the ruse. Maybe she'd ask for more money once he was deep in treatment.

"Now, if you please." Her words had an edge. The bonesetter was not a patient woman. "It is time for my next appointment."

Griff reluctantly came to his feet. He wanted more time with this woman, his only lead after all these years into who killed his parents. "When shall I return?"

"In a week's time. Until then, please apply the neatsfoot oil daily."

"And when I come back?"

"I will begin the process of setting your body back to rights."

She said it with such conviction that Griff almost believed her.

Almost.

HANNA USHERED MR. Thomas out of her office. Unfortunately, there was no avoiding *Citi*. The front door was by the parlor where the old woman perpetually perched in her worn leather chair by the hearth. The mouthpiece connected to her hookah dangled from the side of her mouth.

The patient paused on his way out. "Good day, madam," he said politely to *Citi*.

Surrounded by a silvery haze of smoke, her grandmother raised a corner of her upper lip in response. *Citi*'s face was always pursed in a permanent scowl, even when she did not disdain you. "*Yikhrib baitak*," she muttered in Arabic. "May God destroy your house."

Mr. Thomas gave *Citi* a slight bow. "What did she say?" he asked, his lips curving into an arctic half smile.

Hanna avoided looking at her grandmother. "She hopes God will bless your house."

"That is very kind of you," Mr. Thomas responded to *Citi*. "And I wish the same for you."

The old woman glared at him as she took a heavy puff of the water pipe. A crosshatch of lines framed her thin lips. "*Maleun*. I don't trust him," she responded, still speaking in Arabic. "He's playing with you."

Hanna ushered Mr. Thomas out and then rejoined her frowning grandmother.

"You are an unmarried girl." *Citi* pounced the moment Hanna returned. "And you were alone in a room with a strange man? Where is Lucy?" Mama and *Citi* insisted that their maid of all work be present whenever Hanna treated a male patient.

"She was at the store."

"*Abe, Citi, abe.*"

"How can helping people be shameful? All I did was treat a patient with a badly injured shoulder. Why do you think your son taught me the art of bonesetting? Baba wanted me to help people."

"My son—*Allah yerhamo*, may God have mercy on his soul—was too easy on his daughters. I was married at fourteen. No one asked for my opinion. I'd only met your grandfather once. But I did my duty." *Citi* shook her head. "You are twenty-six. So old. *Raahut alaikey.* You turned down too many good offers from nice Arab boys. The only option now is to wed a widower who needs a wife to look after his children."

"If I'm too old to attract a husband and time has truly passed me by, then I shall be a spinster. I'll be able to continue helping people without anyone telling me what I can and can't do."

Citi harrumphed. "*Wallahi,* I swear to God, talking to you is impossible. In my generation, girls listened to their elders."

Hanna bent to kiss her grandmother's weathered cheek. "You do deserve a more obedient granddaughter, but you shall just have to make do with me."

"I don't know what I did in my life to deserve this." Shaking her head, *Citi* settled back in her worn leather chair and reached for her hookah, effectively dismissing Hanna.

Seizing her chance to escape, Hanna stole away to Baba's office to develop a detailed treatment plan for her new patient.

Chapter Three

"Whatever possessed you to go and see a bonesetter?" asked Dr. Norman Pratt that evening at supper with Griff. "They're cheats of the very worst sort who prey on the sick and the desperate."

"I was curious." Griff opted against being completely honest with the man who'd been a surrogate father to him since his parents' deaths. Norman would not approve of Griff's searching for their killer. He encouraged Griff not to dwell on the murders. *You cannot move forward if you are stuck in the past.*

"I hope you're not letting her treat you." Norman peered at Griff over the bridge of his round wire spectacles. "Heed me on this. Have I ever steered you wrong?"

"Never." Griff felt a rush of gratitude for his father's cousin, a man who'd stood by him even when his own sisters had not. "Thank goodness Papa designated you as my guardian in his will."

Norman's craggy face softened. "You were always a good lad. And a strong one. You'd have eventually found your way."

"I'm not so certain."

"I am," Norman said firmly.

Griff stared into his half-empty wineglass. "It is not as though Maria, Dorcas or Winifred were clamoring to take me in."

After the deaths, Griff had assumed he'd live with one of his three older sisters, all of whom were wed with families of their own. But not one of them, not even his favorite sister, Dorcas, volunteered. Even now, Griff never saw them. He'd lost his entire family on one devastating evening fourteen years ago.

"Your father, Jeffrey, was not only my cousin but my closest friend," Norman said. "There is nothing I would not do for him. Or for his son."

"I am grateful."

"It was my duty." Norman's knife scraped the porcelain plate as he cut his fowl. "As to this bonesetter, you are a grown man, and I would not presume to tell you what to do. But I must warn you that people of that sort are known to trade on the weakness and desperation of the poor and ignorant."

Griff had every reason to trust Norman's word. The man served as lead physician at the local charity hospital. He devoted his life to caring for the sick and less fortunate. They quieted for a moment as Annie, the young daughter of Norman's housekeeper, appeared to refill their glasses.

"Thank you, Annie," Norman said. The girl was about twelve and walked with her body tilted to one side.

"Is there nothing to be done for her back?" Griff asked once the girl was gone.

"It's a curvature of the spine, a deformity that cannot be helped," Norman said absently while applying himself to his food.

"Have you heard of Mrs. Zaydan?"

Norman shrugged. "Only by reputation. I understand the chit learned chicanery at her father's knee. It appears she is carrying on the family swindle."

Griff wouldn't allow Mrs. Zaydan to do further damage to his shoulder, but he needed to know why she possessed his mother's necklace. "I've nothing to lose. I've seen the best doctors—present company included."

Empathy lined Norman's face. "The muscles in your shoulder have been permanently strained. It is unfortunate that you are in pain, but it will eventually repair itself."

"It's been two years. Maybe I need a magic spell to speed the healing along."

"Your recovery is taking more time than I expected. I suppose rheumatism must be considered. Or possibly neuralgia."

"I know the former is a disease of the joints, but dare I ask what, precisely, is neuralgia?"

"It is nerve pain. The cause is often unknown."

Griff swallowed the last of his wine. "That doesn't sound very encouraging."

Norman studied Griff's face. "What aren't you telling me?"

Griff kept his focus on his food, partridges in white sauce. "What do you mean?"

"You are up to something. I know you too well. Is there more to this business with the bonesetter than you are saying?"

Griff paused, eager to divert the conversation. "The bonesetter is rather . . . appealing."

Norman's eyes widened. "You want to bed her."

"She is rather comely." It wasn't a lie. The bonesetter was extraordinarily attractive, but the main thing Griff wanted from her was answers.

"Your carnal interests run toward the exotic, do they?" Norman lounged back in his chair, an amused expression lighting his face. "Where did she examine your injury? In her bedchamber?"

"In an examination room."

"Were you alone together?"

"Yes."

Norman barked a laugh. "Not exactly respectable, is she? I am beginning to see the full picture. By all means, swive her if you like. That's what those sorts of women are for."

Griff's forehead puckered. "'Those sorts of women'?"

"The laboring classes. She's a Levantine as I understand it. Comes from a family of Arab cotton traders who operate out of Manchester." Norman interlocked his fingers and rested his joined hands on his chest. "Enjoy her charms, son, just don't allow her to treat your shoulder. God only knows what damage she could cause."

Griff couldn't imagine being in worse agony than

he was at the moment. He felt like an invading army was slowly taking over his body. With each passing day, it became harder to remember a life free of physical pain.

He pushed away from the table. "I'm for my bed." He contemplated how many glasses of brandy it would take to blunt the throbbing in his shoulder long enough for him to fall asleep. He couldn't remember the last time he'd slept through the night.

"So early? But we haven't even had our port yet."

"It's been a long day."

"Is it your shoulder? Let me give you a dose of laudanum to ease your discomfort," Norman offered, not for the first time.

"The last thing I need is to become an opium eater. I've seen what it can do to a man." More than one of his fellow soldiers had turned to opium to dull their pain. As a result, too many became insensible and dependent on the substance.

"Drinking yourself to sleep is better?" Norman asked.

"Not better. Just more manageable."

GRIFF SLEPT IN the bedchamber that had been his ever since Norman became his guardian.

Haven House, the family townhome on Cavendish Square, had been shuttered immediately after the murders and remained so, except for a skeletal staff that maintained the residence. Griff spent most of his time at Bell Cottage, a minor family property in Devon that he'd never visited before the murders. The modest house suited him primarily because it held no happy or tragic family memories. On the rare occasion he came to London, Griff stayed with his former guardian.

Climbing into bed, Griff poured a generous amount of brandy down his throat and thought of the bonesetter. Her eyes were remarkable, as black as coal, her hair a beguiling, matching shiny sable. Her hands were precise and confident, her unadorned fingers topped by clean, trim nails. Remembering the feel of those clever fingers gliding over his skin, he slipped his good arm under the counterpane. Closing his eyes, he pictured the woman taking him in hand and stroking him with determined but gentle strength.

He drifted off but awoke sometime later to the sound of barking. Griff leaped up to protect himself, fear slicing through him like a guillotine. A pack of snarling bulldogs charged him. He tried to beat them off with a club, his left arm hanging useless by his side. His heart slammed against his ribs so hard that it hurt. The wild beasts closed in, growling and salivating. One of the animals suddenly developed the head of a snake. The creature whipped forward and latched its fangs into Griff's useless arm.

Griff came awake with a start, his nightshirt damp, his heart beating wildly. It took him a moment to orient himself, to realize he'd had another of the frightful dreams that plagued him almost nightly.

Forcing himself to relax back against the feather pillow, his mind raced with the same thoughts that often consumed him on sleepless evenings. Would

Mother and Father still be alive if it weren't for him? His sisters' continued absence spoke volumes about what they thought. Maria, Winifred and Dorcas must believe the rumors. Nothing else could explain their silence. Like everyone else, they didn't believe he'd slept through the violent and noisy murders of their parents.

Because he hadn't.

The agony in Griff's left arm ratcheted up. He gritted his teeth to keep from making a sound. He was accustomed to suffering quietly, retreating to his bedchamber when the torment became almost too much to bear. He rarely accepted invitations. Not only because of the rumors of his involvement in the murders but also because he preferred to deal with his affliction in private.

Griff closed his eyes. The lids burned against his eyeballs. The result of too many sleepless nights. This wasn't much of a life. For the first time in two years, Griff seriously contemplated taking extreme measures to ease his suffering. More than one doctor had suggested amputation, but Griff hadn't seriously contemplated such drastic action. Maybe it was time to face reality. His arm was of no use to him. It was nothing but a source of torment.

He took a deep breath and tried to clear his mind of dark thoughts. Surely his situation would not appear as grim in the morning.

SHE WAS GOING to kill him. The bonesetter spent the initial half hour of Griff's first scheduled appointment rubbing an embrocation into his shoulder and massaging the injury with the strength of a stevedore.

She stretched. She pulled. She twisted.

Seated shirtless on a three-legged round wooden stool, Griff bit his lip to keep from crying out. Yet, despite the torment, his body still noted her nearness. Her lemon scent, combined with the slightest note of exertion, washed over him. "Are you certain you should rub so hard?"

"Quite certain." Her focus remained on her task as her hands roamed purposefully over his muscles. Her hands were not thin and delicate. They were strong and determined. Capable. "The tissues around your shoulder have lost their natural softness and flexibility."

Beneath a pristine white apron, she wore another modest gown. The garment was yellow and square-necked, with a plain white scarf tucked into her décolletage. On any other woman the ensemble might appear dowdy. But not on the bonesetter.

They were not alone this time. A young servant girl stood quietly by the door.

"Before I can mobilize the joint," the bonesetter continued, "the tissue that's keeping the joint from being properly aligned must be loosened."

"At this rate, you'll loosen the muscle right off my shoulder," he muttered mostly to himself.

She attacked his poor flesh again, edging around his seated body as she worked. Her skirts brushed against his arm, and he got a fleeting sense of the curve of her hip hidden beneath. The world swirled a little. Griff couldn't discern whether the pain or the bonesetter's proximity made him dizzy.

She dropped her hands. "Now, raise your arm as if you are a pupil in class waiting to be called on."

"I have been told to keep my arm still while it healed."

She scoffed. "Not moving your arm worsens the injury." Her words were brisk. A strand of glistening dark hair had escaped its pins, sweeping enticingly over one kohled eye. "Disfunction, pain and stiffness are the result of keeping your arm still."

He attempted to do as she asked. To Griff's surprise, he managed to lift his arm higher than usual before the discomfort became unbearable. "That's the best I can do."

"Very well." Her warm hand settled on his bare shoulder, while the other gently cradled his elbow. "Now let's pull your arm in front of you, across your chest."

"That's impossible. I told—" He clenched his teeth as she moved his arm across his chest. She repeated both motions a few times, first raising his arm and then gently crossing it over his chest while Griff tried not to black out.

After a few minutes, she spoke again. "You are ready."

He tensed. "Ready for what?"

She dug her thumb into his shoulder joint. "Does this hurt?"

"Yes." Griff's gaze followed the V in her hairline

down to the angle of her cheek and farther still to her plump mouth. She bit the corner of that plush lower lip when she concentrated. "It hurts so much so that I'm fairly close to calling out for my mama."

Her mouth quirked. Satisfaction rippled through him at having almost drawn a smile from the stern taskmaster. Without a word of warning, she gave his arm two turns and twisted it around in its socket.

Pain exploded in his shoulder. Griff blurted out a string of colorful curses no gentleman should ever utter in the presence of a female. "Goddammit, woman! Are you trying to kill me?"

"No, indeed." She stepped away, her cheeks flushed, a satisfied smile adorning her striking face. "How is your shoulder?"

"How do you expect?" he snapped. Griff's ire was mostly directed at himself. He'd been too busy ogling the bonesetter to worry about her doing damage to his arm. "You've likely caused irreversible harm." He gingerly moved his shoulder, afraid to discover just how seriously she'd mangled it.

To his surprise, his arm moved easily in the socket. He blinked, momentarily disoriented. Then he dared raise his arm as she had a short while ago. It took him a moment to register the near absence of pain in the joint. He crossed his arm over his chest. His elbow and wrist still throbbed. But his shoulder, although sore, was blissfully quiet.

"What did you just do?" he asked. "Surely, it's not possible—"

"It certainly is possible." The bonesetter was at the

porcelain bowl rinsing her hands. "Your shoulder was out of joint. I put it back in."

"I cannot believe it." He circled his arm above his head and behind him. Some discomfort remained, the joint felt stiff, but it had been forever since he'd been able to move his arm from the shoulder with such ease.

"The shoulder joint will be somewhat rigid for the next fortnight or so. I shall suggest some gentle exercises for you to do on your own."

She continued with the instructions, but Griff barely heard her. What had just happened? He shook his head, unable to process the absence of agonizing shoulder pain that had plagued him for two years.

"Extraordinary. I don't know how to thank you."

"Payment in full once all services are rendered will be all the thanks I need."

Still in partial disbelief, Griff stood and reached for his shirt, pulling it over his head. He caught her gaze moving over his torso before she blinked away. *She liked what she saw.* Griff forced himself to remember that the bonesetter was married and he had a serious purpose for being here. He needed to keep his thoughts out of his trousers.

"How did you manage to repair my shoulder?" he asked to distract from any indecent thoughts.

"The art of bonesetting might not be taught in schools," she said briskly, "but it is as old as Hippocrates."

"Where did you learn the . . . erm . . . art?"

"From my father." She reached for a cloth to dry her hands. "The rest of our relatives are in textiles.

Both sides of the family, the Zaydans and the Atwans, are prominent cotton merchants in Manchester. Our primary enterprise is exporting cotton to the Levant."

"But not you."

"Nor my father nor his father before him. Beginning with my great-grandfather, I come from a long line of bonesetters." She lifted her chin. "I practice an art as old as civilization itself."

"I hadn't realized." He'd assumed that bonesetting was one grand swindle.

She settled behind her desk. "Next, we shall work on your wrist. And after that, your elbow."

"And in the meantime?" he asked, trying to manufacture a reason to prolong their conversation.

"Rub neatsfoot oil into your wrist just as you did for your shoulder. When you return next week, I shall put your wrist back in as well." She reached for her pencil, opened her ledger and began scribbling some notes on the page. "Good day, Mr. Thomas."

Disappointment flooded him. He wanted to stay and talk to her. The bonesetter had succeeded in eliminating the blinding pain that racked his shoulder for two years. But she did not appear to be in any mood to celebrate. Or to have anything further to do with him.

Griff paused. "Just a few days ago, I seriously considered having my arm removed. Now, thanks to you . . ." His throat swelled, making it difficult for him to complete the sentence.

She looked up, her face softening when she registered his emotional state. "Mr. Thomas, I am a healer." Compassion lit her eyes. "You owe me no further thanks for doing what I am trained to do. I help people. It is my work and my duty."

He took in the full extent of the bonesetter's beauty. Smooth skin draped over magnificent cheekbones flushed from exerting herself on his behalf. He could stare at her forever. Her husband was a fortunate bastard. "I just didn't imagine for a moment—"

"That I could help you?" She smiled. It was the first time he'd witnessed a true smile from her, and it animated her entire face. Her eyes came alive, throwing aside the curtain that normally shielded her true emotions.

"You're not offended?" he asked.

"I am well aware that many people view bonesetters as charlatans."

"I should think you'd resent that."

"Physicians and surgeons put themselves above people such as myself. I have no formal institutional training. As a woman, that avenue remains closed to me. The skills I've acquired were handed down through the generations."

"You could help so many. If only they knew." *If only Norman understood.*

"I do help them now." A muscle ticked in her jaw. "But I confess it is not easy when the traditional medical community does its best to frighten patients away from bonesetters."

Frustration rippled through Griff. If he'd come to her directly after the accident, he might have avoided two years of misery. "I will recommend your services to those of my acquaintance."

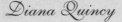

"As you wish," she said, but he saw that his words pleased her.

Her eyes met his. And caught. Her pupils widened. Electricity arced between them. The jolt struck Griff like a thunderclap. Need, potent and unexpected, exploded in his veins.

Alarm glinted the healer's gaze. She felt it, too. This buzz of seductive energy zipping between them. She hastily blinked away. Putting her back to him, she returned to the protection of her desk. Picking up her pencil with a trembling hand, she resumed writing her notes. "Until next week, then, Mr. Thomas."

She did not look up while Griff followed the servant out of her examining room.

Chapter Four

 $\mathcal{W}$hat use would I be on the hospital board of governors?" Griff asked Norman. "I don't know the first thing about managing a hospital."

"Most governors don't. You wouldn't be expected to do much." Norman watched Griff massage neatsfoot oil into his wrist. "What the devil are you doing?"

"What does it look like? I'm rubbing this ointment into my wrist."

"Whatever for?"

"It relieves some of the pain." Given Norman's disapproval of the bonesetter and her techniques, Griff refrained from mentioning Mrs. Zaydan.

"Laudanum would be more effective."

"You know I don't want to use opium. I prefer to keep my wits about me."

"Suit yourself," Norman said mildly.

Griff longed to illuminate his former guardian. To shout from the rooftops that the bonesetter had essentially saved his life. Miraculously, at night he could sleep a few hours at a time now. His shoulder no longer felt like an enemy combatant attached to his body.

But Griff intended to wait and see if the bonesetter could repair the rest of his arm before telling Norman the truth.

The doctor filled two glasses of port. They were having after-supper drinks in the parlor rather than the dining room. It was a ritual they'd established soon after Griff had moved in and now continued whenever he was in London.

"As I was saying, having a nobleman on the hospital's board of governors could mean a great deal. It would certainly assist with fundraising." He handed a glass to Griff. "We are a charity hospital. We depend upon the generosity of our benefactors."

"What would I have to do?"

"Attend board meetings four or five times a year, and host the occasional fundraiser." He sipped his port. "Your father was on the board."

Griff flinched. "You and I both know that I do not deserve to take his place."

Dismay flooded Norman's face. "I told you back then, and I am telling you now, you are *not* to blame."

"We'll never truly know, will we?"

"Yes, we damn well do. You did not wield the knife that killed your parents."

"If only it were that simple."

"It absolutely is. You were young. Boys get up to mischief. That is all." It was a familiar refrain that Griff had heard repeatedly since confessing the truth to his guardian shortly after the crime.

"We weren't even supposed to be there, Mother and I." His fists clenched. "Father had to make an unexpected visit to the country house. I convinced Mother that we should go, too."

"It was a terrible twist of fate. You are not to blame for any of it."

Griff gulped a generous amount of port to ease the ache in his throat. "How deeply involved was Father in the running of the hospital?"

"Very. More than most governors. He paid careful attention to finances and cared deeply about patient care. Joining the board would be a way for you to honor your father's legacy."

Unlike his father, Griff didn't sit on any boards. He mostly ignored his position and the influence that came with it. He'd acquired the title as a result of an unspeakable tragedy. One Griff blamed himself for. Any donations Griff made were given quietly. But maybe it was time to put his title to use to help people on a wider scale.

"Very well." He sucked in his cheeks. "If you believe I can be of service."

"Excellent." Norman lifted his glass. "Here's to your joining the board. And to your father, Jeffrey Ellis, the late Lord Griffin. A thoroughly decent man— sometimes to his own detriment."

"How so?"

"Your father was idealistic, naive even. He found it hard to accept some of life's darker realties. For example, he cared deeply, perhaps too deeply, about the fate of our patients."

"Is it possible to care too deeply? Surely the poor deserve good medical care."

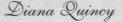

"You are like your father in that way, too tender-hearted. As a doctor, I understand that loss of life is sometimes inevitable. Physicians must accept that they will not be able to heal all patients."

Griff paused. It was unwise to mention the bonesetter, but he couldn't resist. "What about others, people of skill other than physicians, who might be able to heal patients?"

"To whom do you refer?"

"There are physicians. There are surgeons. Each has his own specialty. Is it possible that a bonesetter might have his or her own area of expertise?"

Norman cackled and shook his head. "What is this about? Are you swiving the bonesetter? Has she gotten in your ear as well as your trousers?"

"No, I am not bedding Mrs. Zaydan. Her husband might take issue with that."

"There is no husband as I understand it. She styles herself as a married woman to appear respectable."

A thrill shot through Griff. *She wasn't married.* "What else do you know about Mrs. Zaydan?"

"I've made some inquires. The woman is short-tempered, hardheaded and potentially dangerous."

Griff scoffed. "Please. The woman is no more dangerous than I am."

"She apparently put out the wrist of some young lord after she was called to tend to his injury. He is said to be in excruciating pain."

"Maybe he deserved it."

"I do not begrudge anyone who works to put food on their table," Norman said. "But I must stand against supposed healers who peddle false promises to vulnerable people."

"I doubt the young lordship was helpless. His papa's fortune and position no doubt provide quite a nice cushion."

"I would be careful around her if I were you."

Griff understood Norman's skepticism. But the bonesetter wasn't a complete fraud. Griff's shoulder proved that.

HANNA TRIED TO concentrate as she worked on Mr. Thomas's wrist. Even as the warm woodsy scent of his shaving soap drifted over her.

They sat opposite each other at a corner of her desk, which allowed her easy access to his wrist. Proper treatment required proximity, which was never an issue with Baba's male patients. But Mr. Thomas was not the usual specimen. His nearness prompted delicious anticipation to swirl through her. And the shiver that ran down her spine when she first put her hands on Mr. Thomas had nothing to do with the room temperature.

If anything, she felt overheated. If she weren't intent on preserving her modesty, she'd cast off her fichu to feel blissful cool air against her bare skin. The practical part of Hanna's brain understood that this attraction was purely biological. An undeniable part of life. Yet that didn't keep Hanna from feeling flustered whenever Mr. Thomas drew near.

"How much mobility will I have in the wrist once you're done?" he asked.

She could sense his direct gaze on her face. She kept hers on his wrist. To meet his eyes, to look into them, when they were so close to one another felt too intimate. "I expect you shall have almost complete mobility. Once your wrist is restored, the pain should diminish considerably. Or it could disappear completely."

His cool gaze went to the drawing of the skeleton on the wall. "That's a macabre piece of art."

She glanced up. "It's a Bidloo drawing."

"A friend of yours?"

"Not exactly. He was a Dutch anatomist and royal physician who lived in the last century. I find his work fascinating. That's a copy, of course, not an original work."

Applying pressure, her fingers traced a path over his palm, past his wrist and up his inner forearm. Mr. Thomas cut a formidable presence, but this part of a man—so soft, pale and smooth to the touch—spoke of vulnerability, contrasting sharply with the quiet physical strength of the rest of his body.

"I am still amazed by what you were able to accomplish with my shoulder," he said.

"How is the pain?" At least her voice, strong and brisk, didn't betray the flighty way she felt inside.

"In my shoulder? Almost completely gone."

His wrist was ready. The sooner she got this man out of her examining room, the more quickly her usual rational thinking and clinical detachment would reassert itself. "Please stand."

He came immediately to his feet, showing none of

the hesitation or skepticism from his previous visit. He remained aloof, an invisible shield between him and the rest of the world still firmly in place, but she sensed his blossoming confidence in her skills. The realization delighted her, even though Hanna shouldn't care what this arrogant man thought of her.

Standing at his side, she took his left wrist in one hand and wrapped her right hand around his thumb, her fingers pressing into his palm.

"Will you warn me before you do your worst?" he asked.

"Do not worry." She pressed her thumb into a point in his wrist. "Does this hurt?"

He gritted his teeth. "Like the devil."

"That's the joint that is out of place." Exerting steady traction, she rotated his hand slightly downward. "Try to relax."

Very quickly, before he could draw another breath, she flexed the joint to its full extent until his fingers faced downward. Then, just as sharply, she brought his hand up again so that it was completely extended, all the while keeping her thumb pressure on the sore spot.

He grunted from the unexpected burst of pain. "You promised to warn me," he rasped.

"No, I did not promise."

His mouth drew flat. "You gave me your word."

"Actually, I did not. I believe I said something along the lines of 'Do not worry.'"

"You deliberately misled me."

She suppressed a smile in the face of his outrage.

"Since when do men of your sort believe a woman's word is of any worth?"

"Yours certainly isn't," he muttered, still clearly affronted. "And what do you mean by 'of my sort'? What sort is that?"

"You were clearly born into privilege."

He stiffened. "Why do you say that?"

"It is not something a person can easily hide. It is evident in how you speak, the words you use, how you carry yourself. Your clothes, while not flamboyant, are well-made and of good quality. Should I go on?"

"Only if it will keep you from bending my wrist in unnatural ways." He paused, examining her face. "You've certainly noted a great deal about me. I didn't realize that I was being examined so closely."

"You weren't." She flushed and shifted her attention down to his arm. "Please move your wrist. If you are quite finished with your complaining."

"It's done?" He tested his wrist, gently and slowly flexing and extending it. "It's . . . incredible . . . The pain is gone."

"You must begin moderate use of that joint immediately. If you do not bend your wrist on a regular basis, your former troubles will be restored."

Wonder filled his voice. "I cannot remember what it is to move this wrist without considerable discomfort."

"Do not forget to keep moving it. How do your fingers feel?"

"At the moment? They're tingling."

"Very good. That means the flow of blood is as it should be."

He lifted his gaze to meet hers. "You amaze me."

They still sat close to one another. She should move away. Her work was done. But she stayed put. "I have done what any skilled bonesetter would."

"I don't know about other bonesetters." He brushed a loose tendril away from her face. "But I do know that you are remarkable."

The tenderness in his eyes swathed Hanna in sweet heat. Sitting this close, she could make out the unique details of his gaze. A distinct sunburst bathed in amber and white shot out from the darkness of his pupils, overlaying the icy blue.

He drew nearer, his gaze dropping to her lips. Hanna's skin prickled. Normally, she easily sublimated feelings of physical desire. A price she willingly paid to be able to practice her craft. What man would want a bonesetter for a wife?

Swallowing her physical impulses, those feminine urges, was never truly a challenge. Until now. With this man, her body rebelled against her mind, determined to have what it craved. Hanna licked her lips.

Mr. Thomas's eyes blazed. She was tempted to let the moment play out, to allow him certain liberties. How would it feel to kiss a man? This man. She'd never wondered that about anyone else. He inched closer, his intense blue gaze locked with hers.

But then she heard Baba's voice. Almost as clearly as if he were there in the room with them. *One day,*

Baba, you will be the finest bonesetter in all of London. Hanna didn't know where her dream ended and she began. Being a bonesetter was as much a part of her as her arm or leg. Any hint of impropriety could destroy her tenuous hold on the life she wanted so badly.

Breaking eye contact, she drew back with a trembling breath. "I shall see you next week, Mr. Thomas."

Chapter Five

When Griff returned the following week, the bone-setter was wearing his mother's sapphire.

The necklace swayed on its gold chain as she worked on Griff's elbow. Mesmerized, he followed the pale gem's back and forth movements as intensely as a man under a hypnotist's influence.

Mrs. Zaydan was more aloof today, after he'd almost kissed her at their last meeting. He would have done so if she hadn't pulled back. It was just as well. He needed to keep his focus where it belonged. Out of his trousers and on the necklace.

His eyes on the sapphire, Griff barely noted the pain Mrs. Zaydan inflicted on him with determined, decisive strokes. She massaged his elbow with the same relentlessness she'd employed to attack his shoulder and wrist.

The sound of cracking bone jolted Griff back to what was being done to him. The bonesetter held his crippled arm just above the elbow with one hand and just below it with the other. Determined not to make a sound, Griff gulped down some of the ale she'd set before him. But the sound of his bones being jangled about proved to be too much.

"This feels"—*and sounds*—"very different from what you did to my wrist and shoulder."

"Yes." Her face was red with exertion due to the fierce battle with his elbow. "I need to break the callus that has formed in the dislocated joint."

"The callus?"

"The bone that has rebuilt there."

The idea of her breaking bones in his elbow drove Griff straight back to his ale. He bottomed out the tankard. Then forced himself to breathe while she manipulated his elbow.

"There," she said after a few minutes that felt like forever.

"There?" he asked.

She bent Griff's arm toward his chest and then slightly away. "Done."

"Really? Shall I attempt to move it?" After living with an immobile elbow for two years, Griff was reluctant to put it into motion.

"Not yet. You require a sling to keep your elbow still for a fortnight. After that, I shall give you some daily exercises that you must do without fail."

A pounding at the front door reached them. The young maid by the door exchanged glances with Mrs. Zaydan, who dipped her chin. The servant slipped out to see who was calling.

"Now, as I was saying," Mrs. Zaydan continued, "in about two weeks' time, you may remove the sling. If you have any further problems with your arm, you should return to see me. But I doubt that will be necessary."

"So that is it?" He blinked. "This is our last appointment."

"We shall schedule one final meeting. Unless you have any other joints that are out or broken bones that need to be set, you may rest assured that the worst is over."

Instead of relief, disappointment swamped Griff. He told himself it was because he'd already met with the bonesetter four times and still knew nothing about where she'd gotten his mother's sapphire. "That's a beautiful necklace. It's rather unusual."

"Is it?" She spoke in a distracted manner as she fitted his arm with a sling. "I'm rather partial to it."

"Was it a gift from your husband?"

Those dark, serious eyes briefly met his gaze, but he couldn't tell what she was thinking. "No."

"Where did you get it?"

She paused to regard him with some surprise. Griff cursed himself. He'd done a poor job of hiding his interest in the necklace. They were distracted by a loud, unruly male voice in the corridor just as the bonesetter finished tying the sling around his neck.

Griff's brows went up. "Your next appointment?"

"I am not scheduled to see anyone else today."

The verbal disturbance grew nearer. "Where is she?" an inebriated man's voice called out. "Where is that she-devil?"

Lucy's voice pleaded with the man. "You cannot go in there, sir. Mrs. Zaydan is with someone."

"I'll just bet she is," the interloper snarled. The door burst open. A well-dressed young man stood on the threshold holding one bent arm over his chest. He flushed when he spotted Mrs. Zaydan. "You did this to me, you bitch."

Griff stiffened. It took him a moment to place the face. And then he realized who the boy was. *Mansfield.* The tadpole whose wrist the bonesetter had put out at the coffeehouse.

Griff stood. "Settle down," he said coldly. "And then apologize to Mrs. Zaydan."

"That's not necessary," she said.

"It damn well is. I saw what happened at the coffeehouse." The words slipped out before Griff realized what he'd revealed.

Surprise flickered in her eyes. "You did?"

"I tried to keep him out, miss." The servant girl came in behind Mansfield. "I really did."

"That is all right, Lucy," the bonesetter said soothingly before turning to the whelp. "Good afternoon, Mr. Mansfield. How may I help you?"

Outrage colored his face. "What did you do to my wrist?" He vibrated with menace. "You're going to pay for what you've done, you witch. I visited four doctors, and no one's been able to help me."

Griff stepped between them. "Mind your manners."

"And if I don't?" Mansfield's disdainful gaze dropped to the sling cradling Griff's elbow. "What will you do about it?"

Griff's good hand whipped out, grabbing Mansfield

by the throat, forcing him to stumble backward until Griff had him up against the wall. "I will break your useless little neck, you insolent puppy."

Mansfield gagged. "Now, see here—"

"Apologize." Griff tightened his grip.

"Truly, Mr. Thomas, this is not necessary," Mrs. Zaydan said from behind him.

Mansfield tried to peel Griff's hand away from his throat. "Do you know who I am?" he gasped. "My father will have your head."

"I know exactly who you are." The idiot's father was a viscount, just like Griff. "Apologize now."

"I do not require an apology," Mrs. Zaydan said. "He is in pain. I can help him."

Griff didn't relax his hold. "I find it very necessary that he apologize for his rudeness."

"I apologize," Mansfield finally said in a strangled voice.

"Good." Griff released him. "Now, make certain you mind your manners in Mrs. Zaydan's presence." He caught sight of the servant girl watching the unfolding scene with wide eyes.

"Now," the bonesetter said to Mansfield, "if you'd care to take a seat on my examining table, I'll put your wrist back in."

"As if I'd let you touch me," Mansfield snapped. "Well," he amended, "I wouldn't let you touch my wrist, but if you'd care to put your hands elsewhere—"

Griff's temper flared. "Do not tempt me to thrash you."

Mansfield flinched. "I meant no disrespect."

"You damn well did," Griff growled. "Do it again and your other wrist will need fixing as well."

"Thank you for your gallantry, Mr. Thomas," the bonesetter interjected. "You must have other things to do with the remainder of your afternoon. I am certain Mr. Mansfield and I will manage to be civil."

"I'm staying as long as Mansfield is here. I'm not leaving you alone."

She looked skyward. "Very well." She faced Mansfield. "I thought you would come to me right away to put your wrist to rights. Why did you wait so long?"

"Because everyone knows bonesetters are fraudsters," Mansfield retorted. Griff made a warning hum with his throat. Mansfield hastily added, "Ma'am."

"If you allow me to treat your wrist," she said, "you will leave this office free from pain."

Mansfield's doubtful gaze bounced from the bonesetter to Griff. His eyes went to Griff's sling. "You let her treat you?"

"I did. My wrist was put out, and Mrs. Zaydan put it back in."

Mansfield's eyes bulged. "She put out your wrist, too?"

Griff actually laughed. "No. My wrist was out for the better part of two years."

Mansfield's uncertain gaze traveled back to Mrs. Zaydan. "You won't hurt me?"

"Putting any joint back in is painful. But it will be over before you know it." Her tone was almost cajoling now, as if Mansfield were still a boy in apron-strings who needed to be coaxed into taking his medicine.

"Stop wasting her time," Griff warned. "Either allow Mrs. Zaydan to treat you or leave."

"Very well." Mansfield edged toward the examining table. "If you promise not to make it worse."

Mrs. Zaydan followed him. "Do not worry."

Griff suppressed a snort. He knew what happened when the bonesetter told a patient not to worry. Mansfield settled on the table.

"Roll up your sleeve," she instructed. "We'll have you put to rights in no time."

She took the pup's affected wrist in one hand and wrapped her right hand around his thumb, her fingers pressing into his palm. "Does this hurt?"

"Ouch!" Mansfield gasped. "Yes, it damn well does."

"Watch your manners," Griff warned.

He watched, fascinated, as the bonesetter rotated Mansfield's hand slightly downward. Now that he wasn't the patient enduring the pain, he could fully appreciate Mrs. Zaydan's skills.

"Try to relax," she urged the patient. Griff's eyes crinkled at the corners. He'd heard that before, too. Right before the worst of it. And, just as Griff expected, the bonesetter flexed and extended the joint in a flash, her thumb pressure remaining on the impacted joint during the procedure.

Mansfield yelped. "Goddammit to hades!"

Griff allowed the cursing to pass unchecked. After all, he knew the pain of having a joint put back.

"Very well, Mr. Mansfield," she said. "Your wrist is back in. You should have no further trouble with it."

Cradling his wrist, Mansfield regarded her with suspicion. "What are you saying?"

"You may now move your wrist."

Mansfield's gaze dropped to his arm. He flexed and extended his wrist in slow, uncertain movements. "By God, it works."

He hopped up from the table, keeping his distance from both Griff and the bonesetter. "I'll be on my way."

Griff stepped in his path. "Not quite yet. You haven't paid the lady."

Mansfield curled his lip. "Why should I pay her for fixing the damage she caused?"

"Because I told you to."

"No." The bonesetter set her jaw. "Payment is not required."

Griff paused. "You may thank Mrs. Zaydan before you leave."

"My sincere thanks." Mansfield ground out the words. He shot a glance at Griff. "Satisfied?"

"Just barely." He motioned toward the exit with his chin. "You may go now." Mansfield was through the door before either of them could draw another breath. Lucy followed Mansfield to see him out.

Mrs. Zaydan wiped down the examining table. "I could have handled him, you know. I've met with worse."

"You should not have to."

She turned to face him, her expression serious, questioning. "You are keeping secrets, Mr. Thomas."

His heart skipped a beat. "What makes you say that?"

"You said that you saw what Mr. Mansfield did to me. How is that possible?"

A GUARDED EXPRESSION entered Mr. Thomas's eyes. Hanna immediately knew he was going to lie. Or, at the very least, be less than honest. Had one of her detractors sent him to prove she was a fraud?

He glanced down. "I was at the coffeehouse when Mr. Mansfield and his cohorts summoned you. I saw you put his wrist out."

"It wasn't my finest hour. I lost my temper." Her cheeks warmed. "My grandmother says acting in anger will be my undoing."

"Mansfield got what he deserved."

"A healer should do no harm. I must exercise more self-control. But sometimes it feels as if there's a violent storm within me that cannot be quelled."

"With good reason on that particular afternoon. You had no reason at all to temper your reaction. They overstepped. As gentlemen, they were aware that their behavior was abominable."

"Perhaps with ladies of their class. Men of that sort follow a different code with the laboring classes. Not to mention that they hold bonesetters in the lowest regard possible."

"I do not. I hold you in very high esteem. I've seen what you can do. You are mesmerizing."

Her heart thumped. "Few people would call a bonesetter *mesmerizing*."

"I am not referring to the bonesetter. I'm taken by the woman."

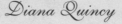

She lifted her eyes to meet his. "You shouldn't say such things."

"Probably not." He paused. "Are you wed?" The words were low. Intimate. Urgent. "Is there a Mr. Zaydan?"

She should lie. But she didn't. "No."

"Are you otherwise promised to anyone?"

"I am not." He shouldn't ask such personal questions. Moreover, she should not answer. Mr. Thomas was a patient. "I am wedded to my work."

His gaze dipped to her lips. He stepped closer, near enough for her to feel his body heat. Near enough so that she suddenly couldn't catch her breath. "Why would you come to me"—her words came out in a whisper—"after seeing me deliberately injure Mr. Mansfield?"

"I saw what your hands could do. I witnessed your fiery nature. You impress me."

Why was the room so hot? Perspiration gathered in her armpits. Hanna's breasts felt sensitive. And exquisitely connected to the place between her legs. Mr. Thomas wasn't touching her, yet he invaded her body. She felt him in the quickened beat of her heart and the hard rush of her blood.

"I got it from my father!" she blurted out.

He blinked. "I beg your pardon?"

"You asked about my necklace." She held up the pendant, dangling it between her two fingers, just as a bullfighter waves a red flag in front of a bull. The sky-blue stone sparkled. She'd said the first thing she could think of to break this strange spell between them.

It worked. Mr. Thomas was instantly distracted. "Your father?"

"Yes."

"It's an expensive piece." His eyes fixed on the jewel. "I didn't realize bonesetters were paid so handsomely. Do you know where he purchased it?"

"Why? Would you like to buy it as a gift for Mrs. Thomas?" It wasn't her concern. And yet, she wanted to know. *Badly*.

"There is no Mrs. Thomas," he answered instantly, reflexively.

Relief filtered through her. "Then why are you interested?"

After a long pause, he said, "Because there is a lady for whom I might wish to buy such a gem."

Hanna blinked. He might as well have dropped a boulder on her. "I see." Such an expensive gift suggested he had serious intentions toward the lady. Which made Hanna what exactly? A lowly nobody he wanted to dally with? She felt a rush of shame. Thank goodness she hadn't allowed the kiss. "That certainly explains your interest."

He couldn't take his eyes off the jewel. He seemed transfixed by it. "Do you know where your father purchased the necklace?"

Her voice cooled. "I have no idea."

"You must have some knowledge about it," he pressed.

"I assure you that I do not."

"Your father didn't say anything about where he got it when he gave it to you?"

She stepped back. "He didn't exactly give it to me."

He edged closer. "What do you mean?"

"I found it among my father's things after he died. I'd never seen it before."

"When did your father die?"

"Almost three years ago."

"Three years ago." He looked beyond her, a contemplative expression on his face. "Did you find anything else of interest?"

"Such as?" She declined to mention the gold ring she'd anonymously returned to its owner a few weeks ago. She hadn't given the parcel much thought since posting it to some toff in Richmond. But now she wondered. *Where had Baba gotten the jewelry? Why had he kept the valuable pieces hidden away? And why was Mr. Thomas so interested?*

"Anything at all?" He stood too close. Mr. Thomas didn't frighten her, but his intensity made her uneasy. "What else did you discover along with the necklace?"

"Nothing." She squared her shoulders. "You are making me uncomfortable."

He blinked. "Am I?" That seemed to snap him out of whatever reverie gripped him. He immediately retreated. "I beg your pardon."

She glanced from the sapphire pendant dangling at her waist up into Mr. Thomas's soft blue gaze. "I just realized the color of this gemstone perfectly matches your eyes."

"I noticed that as well." He paused. "I have my mother's eyes."

Chapter Six

*T*he following morning after a sleepless night, Hanna grabbed the blue-and-white shawl *Citi* had embroidered for her and stepped out the front door.

She needed fresh air. Thoughts of Mr. Thomas, both her interest in him and his interest in the necklace, had consumed her all night. Not to mention the revelation that he was courting a lady who he gifted with expensive jewels. Mostly, though, she couldn't get what *Citi* had revealed about the necklace out of her mind.

It was probably stolen.

Last evening at supper, she'd asked *Citi* about the jewelry and learned that Baba never turned any patients away. Not even criminals who sometimes insisted on paying with stolen goods. Whenever possible, Baba returned the goods to their owners, the way he'd intended with the gold ring that belonged to a toff called Lord Griffin.

Hanna had discovered the signet ring with a lovely carved band in the same drawer as the necklace. But unlike the necklace, it was packaged and addressed to this Lord Griffin. She'd opened the package to find the band inscribed with the words *Lady Griffin*. Then she'd rewrapped the package and sent it back to its rightful owner, a viscount in Richmond, just as her father had intended.

"Escaping your grandmother?" an amused male voice called out from behind her.

She turned to greet her friend Evan, a lanky man with a friendly face. "As if anyone could outrun her."

"You're out early."

"I needed some air."

"May I join you?"

"Of course."

He fell in step beside Hanna. "I understand that patient I referred last week is doing much better."

Hanna nodded. "It was a broken leg, a relatively simple case." She'd first met Evan two years ago when he dislocated his knee. Hanna had put it back in, and they became fast friends. Evan was young and possessed a sharp and curious mind. Before long, they'd hatched a plan to one day open their own dispensary—a doctor and bonesetter working side by side to give patients the best medical care possible.

"Have you heard that Mrs. Lockhart is at the hospital?" he asked.

"No. What ails her?"

"Her malady of the lungs has worsened considerably. Dr. Pratt, the lead physician, is keeping her there for a few nights."

Hanna was not an admirer of Dr. Pratt, who had tried his best to steer patients away from Baba, but she hoped for Mrs. Lockhart's sake that he was a capable doctor. "I must get over to visit her."

As much as she wanted to avoid Dr. Pratt, Hanna felt obligated to check in on the older woman. A hospital stay must be lonely for a widow with no children.

"I was given to understand that you prefer to stay away from Margate Hospital," Evan remarked.

"Normally, I do." She tightened her wrap around her. "But what choice do I have?"

"Now," THE BONESETTER commanded after massaging Griff's arm for the better part of an hour, "move your arm."

Griff struggled to keep his body calm as Mrs. Zaydan's warm hands slid over his bare skin. Whenever she touched him his blood temperature soared. He did as she asked, straightening his elbow and then bending his arm in toward his chest.

The bonesetter behaved in a businesslike manner two weeks after their last encounter when he'd asked her about the necklace. Her manner was completely professional and somewhat removed. Not unlike their very first visit.

Not that Griff blamed her. She probably thought him a cad. After all, he'd told her outright of his intention to buy an expensive bauble for some imaginary lady. She'd caught him off guard, so he'd spouted the very first lie that slipped into his head. The truth remained that the only woman to occupy his thoughts these days was the very unapproachable healer before him.

"Move your wrist," she said.

Under her watchful gaze, he did as she asked.

"Very nice." She crossed her arms.

Extending his arm high over his head, Griff did windmills with it. He was still stiff. His range of motion limited. But the pain that had become as much a part of him as his skin was blissfully absent. "I cannot believe what you've managed to do with my arm."

"I am pleased with the result," she said briskly. "Your arm was quite mangled, but you are young and healthy. Your overall youth and physical fitness assisted in your recovery."

He stared at her. "You are a miracle worker."

She dropped her gaze. Her thick long lashes fanning over her cheeks. "Hardly. Bonesetting is not only an art, but also a science. We study the joints and how to manipulate them."

He wanted to continue talking to her. To know her better. "How did you come to learn the art from your father?"

"I was fascinated by it. He let me watch, and I assisted him when he needed a second pair of hands."

"And not your brothers? Do you have brothers?"

"I have three brothers who weren't interested in my father's work. They immersed themselves in the family business of cotton exports."

He tried to imagine her as a little girl. The image of her bossing her brothers around came into his head. "But not you."

She relented. Her passion for her work loosened her tongue. "As my father's apprentice, the functions of the human body captivated me from the very first." Her face brightened when she talked about her work. She was incandescent. "Being able to help people struck me as the most worthwhile profession in the world."

He swallowed. Hard. Unnerved by his intense attraction to her. "Clearly, your father taught you well. What you've done for me is a miracle."

"It is the human body itself that is the miracle. The way we're put together, the bones, tendons and tissues." Her dark-rimmed eyes shone. "The fact that our heart continues to beat day in and day out."

She seemed to catch herself and retreated, reminding him of a crab going back into its shell. Only in this case, the bonesetter's carapace was her desk. She returned to sit behind it and picked up her pencil, as a soldier might wield his armor, signaling her dismissal.

Griff's heart sank. He rose, pulling down his shirtsleeves. He was running out of time. This was their last scheduled appointment. He needed a reason to keep seeing Mrs. Zaydan. Short of dislocating his other shoulder, he couldn't immediately think of one.

He reached for his tailcoat. "And our next appointment?"

She kept her focus on her writing. "As you know, we are finished. If you continue with your exercises, you should recover complete range of motion."

"Will you at least let me escort you to a tea shop as a way of showing my appreciation?"

"That is very kind." She spared him a quick glance before going back to her notes. "But payment in full is all the thanks I require."

She'd asked for two guineas. He set five times that amount on her desk.

She examined the sum. "That is not the fee we agreed to."

"What you've done for me is worth ten times that amount. Twenty times." He meant every word. "You've given me my life back."

"All the same. Two guineas will suffice."

He wanted badly to repay her. To do something that would convey the full extent of his appreciation. But the stubborn set of her jaw suggested that she wouldn't allow it. "Then, please accept the money to cover future patients who might not be able to afford your fee."

"I see you intend to be very mulish about this." She finally looked up from her writing.

"*I* am hardly the stubborn one here. Your skills are worth more than two guineas."

She relented. "I will accept the extra funds for patients in need."

"Very good." He paused. She waited expectantly. This was when he should make his exit. In her mind, any business between them was over. In his mind, it had just begun.

"About the necklace," he said.

"The necklace?" She made a show of appearing uninterested, but he noted how her fingers tightened around the pencil.

"Yes, the one with the blue gemstone that you wore the other day. Did you learn where it came from so that I might buy one that is similar?"

"No." Her voice was resolute. "There is absolutely nothing more I can tell you about the necklace."

THAT EVENING, GRIFF had supper with Hunt at the duke's home on St. James Place in Mayfair.

"By God, it's a miracle," Hunt pronounced after Griff demonstrated the newfound mobility in his left arm. "How did you manage it?"

"Remember the bonesetter who had my mother's necklace?"

"Are you jesting?"

"I am as serious as an apoplexy. She's remarkable. She knows everything about joints. The bonesetter not only fixed my arm, wrist and shoulder, but I also saw her repair Mansfield's wrist."

"Mansfield? The pup from the coffeehouse? Payton is up in arms over what happened."

"Payton?" It took Griff a moment to place the name.

"Viscount Payton. Mansfield's father. He is demanding the bonesetter be held to account."

Griff bristled. "That whelp got exactly what he deserved."

"I agree." The duke paused, studying him. "You seem different."

Griff sipped his drink. He felt different. "Do I?"

"Most definitely."

"Maybe you're not used to seeing me rested. I am finally sleeping through the night. It's been two years since I slept more than two or three hours at a time."

"It's more than that. You seem less . . . burdened."

He considered that for a moment. "I suppose living

in pain adjusted my perspective. Before my accident, I was so caught up in what happened to my parents that I barely paid attention to actually living a full life."

Hunt nodded. "It always seemed to me that you felt you didn't deserve to enjoy your life while your parents were not present to enjoy theirs. I feared you joined the army because you had a death wish."

"Maybe I did," Griff admitted. "But my injury changed my outlook. Now that I am free of pain, I can't believe how much of my life I've squandered."

"And now what? Do you have a grand plan for the future?"

"I have no idea. I just feel compelled not to waste it as I did before the accident."

The butler appeared to summon them in to dinner. The men took their drinks into the dining room with them.

Griff was surprised to see two place settings. "Is Her Grace not joining us?"

"My wife is off visiting her relatives again. There are innumerable aunts and uncles and cousins and second cousins—that every time I turn around, there seems to be another family wedding or other function to attend."

Griff wasn't well acquainted with his friend's wife, the daughter of a marquess and a merchant's daughter. Their marriage had caused a mild scandal in London. But Hunt, who once placed propriety and decorum above all else, seemed happy. The duke had conveniently missed most of the scandal by accompanying his new wife, a travel writer, to Morocco.

"Now you must catch me up on the necklace," the duke said. "Did the bonesetter tell you where she got it?"

"No, I made a hash of things when I tried to learn more about it." Griff swallowed a spoonful of white soup, creamy chicken and veal augmented by toasted almonds. "The problem I face now is that my treatment is concluded, and I've learned nothing about the necklace except that she supposedly found it among her father's things after his death."

"The old man must have been aware the necklace was ill-gotten. Otherwise, why hide something so expensive?"

"I need to see the woman again. But she refused my offer to escort her to a tea shop as a way of expressing my gratitude."

Hunt chuckled. "From what you've told me of her, your bonesetter is not the tea-shop sort."

"I'm not sure of what to do now."

"Be resourceful." Hunt finished the last of his soup. "Do your homework. See what interests her. Extend an invitation that would be hard for her to refuse."

"What kind of invitation would that be?"

"Ah," the duke said, "but that is for you to decide. I am ready for my soused lamb." He signaled the footman. "Bring in the next course."

Chapter Seven

Griff stretched, feeling supremely rested after seven hours of uninterrupted slumber.

He couldn't recall the last time he'd slept so deeply and painlessly. Or experienced a blissfully dream-free night, with no snake-headed wild dogs tormenting him.

As he dressed, he thought about Mrs. Zaydan and the necklace. He needed an excuse to see her again. He told himself he was eager to see her to learn more about the necklace and not because he missed her company.

Griff trotted down the stairs and into the dining room to find that Norman wasn't there.

"Is the doctor not joining me?" he asked Mrs. Peele when the housekeeper appeared with Griff's coffee.

"No, my lord," she said as she filled his plate, just as she'd always done. "He was called to the hospital early this morning."

He watched her pile more food onto the plate than he could ever hope to eat. "You don't need to fill my plate any longer, Mrs. Peele. I am grown, you know."

"Still far too thin for my liking." She set the food

before him. Mrs. Peele had worked for Norman ever since Griff first came to live with him. She'd always had a soft spot for the parentless boy. Even after he'd grown into a man.

Griff paused between bites. "How is young Annie doing?"

"As well as can be expected. The girl will likely stay with me forever. Few men will wed a girl with a curved back."

Suddenly it hit him. It was so obvious. Why had it taken him so long to think of it? "Have you considered taking her to see a bonesetter?"

Mrs. Peele's eyes rounded. "Certainly not, my lord. Dr. Pratt says bonesetters are swindlers."

"Maybe some are." He moved his arm around. "But I was treated by a bonesetter, and the pain in my arm is gone."

"Heavens!" She stared as he stretched his arm wide and bent it at the elbow. "You can move it? Does Dr. Pratt know about this?"

"Not yet. He's been working such long hours at the hospital that I've barely seen him. But as soon as I do, I intend to demonstrate the full extent of my recovery. Then he will understand that some bonesetters are very capable."

Mrs. Peele appeared unconvinced. "Do you think this woman can help my Annie? Really and truly?"

"She might be able to. She helped me, and I saw her assist another man whose wrist was dislocated." He neglected to disclose that the bonesetter was why Mansfield's wrist was out in the first place. "None of the other doctors have been able to help your girl. Perhaps Mrs. Zaydan can."

Cautious hope flashed in her face. "But Dr. Pratt won't approve."

"You needn't tell him until after you've seen whether Mrs. Zaydan can assist Annie." He felt no guilt using the girl as a means to see the bonesetter again. He truly believed the healer could help.

"Maybe Annie and I will call on this bonesetter of yours." Mrs. Peele's voice wavered. "If you think my Annie's back can be fixed. Will you give me the bone-setter's direction?"

"I shall do better than that. I'll escort you there myself."

"CAN YOU HELP my daughter?" Mrs. Peele asked.

Hanna nodded. "I believe so." The girl had a dis-location of the spine that made her back curve to the right. "It will require some adjustment of the spine and manipulation of the soft tissues, but I do think I'll be able to help Annie."

The girl sat on the examining table, listening in-tently. Hanna and Mrs. Peele stood on either side of her. "It hurts sometimes," the girl said. "A great deal."

"Don't worry, Annie," Hanna said gently. "I'm go-ing to help you. My treatment will ease the pain. And then I shall give you some exercises to perform daily to help keep the hurt away."

"Thank you, miss!" Hope brightened the girl's nar-row face. "'Twould be a dream come true if my back weren't paining me all the time."

"It is just . . ." Mrs. Peele paused.

"Yes?" Hanna prodded.

"Is it very expensive? I have heard bonesetters ask for a great deal of money for their potions."

"I assure you that there are no potions. Furthermore, I can adjust the rate for my services as needed." Hanna understood that a housekeeper would naturally be concerned about costs. "The important thing is to make certain that Annie feels better."

There was a knock on the door. Lucy appeared. "Pardon the interruption, miss."

"What is it?"

"Mr. Thomas is here," Lucy informed her.

"He is?" Hanna straightened, all of her nerve endings suddenly on alert. But then she remembered herself. "Obviously, I cannot see him. I am in the middle of a session."

Hanna hated the way her entire body perked up when she heard Mr. Thomas's name. Or the way the mere mention of him transformed an otherwise lackluster day into one that suddenly seemed bursting with possibility. Her reaction was ridiculous. She needed to stay away from the man.

"Mr. Thomas says he is here for an appointment," Lucy said.

"He doesn't have an appointment."

"But Mrs. Peele and Annie do," Mr. Thomas said as he walked in behind Lucy. "And I am accompanying them. They are here on my recommendation."

Hanna was impossibly pleased to see him. Even though she shouldn't be. If he learned the necklace was stolen, he might accuse her of being a fence. Or, worse, assume that Baba had dealt in stolen goods. The Dr. Pratts of the world were just waiting for her to slip and make a mistake. The doctor would take great pleasure in smearing Baba's reputation.

"Is that true?" she asked Mrs. Peele. "Are you here on his recommendation?"

The housekeeper nodded. "Yes, miss. Lord . . ."

Mr. Thomas interrupted. "My friends call me Griff. Can I convince you to do the same, Mrs. Zaydan?"

It was an intimacy that she should not allow, but she did. "As you wish."

"Excellent. I've known young Annie practically since birth. I knew you could help her."

Hanna could hardly fathom that he'd actually sent a patient to her. *He believed in her.* "I would never have imagined the skeptical man I encountered at our first meeting would send patients to me."

"What can I say?" His eyes twinkled. "You won me over with those talented hands of yours."

Her cheeks felt hot. Was Griff flirting with her? "And how do you know Mrs. Peele?"

"Mrs. Peele is our housekeeper."

Our housekeeper. That meant he lived with someone. His parents perhaps, since he'd informed her that he wasn't wed.

She soaked in the sight of him. It had only been a fortnight since their last meeting, but the man was even more handsome than she remembered. His dark hair was short and neat. His complexion clear and bright. The dark smudges under his eyes were gone, and the lines bracketing his mouth much fainter.

"You look well," she said.

"It is all thanks to you. For the first time in two years, I am actually sleeping through the night. I've never felt better."

His renewed vigor was apparent. Vitality poured out of him. He seemed . . . transformed. This renewed Mr. Thomas . . . Griff . . . was even more appealing.

"His eating has improved as well," the housekeeper put in.

"Mrs. Peele has been trying to fatten me up ever since I was a boy," Griff said warmly.

"Mrs. Zaydan says she can help my Annie," Mrs. Peele informed him.

The girl piped up. "She says I won't always be hurting after she cures me."

"I'm very glad for that, Annie." His eyes caught Hanna's. "The opportunity to live life free of physical pain is one of the greatest gifts a person can receive."

"I'd like to make payment now." Mrs. Peele withdrew a knitted coin purse from her pocket and loosened the drawstring. "I must return to the house. I've much work to do."

Griff put a hand over Mrs. Peele's coin purse, stopping her. "None of that now. You and Annie run along. I shall settle up with Mrs. Zaydan."

The housekeeper paused. "I couldn't possibly allow—"

"Don't be ridiculous. I insist." Mirth danced in his

eyes. "Besides, I happen to know that Mrs. Zaydan drives a very hard bargain."

The housekeeper finally acquiesced. "That is very generous of you, sir." She looked to Hanna. "He's always been most thoughtful. Even as a boy. Come along, Annie." The girl scooted off the examining table to follow her mother.

Hanna escorted them to the office door. "I shall see you both first thing on Monday to begin Annie's treatment."

Lucy quit the room to see them out, while Hanna faced Griff. "I drive a hard bargain?"

"Yes, indeed." He examined the Bidloo sketch on the wall behind her desk. "You won't accept what you're worth."

"You mean what my services are worth."

"They are one and the same to a man who's been given another chance at life." He turned away from the drawing. "One I do not intend to waste this time." The words were wistful.

"You make it sound as if you were squandering your life before your injury. Were you living the life of a privileged wastrel?"

"Hardly." His face darkened. "I allowed a childhood tragedy to color my life. I felt guilty for being alive after my mother and father died when I was fifteen. I think that's why I went to war. I didn't think it mattered if I died, too."

"I beg your pardon." Her heart ached for him. "I didn't know about your parents."

He studied her face. "Did you not?"

"How would I? You just now told me they died when you were a boy." Nausea churned in her belly at the thought of Griff suffering such a dreadful loss as a young boy. "I'm terribly sorry."

His probing gaze fixed on her. Almost as if he expected her to say something more. Something of more interest than the usual platitudes. But then he seemed to remember himself, and his strange mood evaporated just as swiftly as it had appeared.

"My apologies," he said, his words lighter and brighter. "Sometimes the old melancholy still intrudes. Now, how much do I owe you? My intention is to pay for all of Annie's treatment."

"The extra fee you gave me last time will suffice."

"I prefer that you keep that for someone else who needs it. I want to take care of Annie. Mrs. Peele looked after me after my parents passed."

"Beneath all of that ice, there is a heart after all."

"I beg your pardon?"

"You are obviously fond of your housekeeper. Most aristocrats take no notice of their servants." Or any member of the laboring class.

"I was in the army. I served with men from all walks of life and was privy to their challenges, particularly their financial struggles."

That explained his desire to ease the housekeeper's burden. "My fee for Annie is the same as yours. Two guineas."

He pursed his mouth as he withdrew the sum from his pocket. "I still say you should charge triple what you do."

It was tempting. If she did, she'd have more money to put toward opening the dispensary. But most of her patients were not as well-to-do as Griff and could ill afford higher charges.

"Well, I suppose that is it." He paused, and she could feel him thinking. Was he attempting to prolong the moment? She should want him gone, but she didn't. She tried to think of something to say so that he wouldn't leave so quickly.

He gestured toward the wall. "You said that sketch was done by a fellow named Bidloo."

"Indeed."

"Very well. Since you will not allow me to compensate you as you deserve after curing me—"

She interrupted on a sigh. "We aren't truly going to have this fruitless discussion again, are we?"

"If you would allow me to finish?"

With a sweep of her arm, she gestured for him to continue. "By all means."

"As I was saying, since you won't take money, perhaps you will allow me to escort you to see a collection that includes this Bidloo fellow's works."

Her eyes snapped up to meet his. "And where would this collection be?" She didn't know of any museum or society in London that carried Govert Bidloo's works.

"Nearby."

"How nearby?"

"Ah, you will just have to agree to allow me to accompany you there."

"When?"

"Tomorrow afternoon?"

She hesitated. She shouldn't go anywhere with the man. She should politely thank Griff and send him away. But the opportunity to see Bidloo's works was too tempting.

"Very well," Hanna said. "Tomorrow it is."

Chapter Eight

"Where are we?" Hanna peered up at the redbrick townhome in Holborn.

"Lincoln's Inn Fields." Griff led her up the narrow steps to the entrance. It felt strange to be out with him. He was very appealing in his beaver hat, charcoal tailcoat and smart white cravat.

"Yes, I know full well that we are at Lincoln's Inn Fields." They were only about three miles from Hanna's house. "But why are we here?"

"To see the Dutch fellow's works." He led her up the steps. The servant girl trailed them. "Surely you haven't already forgotten."

"But this is a private home."

"It's a privately held collection." He rapped on the bright red door. "I haven't seen it myself, but I'm told the artworks are quite popular with people in your field."

"My field?"

"The medical field." His casual reference to her as a professional took Hanna off guard. And delighted her.

The manservant who let them in did not seem surprised to see them. "The master said you're here to see the collection, sir."

"Indeed, I am."

He showed them the way and then excused himself. Griff offered Hanna his arm. "Shall we?"

"Does a friend of yours live here?" She surveyed the dark-paneled hallway as she pulled off her gloves and stuffed them into her reticule. Artifacts, bits of carvings and sculptures, were affixed to every inch of wall and the ceiling as well.

"No, indeed. This house belongs to an associate of my guardian, the man who took me in after my parents died. As you can see, he is quite a collector."

A door off the hall opened onto a chamber that ran the length of the house. A salon was to the front and the dining room beyond it. Here, too, were curiosities stacked atop book-lined shelves. Drawings lined the walls. And then she saw it.

Her eyes widened. "Is that a Ruysch diorama?" She crossed back to the dining room for closer inspection. From afar, it appeared to be a sculpture, but up close, it became apparent the artistic arrangement was made of human parts set atop a pedestal. Two full skeletons flanked the sculpture.

Lucy screeched. "Are those pieces of people's bodies?"

"Perhaps you should wait out in the foyer," Hanna said to the girl.

"Yes, miss." Looking relieved, Lucy dipped a quick curtsy and hastily retreated.

"You can hardly blame the girl for running away," Griff remarked. "This is a house of horrors."

"Ruysch was a Dutch anatomist," Hanna explained. "He pioneered ways to preserve organs and tissue."

"I do not know if I've ever seen anything more disturbing. And in a dining room, of all places."

She absorbed the details of the piece, the full skeletons flanking a landscape of trees and grass. "I've viewed etchings of Ruysch's work. I never expected to see one of his works in person."

He came up beside her, staring at the arrangement. "Are the botanicals supposed to make the skeletons more palatable?"

"The trees are actually constructed of hardened major veins and arteries."

He grimaced. "Dare I ask what the grass is made of?"

She examined the greenery more closely. "Lung tissue, I believe. And smaller vessels for the bushes as well."

"Ugh." He moved away to examine a sketch on the wall. "I see the morbid theme lingers throughout this particular collection."

She straightened, looking over to see what had caught Griff's attention. The drawing depicted a skeleton standing in an alcove. "That's a Bidloo."

"I gathered. It's similar to the one in your examining room." He shook his head. "These two Dutch fellows must have been a bucket of laughs at a party."

Hanna scarcely heard him. A life-size sculpture drew her away.

"I suppose that's one way to be half-dressed," Griff remarked, following her. He came to a stop next to her.

The left half of the woman's body was a full-color

wax skeleton, including some muscles and ligaments. The other half depicted a living woman in fine clothing. It was as though she'd been split down the middle. The left side of her entire body dead, the right side alive and thriving.

Hanna examined the details of the muscles and the way they roped around the bone. She reached out to touch the skeletal shoulder. "This is where your pain came from."

Griff leaned forward, his interest piqued. "That's the joint that was put out?"

"Yes." Her fingers drifted a few inches. "It was here. I had to move it back in."

"Fascinating. And my elbow and wrist?"

She showed him his injuries, where bone had formed in his elbow that she'd cracked in order to move his elbow back to where it needed to be. She pointed out the muscles that had tightened, that she'd massaged and manipulated in order to put his dislocated elbow back where it belonged.

Griff's hand moved to his shoulder, his fingers sliding along muscle and bone. "Here?"

"Here." She moved his fingers, settling them in the right place. His hands were large, his fingers long and solid. They were a gentleman's hands. Untouched by physical labor, warm to the touch and very lightly dusted with fine hairs. She'd never found a man's hands so fascinating before. They'd certainly never stirred her. But Griff's were different. Everything about this man was different.

His hand closed over hers, where it rested on his

shoulder. "I cannot thank you enough for what you did for me."

The impact of his touch arrowed up her arm like an electrical current. "Any healer would do the same."

"But, before you, none of them could." He turned her hand over in his, laying it flat in his palm, treating it as a masterpiece. With his other hand, he traced the lines of her palm. "So much mastery here," he murmured. "And exquisite beauty, too." He lowered his face to press warm, soft lips against her bare palm.

Hanna's knees almost buckled. The sensation of his lips against her sensitive skin melted her bones.

"I should have kept my gloves on." The words came out breathy and uneven. She didn't sound like herself.

His hot gaze met hers. "How fortunate for me that you did not."

A wildfire raged inside of Hanna. Once ignited, containment was impossible. She did not move away. When Griff's serious, captivating face moved closer to hers, she closed her eyes and raised her lips up to meet him.

His hands cradled the back of her head as his mouth dipped down to settle on hers. His kiss was light and sweet, but not at all unsure. He took small nips. As though he was prepared to release her if she objected. Which did not even cross her mind. If anything, she wanted more.

Griff pulled her closer, his lips moving in gentle movements over hers. He angled his head so that they fit together perfectly. His lips were both soft and firm, guiding her more deeply into the kiss.

He nibbled on her bottom lip. She swayed on her

feet, floating into the seductive cocoon he spun around them. If she'd known kissing could be so divine, Hanna wouldn't have waited so long to experience the intimacy.

He rubbed the back of her neck with tender fingers. Pleasurable chills rushed down her spine. She opened her mouth on a sigh, and his tongue slipped between her lips. He stroked her tongue in slow, caressing movements.

The kiss was a conversation unlike any Hanna had ever had. She was learning him. The texture of his tongue. The taste of him. The small hum of approval in his throat when she tentatively stroked her tongue along his.

She held on to his forearms to keep herself steady. Her fingers closed around ropey muscles over bone. She knew his arms. They were strong and capable. He was the port in the storm. But he was also the storm, throwing her off balance, while keeping her steady and safe.

Safe. The realities of her situation filtered back in. The only way to keep herself protected was to deny Griff, or any man, any liberties. A scandal could destroy Hanna's bonesetting practice. But that didn't compel her to stop. Instead rebellious thoughts gathered in her mind. Why should she have to relinquish being close to a man in exchange for pursuing her calling? Why couldn't she have both?

But then she remembered the woman Griff was courting. The one he gifted with expensive jewels. "Stop."

He released her immediately, searching her face. He

was breathing fast. His voice strained. "I am not sorry for kissing you. But I will apologize if I offended you."

Ribbons of pleasure continued to unwind in her chest and belly. "Will you also apologize to the lady you are courting?"

He scrunched up his face. "Meaning?"

"The lady for whom you intend to purchase an expensive necklace. Have you forgotten her already?"

"Oh, that." He flushed. "I overstepped. My apologies." He put distance between them and addressed her with scrupulous courtesy. "Would you prefer that I wait outside while you view the collection? Perhaps that would make you more comfortable."

No. "Yes." She squared her shoulders. "That would be for the best."

Disappointment clouded his gaze. "Very well. Please take all of the time you need to fully enjoy the collection." He paused. As if he wanted to say more.

Hanna waited. Anticipation trembled in her veins. Would he deny the existence of another woman? They stared at each other. But then Griff clamped his jaw shut, politely dipped his chin and strode away.

She did not turn around to watch him leave.

GRIFF STEPPED INTO Norman's study and discovered that he had company. A man with long and haphazard hair stood beside Norman peering at an open book in his hands.

"Griff, come in." Norman looked up as he entered, snapping the book shut. "You remember Lionel Shaw."

"Of course." Mostly Griff recalled the man's hair,

which had apparently never met a comb. "How are you, Doctor?"

"Very well. Work keeps me busy." The man stepped away from Norman. "Speaking of which, I was just leaving. If you'll excuse me."

Griff moved aside for Dr. Shaw to pass through the open door. He watched him continue down the corridor. "He edits a medical journal, doesn't he?"

"Not just any journal." Norman set the book down. "*Medical Facts and Observations* is perhaps the most influential medical publication in London."

"What sorts of things does he write about?"

"Mostly intriguing or interesting cases that will help advance the cause of medicine. Are you ready to go?"

Griff was about to attend his first board of governors meeting. "Not just yet. We have some time." Griff carefully closed the door behind him. "I thought you might like to see the progress that's been made in my recovery."

"Feeling improved, are you?" He examined Griff's face. "You do seem well rested."

"I've never felt better." It was true. Hanna had given him his life back. The years he'd wasted feeling guilty about his parents' murders, allowing melancholy and anger to consume his days, were behind him. He was alive and pain-free. He intended to make the most of his second chance.

"Let's have a look at that shoulder."

Griff lifted his arm up over his head. "I cannot get my arm totally straight."

"Still, you've clearly made excellent progress. And the pain?"

"Almost all gone."

"How about the elbow and wrist?"

Griff moved his wrist around. "As you can see, almost back to normal." He removed his tailcoat and set it over the back of a stuffed chair. Rolling up his sleeve, he bared his arm so that Norman could see that his elbow no longer appeared deformed now that it was back in place.

Norman approached to examine him more closely. "Excellent. Just as I told you. The cure would come with time."

"It wasn't time, it was a bonesetter."

Norman's eyes snapped from Griff's elbow to his face. "What the devil are you talking about?"

"I had several sessions with the healer. She said all three joints were out of place. My shoulder, my elbow and my wrist. She put them all back in."

"No, my dear boy." Norman shook his head like a kindly uncle. "It was simply fortunate timing for the bonesetter that your healing occurred over the weeks that you visited that woman."

"She cured me. I am telling you, Norman, you should work with her, collaborate with her. Imagine if I had put myself in her care right from the start. I wouldn't have spent two years in agonizing pain. Think of how many of your patients she could help."

Exhaling loudly, Norman removed his spectacles and pinched the bridge of his nose. "It pains me to see an intelligent young man made the fool by a well-known charlatan simply because she fluttered those long, dark lashes and allowed you to sample what's beneath her skirts."

"There's no need to be crass. Hanna is a respectable woman."

"*Hanna*? I see you are on very familiar terms. I credited you with better sense than that."

"I haven't bedded her. And I will ask you to refrain from insulting her." His voice was hard. "At first, I thought as you did, that she was a fraud."

"Then, why did you go and see her in the first place?"

"Because she has Mother's necklace."

Norman cocked his head. "What?"

"I saw her at a coffeehouse near Red Lion Square. She was wearing the blue sapphire that Mother always wore."

The blood drained from Norman's face. "The stolen necklace."

"The one taken from Mother on the night she died."

The air around them felt very fragile, as if it could shatter at any moment. "Where did the bonesetter get the necklace?"

"She says she found it among her father's things. She doesn't know where he got it."

"There *were* rumors that the old bonesetter was a fence."

"I don't know anything about her father, but I believe Hanna is innocent of any wrongdoing." He paused. "I am also convinced she is an extremely skilled healer who can help people who are suffering."

"People like Mrs. Zaydan are known to cause suffering," Norman said patiently, as if explaining a complicated concept to a child. "That is why they are so dangerous."

"You should at least speak to her. Meet with her, and some of her patients. Learn about her techniques so that you can come to your own, informed opinion of her."

"My opinion is informed." Norman put his spectacles on. "I attended the Medical College at the London Hospital and received one of the finest educations available. The Medical College is a pioneering school that teaches all of the latest techniques. My opinion, unlike yours, is informed."

"I might not be a physician," Griff said, "but my opinion is informed by my hands-on experience with the woman. She is a talented medical professional."

"Medical *professional*?" Norman shook his head. "Now, I have truly heard it all. For you to refer to any bonesetter as a *medical professional* defies all logic and good sense."

"Please say that you will at least consider what I've told you. I have always known you to approach matters with an open mind."

"Exactly. That is why you should heed what I am telling you about the bonesetter." Norman picked up Griff's tailcoat and handed it to him. "Put this on. We must depart. You don't want to be late for your first meeting of the board of governors."

"I should like to continue this conversation later."

"As you wish." Norman led the way out the door. "But please, whatever you do, make no mention of the bonesetter at the meeting. I don't want the board members to think I've asked a bedlamite to join the hospital board."

Chapter Nine

That day Hanna set out for Margate Hospital to visit Mrs. Lockhart.

Normally, she stayed clear of Margate, preferring to avoid any encounters with its principal physician, Dr. Pratt, the sanctimonious prig who made no secret of his aversion to Baba and all other bonesetters. But because Mrs. Lockhart was alone in London, Hanna felt obliged to see how she fared.

Carrying a large bouquet procured from street urchins selling flowers near the hospital, Hanna passed through clean wards with generous windows and single beds arranged under high ceilings. The tidy surroundings impressed her.

Margate, a charity hospital, took in patients of limited means who could rarely pay for their care. However, once admitted, patients and their families had no say in their treatment. That would not be the case at her dispensary, if Hanna ever had the opportunity to open one with Evan. Their patients would be actively involved in any decisions regarding their own care.

She was directed to the matron, a respectable-looking woman of middle age who presided over the ward. "My, but that's a large bunch of flowers," the matron exclaimed when Hanna approached her.

"There were three children selling them, so I felt obliged to buy from each of them," Hanna said with a rueful expression. "In any case, Mrs. Lockhart is very fond of spring flowers."

The matron's smile slipped. "Mrs. Lockhart?"

"Yes, Mrs. Claudia Lockhart." When the matron paused, Hanna added, "She was admitted suffering from a lung ailment."

"Are you . . . a family member, dear?"

"No, I am a neighbor. Mrs. Lockhart is a widow and doesn't have any family in Town so I thought I'd look in on her. Could you direct me to her bed?"

Sympathy filled the matron's jowly face. "I am sorry to inform you that Mrs. Lockhart has gone to be with the Lord."

"What? When?" Hanna felt like she'd been slapped in the face. "Are you certain?" Mrs. Lockhart wasn't that ill when Hanna last saw her. Could she really be gone?

"Are you all right, dear?" the matron said. "Would you like to sit for a moment?"

Stunned, Hanna allowed the matron to lead her to a seat at her desk. "It's just that . . . it's quite a shock." She set the flowers on the desk. "I hadn't realized Mrs. Lockhart was so ill."

"Lung ailments can be merciless." She poured a glass of water. "It was very swift. I can assure you that she did not suffer."

"When did she succumb to her ailment?"

She set the water before Hanna. "It's been almost a week now."

Guilt gnawed at Hanna's stomach. Dreading a visit to Dr. Pratt's hospital, she'd delayed seeing her neighbor. She hadn't been terribly close to the older woman, but she hated to think of Mrs. Lockhart dying alone.

She drank some water. "I must find a way to tell her family."

The matron patted her hand. "No need, dear. The relations are aware. They came for the body."

"Oh, did they?" Relief whooshed through her. She wouldn't have to run Mrs. Lockhart's family to ground. "Do you know anything about the arrangements? I would like to pay my respects."

"No, dear, I understand they intended to lay Mrs. Lockhart to rest back in her village."

Hanna took a deep breath. She was glad Mrs. Lockhart's family had come for her and that her final resting place would be among her loved ones.

"My thanks." She rose, automatically reaching for the flowers. "You've been very kind."

"Not at all, dear. Good afternoon."

Her head still spinning, Hanna took her leave. She'd almost reached the exit when she realized she should have left the flowers for the patients. As she pondered going back, she spotted a familiar figure.

Griff.

Only it wasn't. He normally dressed in well-made clothes, but his attire now—the navy tailcoat and pale paisley waistcoat—were on an entirely different level.

They were the expensive clothes of a gentleman. And not just a mere gentleman, a noble of the highest ton. Why was he here? It certainly couldn't be to visit a friend or member of his family. Margate's patients were among the neighborhood's least fortunate.

He was accompanied by a small group of men. Clearly men of means, but none stood out the way Griff did with his fine physique, splendid clothing and broad shoulders. He walked as if the world was at his beck and call. It was Hanna's first opportunity to see Griff in his own element, among his own associates. The effect was tantalizing.

When his gaze landed on her, Griff's face brightened. "Mrs. Zaydan," he called out as he drew nearer to her. "This is a surprise."

"I came to see a friend." One of the men from his party separated from the crowd. Unease sliced through Hanna. *Dr. Norman Pratt.* Why was Griff with Dr. Pratt?

"My lord," called another of the men, "we'll go on ahead to the meeting room."

Griff waved the men on. "I'll join you shortly."

"What?" Hanna stared at the man and then at Griff. "Why did he refer to you as *my lord*?"

"Lord Griffin," said another man, "see you inside."

Griff nodded.

Hanna stared at him. *Lord Griffin*? Mr. Thomas—Griff—was *Viscount Griffin*? A dozen images shuffled through her mind. The package labeled by her father. Addressed to Lord Griffin, the viscount in Richmond. The gold ring within. The inscription. *Lady Griffin.*

"You're—" she asked, her voice drowned out by her pulse pounding in her ears.

"I can explain." That hooded blue gaze watched her carefully.

"Tell me you are not Lord Griffin."

"If I told you that, I would be lying. And I do not want to lie to you."

"It's too late for that." She could barely choke out the words. *Griff was Lord Griffin.* And he was obviously associated with Dr. Pratt, a man who'd tried to ruin Baba and would happily destroy everything Hanna had worked so hard to achieve. Had they partnered together to plot her downfall? To accuse her of stealing the ring and necklace? To prove that she was a fraud?

"It's not what you think," Griff . . . Lord Griffin . . . said quietly, urgently.

Hanna felt very cold inside. Despite the sun streaming in through the window, trapping her in its rays. "How would you know what I think?"

"Griff." Dr. Pratt came up behind him, his interested gaze finding Hanna. "And who is this?"

"A friend," Griff responded.

"No, not a friend," Hanna corrected.

The doctor's eyebrows lifted. He scanned her from head to toe. "Do not tell me that this is your bonesetter."

"This is Mrs. Zaydan." Griff cut Dr. Pratt off. "The very skilled bonesetter who repaired my shoulder."

Dr. Pratt flushed. "Forgive me, but I must speak plainly. Mrs. Zaydan knows as well as I that she had nothing to do with your recovery. I understand that the two of you might need a respectable pretext for your meetings, but I cannot in good conscience allow medical falsehoods to go unchallenged."

Hanna gasped at the implied insult to her virtue.

Griff's face went white. "Mrs. Zaydan is a respectable woman."

"I did not mean to imply otherwise," Dr. Pratt responded evenly. "The meeting is about to begin. If you will excuse me. Griff, please don't be too long."

Griff didn't acknowledge the man's words or his departure. His intense gaze remained fixed on Hanna. "I am sorry." His features were drawn tight. "Norman . . . erm . . . Dr. Pratt was out of line."

"Did you tell him that?" Her voice trembled with fury. "Did you tell him we are engaged in a liaison?"

"No. Of course not."

"Then, how did he come up with that notion?"

"Please let us go someplace where I can explain." He reached for her. "Once I tell you the truth—"

"Don't *touch* me!" She jerked her arm away when his fingers brushed her elbow. "Answer the question. Why does Dr. Pratt believe we are conducting an illicit affair?"

"You must know that I have the utmost regard for you. I would never do anything to tarnish your reputation."

"Then, why would Dr. Pratt say something like that?"

He clamped his mouth shut. Then sighed. "Men talk. I mentioned that I found you to be very appealing. Norman made some unfortunate assumptions."

She nodded her head in slow, deliberate motions as his words sank in. "I see." She spoke through clenched teeth. "You discussed me in a manner that made Dr.

Pratt believe that if you were not already bedding me, you would be soon."

"It wasn't like that—"

"Do you expect me to believe anything you say?"

"I never told Dr. Pratt that you and I were—"

Fury clouded her vision. "No, you only implied it." She lashed out, bashing him in the head with the bouquet of flowers. The tips of the broken stems fell with a thud. Loosened petals fluttered to the ground. "How many people have you told that I'm a strumpet to be had for two guineas?"

"None. I swear it."

"You're a liar. You lied about who you are and who knows what else. I cannot trust a single word that comes out of your mouth." She swung out at him again. The bunch of flowers were now just forlorn stems, looking as disillusioned as Hanna felt. He ducked, putting up his hands to defend himself. Although the effort seemed half-hearted. He made no move to stop her. Even though he could have. Easily.

"How dare you?" She struggled to hold back tears of indignation and hurt. A few careless words could ruin her before she even truly started. How many other men had Griff discussed Hanna with? Recalling their kiss made her burn with shame. "How dare you impugn my name? My livelihood? My reputation?" She hurled the remaining stems at him.

He took a step toward her. "Please, Hanna—"

"Don't you ever say my name again. You have no right." She backed away. "Stay away from me." Her voice broke. "I never want to see you again."

She fled without a backward glance, leaving him standing in a puddle of loose petals and tangled stems.

GRIFF COULD BARELY make it through his first board of governors meeting. Not only had his own behavior with Hanna been less than honorable, but Norman's insulting manner made everything immeasurably worse.

He kept seeing Hanna's face, the hurt, the anger, the disbelief. Tomorrow he would visit her and explain everything. He'd even tell her about his mother's ring. And the necklace.

His thoughts full of Hanna, Griff barely heard himself agree to host a fundraiser for the hospital. It was his role. The point of having a peer on the board was to prevail upon his wealthy friends to loosen their purse strings.

"Your behavior was less than courteous," he said to Norman after the meeting as they walked back to the waiting carriage.

"What was your friend doing in my hospital?"

"I have no idea. She said she was visiting someone."

"It is not my place to tell you who to associate with, but I don't want the young woman anywhere near my patients."

"I'm hardly her keeper," Griff retorted. "Do you really intend to keep a perfectly respectable woman from visiting her infirm friends and relations?"

"Perfectly respectable?" Norman exhaled. "For the love of God, if you haven't swived her yet, do us all a favor and get it over with. Once you wet your prick, perhaps you'll come to your senses."

Shocked by Norman's vulgarity, Griff watched the older man climb into the carriage. Norman was usually gentle and mild-tempered. Above all, Griff always found Norman to be a man of reason.

"I am baffled. Why do you hold Hanna in such deep contempt? You don't even know her. Is it because she is an Arab?"

"It is quite simple. Your bonesetter is a dangerous woman. She put out the wrist of Lord Payton's son. The young man was in pain for weeks." Norman landed hard on the carriage's forward-facing stuffed seat. "And I do worry that she might be cunning and manipulative. Look how she's already turning you against me."

Griff settled across from his former guardian. "Do not be ridiculous. She could never do that."

"I wonder," Norman said. "You have never spoken so harshly to me."

"Nobody could ever turn me against you." Griff felt a stab of guilt. He was blaming Norman for a situation that was his own fault. None of this would be happening if he hadn't lied to Hanna from the very beginning.

"There is now talk that she intends to open an infirmary."

"Mrs. Zaydan is? I hadn't heard that." That struck him as more respectable than seeing her patients at home. "Good for her."

"It could hurt Margate. She will likely open her dispensary near the hospital. Look how easily she turned your head. If she flutters those long, Levantine lashes convincingly enough, our donors could decide to give her *our* donations. That would be ruinous for a charity hospital. Margate lives and dies by donations."

Griff scoffed. "How could a small dispensary compete with a full-fledged hospital?"

"I cannot take the risk." He smoothed a wrinkle in the sleeve of his tailcoat. "Margate is my life's work. I will do whatever is necessary to protect the hospital."

It took a moment for Norman's meaning to sink in. "Surely that doesn't extend to ruining Mrs. Zaydan's reputation?"

"My focus is always on the greater good. Nothing must deter Margate from its mission of helping the poor."

"No matter who gets hurt in the process? Isn't that a little ruthless?"

"My dear boy, you have never had to worry about where your next shilling will come from. If you had, you would understand that sometimes being ruthless is necessary for the betterment of the many."

"At the expense of the few?" The cool detachment in Norman's approach jarred Griff. "I won't stand by and let you hurt her."

"Do calm yourself. I don't intend to do any harm to your bonesetter. She will manage that all on her own."

"Meaning?"

"Lord Payton is furious about what she did to his son. Who knows how many other Mansfields are out there? She won't be allowed to continue hurting people. At some point, your bonesetter will be made to account for her transgressions."

Chapter Ten

Meskeena." *Citi* tsked as her fingers moved rapidly, stuffing boiled cabbage leaves and rolling them into neat piles. "Poor thing. To die alone with strangers."

"We don't know if she was alone." They were in the kitchen making Hanna's favorite Arabic dish, cabbage rolls stuffed with lamb and rice, flavored with lemon and garlic. "Mrs. Lockhart's family took the body to her home village. It's possible they came the moment they heard she was ill."

Lucy, on her feet chopping garlic, tipped her bowl so *Citi* could see into it. "Is this enough garlic, *Um* Ali?"

"More. More." *Citi*'s perpetual frown deepened as she switched to Arabic. "That girl is so lazy."

"Yes, ma'am." Lucy returned to her task.

Hanna lined up rice mixed with lamb on a cabbage leaf and carefully rolled it up. "Remind me why we need so much garlic?"

"So that the cabbage won't make you bloated," *Citi* answered. To Lucy, she said, "Cut more garlic," even though the girl was already doing just that.

"*Salam*." Hanna's brother Rafi wandered in looking like he'd just tumbled out of bed.

"When did you arrive?" Hanna asked, surprised to see him.

"Last night."

"*Ahlan!*" Their grandmother's face lit up as she greeted her grandson. "Do you want something to eat, *Citi*?"

Lucy frowned. "Why is she calling him *Citi*?" she murmured to Hanna. "I though *Citi* means grandmother."

"It does. But a grandmother will also address her grandchild as *Citi*."

"Why?"

She shrugged. "It's an endearment. My father always called me *Baba*. It's an affectionate way of defining the family relationship between the two people who are speaking."

Lucy twisted her lips. "That's confusing."

"Eat something," *Citi* urged Rafi.

"I'm not hungry," Rafi said. "Is there any coffee?"

Lucy cast an admiring gaze at him. With his chocolate eyes and perfectly symmetrical bone structure, Hanna's eldest brother had an effect on women. "I can make it for you, sir."

"Thank you." Rafi yawned. He stooped to brush a kiss on *Citi*'s cheek. "How's the prettiest girl in the family?"

"*Malaya minuk*. Don't be silly." But *Citi* blushed. "Did you sleep well, *habibi*?"

"You arrived yesterday?" Hanna arranged a few more rolled cabbages in the pot. "I didn't see you last evening."

"Elias and I got here late yesterday morning. We made deliveries to some shops on Bond Street. And then"—he did a wavy little dance with his head—"we went to find some amusement."

"Of course you did." Frustration roiled through Hanna. Her brothers could do as they pleased, which included traipsing about town in the company of less-than-respectable women. Meanwhile, all sorts of restrictions were put on Hanna's ability to do what Baba had trained her to do, which actually helped people. "What time did you come home last night?"

"It doesn't matter. They're boys. It makes no difference." *Citi* beamed at her grandson. "We're making *malfouf* for you." Rafi was tall and much too thin, according to *Citi* and Mama, who constantly tried to make him eat.

"I will definitely be at home to eat." Lucy brought Rafi's coffee over. He strolled out of the kitchen, coffee in hand, pausing momentarily to wink at *Citi*. "I can't miss my *citi*'s cooking."

"*Shottar.*" *Citi* watched him go, adoration shining in her eyes. "He's a good boy."

There was a knock at the front door. Hanna tensed.

"Are you expecting someone, miss?" Lucy asked.

"No."

Lucy left to see who was at the door. *Citi* eyed Hanna. "What's wrong with you?" she asked in Arabic.

Arranging her *malfouf* rolls in the pot, Hanna avoided *Citi*'s probing bloodshot gaze. "Nothing is wrong."

"*Kezaba*."

Hanna's face heated. "Why do you assume I'm lying?"

"You've been too quiet since yesterday, when you came back from the hospital."

"Our neighbor died unexpectedly. Naturally I'm a little upset."

"You are more than upset. You are worried. I hope this is not about Blue Eyes."

"Who?" Hanna avoided looking at *Citi*.

"Your patient. You know which one. Blue Eyes. I don't have to remind you that we stay with our own. You need to marry a nice Arabic boy."

"There is no danger of my wedding Mr. Thomas or any other man. Arab or not." She'd had offers of marriage from within the Arab community. She'd even briefly entertained one. Nabeel had kind eyes and a generous nature, but he hadn't come close to tempting Hanna into giving up bonesetting. Which she would have to do. No husband would let her treat half-clothed men. "I'm too old. Besides, I'm wedded to my work."

"That won't keep you warm at night. Every woman needs a husband."

"You always say that *Cidi* was a headache."

"True. Your grandfather tired me out. Life with him was not easy. But a woman in this world is nothing without a man." *Citi*'s probing gaze stayed on Hanna. "If it's not the stranger with the blue eyes, then what *is* bothering you?"

Hanna debated telling her grandmother everything. *Citi* was right to be suspicious of Griff, while Hanna was busy obsessing about the man's physique and warm gazes. "When I was at the hospital—" she began.

Lucy reappeared. "There's someone to see you, miss."

Hanna rose, relieved by the interruption. "Who is it?"

"A solicitor. He says it's a matter of great importance."

Hanna's stomach lurched. Her thoughts immediately flew to Griff. Maybe he sent his solicitor to deliver some sort of warning. Had he already traced the package containing the gold ring back to her? Would he accuse Hanna of having stolen goods?

She removed her soiled apron. "Did you show him to the parlor?"

"Yes, miss. Shall I serve tea?"

"No tea." *Citi*'s assessing gaze clung to Hanna like a heavy mantle. "What does he want? Does it have to do with why you are worried?"

"How would I know what he wants?" Hanna smoothed a nervous hand down her bodice. "I suppose I should go and find out."

The solicitor stood by the bow window in the front parlor. Thin and rumpled, what little remained of his hair ran askew atop his head. He was not the type of solicitor Hanna expected the Quality to employ.

"Are you Miss Hanna Zaydan?"

Her heart pounded so loudly she could barely hear her own answer. "Yes, I am."

"Good day. I am Mr. White. I am settling the estate of Mrs. Claudia Lockhart."

"What?" Relief rolled through Hanna. This visit had nothing to do with Griff. "Oh. I see. But what does that have to do with me?"

"Mrs. Lockhart had no children."

"Yes, I know."

"She left something to you."

"She did? I wasn't aware that Mrs. Lockhart had anything to bequeath to anyone."

"Mr. Lockhart, her late husband, purchased the building that houses the grocery."

"I had no idea that Mrs. Lockhart owned the building."

"She did. She left the building to her nephew. He will receive the rents from the two apartments located above the shop."

"Forgive me, Mr. White, I fail to see what any of this has to do with me. Mrs. Lockhart was a neighbor and one-time patient, but we were not particularly well acquainted."

"Well, you must have made an impression on her. Although the building belongs to the nephew now, Mrs. Lockhart stipulated that you should have use of the ground-floor shop space."

"Me?" Hanna pressed a hand flat against her chest. "Whatever for? I am a bonesetter, Mr. White. I have no interest in operating a grocer's shop."

"She wanted you to have that space, free of rent, to set up your dispensary."

"My dispensary?" Her mouth fell open. "Are you certain?"

"Absolutely. I drew up the will quite recently."

"She wanted me to use the space for free? For how long?"

"As long as you wish to operate a dispensary that sees to the medical needs of this community, including the less fortunate. If you wish to run a dispensary for the next twenty years, it is your prerogative to do so."

Tears stung her eyes. What a generous gesture! And from a woman Hanna hadn't spent a great deal of time with. "I can hardly believe it."

He withdrew something from his pocket. "Here is the key."

Still in disbelief, Hanna stared at the brass skeleton key.

"Of course, you do not have to accept the offer." He began to withdraw his proffered hand.

"Oh no. I'll take it." Hanna reached for the key. "Thank you. I absolutely accept Mrs. Lockhart's generous offer."

She grinned as the reality set in. "I'm going to open my own dispensary."

Two DAYS AFTER his encounter with Hanna at the hospital, Griff examined the green sign with black lettering above the bow window. *Lockhart Grocers.* He'd just called at Hanna's residence. Her maid directed him down the street to this corner shop on the same block.

He waited to see her in hopes that her temper might have cooled a little. Filled with remorse, he was eager to talk to her, to explain that he'd never intended to harm her. He hadn't slept well. Regret had gnawed at him since their last meeting.

Pushing the door open, he peered inside. It wasn't much of a grocer. There was no food anywhere. Just some empty tables and shelves. And Hanna. And another man Griff didn't recognize.

"It's an excellent space." The man turned in a circle staring upwards. Tall, with even features, he wore a neat brown suit tailored to his long, lanky form.

"How much of it should we leave open?" Hanna said to the man. She wore a lavender gown, her hair tied in its severe knot at the base of her neck. "We do have the office in the back for private consultations."

"What do you think of partitions out here as well?"

She gestured with her hand. "Perhaps on this side."

The back of Griff's neck heated. He did not care for the obvious warmth between them. Nor for how easily their conversation flowed.

"The waiting room should be near the entrance." She glanced toward the door and stopped short. She'd spotted him.

"Good afternoon." He stepped inside. Closing the door behind him, he removed his hat.

"Keep it on," she said coldly. "You're not staying."

"I need to speak with you." He tried to keep the desperation out of his voice. "I can explain everything."

"I have no interest in hearing it. Our business is concluded. We've no reason to speak with each other."

He would beg if he had to. "Hanna, please—"

"That's *Mrs. Zaydan* to you." She turned away, dismissing him. "What about examining tables?" She spoke to her male companion. "How many do you think we'll need?"

The man looked from Hanna to Griff and back to Hanna. "Two? Three?"

"Perhaps we should start with two," Hanna said.

Griff pleaded with Hanna's back. "I am asking for just five minutes of your time. I want to explain why I initially came to you under false pretenses. Please hear me out."

She rounded on him, temper flashing in her dark-rimmed eyes. "I am not one of your servants who must do your bidding, *my lord*."

"Anyone who's ever met you knows that Hanna Zaydan doesn't do anyone's bidding but her own." He paused. "It's one of the qualities I most admire about you."

"Why are you still here? I asked you to leave."

"I am asking, humbly, that you give me a few minutes to explain."

"So"—she tilted her head—"you understand that I do not have to speak with you."

"You don't, but I wish you would."

The man interjected. "No disrespect, sir, but Mrs. Zaydan has made it clear that she doesn't wish to speak with you."

Griff fixed a cold stare on the man. "And who are you?"

"That's none of your business," Hanna snapped. "Don't let him intimidate you, Evan."

The man kept his gaze even with Griff's. "He doesn't."

Griff ignored him. "Hanna, if you would hear me out. I need to tell you everything."

"I would have been very happy to hear you out before I discovered what a liar you are. The only reason you want to explain anything to me now is because I caught you in your deception."

"I know I should have been honest with you earlier but—"

"I've had enough." Hanna crossed over to a table and reached for her reticule. "If you won't leave, I will." She marched out toward the street, slamming the door behind her.

"Now, then," said the man she'd called Evan. "Is there something I can help you with?"

"Go to perdition." Griff followed Hanna out the door, making certain to slam it even harder than she had. He watched her walk away, her shoulders set and proud. He couldn't force her to talk to him.

He'd have to find another way to show Hanna just how remorseful he was.

GRIFF STARED UP at the gracious redbrick town house off Cavendish Square and tried to quash the emotions welling up inside him.

It had been more than a dozen years since he'd stepped foot inside of Haven House. A place that held happy memories of his parents and sisters. But his parents were not inside and never would be again. His throat swelled. He should meet Dr. Shaw at his club. But he couldn't risk being seen by anyone who might report back to Norman before Griff had a chance to set things right with Hanna.

Two weeks had passed since he'd last seen her. Since then, he'd called twice at her home, and she'd refused to see him. The three notes he sent came back unopened. He couldn't force Hanna to meet with him. But this was one thing he could do for her in order to begin to make amends.

Taking a deep breath, he refocused on the house and forced himself to approach the glossy black front door. It swung open immediately.

His parents' butler—his butler now—appeared. "My lord. Welcome home."

"Wright." Griff swallowed. He felt a rush of gladness. Wright was the butler of his childhood. "You're still here."

"Indeed, my lord. Where else would I go?"

"To an employer where a family is actually in residence?"

"Why would I do that, my lord?" The corner of the man's mouth turned up. His face was the same, only more weathered now. Gray hair framed his lined face like a lion's mane. "It's a great deal less work when one's master remains absent for fourteen years."

Griff stared at the man. "Is that humor I detect, Wright?" Throughout his childhood, he'd never seen Wright wear anything other than an inscrutable expression. "And the beginnings of an actual smile?"

"It might very well be, my lord. It isn't every day one's master leaves as a boy and returns a grown man."

He handed his hat to the butler. "I might need a moment to recover from the shock of discovering that you have feelings."

"I do my best to conceal that weakness, my lord."

"Your secret is safe with me." He paused for a moment to take in his surroundings. The marble floors he'd skidded across. The curved staircase with the banister he'd slid down when his mother wasn't around and Wright pretended not to see. As the youngest of four and the only son, they'd all indulged him far more than they should have.

Griff's solicitor oversaw all operations and expenses at Haven House. Griff signed off on the expenditures, but otherwise knew nothing about staffing and day-to-day operations. For his own survival, he'd steered clear of this place and its memories. Until now.

"The maids have prepared your bedchamber, my lord." The butler paused. "The master's chamber, of course."

His father's chamber. "I won't be staying," Griff said quickly. "I am just here for a meeting."

"As you wish, my lord." The words were mild, but Griff thought he detected disappointment. "Once I received your note, I had both the parlor and your study prepared for your arrival."

His study. Wright meant his father's study. The late viscount's private domain. A room Griff hadn't been allowed to enter unless his father was present. "Not the study. The parlor will do nicely." He'd never spent any time with his parents in the parlor, a formal space reserved for guests and grown-ups. It was easier to meet Dr. Shaw in a room where memories of his family didn't cling to the walls like English ivy.

"Very good, my lord."

Griff made his way to the parlor. A footman stood by to open the door for him. "Welcome home, my lord."

"Thank you." Griff paused to study the tall, well--built man in his late thirties. There was something familiar about the footman. "Felix?"

"Aye, my lord." The man beamed. "It is I."

"You're still here?"

"Yes, my lord. My father served your father. And I serve you. My family has served yours for at least three generations."

"Is that right?" Griff hadn't known that. He remembered Felix, who'd been in his early twenties when Griff was a teenager. He'd slipped Griff a chcroot more than once and had never revealed the evenings when he caught Griff stealing away to meet friends.

"I'm glad you're still here, Felix." His parents were gone, but Wright and Felix were part of his old life. Maybe home was more than just his parents and sisters.

"Thank you, my lord. It is a pleasure to have you back at last."

Griff entered the parlor. It was as he remembered it. With too much furniture and an abundance of porcelain figurines and drawings of birds that his mother had so adored. He reached for one figurine on the nearest gleaming tabletop. A bluebird perched on a branch. It was cool in his hand. His father had often bought bird-themed gifts for Griff's mother. *If it's got anything to do with birds, Caroline will love it,* Papa would always say. And he was right. Mother had loved them all. Or, if she hadn't, at least she'd pretended to.

Behind him, Wright cleared his throat.

"Dr. Shaw, my lord."

Griff turned to find the editor of the medical journal standing beside his butler. "Dr. Shaw, come in. It was good of you to meet me here."

"When a viscount beckons, few in my position would refuse." He took the seat Griff indicated. "Curiosity alone would induce me to attend you."

"Whatever the motivation, I do appreciate your coming."

"What can I do for you, Lord Griffin?"

"I was wondering whether you've ever written about bonesetters."

Chapter Eleven

*E*van appeared unexpectedly and dropped a booklet on Baba's desk. "It appears that funding our dispensary should no longer be a problem."

"Hello, Evan." He'd interrupted her review of notes from Annie Peele's most recent appointment. The girl's treatment was progressing well. Griff had stayed away. She'd half expected the man to try to accompany his housekeeper's daughter to the appointments in order to gain an audience with Hanna. "Dare I ask what you are talking about?"

"This."

Her gaze fell to the journal he'd dropped in front of her. "*Medical Facts and Observations*?"

"Have you read it?"

"No. Should I have?" She paused. "Wait, what did you mean about funding no longer being a problem? Have you found a wealthy donor?"

"No, but you have. It appears that your viscount has delivered the goods."

She stiffened. "He is not *my* anything. And I'm not taking a shilling from him."

"You won't have to. It's not money that he's offering."

"It's not? Then what is it?"

"Your erstwhile suitor—"

"He is not my suitor."

"—has given an interview to the most prestigious medical journal in London extolling the virtues of the bonesetter who cured him when his own former guardian, the venerable Dr. Norman Pratt, the epitome of the medical establishment, could not."

The blood left Hanna's face. "He wouldn't do anything so foolish."

"He no doubt expects you to fall at his feet in gratitude now that a viscount, one of the most respected citizens in the land, has vouched for you." He leaned in, his hands flat on her desk. "The man put his own reputation on the line to speak up for you and your skills. I don't have to wonder what he expects in return from you."

Hanna barely heard him. "He shouldn't have done that."

Evan snatched the journal up from the desk and leafed through it. "Ah, here it is. He says he was cured by powerful manipulation and that, and I quote . . . *there is no denying that Mrs. Zaydan has a gift. She seems to intuitively know when a joint, muscle or tendon is out of place.*"

"Let me see that." She practically snatched the journal from Evan. *The first step is recognizing that this gift exists and could be an important component of future medical care*, the author had written. Hanna felt sick. "He has no idea what he has done."

Lucy appeared. "You've a visitor, miss. It's the toff." The maid spoke in a bored tone. She and Hanna had replayed this scene a number of times in the last fortnight. "I suppose you want me to send him away again."

Hanna tossed the journal onto her desk. "No, I shall see him."

Lucy straightened. "You will?"

"Please send him in."

"Yes, miss." Lucy shot Hanna a skeptical glance before quitting the room.

"Do you want me to stay?" Evan asked.

"No." She couldn't avoid Griff any longer. Who knew what damage the infuriating man could do in his quest to make amends? Or whatever he was truly after. "I shall see him alone. This is something I must take care of by myself."

HANNA CAME TO her feet as Griff appeared. She hated the way her heart shifted at the sight of him. Only a fool would pine for a man who'd not only lied to her but was also totally unsuitable. As a viscount, Griff was destined to wed a lady of quality, and if Hanna married at all, it would be to an Arab boy approved by her family.

And yet Hanna's mood lifted as Griff approached.

"Hanna, thank you for seeing me." He was handsomely dressed. Not in an extravagant way, but the fabrics and tailored pieces were more suited to the viscount he was, rather than the former soldier he'd pretended to be.

She came around Baba's desk. "I see you're not bothering with your disguise any longer."

He regarded her warily. "My disguise?"

She settled her hips against Baba's desk, her palms resting on the wooden surface on either side of her. "That tailcoat probably costs what I earn in a year."

He watched her carefully. "Do you expect me to apologize for who I am?"

"No, simply for lying about it, *Lord Griffin.*"

He winced at the emphasis she placed on his true name and title. "I didn't intend to deceive you."

"Of course you did. You very deliberately did not tell me who you are."

"My title is irrelevant to who I am as a man."

"It is not meaningless in terms of-the power you wield as a nobleman."

"Influence that I have exerted on your behalf."

Lucy returned after seeing Evan out and took her post by the door.

Griff glanced down at the medical journal on her desk. "You've seen the piece, then?" He regarded Hanna expectantly. "Did you like it?"

"No, I don't like it," she snapped. "Are you truly so removed from ordinary life that you don't realize you've made me a target?" She stopped and took a moment to rein in her temper.

"I am fully acquainted with life's hardships." His face hardened. "I am not inured from pain and loss."

She tapped her chest. "I stand to lose my livelihood."

"How so?"

"You have made Dr. Pratt a laughingstock."

"I have done no such thing." He drew back. "I set a condition with the editor of the journal that Norman not be named in the article."

"He doesn't need to be mentioned. You were in his care. You sit on the board of his hospital. Everyone will know of your association. He treated your shoulder, did he not?"

"Yes, but that's not in the piece—"

"If I had known that you were associated with Dr. Pratt, I would never have agreed to treat you that first day."

"I don't believe that. You would not have allowed me to continue suffering."

"What is your relation to him?"

"Dr. Pratt? He is my guardian, my former guardian. He looked after me after my parents died."

Hanna blinked. His *guardian*. Griff had lived with Dr. Pratt. She hadn't even begun to imagine that the two men could be so close. "Was his intent to prove to all of London that I am a fraud?"

"No, that—"

"But then I actually cured you." She gave a mirthless laugh. "Did you undergo a conversion? The charlatan surprised you by relieving you of your pain. Is that when you had an epiphany? Did you decide I wasn't a fraud after all?"

"Dr. Pratt had nothing to do with this. In fact, when he learned I was seeing you, he expressed concern and warned me to stay away from you."

"Why didn't you?"

"Because of the necklace."

"The sapphire?"

"I've been wanting to tell you the truth. I just didn't know how."

"What is your interest in it?"

"The sapphire belonged to my mother."

She froze. "What?"

"Your necklace was stolen from my mother's body the night she was murdered."

"MURDERED?" HANNA GRIPPED the overhanging edge of Baba's desk. "Your mother was *murdered*?"

He nodded, grim-faced. "As was my father."

"Oh, Griff." Sorrow filled her at the thought of what he'd endured. "How awful. I'm so sorry."

"Gor!" Lucy blurted out at the same time. They both turned to her. Lucy's eyes rounded, and the flat of her hand flew to cover her mouth when she realized she'd spoken aloud.

"You may go, Lucy," Hanna said.

"But I'm not supposed to leave you alone with—"

"*You may go*," Hanna said more firmly. Lucy looked like she was about to object but then sullenly turned and left the room.

"Is that wise?" Griff watched after the girl before turning back to Hanna. "Won't your grandmother object to us being alone?"

"Yes, but she's away." *Citi* was visiting her cousins. "My brothers are here for a few days. She left them to chaperone."

"Won't your brothers object?"

"They can barely look after themselves, much less

be bothered with what I'm getting up to." She gentled her voice. "Now, tell me about your mother's necklace."

"She wore it the night she died." Pain clouded his gaze. "We weren't even meant to be there that night. Mother and I originally intended to remain in London while Father traveled to our country estate for a couple of nights to see to some business. I convinced Mother that we should go with him. There was a friend there who I wanted to see. It's my fault that we were even there."

"Surely the only person at fault is the man who actually harmed your parents."

He gave a sad smile. "At least Mother might still be here, if only . . ." Taking a deep breath, he continued. "As to the necklace, Mother wore it all the time. When I picture her in my mind, she's wearing the sapphire around her neck."

"No wonder you reacted as you did the day I put your elbow back in."

"I saw you with the sapphire before that. At the coffeehouse." He paused to pull something from his pocket. "This was my mother's as well. She rarely took it off."

Hanna stared down at the gold signet ring in Griff's palm. The one with the carved floral band she'd so admired.

"The reason I was at the coffeehouse the day you put Mansfield's wrist out," he explained, "was that I'd just come from the post office off Red Lion Square, the one that stamped the package containing Mother's ring. I tried to find out who sent it."

Hanna licked her dry lips. She'd dispatched Lucy to mail the package. "What did you learn?"

"Nothing at all. They didn't remember anything about the package or its sender. I visited the coffee-house after that to contemplate what to do next. And then you walked in wearing my mother's necklace."

Understanding dawned. "Which is why you came to see me."

"It was deuced convenient that my injury gave me a plausible reason for seeking you out."

"I wondered why you came to me when it was obvious you were skeptical from the start." She recalled his surprise upon learning about her modest fee. "You thought I was a charlatan."

He colored. "I did. Yes."

"You came to me because you thought I mailed the ring."

"I suspected." His gaze met hers. "Did you?"

"Yes."

He exhaled long and slow. "It *was* you."

"I found the ring and the necklace among my father's things. He'd already packaged the band. Your name and direction were on it. It's clear that Papa intended to send your mother's ring back to you."

"Where did he get it?"

"Papa's patients sometimes paid with goods when they didn't have money. Afterward, he must have seen the inscription inside the band and realized the ring belonged to you."

"Why do you think he didn't include the necklace?"

"It's possible he didn't know the sapphire belonged

to the same person who owned the ring. There's no inscription on it."

"That makes sense." His shoulders hunched. "Your father is no longer with us. There's no way to know who gave him the ring and necklace."

Hanna drummed her fingers against her skirt. "Actually, there might be."

He straightened. "How?"

"Every patient and each payment are recorded in my father's ledgers."

"My parents were killed fourteen years ago. Do you have records that go that far back? Would you even know where to begin to look?"

"I've kept patient records for my father since I was twelve. He always said my handwriting was better than his." She brightened at the memory. "I might not have been the one to write down this payment, but I know exactly how Papa did things. He was meticulous, and he taught me to be so as well."

Griff rubbed his hands together. "Where do we start?"

"ANYTHING YET?" HANNA asked.

They'd spent hours poring over the old ledgers they'd brought up from the basement cellar. Hanna working behind Baba's desk with Griff sitting opposite. Her father's study was overly warm, thanks to the late-afternoon sun which cast dark shadows over the stone-flagged floor. It was getting late.

"Nothing." Griff stretched his stiff neck from side to side. "You?"

"No. We'll just have to keep searching."

Griff discovered that Hanna was right. Her late father kept excellent notes. Neat columns and careful handwriting detailed each patient's name, symptoms, diagnosis and treatment. The final note on the patient's record documented the amount paid for treatment and the date.

Griff also learned that Hanna's father hadn't been greedy. He'd accepted just about anything as payment. A rooster. A pail of onions. Fresh-baked pies. But so far, no gold rings or sapphire necklaces.

The servant girl appeared in the doorway. They'd taken care to leave the door ajar. "Supper is ready, miss."

"Coming, Lucy." Hanna rose. Griff realized she had removed her fichu at some point during the long afternoon. Even divested of the chest kerchief, the modest cut of her gown ensured she displayed no more of her décolletage than any other respectable woman. Still his eyes were drawn to the delicate bare skin on her chest. And the dark beauty mark above her left breast. A sight hidden from his view until now.

She stretched after sitting for so many hours, arching her back. The cotton bodice of her gown pulled tight, outlining pert, round breasts.

"Would you like to join me?" she asked.

"What?" He blinked and forced his gaze up to her face.

"Would you care to join me for supper?"

"It would be my pleasure. But your brothers—"

"Are not at home, and I have no idea when they will

be." She stacked the ledgers on the desk. "Besides there is nothing scandalous about our taking a meal together. Lucy is here."

True, but they both knew she was taking advantage of her grandmother's absence by pushing the boundaries. Griff was in full support. The old woman's scowl could frighten the most battle-hardened soldier.

He paused. "Before we go in to supper, I want to assure you that I never told Dr. Pratt that I'd bedded you. It is important that you know that."

She paused, one forearm resting on the stack of ledgers. "Then where did he get that idea?"

"I knew he'd object to your treating my injury, so I led him to believe I might be more interested in . . . erm . . . other attributes."

She flushed. "I see."

"It wasn't to impugn your reputation," he quickly added. "I would never do that. I just wanted to get Norman off the topic of my being treated by a bonesetter."

"I don't approve of what you said, but I understand why you spoke as you did. Goodness knows, I've wanted to divert my grandmother's conversation often enough." She came around the side of the desk. "Shall we eat?"

He followed her through the passage into the dining room. A round table with tapered legs was in the center of the room. A mahogany sideboard stood along one wall and, for some reason, a yellow sofa was pushed up against the other. Half-open folding doors led to the front parlor where Hanna's grandmother often planted herself, smoking the strange water pipe of hers.

He surveyed the crowded bookshelves tucked between the sofa and an adjacent wall. Sketches, prints and needlework adorned the space. "This is an interesting room," he remarked as they took their seats.

She glanced at the sofa. "We have a large family. We put seating wherever we can manage. There's never enough room when the entire family is together. We're practically sitting on top of each other."

Griff wondered what it would be like to always be surrounded by family. The home wasn't large, but it was a comfortable, middle-class abode. From what he could discern, there were four floors. The maid brought the food up from the basement kitchen.

The tray was laden with open-faced meat pies, cheese and fruits all to be washed down with ale. The maid also set out small plates of olives, radishes, cucumbers and pickles. The tantalizing aroma of fresh-baked meat pies filled the air; they were unusual, with minced meat and pine nuts on individual servings of round flat bread.

"Those smell delicious."

"They're Arabic-style meat pies," she said as they took their seats. "We call it *sfeeha*."

He admired her as she filled a plate for him. Hanna's actions were sure and purposeful. Undaunted confidence lent her a grace that Mayfair debutantes could never hope to attain. She reached for the radishes. Her hands were not the delicate porcelain of a gentlewoman. They were smooth and tan, strong and capable.

Those knowing hands had delivered him from years of misery.

"*Sfeeha* is made with ground lamb, onion and spices mostly," she said. "Nothing too exotic for an English palate."

"Knowing you has whetted my appetite for the out-of-the-ordinary. For the extraordinary."

She flushed as she concentrated on adding two meat pies and some olives, radishes and pickles to his plate. "It's a light supper. Nothing suitably grand enough for a viscount."

"Meals are a hearty but modest affair at Norman's . . . erm . . . Dr. Pratt's house and at Bell Cottage." He bit into one of the meat pies. It was warm, the dough just a touch crispy, the robust taste of lamb subtly enhanced by unusual spices.

"Bell Cottage?" she asked.

"My home in Devon."

She popped an olive into her mouth. His gaze lingered on her lips. Her mouth was wide and plump, the bottom lip fuller than the top. "You live in a cottage in Devon?"

He tore his eyes from her mouth. "Yes, I seldom come to London. On the rare occasion that I am in Town, I stay with Dr. Pratt."

Mirth danced in her eyes. "I thought viscounts lived on grand country estates with dozens of servants."

"I prefer something more intimate." He paused. "It is, after all, just me."

"Do you have any sisters or brothers?"

"Three sisters."

"Do you see them often?"

He swallowed a too-big bite of meat pie. "No. All are married and busy with their own families."

"Really?" She frowned, a delicate number eleven forming between her full brows. "You should make time to see them. They are your family."

"Our lack of connection is not my doing," he said tightly. "It is their choice."

"Oh." She searched his face, but what she saw there did not invite more questions about his siblings. "And Dr. Pratt?"

"Norman is not only my former guardian, he is also family. He and my father were cousins."

He registered the distaste on her face before she quickly concealed it.

"I realize Norman made a terrible first impression," he said. "He was unaccountably rude to you, but he's been very good to me."

"I'm happy Dr. Pratt treated you well. You deserved that. But I have my own experiences." Anger clouded her luminous eyes. "He tried to ruin my father's reputation. He did everything he could to make certain my father had no patients."

Griff frowned. "I had no idea a previous association existed between Norman and your family. He never mentioned it."

"Purposefully, I am sure." She scoffed. "My father successfully treated a patient that Dr. Pratt was unable to cure. Your guardian was furious. He warned Papa to stay away from his patients. Dr. Pratt threatened to ruin Papa, to see to it that he never practiced bonesetting again. We are simple people. An influential man such as Dr. Pratt could easily have ruined my father."

A chill rippled through Griff. "And history has just repeated itself." He finally understood the grave error he'd made in speaking to the medical journal. "Only this time with you, the bonesetter's daughter."

"Exactly. You told all of London that a bonesetter bested Dr. Pratt, and a female daughter of foreigners at that."

"I do beg your pardon." Regret panged through him. "I would never purposely put you in harm's way."

"Nonetheless, you have done so." The words were matter-of-fact, rather than accusatory. But they stung, nonetheless. "Now it is only a matter of time before Dr. Pratt retaliates. He will want to see me ruined."

"I won't let him harm you." He slid his hand across the table to cover hers. Her skin was smooth to the touch. "I swear it."

Her color deepened. "It is probably already too late."

Griff stared at their joined hands, his focus on the delicious weight of her warm fingers in his palm. He was overcome with the urge to touch more of her. To feather his fingers over the beauty spot on her décolleté. To feel the urgent press of her lips against his. To taste her. Knowing her grandmother was nowhere in the vicinity made him reckless.

Her eyes met his. "I shall have to be on guard."

He blinked, sensing she was no longer talking about someone else. "Against?"

"Apparently from all of the men in your family," she

said. "And not just your father's cousin, who clearly detests me."

"You cannot believe *I* mean you any harm. I would do anything to protect you."

"That is why you are perhaps even more of a danger to me. To my sense of self-preservation." He registered the banked heat in her gaze, the dilated pupils, the high color on her cheeks. Her fingers pressed against his. "When you touch me, I am tempted to do your bidding. Even though it could destroy everything I've worked for."

Heat slid across the surface of his skin. He could have free rein. Do what they both so clearly wanted. He had nothing to lose by taking her to bed. But she would be risking everything. Her reputation. Her livelihood. He could not subject her to that.

Griff slowly, regretfully, withdrew his hand. She briefly tightened her grip, startling him by momentarily prolonging the physical contact. Then she let him go.

He struggled to gather his thoughts. "On the subject of Norman, there is something I must tell you."

"What is it?"

"Norman knows about Mother's necklace."

"Knows what exactly?"

"That it is in your possession. That you found it among your father's things."

She pressed her lips inward so that they all but disappeared. "And how did he react?"

"He accused your father of being a fence. We only discussed it briefly once. It's entirely possible that

Norman has already forgotten about the necklace. He hasn't mentioned it to me again."

"Perhaps." But he could tell by the somber expression on her face that she didn't think so. Neither did Griff.

Chapter Twelve

*N*orman was waiting for Griff when he returned to his former guardian's home.

The moment Griff stepped through the door, Norman appeared in the front hall, his wrinkled shirt untucked from his trousers. Norman's rumpled appearance surprised Griff. The man prided himself in always looking neat and tidy. He said patients had more confidence in an orderly-looking physician than an unkempt one. "Where have you been?"

"Here and there." Griff shrugged off his coat. "I had matters to attend to."

"Were you with her?"

"Need I remind you that I am a grown man? My whereabouts are not your concern."

"Please come to my library," Norman said tightly. "I should like to have a word with you."

"I'm exhausted." Griff headed for the stairs. "Can we speak in the morning?"

"I would prefer that we talk now."

Out of respect for all Norman had done for him, rather than fear, Griff turned in the direction of the library. As soon as they entered, Norman rounded on him.

"Have I been good to you?"

Griff edged around Norman to settle into a stuffed chair. "You know you have."

"And yet you see fit to insult me before my peers, before all of London."

Griff rubbed his eyes. "I gather this is about the medical journal."

"You know damn well that it is."

"What would you have me do, Norman?" he asked, exasperated. "You insulted her in public. Impugned her reputation. You practically called her a whore."

"It might not have been my finest moment, but you are overreacting." Norman perched on the edge of his chair. "She's a member of the laboring class. It isn't as if I insulted a lady."

Griff clamped his mouth shut, struggling to keep his temper in check. "I don't want to hurt you, Norman. You and I both know that you are the only family I have left."

Norman flushed. "And yet, this is how you treat me."

"I told the truth. I had to counter any damage to her reputation done by your attacking her in public."

"I stood by you when no one else did."

"Yes, you did. And I am grateful."

"I don't want you to feel indebted. You're like a son to me. All I ask for is a little loyalty."

"You have it. Unreservedly. But I will not stand by and watch you ruin the reputation of a woman who has done nothing to deserve it."

"Can you not see that she is dangerous?" Norman entreated. "Or at the very least inept. She put out Mansfield's wrist!"

"Maybe it was no accident."

"What are you saying?" Norman squinted at him. "You believe the bonesetter intentionally dislocated Mansfield's wrist? That is even more concerning."

"I am not saying anything. All I mean to suggest is that you've only heard Mansfield's side of the story."

Norman threw up his hands. "I give up. There is no talking reason into you where she's concerned. At least your association with the bonesetter is at an end. Your treatment is complete, is it not?"

"Yes."

"Dare I assume you won't be seeing her again?"

"I am a grown man," he said coldly. "I alone decide who I wish to associate with."

"Meaning you intend to continue to consort with the bonesetter."

"Do not make me choose, Norman."

"Make you choose?" Disbelief flooded Norman's face. "As if there is a choice between a foreign woman you met a few weeks ago and me, who raised you as my own son since the age of fifteen."

"What do you want me to do? Acknowledge the obvious? That I am in your debt? Pay you for all of the years?"

He tsked. "Certainly not. There is no debt. However, I cannot abide you going from my house to hers. It is the height of disloyalty."

Griff rose. "Very well."

Norman watched him carefully. "Very well what? We are agreed that you will not see her?"

"It is past time for me to stop taking advantage of your kindness."

"What does that mean?"

"I'm moving out."

Norman shot to his feet. "Don't be ridiculous. Where are you going? Do you mean to set up house with that woman?"

He headed for the door. "No, I am going home."

"To Bell Cottage, out in the country?" Norman followed him. "You're leaving London?"

Griff paused. Turning to face his former guardian, he set a hand on Norman's shoulder. "I thank you for your care of me. I shall be forever grateful. But the moment has come for me to stand on my own. We both know it's long overdue."

"But where will you go?"

"I am returning home to Cavendish Square. It's time to reopen Haven House."

"STILL NOTHING. No one who paid for your father's services with jewelry."

Hanna looked up from the latest ledger containing Baba's patient records. "There are plenty of more files to go through."

She and Griff decided to meet at the dispensary to continue going through the ledgers. Both were eager to escape *Citi*'s critical gaze now that she'd returned from visiting her cousin.

He set a ledger aside. Hanna was acutely aware of

Griff's every move, every breath, every sigh. It would be easy to get carried away but for Lucy, who was sitting out front in one of the waiting chairs near the entrance.

"It would help if we knew when your father received the jewels," Griff said.

"But we don't know how long he had them." Hanna turned the page, continuing her examination. "So we need to go through all of the records in the time period between your parents' deaths up until my father died."

Griff nodded. "Your father could have received the jewels at any time in those intervening years." He tossed the ledger beside him on the examining table where he was sitting. "But I'm afraid we'll need to take this up again tomorrow, if you are available."

"You're leaving?" Disappointment lashed through her. "So soon?"

"I'm afraid so. It's moving day for me."

Her stomach dropped. "You're leaving London?"

"No, just Dr. Pratt's house."

"You are?"

"It is time," he said briskly.

"It's because of the interview you gave to the medical journal, isn't it?" Hanna disliked Griff's former guardian, but she understood that he was Griff's only real family because his sisters chose not to be in his life. "I am sorry if this has caused a rift between you."

"Don't be. It is past time that I returned to Haven House."

"Haven House?"

"My family home . . . erm . . . my townhome in Mayfair. I am used to regarding it as my parents' house. But it is mine and has been for more than a decade. It is time to reclaim my heritage."

"If you have your own house here, why do you stay with Dr. Pratt when you are in London?"

He grimaced. "Both Haven House and Ashby Manor, our country seat, were closed up after the murders. I couldn't bear the thought of returning to places where I'd once been so happy."

She followed him out of the office to the main floor. "Why don't you see your sisters more often?" Hanna saw her own family all the time. Far too much. She often felt like she couldn't get a moment alone. "You could be a comfort to each other."

His jaw tensed. "As I mentioned previously, it wasn't my choice. In any case, my things are being taken over to Haven House as we speak, so I must go."

The bell over the door sounded. Evan came in carrying a package. "Another delivery. More supplies. Someone left it outside."

"Evan, you remember Lord Griffin," Hanna said.

Evan and Griff faced each other. "Yes, of course." Evan bowed. "Good afternoon."

"Hello." Griff's icy gaze traveled over him. "Are you here for an appointment?"

Evan flashed his teeth. "No, indeed. We are not seeing patients yet."

"*We*?"

"Dr. Bridges is my partner," Hanna said. "We shall be working together once we open the dispensary."

"I hadn't realized." Griff wasn't pleased. "And your grandmother approves?"

"Of course not. She also did not approve of my treating you, either, but I am hoping to nudge her along."

"I see." Griff kept his gaze on Evan, who returned it, unblinking.

"Griff," Hanna said, "you mentioned that you must leave, did you not?"

"Yes, I must." He spared Evan one final glance. "Good day."

Evan peered through the bow window, watching Griff head down the street. "How much do you know about that man?"

"I'm not sure what you are getting at." Hanna started unpacking books she'd brought from Baba's office to the dispensary. "You know he's a former patient."

Evan's brows lifted. "And that is all?"

"Is this an interrogation?" she asked lightly. Hanna didn't know how to fully answer Evan's question. She wasn't going to mention the jewelry.

"I made some inquiries. Do you still wish to rearrange the examining tables?"

"Yes, I think so." She watched him push the patient table. "What sort of inquiries?"

"I asked about the man and his reputation. How's this?"

She surveyed the positioning. "Maybe move it a bit more to the left. You made inquiries into Lord Griffin?" She set down the book in her hand. "And? What did you learn?"

"His parents were murdered."

"He told me."

Evan shifted the table to the left. "Did he also tell

you that it was a brutal knife attack? That they fought for their lives?"

"No." She shivered. "Naturally, he wouldn't go into that kind of detail. It's hardly a subject for polite conversation."

"Perhaps he prefers not to speak of it because most of society believes he committed the murders."

"What?" She gave an incredulous huff. "That's ridiculous. He was just a boy."

"Fifteen years old. Young certainly, but not a child." Evan straightened and surveyed the examining table. "Griffin claimed that he slept through the attacks. That he saw and heard nothing. Even though it was clear that the parents did not go quietly."

"If my brothers are any indication, boys that age can sleep through just about anything."

"There was no sign of forced entry. No broken windows or doors. The servants told the magistrate that the doors and windows were always locked before the household retired for the evening."

"You are saying it was someone who was in the house at the time who was responsible? What about the servants?"

Evan gestured toward the table. "Good?"

She nodded. "Perfect."

"Most of the servants were off. One of the footmen was getting married in the village, and the staff had a few hours' leave to attend the festivities. The only member of the staff who was home that night was a housekeeper. She didn't hear anything. Her quarters were far away from the family wing. A woman alone could hardly attack and kill two people who fought back. There wasn't a scratch on her. But the same couldn't be said for your viscount."

"What do you mean?"

"There were fresh scratches on his back. He claimed he'd brushed up against some tree branches."

"It seems like you'd get more than some scratches on the back if you attacked and killed two people with a knife."

"You certainly are an ardent defender of the man."

She looked away. "It is ghastly to assume a boy could kill his own parents in such a terrible way."

"I just thought you should know."

"It sounds like you went to a great deal of trouble to learn vile gossip about Lord Griffin."

"He seems to be coming around you a great deal."

Hanna declined to give Evan the details into their examination of the records. "We have some unfinished business. That is all. Once this matter is concluded, Lord Griffin will return to Mayfair, and you and I shall be here, treating patients."

"Considering the way that man ogles at you, I doubt you will be rid of him so easily."

"Don't be ridiculous. He does no such thing."

"If you say so."

She studied Evan. His color was high. "What is the matter with you?"

"I don't know what you are talking about," Evan said lightly as he shifted the second examining table.

Chapter Thirteen

"Have you hired a valet, my lord?" Wright, the butler, asked Griff.

Griff surveyed his father's bedchamber. *His* bedchamber now. The wardrobe that had appeared massive to Griff as a boy no longer seemed so. The familiar four-poster bed certainly wasn't as enormous as in his memory. His eyes locked on the burgundy paisley canopy. "Have you changed the bed coverings?"

"Certainly, my lord. The others were quite old."

"Of course." In Griff's mind, Haven House had frozen in time, unchanged from the moment fourteen years ago when he and his parents departed for a few unexpected days in the country. He inhaled the clean scent of lemon and beeswax and felt the warmth of the late-afternoon sun filtering through the windows.

For years, he'd put off returning to this place where some of his fondest family memories were enshrined. But the house didn't feel like a mausoleum. To his surprise, it still felt like home. "And no, I don't have a valet."

"Would you like me to advertise for one, my lord? In the meantime, I can assign a footman to assist you."

"Could you send Felix?" he asked, recalling the favorite footman of his youth. "He is available, is he not? I saw him the other afternoon."

"Certainly, my lord." He paused. "I did not assemble the staff to greet you upon your official return to Haven House. I thought you might prefer to decide when to address the staff. When you are ready, that is."

Normally, whenever Griff's father had returned from the country, the staff would line up in the front hall to greet him. Griff was relieved Wright hadn't gathered the servants. Just being back at Haven House was overwhelming enough.

"Yes, thank you, and Felix will do nicely," Griff said. "It will be good to have a familiar face around."

"You will find, my lord, that there are several members of your staff who remember you with great fondness and are eager to welcome you home."

It never occurred to Griff that he might be missed by his father's servants. *His* staff now. What would it have been like to return home to Haven House directly after the murders? At the time, he'd been drowning in grief and guilt. Maybe being home would have helped. Maybe his sisters would still be in his life.

His gaze caught on the closed door that led to Mama's adjoining chamber. "And the viscountess's rooms? Have they also been changed?"

"Yes, my lord. The housekeeper replaced the bed coverings and upholstery."

He walked over and put his hand on the brass door

handle. Pausing, he took a deep breath. Then he turned the knob and pulled open the door to his childhood.

He'd spent a great deal of time in this bedchamber. Playing on the floor while his mother dressed. Cuddling in bed with both of his parents whenever he escaped Nurse in the middle of the night after a bad dream.

Mother's dressing table was still here. But the lotions and hairbrushes that used to neatly line its mirrored surface were long gone. Griff looked for the stuffed chair by the window. Papa's chair. It was still there but was covered in a new fabric. One with birds.

"Birds."

"Indeed, my lord. Mrs. Tanner and I thought it might be an appropriate way to honor the viscountess."

"Mrs. Tanner? The housekeeper? Is she still here?"

"No, my lord. She left to serve Lady Dorcas several years ago."

"She works for my sister now?"

"Yes, my lord. Mrs. Tanner said the house was far too quiet after . . ." Wright didn't finish. He didn't need to.

Griff opened the wardrobe. It was empty. "My mother's things?"

"The Ladies Maria, Winifred and Dorcas came a few weeks after . . . the tragedy . . . and they sorted through everything."

"My sisters were here?"

"Yes, my lord. They took what they wanted and distributed the rest. They were most generous with the staff."

They hadn't asked Griff to join them? *Because they blame you.* He swallowed. Griff couldn't fault them for wanting nothing to do with him. But Dorcas's defection stung the most. He was closest to her. They were just four years apart. Maria and Winifred were much older.

"Except for the family jewels," Wright added. "Naturally, those remain in the family safe. They belong to your future viscountess and to future holders of the title."

"And my father's things?" Griff closed the wardrobe door. "Did Maria, Winifred and Dorcas dispose of those as well?"

"No, my lord. Your sisters asked that his lordship's things be boxed up and put aside for you to dispose of as you saw fit." Wright cleared his throat. "Naturally, we did not expect you to stay away so long."

"I've clearly been remiss." Griff had been so wrapped up in his own grief that he hadn't realized there were people depending upon him. Maybe it was time he stopped disappointing them. Taking a deep breath, he turned to face the butler. "I am here now. And I intend to see to my duties."

Wright's eyes lit up. "Very good, my lord." He bowed and walked toward the door. He paused and turned back to Griff. "If I may say, my lord, how pleased we are to have you back with us at last."

"Thank you, Wright." Griff surveyed Mama's chamber. Her presence lingered. He could almost smell her perfume. "It is good to finally be home." To Griff's surprise, he meant it. "And, Wright?"

The butler paused. "My lord?"

"Please assemble the staff. I'll meet them in the front hall in a quarter of an hour."

HANNA WAS IN the back office at the dispensary examining Baba's records when the bell over the front door sounded. Her spirits lifted. It must be Griff. He'd stayed away for three days.

"I'll be right there," she called out, moving at a fast clip, straightening her bodice and shaking out her skirts. She wasn't expecting anyone else. Evan was busy seeing patients at his old office.

"I was wondering where—" She stumbled to a halt. *Citi* and her brothers Rafi and Elias stood in the middle of the dispensary. "Oh, hello."

"What were you wondering?" Rafi asked.

"I was wondering . . . who it was." She tried to keep the disappointment out of her voice. "I wasn't expecting anyone."

"You sounded pretty cheerful," Rafi observed.

Elias pursed his lips as he took in his surroundings. "This seems like a real clinic."

"It should," she responded. "That's exactly what it is."

"Very nice." Rafi hopped onto an examining table. "Did you really learn enough from Baba to be able to fix patients on your own?"

"I apprenticed with Baba for more than a decade, since I was eleven." Hanna kept her gaze on *Citi* as the old woman shuffled about the space, taking everything in. "I was by his side for practically every patient."

Citi passed a hand over the examining table across from the one Rafi sat on. "The whole time Ali was teaching you how to be a bonesetter?"

"Yes." Hanna leaned her hips against the table next to Rafi. "He said I had a natural talent for it."

"Your Baba told us you were just playing." *Citi* paused to examine the jars and instruments laid out atop the commode table.

"I know." Hanna crossed her arms over her chest, her nerves taut. "He said we should keep it a secret because you and Mama didn't approve."

"But the entire time you were watching and learning." *Citi* pulled the top drawer of the commode table open and nodded briefly to herself as she scrutinized the neatly stacked clean linens and bandaging. "You were both lying."

"Watch out," Elias murmured as he settled on Hanna's other side. "She's going to blow at any moment." Even as her brothers teased, they'd lined up on either side of Hanna, silently bolstering her.

The muscles across the back of Hanna's shoulders tightened. She'd never explicitly asked for her family's blessing to move forward with opening the dispensary. It would be harder for them to object once the clinic was open. She didn't want to give them the opportunity to forbid it.

It was a gamble. But she'd thought it through. At twenty-six, she was a spinster. Over the years, offers from eligible Arab men had dwindled. *Citi* and Mama couldn't seriously expect her to make a decent match at her age. They could focus on marrying off her younger sister, Fiona Kate, while Hanna ran her dispensary.

"Baba was just trying to keep the peace," Hanna said to *Citi*.

"And you?" For the first time since entering the dispensary, *Citi* looked her granddaughter square in the eyes. "What were you doing?"

"At least you're faster than her," Rafi said under his breath. "If you decide to run."

Hanna felt like a hundred fluttering butterflies were trapped inside her chest. "When I was fifteen, Baba allowed me to start treating some of the patients while he supervised. I learned it is my destiny to be a bonesetter." She winced as she finished the sentence that could truly set *Citi* off.

A muffled sound of shock came from Elias's throat. "Now you've done it. It's a good thing she can't slip off her shoe fast enough to launch it at you."

They'd spent their childhoods trying to evade *Citi*'s and Mama's flying slippers. Both women showed excellent precision when it came to aiming their airborne shoes at whichever child showed disrespect or broke a rule. Adding to the indignity, the offender would then have to return the shoe to its owner and risk getting hit again, only this time at close range.

"In my day, we never had a choice." *Citi* settled heavily into a seat in the waiting area. Her voice was wistful. "We had to marry, have children, cook and clean. We never could choose."

"What is happening?" Rafi muttered. "No projectiles? No cursing?"

Citi stared out the bow window. "No one ever asked the *binat*, us girls, what we wanted."

"To be fair," Elias murmured to Hanna, "no one asked you what you wanted. You just took it."

Citi's strange mood, reflective rather than condemnatory, unsettled Hanna. This was a side of her grandmother she'd never seen. Feeling less fearful of having a shoe flung in her direction, she crossed over to sit next to her.

"I never intended to lie or be disrespectful. I got caught up in it. I took to bonesetting from the very beginning. I was good at it. It made me proud to excel at a craft that helps people."

"A girl should get married. She is incomplete without a husband and children."

"*This* is my dream," Hanna said. "Girls deserve to have dreams, too, don't they? And to try to make them real. What were your dreams?" It had never occurred to Hanna to ask before.

"*Indari*, *Citi*, I don't know." The old woman released a long breath. "I don't remember. No one expected girls to have dreams back then, so we didn't bother."

Love for her grandmother swelled in Hanna's chest. "I just want to be a bonesetter." Hanna put her hand over *Citi*'s vulnerable-looking, veiny hand. "I'm very good at it. Baba said so all of the time. You understand, don't you?"

"It doesn't matter if I understand." *Citi*'s gaze met hers. "Just wait until your mother finds out."

"MY LORD, YOU have a visitor."

Griff barely heard the butler. He was too immersed in the past, having spent two days going through his father's things, rediscovering the person Griff hadn't had the chance to know as a grown man. Wright had saved everything. More than a dozen cravats, several pairs of gloves, the dark evening clothes and wool day tailcoats. And Father's fob.

Father never left home without the distinct gold-and-silver timepiece attached to a deep burgundy ribbon. Countless times, he pulled the timepiece from his fob pocket at his waistband to stare at while waiting for Mother at the bottom of the stairs.

"It is quarter past, Caroline," he would call up to her. "We were meant to be there by now." Mama tended to run late. She used to tease Father for always insisting they arrive unfashionably early.

Wright cleared his throat. "My lord."

Griff tore his attention away from Father's watch. "Yes?"

"You have a visitor."

"I do? Who even knows I'm here?"

"Everyone in Mayfair, my lord."

"What? How?"

"News travels like a speeding carriage among the ton."

"You are saying that the entire city knows I've taken up residence at Haven House?"

"I believe that would be an accurate assessment of the situation, my lord."

"Who is it? Who's here?"

"Lady Winters is calling."

"Who the devil is Lady Winters?"

"My lord will perhaps remember her as Lady Selina."

Griff stiffened. "Selina is here?" His past was catching up with him all at once.

"Would you like me to tell her that you are not at home to visitors?"

"No, that won't be necessary." He came to his feet. "Where did you put her?"

"She is in the front parlor at the moment, my lord."

Selina would laugh if he chose to greet her in such a formal room. "I'll see her in the upstairs sitting room." Just like before.

"Very good, my lord. Shall I have tea brought in or"—he paused meaningfully—"an entire tea tray?"

Griff tried to decode the butler's intent. "Which do you advise?"

"It depends upon how long you wish the visit to last. Tea alone with a single plate of biscuits is generally more expeditious. If you take my meaning."

"I do, indeed." He hadn't seen Selina in fourteen years. Maybe she'd become a termagant. Although he couldn't imagine that. Still. "Perhaps we should err on the side of expedition. Just to be safe."

"Very good, my lord. Tea and biscuits it is."

A few minutes later, Griff joined Selina in the family sitting room. She immediately approached, a huge smile wreathing her face. With her golden hair and noble features, his childhood partner in crime had grown into a handsome woman.

"Tommy," she said.

"Selina." He took both of her hands in his and kissed her soft cheek. She smelled of expensive perfumes and hair rinses. Like a grown woman rather than the scruffy tomboy he remembered. "How good it is to see you." And he meant it. Rather than dredging up the worst memories, as he'd feared, Selina's presence recalled happier times.

"It has been entirely too long." She held his hands apart as she assessed him. "Look at you. Mama always said you'd grow up to be handsome."

"Did she?" Their mothers had been the best of friends. "And what did you say?"

She released his hands. "I was a bit more skeptical."

He snorted. "I see you haven't changed. How is your mother?"

"As industrious as ever. She's the one who told me you'd finally opened Haven House."

A footman came in with the tea and set it out under Wright's watchful gaze. As soon as they were alone again, Selina burst out laughing.

"Just tea and biscuits? Planning to be rid of me quickly, are you?"

His cheeks warmed. "Is that a common practice in the ton that I am unaware of?"

"No, it was Lady Caroline's way. She and Mama used to giggle about it."

"Really? My mother used to offer lesser refreshments to callers she wanted to be quickly rid of? I had no idea."

"You were a boy. Boys don't notice such things." She paused. Her expression growing more serious. "How are you? Truly?"

"I am well." It was the truth. His shoulder wasn't the only thing that was healing. "I regret not coming home sooner."

"Why didn't you?"

"I thought the house would be full of ghosts. Instead I find it's full of pleasant memories."

"I was hesitant to visit. I feared you might blame me."

"That's ridiculous. You did nothing wrong."

One of her eyebrows shot up. "We both know that is not true. But I don't regret it."

"Neither do I." Looking at her, he felt a rush of fondness. Selina had been in his life for as long as he could remember. "You honored me."

"You paid the price."

"One of us had to."

"I'm sorry it had to be you. I should have been braver."

"Nonsense. That would have been disastrous." He took her hand and led her to the sofa. "Let's not dwell on the past."

Her eyes twinkled. "Parts of it were quite memorable."

"I remember." He felt himself blushing. "I was there."

She laughed, and he squeezed her hand. All of the years they'd spent apart vanished, leaving the comfortable familiarity. Selina was still her old self. And by some miracle, Griff was beginning to feel like himself again, too.

"Let's have our limited ration of tea and biscuits while you catch me up on everything."

She settled next to him on the sofa. "What do you want to know?"

"Everything. How have you been? Is your husband good to you?"

"He was."

"Was?"

"Yes, I am quite unattached at the moment. I am a widow."

HANNA STARED UP at the vision coming down the grand staircase on Griff's arm.

She was blonde, fair-skinned and very finely dressed. Obviously a lady. Griff's face shone as he chatted intimately with the woman, their heads tilted together. His hand covered the lady's where it rested on his arm. They were so wrapped up in each other they didn't take immediate notice of Hanna and Rafi standing in the front hall.

The scene before her hit Hanna like a punch to the belly. This regal woman explained why Griff had been absent for several days. What a fool Hanna was to worry about him. He'd obviously been otherwise occupied.

She regretted cajoling her brother into accompanying her to Cavendish Square under the guise of returning the necklace. Griff lived in the finest section of London's finest neighborhood. He was as elite as one could be without being actual royalty. It was a reminder she and Griff lived in two different worlds that might collide but could never blend.

The grandness of the house was intimidating enough. Not to mention the impossibly distinguished butler who'd stared down his nose at them when they'd asked to see Griff.

I shall see if his lordship is receiving. From his imperious tone, it was obvious the stuffy man expected the answer to be a resounding no. And now, seeing this lady on Griff's arm—

"*Zay il umar,*" Rafi murmured as he stared up at the woman. "She's beautiful like the moon."

When Griff finally spotted them, delight sparkled in his eyes. "Han—Miss Zaydan. This is certainly an afternoon for unexpected pleasures."

Hanna didn't know exactly what that meant, but she didn't like the way it sounded. One didn't need to be a genius to surmise what the two of them might have been up to. The butler, who'd started up the stairs, halted.

"My apologies, Lord Griffin. This young woman insisted upon seeing you." The words dripped with disdain. "I was just coming to inquire."

"Do not concern yourself, Wright. Miss Zaydan is most welcome here."

"Very good, my lord," the butler said dubiously before discreetly fading into a nearby corner.

Griff's eyes crinkled at the corners. Her stomach fluttered. Griff was not a naturally warm man, but his smile ignited a furnace inside her. Griff's gaze cooled when it settled on Rafi. "I'm afraid I haven't had the pleasure."

"This is my brother. Rafi."

"Ah." Griff perked up. "How do you do?"

"Well enough," Rafi answered.

Griff and the lady joined Hanna and Rafi in the front hall. "Allow me to present Lady Winters."

"My pleasure," Rafi said, his eyes wide. Hanna resisted the urge to elbow him hard in the side. The woman wasn't that stunning. Except that she rather was. She wore a cheerful chintz gown topped by a stylish pelisse and hat. In her drab muslin dress, Hanna felt like a dowdy washerwoman next to Lady Winters.

"How do you do?" the woman said with a friendly tilt of her chin.

"This is Miss Zaydan," Griff told her. "She fixed a shoulder injury that plagued me for two years."

"Is that so?" Lady Winters regarded Hanna with interest. "Are you a healer of some sort?"

Hanna put her shoulders back. "I am a bonesetter."

"A bonesetter?" Lady Winters's delicate amber brows lifted. "How intriguing."

"The finest one in all of London," Griff added.

"I confess to not knowing a great deal about bone-setters," Lady Winters remarked. "How were you able to help his lordship?"

"It was a simple procedure," Hanna said. "The joints in Lord Griffin's shoulder and arm were out. I put them back in."

"Miss Zaydan is being modest," Griff said. "I saw several doctors, and not one of them managed to accomplish what Miss Zaydan did in just a few short weeks."

"I see that we are disturbing the two of you," Hanna said, eager to end the awkward encounter. They'd obviously interrupted a private moment. "We shall go."

Griff took a step toward her. "Don't leave let."

Rafi spoke at the same time. "Aren't you going to give him the necklace? Isn't that why we're here?"

"The necklace?" Griff repeated.

"You all must excuse me." Lady Winters turned to Griff. "I am due at Mama's. She'll have my head and yours, too, if I don't turn up."

"Is your carriage waiting?"

"No, you'll recall the house is just four doors down," Lady Winters said. "I shall walk."

Griff frowned. "Alone?"

"I would be happy to escort Lady Winters home," Rafi blurted out so eagerly that Hanna wanted to kick him in the knee.

"There's no need," Griff said. "I shall accompany the lady."

"You stay and settle your business with Miss Zaydan." Lady Winters's firm tone did not invite contradiction. "I am happy to accept Mr. Zaydan's offer of escort. It is a two-minute walk at most."

Rafi seemed dumbstruck by his sudden good fortune. "It would be my honor." Hanna had never seen her brother all agog over a woman before. It was beyond aggravating. Usually the girls clamored for Rafi's attention, rather than the other way around.

Her brother offered Lady Winters his arm. "Shall we?"

"Absolutely."

They said their farewells, and Lady Winters floated out the door on Rafi's arm like a princess in a fairy tale.

Mirth danced in Griff's eyes. "Your brother seems awfully pleased."

"Deliriously so," she said sourly. "He completely forgot that he is supposed to be my chaperone."

Griff laughed out loud. He seemed so carefree. "Selina can have that effect on people."

"Selina?"

"Lady Winters."

"I see." Her toes curled. They certainly were on familiar terms.

Seeing how happy and unburdened Griff looked, no doubt thanks to *Selina*, made Hanna feel like a complete *habla* for worrying about him. "I came to see you because I was concerned about you," she blurted out. "It's been three days."

He grinned. "Did you miss me?"

"Certainly not." She kept her head high, resisting the urge to hide behind the nearest potted plant. "You seemed so eager to go through Papa's records that I could not help but wonder what became of you."

"Are you certain you didn't miss me just a bit?"

How dare he flirt with her when the lady he was obviously courting had just walked out the door? She spun toward the exit. "I'll wait for my brother outside."

"No, no." He rushed to her and put a gentle hand on her arm. His touch burned through her sleeve. "My apologies. Stay. Please. I would like to talk with you."

"About what?"

"I apologize for my absence. I've been settling in. Learning about the viscountcy, my properties. There is a great deal I have neglected."

Including Lady Winters? "You are under no obligation to explain yourself to me."

"Nonetheless, I want you to know why I've been absent. I didn't mean to vanish on you."

"I suppose it is the natural way of things." She saw with her own eyes what, or *who*, kept Griff occupied at Haven House. "You've returned to the world into which you were born." One that might as well be a thousand miles from Red Lion Square.

"Your brother said you came to deliver the necklace." He studied her face. "Why?"

"It *is* yours." She withdrew the necklace from her reticule and felt a pang of regret at its loss. Especially knowing it would soon adorn Lady Winters's long and graceful neck. "Now that you know the necklace belongs to you, you won't have to purchase one for Lady Winters. You can give her this one."

He accepted the sapphire. "Why would I give my mother's necklace to Selina?"

"She is obviously the lady you are courting. Now you can gift the necklace to her. There's no need for you to purchase another like it."

The door swung open and Rafi rushed in. The wild-eyed expression on his face suggested he finally realized he'd left his sister unchaperoned in the home of a bachelor. "Hanna, there you are." He exhaled, obviously relieved. "Are you well?"

"*Now* you ask?" Hanna retorted, supremely irritated with both men and their fawning infatuation with Lady Winters. "I am ready to go."

"Wait," Griff said. "Don't leave so soon."

"Our business is concluded. Good afternoon." Eager to escape, Hanna ushered her brother out the door without a backward look.

Chapter Fourteen

$\mathcal{N}$ow touch your toes," Hanna instructed.

Peeking in through the half-open dispensary door, Griff took a moment to watch the scene unfolding inside the clinic before announcing his presence.

Annie Peele folded at the waist, her fingers stretching toward the floor. "Like this?"

"That's good, isn't it?" Mrs. Peele asked Hanna.

"Yes, excellent. Now straighten up and bend slightly backward." Hanna wore a lilac dress that might appear frumpy on another woman. But not on her. Nothing could diminish her proud stance and strong form. Or the easy command with which she wielded her knowledge to help others.

Annie complied with Hanna's directions, stretching her hands high in the air as she performed a slight backbend.

Hanna took notes as she watched the girl, her brow adorably furrowed. They appeared to be alone at the dispensary.

"What next?" Annie asked excitedly. "How do I keep the pain away?"

"Exercise and stretches will help. You will come and see me a few times a year for a massage to keep everything in place."

Griff pushed the door farther open, choosing that moment to make his presence known. The bell over the door sounded. "Well, if it isn't my favorite ladies all in one place."

Hanna looked in his direction, and his heart somersaulted. Her dark gaze dropped to the massive bouquet of flowers in his arms. "Hello, Lord Griffin."

"Congratulations." The formal address told him all he needed to know about her mood. "I understand you opened your doors to patients this morning."

"It's a relief to treat patients without my family traipsing in and out of my office. Or patients having to run the gauntlet of *Citi*'s inspection every time they visit."

"Your grandmother is not for the faint of heart." He extended the flowers. "These are for you to mark this special occasion."

"Thank you." She accepted the bouquet, yet her old reserve from when they'd first met was firmly in place.

Griff looked past her. "And how is Annie doing?"

The girl beamed. "Much better, my lord. Parts of my back were out of position, but Miss Hanna has put them back in."

"She's a miracle worker," Mrs. Peele said.

Griff's tender gaze met Hanna's. "She certainly is."

"Nonsense." Hanna busied herself arranging the flowers in a water pitcher. "Bonesetting is not about miracles. I use time-tested treatment methods."

"Well, it's miraculous to us. But now, we really must go." Mrs. Peele ushered Annie toward the door. "Dr. Pratt will be wondering where I am."

"I miss your cooking terribly, Mrs. Peele," Griff said.

"Then, you shall have to come to dinner. Dr. Pratt is quite lonely without you."

"I will do so," Griff said. After mother and daughter said their goodbyes and departed, Griff faced Hanna. "How are you?"

"I couldn't be better." She put her shoulders back as if he'd challenged her in some way. "And you?"

"Better now that I'm here with you." He scanned the clinic. "Where is your partner?"

"Evan had to pay a house call."

"And the servant?"

"Lucy is running an errand. She will return at any moment."

"We are alone. Finally."

Avoiding his gaze, she wiped down the examining table. "But I am quite busy, so if you don't mind—"

"Are you?" He made of show of looking around the empty dispensary. "Busy, I mean."

She faced him. "Do you want me to come right out and say that I'd like you to leave?"

"At least that would be honest."

"Have you been honest with Lady Winters?"

"About what?"

Temper flashed in her luminous eyes. "Does your high-born lady know you have a taste for dallying with the lower classes?"

He stiffened. "No, she does not."

"Just as I thought." Turning her back to him, she strode toward the back office. "You may see yourself out."

His neck burning, he followed her. "I'm not leaving." His voice was hard. Cold.

He found her facing the desk, her palms face down supporting her body weight.

"There is nothing left for you here," she said.

"We both know that is not true."

She pivoted to look at him. "Go back to Lady Winters."

She was jealous. Delight streaked through him. "I am not engaged in a liaison of any sort with Lady Winters. I do not love Lady Winters. I am not betrothed to Lady Winters." He stepped closer. "Nor do I ever plan to marry her. She is a childhood friend. I do not think of her in that way."

"Why not?" She folded her arms over her chest. "She's clearly beautiful."

"You are the only woman I can see."

Her face softened. "You shouldn't say such things."

"And I am not dallying with you. For you to even suggest it is an insult to us both." He barely contained the anger in his voice. How dare she believe that of him? Of herself. "You are not a woman a man trifles with. You are the kind of woman a man never wants to leave."

She stared at him. "That's ridiculous."

"Why?" He stepped closer, his pulse bounding strong and hard at the base of his neck.

"Because there can be nothing real between us."

"This feels very real to me."

"I am a laboring girl. A bonesetter. The daughter of foreign merchants. You are a viscount born into privilege. We could not be further apart. Oh!"

He swept her into his arms before she could finish her sentence. "What are you doing?" she asked breathlessly.

"Unless you tell me to stop, I am going to kiss you."

She clamped her lips together. A thrill shot through him as he settled his mouth on hers. This was not the gentle exploration of their last kiss. His tongue was immediately in her mouth, stroking, seeking, devouring. "We don't feel very far apart now, do we?" he murmured against her soft lips.

"Mmm." She responded as if he were some delicious treat. She kissed him back, hard, determinedly, inexpertly. As if desperate for every taste of him, every part of him. Even if it was just for this moment.

Griff wanted this encounter to last forever. But reason slowly, reluctantly, reasserted itself. This could go no further. Griff pulled away.

She protested. "Don't stop."

"We must."

She stiffened. "If you'd prefer not to—"

"There's nothing I'd rather do." He tightened his arms around her. "But I don't want to take advantage of you."

"You mean to protect my virtue." She blew out a frustrated breath. "It's ridiculous."

"What is?"

"Being expected to guard my maidenhead as though it's the most important thing in the world to a woman."

"You are not making it any easier for me to remain gallant. It's already deuced annoying as it is." The discomfort in his pantaloons attested to that. "But I will not put you in jeopardy to satisfy my urges. No matter how strong they are."

"What about my urges?"

He blinked. "I beg your pardon?"

"I am too old to marry. If anything, I am wed to this dispensary and my work. Few husbands will accept a bonesetter as a wife."

"Any man who would not want you is an idiot."

"But I am still a woman," she continued, "with a woman's urges. I'd like to experience physical intimacy with a man."

Griff's muscles pulled taut across the back of his shoulders. "Do you have a particular man in mind?"

"A very specific gentleman." She peered at him from beneath a fringe of long, dark lashes. "The man who awakens things in me that I never knew existed, who makes me question the sacrifices I've made to practice my craft. And prompts me to reconsider some of my choices."

Desire saturated his blood. "Such as?"

"I'll never give up bonesetting. But I want to know what it can be like between a man and a woman. And since I don't plan to marry, why not take pleasure in each other? Discreetly, of course. No one else need ever know."

His breathing accelerated. "But your reputation—"

"—will remain unblemished so long as nobody finds out."

She made it sound so simple. Nothing in Griff's life had ever been simple. "I never want you to think I don't respect you."

"Truly respecting me means acknowledging that I am a grown woman who knows what she wants, and at the moment I want you."

He swallowed hard. "You certainly make it difficult for a man to remain a gentleman."

She closed in on him until their bodies were touching. "Then don't," she whispered, her lips coming up to meet his. Griff immediately gave in. After all, he wasn't a saint and nothing was as irresistible as Hanna when she took control.

His lips crashed down on hers. They explored each other with their tongues, mating, tangling, stroking: the kiss became less gentle and more heated, more demanding on both of their parts. He kissed his way down her neck, nuzzling, licking, tasting her tender skin.

His insides broiling, he bent her back over the desk, pressing his hips into hers, grinding into her sweet softness. She spread her thighs, cradling his erection through her skirts. Her boldness made him even more aroused. He whipped her fichu from her dress, baring her décolletage. He touched his tongue to the beauty spot adorning her chest.

"God, you don't know how long I've wanted this," he groaned, dragging his lips down to the upper swells of her breasts.

Hanna arched into his mouth, practically offering her breasts to him. "And I. It feels like forever."

Blood surged to his groin. His fingers touched her neckline, her skin soft and warm against his fingers. He tugged until her breasts were freed. He paused to stare at the fleshy mounds with their pointed caramel tips.

"I am the most fortunate man alive." He murmured as his mouth closed over the pert tip of her breast, his tongue flicking her nipple. She tasted sublime. Sweet yet earthy. Uniquely her.

She cried out as he sucked on her nipple. He caressed her other breast with his hand, filling his senses with the touch, taste and feel of her. Hanna thrashed beneath him. A sob erupted from her chest.

Griff froze. "Have I hurt you?"

"No." He heard the tears, the emotion, in her voice. "I don't know what's wrong with me. My body feels entirely too wound up. It's like I want you so much that it hurts."

Tenderness swelled in his lungs. "Oh, glorious girl." He kissed away the tears that slid down the sides of her eyes. "Being intimate with someone can be overwhelming."

In truth, Griff felt somewhat overcome himself. He'd been sexually excited before, but this was different. Every touch. Every kiss. Every sigh was heightened with Hanna.

"Truthfully?" she asked. "Is it overwhelming even for you?"

"Yes." He feathered his fingers along her hairline,

following the adorable dip at the center of her forehead. "Absolutely." He kissed her gently this time. She kissed him back with such sweetness, such tenderness, such desperation, that it fleetingly crossed his mind that this must be what love felt like. The kiss deepened, grew more intense. Unbearably pleasurable. He wanted nothing more than to mount her, to find bliss in her sweet heat.

Hanna squirmed beneath him, her body straining.

"What is it?" he whispered.

"I don't know," she said tearfully.

"Am I hurting you?" He brushed her hair away from her temple in a tender motion. "Is it too much?"

She shook her head and looked away. Embarrassed.

"Do you want me to stop?"

"No, please don't stop."

"Tell me what's wrong." He pressed a gentle kiss against her forehead. "Let me fix it."

"It's like I'm seeking something, or my body is, that I can't find."

He kissed her breast. "That's arousal. It's perfectly normal."

"What do I do with it?" she asked, frustrated.

"Ah, but in this instance, that is my duty." His pulse raced. "And my reward."

He lifted her skirts and moved his hands over her thighs until he found the slit in her drawers. She instinctively closed her thighs. "What—"

"I can take away that ache, that frustration." He stroked her thigh softly. Enticingly. "If you will allow it."

She regarded him with such trust that Griff's throat hurt. "Are you going to . . . copulate with me?"

"No, I mean, not right at this moment." God, how he wanted to! It would be heaven to plunge into her sweet warmth. To find his release. But it wouldn't be right. She was still sexually inexperienced. An innocent. And at the moment, neither of them was thinking clearly. "I'll use my fingers to ease you. You'll still be a maiden."

"Oh." She relaxed her thighs.

"Good girl." He touched his mouth to hers again, using his tongue to kiss her so thoroughly it felt like the desk beneath them was floating. His fingers traveled to the triangle of hair between her legs. And then to tender flesh. She was moist. So wet. So perfect. He stroked gently, forcing himself to go slow, to ease her into being touched so intimately.

"Oh," she said, "that feels wonderful."

He laughed quietly. "I see you are a talker."

"What does that mean?"

"I'll explain it to you later." His finger moved to her sweet bud. He circled it gently, moving in a steady rhythm, and saw the need in her start to rise.

"It's happening again." Her voice strained as her back arched off the desk.

"Good," he whispered in her ear. "Let it. Don't fight it."

"I don't know how." Frustration knotted her voice.

"Your body does." He kissed her cheek. "Just breathe, and let your body do the rest."

She let out a guttural sound as something inside her

began to soar. He felt her muscles tense. His finger worked a little faster.

"That's it, sweetheart." His words became more urgent as he put his mouth to her breast and sucked hard. He lightly bit her nipple. "Reach for it."

"Oh . . . oh . . ." She couldn't seem to find any words. Her lower body began to tremble. Griff felt her muscles tense, hold and release. And then the throbbing where his fingers were. Satisfaction rippled through him. Although his cock was hard and swollen, his body agitated almost to the point of pain, watching Hanna come was its own reward. He'd never forget it.

He held her for a few moments before kissing her gently, slow and sweet. "Better?"

"Oh, yes." Her eyes sparkled, her delicately curvaceous body moving with a sweet languor. "Virtue is supremely overrated. You knew exactly what to do."

"What can I say?" He kissed one breast and then the other. "Seeing to your pleasure is my pleasure."

"Why is that happening?"

"What?" He licked her nipple.

"Those pulsations . . . you know . . . down there."

He cupped her breast, still savoring being able to touch her like this. "Those pulsations mean you've achieved your pleasure."

"How fascinating." Her hands were running through his hair. A chill of pleasure ran through him. He could stay here like this with her forever. Unfortunately, he shouldn't. Reluctantly, he pulled away and straightened.

Taking her hands, he helped her sit up. "We should put you to rights before someone comes in."

Her eyes rounded as her hand flew to her mouth. "How could I be so careless?" She scooted off the desk, hurriedly tucking her breasts away.

Griff regretted losing the tantalizing view. But it was for the best. He needed to calm his raging body. He could hardly walk out of the dispensary in his current physical state.

Hanna was too busy tidying her clothing to notice him. "Anyone could walk in and discover us. Evan. Lucy. One of my brothers. Even *Citi*, heaven forbid." She looked around wildly. "Where's my fichu?"

He knelt to get it for her. "Here."

Adjusting the lace scarf around her neck, she tucked it into the neckline of her dress and gave Griff a pointed look. "We have to be more careful. If I were to be publicly compromised—"

"I'd marry you to save your reputation?" The suggestion tumbled out of his mouth before he could consider the implications.

"What?" she stared at him. "Don't be ridiculous. I cannot marry you. My family would never accept it."

"*You* cannot marry *me*?" Most mothers would knock down his front door to offer up their daughters. Even with the rumors about his parents, Griff's rank and wealth afforded him his pick of society's debutantes. "Why wouldn't your family accept me?"

"Because you are not Arab," she said simply. "If I marry at all, I must choose a husband from among my community here in England."

"Are you telling me that your family would prefer to see you wed to a shopkeeper than an English peer?"

"If the shopkeeper is Arab. Yes."

He let out a small laugh. "That's ridiculous."

"It's a way to keep our traditions from being lost. In any case, none of that matters because I'm too old to wed. Hence, our delightful experimentation."

Griff gaped at her. Every woman he'd ever met aspired to marriage. It was the way of things. Ending up a spinster was considered a terrible fate.

The bell to the front door jangled. Hanna started to exit the office but halted and spun back to face him. "How do I look?"

He adjusted her fichu. "Irresistible," he said, still struggling to comprehend how a merchant family could possibly think a viscount wasn't good enough for their daughter.

"Hanna?" a male voiced called out. Griff recognized, with considerable distaste, the partner's voice.

"Back here." She rushed toward the doorway.

Evan's tall frame appeared on the threshold. His gaze settled first on Griff. Then he examined Hanna. "Are you well?"

"Of course," she said calmly. "Why wouldn't I be?"

Griff admired her aplomb. No one would ever guess she'd come apart in his arms just minutes earlier.

Distaste flickered in the man's face. "Griffin."

"Bridges." Griff gave a chilly nod. "If you will excuse me, Miss Zaydan, I'll be on my way."

"My lord." Her eyes met his. "Thank you."

He held her gaze. "You are most welcome."

"For what?" Evan asked.

That seemed to break the spell. Hanna actually

shook her head. "Lord Griffin bought me some flowers. It was . . . they are . . . spectacular."

"The pleasure was all mine," Griff assured her.

Evan glared at him. "I thought you said you were leaving."

"And so I am," Griff replied. "I wish you both a very pleasant rest of the day."

HANNA FOLLOWED GRIFF and Evan onto the dispensary floor on shaky legs. The pleasurable aftereffects of her intimacy with Griff thrummed through her body, making her feel warm and lazy. She just wanted to curl up and take a nap.

The door at the dispensary entrance opened as the three of them emerged from the back office. Hanna's stomach knotted when she saw who it was.

"Norman?" Griff said to Dr. Pratt. "What are you doing here?"

"I could ask the same question of you." Dr. Pratt removed his hat. "But I will not. Ah, there you are Miss Zaydan. It is *miss*, is it not?"

"It is." Any lingering warmth in her evaporated. Nothing good could come of Dr. Pratt visiting her dispensary.

The man stared at her through round spectacles. "You are the reason I am here."

Evan came to Hanna's side. "Why is that?"

She licked her lips. "What do you want?"

"I've come to inform you that in one week's time, you must appear before a commission."

"What kind of commission?" Griff asked.

Dr. Pratt spoke with clinical detachment. "I have no choice but to convene a medical committee to assess whether the bonesetter should be allowed to continue to practice in London."

Hanna's stomach dropped. "Why?"

"Norman," Griff growled, "what have you done?"

"Me?" He laid a hand flat over his chest. "I myself have done nothing. I did warn you she would be made to account for her transgressions."

"And you made certain it came to pass?" Griff retorted.

"Not at all. She brought this on herself," he said evenly. "Viscount Payton is outraged at the damage she did to his son's arm. He demands justice."

"Payton?" Evan asked. "Who is that?"

The blood drained from Hanna's face. "Mansfield's father."

"Precisely," Dr. Pratt said. "You are accused of putting out his son's wrist at a coffeehouse on Red Lion Square. Do you deny it?"

Griff interjected. "Don't answer that."

Hanna cupped her fist with her opposite hand. "Who will be on this commission?"

"A collection of medical experts and notable citizens of influence."

"Will Payton sit on this commission of yours?" Griff asked in a raised voice.

"He will not. He will likely be a witness. As will Mansfield."

"I see." Hanna forced herself to stay upright, to show no outward expression. She wouldn't give Dr.

Pratt the satisfaction. But they both knew her time as a bonesetter in London was as good as over. No one would take the word of a laboring-class immigrant's daughter over that of a viscount and his son, who could probably trace their bloodlines back to the Conqueror. Their blood was as blue as it came. Hanna was powerless against them.

"If that is all, Dr. Pratt," she said calmly. "Or is there more?"

"That is it." Dr. Pratt replaced his hat on his head. "I shall look forward to seeing you at the hearing in a week's time. Good day."

The bell rang over the door as Dr. Pratt departed, passing two people entering the dispensary. A man escorting a woman, Mrs. Baker. Hanna's patient. She suddenly remembered that she had an appointment.

Mrs. Baker surveyed the three of them standing silently in the clinic. "Is this a bad time?"

"Not at all." Hanna recovered herself. She ushered the woman in. "You are on time. Please come in."

Chapter Fifteen

$\mathcal{Y}$our viscount could be behind it all," Evan pointed out.

"I don't have the energy to argue with you." Hanna finished wiping down the examining tables as she and Evan prepared to close up for the night. "I know you dislike him."

"And you don't seem to be able to see him for what he is."

"Yes, I know you suspect he's a killer."

"He might be. I obviously cannot say for sure. But in this case, Dr. Pratt is practically a father to Griffin," Evan pointed out. "The viscount readily admits that he came to see you under false pretenses."

"But then I cured him."

"Why did he come to see you in the first place, if not to expose you as a fraud?" Evan straightened the waiting-area chairs as he talked. "Why else would he seek you out when his guardian has a serious aversion to bonesetters?"

Hanna debated how much to tell Evan. "He came to see me on a totally unrelated matter."

Evan straightened. "What matter?"

"Unknowingly, I had a stolen necklace that belonged to his mother. Griff saw me wearing it. He found out who I was and came to see me in the hopes of discovering where I'd gotten the necklace."

"Where *did* you get it?"

"From my father. Sometimes his patients paid in jewelry and other goods." Hanna felt completely drained. She just wanted to go home and curl up in bed under a blanket. She called for Lucy, who was sweeping the back office. "It's been a long and trying day. I'm going home."

"Keep in mind what I have said about Griffin."

"How can I not?" She pulled the front door open. "I couldn't forget even if I wanted to."

GRIFF RETURNED THE following day. "I'm hosting a fundraiser for the hospital. You should come."

Hanna shut the drawer to the commode by the examining table. "Is that a jest?"

"No." Pacing away from her, Griff glanced at the servant girl cleaning the floor. "Where is your intolerable associate?"

"Dr. Bridges? He is paying a house call to an elderly patient."

Griff was relieved the man wasn't around. "Attending the fundraiser would advance your cause."

"In what way? The purpose of the event is to help your former guardian's hospital. If you'll recall, the man hates me."

"He detests what you represent."

"What is that, exactly?"

"The future of medicine. He's not ready for that. Norman is very tied to the old ways in his approach to medical care. He'll come around."

"By the time he does, it shall be too late for me. I am about to lose my right to practice bonesetting in London. I'll have to return to Manchester and see patients there."

His gut twisted at the thought. He wanted Hanna here. Where he could see her. Where he could be with her. "That is why you must attend. Waiting until the commission hearing to advance your cause will be too late."

Hanna gathered up some patient records and headed for the back office. "How does attending your charity event change anything?"

"Some of the commission members will be there." He followed her. "I'll make the introductions and tell them how you repaired my arm."

"How do you know who is on the commission?"

"I've made some inquiries. Most are physicians. Others are men of influence."

"Men of privilege such as yourself. Peers."

"Yes."

"Men like Viscount Payton, Mansfield's father. He'll be as strong a detractor as you are an advocate. And people will make certain assumptions as to why you are supporting me. Dr. Pratt believes you have very personal reasons for coming to my defense."

"I am speaking up for you because you've done nothing wrong."

"That's not exactly true. I did put out Mansfield's wrist."

"He provoked you."

"But will your commission of nobles and respected doctors see it that way? Or will they see a common woman, the swarthy daughter of immigrant merchants, who has the audacity to stand up for herself? Will they scorn a member of the laboring class who doesn't properly respect her betters?"

Griff made a sound of frustration. "I will make them see the truth."

"They will never take the word of a bonesetter over a viscount and his son."

He rubbed two fingers between his brows. "God, what a mess."

"If the men who run London want to be rid of me, then I am done for."

"It is unfair."

"The world is an unjust place for many."

"It shouldn't be." He forced himself to unclench his jaw. "Please don't abandon all hope without a fight."

"Oh, I am not giving up. I intend to make my case before the commission. I will fight for my right to work in London. But I am also realistic. I am prepared for the panel to rule against me."

"You say you intend to fight. Then, fight," he implored. "Start by attending the fundraiser. Your attendance conveys respectability. If the commission members meet and talk with you, they will see that you are not a charlatan."

"It won't make a difference." She placed the records on the desk. "That sort sticks together."

"I don't. I stick by you."

She gave him a soft smile that made him light-headed. "You *are* special."

"As are you. You must launch your own offensive. Make the commission members see you as you wish to be viewed. Not as the fraud Payton or Mansfield or any of the others wish to paint you."

She made a face. "I don't know the first thing about attending fine parties."

"You won't be the only outcast there." He paused. He needed to be completely honest with her. No matter how difficult it was. "Society doesn't fully accept me, either. Because of what happened to my parents."

She settled her hips back against the desk. "You don't have to do this."

His chest hurt. He slid into a seat. "You don't understand." Taking a deep breath, he forced himself to look up at her. "Half of society assumes I did it. That I killed them." He braced himself and waited for the inevitable reaction. Condemnation. Revulsion. Fear.

Instead of pulling away, Hanna leaned forward, placing her hands on his shoulders. "I know you are not capable of something so terrible."

Relief swamped him. He turned his head to plant a kiss at her wrist. He squeezed his eyes shut, attempting to contain his emotions. She slipped into his lap, putting her arms around his neck. "I don't require any explanations." She kissed his forehead. "I know you."

"How can you be so certain?"

"I just am."

"You should know that my standing by you might not necessarily help." He swallowed against the lump of emotion in his throat. "Because of what people believe. Those old rumors."

"Perhaps you do have the right of it." She straightened and lifted her chin. "I should meet those toffs and snobbish physicians. I shall be at your fundraiser. And I shall be proud to have you by my side showing your support."

"Are you certain?"

"Very." Mischief twinkled in her eyes. "Now that we've settled that issue, you will notice that we are alone."

"And?"

"I quite enjoy kissing you. And would like to experience that again. But we must hurry because Lucy could come back here at any minute."

He grinned. "I am always happy to be of service."

"Which is very fortunate for me." Her face came down to meet his. He pressed his lips to hers and kissed her long and slow, taking his time to savor her. She stroked her tongue along his, tasting him, a bit hesitantly at first but then more boldly. Sliding one hand up to cup her breast through her gown, Griff fondled her while allowing her to control the kiss.

"Miss?" Lucy's voice called from out on the dispensary floor.

Hanna broke away. "Coming," she called out while staring straight into Griff's eyes. Her breathing was heavy, her cheeks flushed. "I must go."

"We were just getting to the good part." Griff's body was heated and primed. He seemed destined to forever be left wanting when it came to Hanna.

"You really are an excellent teacher." Planting one last kiss on his lips, Hanna came to her feet. Her radiant expression made his heart thump hard. And then she was off to see what the girl needed.

HANNA STARED UP at the delicate plasterwork adorning the sitting room. The Duke of Huntington's butler had put her there while he went to inform his mistress that she had a visitor. Sometimes Hanna forgot how grandly her cousin lived. Although she shouldn't. Leela had grown up in a different world. Her mother had married a marquess, and Leela was now wed to a duke.

Hanna couldn't envision ever being at home in this world. The landscape on the wall was probably worth more money than Hanna would earn in her lifetime.

"Hanna, this is a pleasant surprise." Leela crossed the room to embrace her cousin. She pulled back so she could see Hanna's face, her lovely, luminous eyes filled with curiosity. "Is *Citi* well? You haven't come with bad news, have you?"

"No, not at all. I'm sorry to intrude."

"Don't be ridiculous. I'm thrilled to see you. Come and sit." Hanna wasn't surprised that the duchess received her in a faded dressing gown, with her long curly waves haphazardly secured in a low bun. Her splendid cousin didn't care what society thought of her. Ever since causing a minor scandal when they'd wed last year, Leela and her duke did as they pleased. "I could use a respite. Hughes is fetching us something to eat."

Hanna settled on the sofa with Leela. "I don't want to put you to any trouble."

"Don't be silly. I'm starved, and I insist that you eat with me. I was writing and lost track of time." Leela scripted travelogues. Her first three volumes, *Travels in Arabia*, were a London sensation. Her most recent release detailed her and the duke's marriage trip to Morocco. "Your visit could not come at a better time. Hunt and I sail for Athens the day after tomorrow. I am eager to write about Greece."

"You live such an adventurous life."

"It wasn't always so. When I started to follow my heart, rather than society's rules, my life truly began. Enough about me." She patted Hanna's knee. "Now, tell me why you've come."

"I am in need of advice." Hanna bit her lower lip. She hoped she wasn't overstepping. Although Leela was welcoming, Hanna did not know her well. During their childhood, Leela's mother never brought her children—Leela and her brother, Alexander, the heir to the marquessate—to visit their mother's side of the family. But Leela had recently sought out her Arab relatives and seemed keen on becoming better acquainted.

The duchess tucked her legs beneath her and laid an arm across the back edge of the sofa. "I don't know what I'm qualified to advise you about, but I'm happy to try."

"I am attending an event, a fundraiser for a hospital at the home of a viscount. I am hoping you can give me a few tips on etiquette. I don't want to make a fool of myself."

"You could never make a fool of yourself."

"I know you must be accustomed to society affairs. But I have never attended one. And it is very important that I make a favorable impression."

Leela tilted her head. "Is there a particular someone you wish to impress?"

An image of Griff flashed in Hanna's mind. "I am fighting for my professional survival."

She was about to explain when a footman came in with tea and a food tray. To Hanna's surprise, the duchess served her black tea Arabic-style, with mint and plenty of sugar. And an unexpected food was nestled among the delicate cakes and sandwiches.

"Is that *za'atar menaeesh*?"

"Indeed." Leela reached for the freshly baked flat-bread topped with a zesty thyme and olive oil mixture. "It's one of my absolute favorites, so Cook learned to prepare it. Now, what is all this about fighting for your survival?"

"You might not be aware," Hanna hesitated, bracing for the usual skepticism about her craft, "that I am a bonesetter."

"I have heard." Leela nodded encouragingly. "*Citi* says you are very good. That you learned from your father. I am sorry I never met him."

Hanna's mouth dropped open. "*Citi* told you that I am a gifted bonesetter?"

"Yes, but she also said it would be better if you married."

"Now, that sounds more like *Citi*." She grew more serious. "I am six-and-twenty, far too old to marry. All I want is to do my work." She explained her current predicament, starting with the Mansfield incident at the coffeehouse.

"You purposely put out Mansfield's wrist?" Amusement twinkled in Leela's eyes.

"It isn't a laughing matter. I lost my temper." She told Leela about the commission that would decide her fate. "Now I could lose everything. That is why the event hosted by Lord Griffin—"

"Griffin?"

"Yes, do you know him?"

"Not terribly well, but he is a particular friend of my husband's. Wait a moment." Comprehension washed over her lovely face. "*You* are the bonesetter who cured the viscount's war injury?"

Hanna felt a flush of pride. "Yes, that was me."

"Hunt says it's nothing short of a miracle." Leela regarded her with amazement. "Lord Griffin suffered for years, and no physicians could provide him any relief."

"His shoulder, elbow and wrist were all put out. I simply had to put them back in. It's a skill most physicians are not trained in."

"You must be extraordinarily talented." Leela's expression was thoughtful. "Have you formed an attachment to Lord Griffin?"

"Of course not. That would be the height of foolishness." Hanna's cheeks broiled. "He's a viscount, and I am a bonesetter, the daughter of merchants. Besides, you know if I ever wed, my family expects me to marry an Arab. I don't have the same freedom to choose a mate as you did. Your father was an English peer."

"What would you choose if you had the freedom?"

"I have already chosen bonesetting. No man, Arab or English, will wed a woman who touches strange men on a regular basis. Practicing my craft is the life I've carved out for myself. But now the commission could stop me from treating patients."

Leela's expression hardened. "Payton is being a bully of the very worst sort. He's a *hamar*. That donkey is used to getting his way without a care for any lives they ruin. Hunt and I must postpone our journey to Greece in order to attend Griff's fundraiser and show our support."

"Absolutely not." Hanna firmed her lips. "I couldn't ask that of you."

"You are not asking. I am offering. The next ship to Athens leaves in a few weeks. We could book passage then."

"A few weeks! Absolutely not. Organizing such a journey requires months of planning. I won't let you delay on my account."

"You are very stubborn."

"It must run in the family." She relaxed back against the cushions, tea in hand. "Honestly, all I require is advice on how to comport myself. I am not accustomed to the manners of the ton. Members of the commission will be in attendance at the party. It is imperative that I make a favorable impression. My future is in their hands."

Leela assessed her. "You already carry yourself like a princess. With the right dress and hair, you shall have them eating out of your hand."

"My best dress will have to do." She sipped sweet *nana* tea. "I don't have any gowns worthy of a true ton party."

"But I do. And you shall have your pick."

Hanna's mouth fell open. "Oh no!" She set her tea down. "I would never impose on your generosity."

"That is what family is for. I have rather too many gowns, and you are in need of one. We'll find just the right dress. Then my maid will alter it for you. Hasna is a magician with a needle."

"Still, I don't think—"

"*Yalla.* Let's go." Leela rose and reached for Hanna's hand. "We've much work to do."

Hanna came to her feet. Her cousin was a force of nature who swept you along by the sheer force of her considerable charisma. "Let's go shopping in the chamber that holds my gowns."

"You need an entire chamber for your gowns?" Hanna owned a total of six dresses, and they all fit easily in her wardrobe.

"For my ball gowns and other evening gowns. Naturally, my day dresses are in a separate chamber."

"Naturally," Hanna said before her cousin whisked her up the grand marble staircase.

Chapter Sixteen

Griff, come and meet Mr. Lassiter. He is one of our most generous donors."

Griff pasted a welcoming expression on his face. "How do you do?" He'd spent the last hour allowing Norman to lead him about the room like a show pony. Donors paid handsomely to mingle with a viscount in his own home. Griff gave them their money's worth.

Haven House sparkled. Wright and the staff had outdone themselves. Fresh flowers crowded every public room, and Griff had apparently spent a fortune on candles. Every surface gleamed. The staff bearing trays of champagne gracefully wove through the guests like dancers on a stage.

Griff kept an eye out for Hanna all evening. She was late. Had she changed her mind about coming? He spotted Selina and her mother and excused himself to go and greet them.

"I always said you'd grow up to be a handsome boy," Mrs. Waller said as she gave Griff a warm hug. She was an older version of Selina. Her golden hair now streaked with gray. Lines fanned out from lively eyes and lips, suggesting that Mrs. Waller laughed easily and often. Her figure was more comfortably rounded than it had been fourteen years ago.

"You always were too kind and overly generous."

Her eyes shone. "Your mama would be proud. As would your papa."

"I hope to be a credit to their memories." It was all he could do for his parents now.

Selina surveyed the ballroom. "Haven House looks splendid. It reminds me of old times."

Her mother nodded. "We did attend many social events here. Suppers, parties, balls. So many good memories."

Back then, Selina usually accompanied her parents. And when they were young, she and Griff would slip off somewhere on their own. Sometimes to sneak a cheroot procured from Felix.

"I'm so grateful that I visited with your mother on her last night in Town," Mrs. Waller said. "I treasure the memory."

"How was she that evening?" After years of avoiding all talk of his parents, Griff was hungry to hear about even their most insignificant interactions.

"Uncertain about whether to accompany Griffin to Ashby. Your father wasn't keen for you and her to go."

"He wasn't? Why not?"

"Something about him having some business to attend to. He was meeting his cousin there."

"His cousin?" Griff frowned. "Which cousin? Do you mean Dr. Pratt?"

"That's what Caroline said." She peered beyond

him. "I'm starved. Have you laid out a feast? We did give generously to your hospital."

He kissed her cheek. "You were quite munificent. Don't let me keep you."

Selina swallowed the last of her champagne as she trailed after her mother. "I shall see you later."

Griff's mind whirled. Father had met Norman at Ashby the weekend his parents were killed? He hadn't seen Norman prior to the murders. It wasn't until after the bodies were discovered that he'd rushed to Griff's side.

He scanned the room until he found Norman conversing with a group of other doctors. He made his way over. "I need a word."

"Ah, Lord Griffin," Norman said. "Let me introduce you to—"

"Now."

Norman frowned at the expression he saw on Griff's face. He excused himself and followed Griff. "What's this about?" he asked once they were alone in the study.

"Why were you supposed to meet Father at Ashby the weekend he and Mother were killed?"

Norman appeared genuinely puzzled. "What?"

"Mother told a friend that Father was meeting you at Ashby."

Norman's expression smoothed. "I did not meet your father at your country home, and I never had any plans to."

"Are you suggesting that my mother lied? Why would she do that?"

"Not your mother. No."

Griff paused, letting the intent of Norman's words sink in. "You are implying that Father dissembled."

"The dead are dead." Norman rubbed the back of his head with the flat of his hand. "We should allow them to rest in peace."

"What the devil does that mean?"

"That your father's secrets should be permanently buried with him."

"Stop talking in riddles. Why would Father lie about meeting with you at Ashby?"

Norman removed his spectacles and stared at them. "I hoped you would never have to hear this."

"Hear what?" Griff snapped, impatient. "Out with it."

"Your father wanted me to tell Caroline that I was meeting him in the country. I wasn't meeting him, so I refused."

"Why did he ask you to lie?"

"I suspect Jeffrey intended to meet a woman at Ashby." He replaced his glasses, adjusting them on the bridge of his nose. "I took him to task for it. We argued. And then I left."

Griff's mouth dropped open. "Are you suggesting that my father was meeting his mistress?"

"He never confirmed it," Norman said. "But why else did he want me to lie for him? Why was he reluctant to allow you and Caroline to accompany him to Ashby?"

Griff's stomach churned. His parents had always seemed content together. He knew firsthand that they'd spent most nights in the same bed. "Did my father ever confirm the existence of another woman?"

"He did not. I never asked directly. The truth is that I didn't want to know. I never wanted to burden you with this. But I always wondered if his reason for going to the country was somehow related to his death."

"How so?"

"What if there was a jealous husband who didn't expect to find your mother there? Maybe she tried to come to Jeffrey's defense."

"That's quite a leap."

"It explains why he didn't harm you."

"You and I both know why the assailant didn't go after me. I wasn't in the house when it happened."

"You've always refused to say where you were and who you were with."

"And I shall continue to do so." Griff pulled open the study door. "We should rejoin the guests."

GRIFF RETURNED TO find that Hanna had finally arrived.

He blinked, his mouth going dry. He admired her beauty even in her no-nonsense gowns with their modest necklines. But this evening Hanna was a true vision, resplendent in a silk evening gown of the palest blue.

The flowing fabric whispered over her body, like a lover caressing every dip in her feminine form. From the curve of her bosom to the turn of her waist and the flare of luscious hips. The stiff fabric of her everyday gowns did not offer the slightest hint of the womanly bounty that lay beneath.

Not that her gown was daring in any way. She'd selected a military-inspired design, with gold braiding and epaulets. Armor for the evening ahead. Her eyes were dark pools, her cheeks flushed, the lips pink and full. Strangers might see a fully confident woman. But Griff detected the banked defiance glittering behind her kohl-rimmed eyes and in the red of her cheeks.

It took him a moment to notice the man who stood by her side. His lip curled. Bridges.

Griff approached her. "Good evening."

"My lord." She lowered herself. Someone had taught the bonesetter to curtsy with the skill and grace of a lady. When she straightened, her gaze met his, and Griff registered the amusement glimmering in those dark depths.

He reluctantly acknowledged the partner. "Bridges."

The man gave a curt nod. "Griffin."

He returned his attention to Hanna. "You are a vision this evening."

"I see some physicians that I know," Bridges said abruptly. "If you'll excuse me. Unless you have need of me?"

"Not at all." She withdrew her hand from his arm. "Enjoy yourself."

Once he was gone, Griff said, "You look ravishing."

She blushed becomingly. "It's a borrowed gown. I had nothing suitable."

"Blue becomes you. As does silk."

"I don't have much use for silk when I'm tugging on people's limbs." Her full lips quirked. "But it does help me feel less out of place at the moment."

"You seem very at home among these people. If I didn't know better, I'd assume that you are accustomed to balls and ball gowns."

"But I am not," she said simply. "And I do not aspire to be."

"Are you rejecting me before I've even made my advance?"

"Stop jesting," she admonished, looking past him to the guests. "I am here. What do we do now?"

He could think of a million things he'd rather do with Hanna than subject her to the people in this room. But he offered his arm. "Now we circulate. I introduce you and tell everyone how you cured me."

"Will it make any difference?"

"Viscount Payton's allies will align with him. As I am rarely in society, I don't have a great many allies. Payton is much more firmly established in London. But at least you have a viscount suspected of murder on your side."

Her eyes twinkled. "And I cannot deny that I purposely did violence to Mansfield's wrist. We make quite a team, you and I."

He grinned. "Quite." He liked the sound of that, the idea of them as a team. Her lemony perfume filled his nostrils. He was supremely aware of her warmth beside him, the proximity of her body. The delicious memory of his mouth at her breast, of bringing her off, assailed him.

"Griff?"

He shook the delightful images from his head. They had a job to do. "Brace yourself. Here we go."

"YOU ARE COMPLETELY free of pain now?" asked one of the commission members. Hanna couldn't remember his name. The evening was a whirlwind with Griff escorting her from group to group, making introductions to the people who would ultimately decide her professional fate.

"Absolutely." Griff demonstrated, lifting his arm and waving it about—as much as his evening clothes would allow—for about the tenth time this evening. But Hanna never tired of watching him move his athletic form. He was even more appealing than usual in his navy evening clothes and pristine white cravat.

People listened when Griff spoke. For a man who rarely moved in society, he effortlessly exerted his influence. Wielding his power seemed to come as easily as walking or talking.

Hanna knew of course that nobles had power, but she'd never truly seen Griff exercise his until this evening. And it was on her behalf. No one dared cut her or treat her shabbily when she was on the arm of their formidable host. Even Dr. Pratt was polite, although it clearly was an effort for him.

"You are doing wonderfully," Griff murmured as he led her to the next group, the intoxicating scent of his shaving soap flowing over her.

"Are you certain? Or are you just trying to make me feel better?"

"Both." His eyes twinkled. "But, in all seriousness, you answered their questions calmly and thoroughly. By the end of the evening, they shall be eating out of your hand."

"Luckily, no one has directly asked if I put out Mansfield's wrist on purpose."

"That *is* fortunate." He guided her through the door and into an alcove between two adjoining public rooms. "The evening has been a success."

They paused in the shadow of the narrow passage between the two rooms. "What are we doing?" she asked.

"I want you to myself for just a moment."

"Here? Now?" They were just a few feet out of view. Anyone walking from one room to the other would see them.

His eyes twinkled. "As much as I'd like to ravish you right here and now," he murmured close to her ear, "I will force myself to exert some self-control."

She shivered at the feel of his sweetly humid breath against her cheek. "Ah, but will I?"

Banked desire shone in his eyes. "If only we could slip away unnoticed."

Evan appeared in the narrow passage between the two chambers, searching left and right until he spotted them. "There you are, Hanna." He ran a hostile gaze over Griff. "I was worried about you."

Griff stiffened beside her. "She is in good hands."

"Is she?" Evan asked. "There are those who wonder whether she is safe in the company of a man with your history. I am one of them."

"So. It was you." Griff gave a cold huff of laughter. "No doubt you rushed to tell Hanna all about the rumors."

Evan jutted his chest out. "She deserves to know the truth about you."

"She does, indeed," Griff replied. "But I doubt your intentions are pure."

"They are purer than yours." The two men stared at each other like pugilists in the ring.

"This is ridiculous." Hanna moved around Evan to rejoin the guests in the next room. "I am not a piece of meat to be fought over."

"I agree." Griff accompanied her. "Let us get back to the commission members, shall we?"

Evan followed. "You think you can turn her head with your money, your power, your influence." His raised voice drew the attention of nearby guests.

Hanna's cheeks were on fire. "Evan," she warned under her breath, "this is not the place."

"Is that what this is all about?" Griff retorted. "You are jealous because I am a viscount? Must I remind you that I am trying to use whatever influence I have to help Hanna?"

"To *help* Hanna." Evan's words were rich with sarcasm. "More like help yourself *to* Hanna."

"Evan," Hanna said quietly as more guests paused to watch the men. "Stop this."

"It's not that you are a viscount that bothers me," Evan continued. "It's the fact that you killed your parents, and everyone in this room knows it."

Griff froze. All color drained from his face.

A collective gasp came from the assembled guests. The room fell silent.

"Evan!" Hanna's shocked voice rang through the silence. Griff's complexion turned an unnatural shade of gray.

"What?" Evan flushed. "It's the truth. Everybody else here believes it but is afraid to say the words out loud. The hypocrisy makes me ill. Because Griffin is a noble, he not only gets away with murder, but he continues to be accepted, celebrated even, in society."

"Lord Griffin did not kill his parents," a firm female voice called out. "I know because he was with me the evening they died."

Hanna's head whipped around to stare at Lady Winters. Griff's Selina stepped forward, her color high, her shoulders pulled back.

"Selina, what are you saying?" gasped a woman who resembled an older version of Lady Winters.

That seemed to shake Griff out of his trancelike state. "Selina." He spoke sharply. "Don't."

"No, Griff." Lady Winters's gaze met Griff's. An unspoken conversation seemed to rage between them. "I will not allow you to continue to suffer. Not when I alone can prove your innocence."

"What are you saying?" The older version of Lady Winters, presumably her mother, flicked open her fan and fluttered it before her face.

"I met Griff that night. He stayed with me until sunrise so he could not have killed his parents. The reason Lord Griffin didn't hear the murders is because he wasn't home when it happened."

"She's lying." Griff's harsh voice rang out.

"I am not," Lady Winters countered even more

strongly. "We both remained silent about Lord Griffin's whereabouts that evening in order to protect my honor. I've let him suffer horribly to save myself. But I am no longer a girl. It is past time that I spoke the truth. My honor be damned."

"Oh my." Lady Winters's mother swayed. "I don't feel well."

The whispers, the excited murmurs that inevitably accompanied fresh gossip, filled the room. Word of the scandal would blanket London by morning.

Lady Winters hurried to her mother's side. "Come now, Mama. Let's find you a place to sit."

Griff gestured to the nearest footman. "Bring water for the lady." He crossed over to assist the older woman, taking hold of one arm while Lady Winters had the other. Together, they ushered the older woman from the room.

Hanna stared after them, still trying to comprehend what had just happened.

Evan touched her elbow. "Let me see you home."

"No." Hanna jerked her arm away. "You've done enough for one evening."

Chapter Seventeen

*H*anna lingered in the front hall of Haven House.

Around her, guests departed in a quiet flurry, bustling out the door in hushed whispers. She stood with one hand holding the elbow of her opposite arm. She tried not to fidget despite wanting nothing more than to escape Griff and his lies. And his snobbish butler.

But she was stuck.

Once again, her temper had gotten the better of her. She'd sent Evan away in a pique of anger, and now she had no way to get home. She could hardly walk home alone at this time of night. Particularly not in Leela's fine silk gown. And summoning a hackney, much less traveling home alone in one, was entirely unsafe.

"Miss Zaydan?" Griff's butler stared down his nose at her. "May I be of assistance?"

There was nothing to be done for it. She had to ask for the prig's assistance. "Wright, isn't it?"

"Yes, miss, at your service."

"I'd like to have a message delivered to my brother at Red Lion Square."

"Certainly, miss. If you would like."

She forced herself to admit she was stranded. "I need to send word for him to pick me up and return me to my home. My escort . . ." Her voice trailed off. She could hardly reveal she'd been foolish enough to send her escort away, marooning herself in Mayfair. Especially considering that Evan had been right all along. Griff *was* involved with Lady Winters.

"There is no need to trouble your brother, miss," Wright assured her. "I shall summon his lordship's driver to deliver you safely to Red Lion Square."

"Oh, no. I don't want to be a bother."

"I'm certain it is what his lordship would want." He gave a curt nod to a nearby footman, who melted away to do the butler's bidding. "His lordship would understand your desire not to be escorted by Dr. Bridges."

"Oh." Wright had seen her rebuff Evan? "Will Griff . . . erm . . . Lord Griffin be all right?" She hated herself for asking, for caring. But she could not stop seeing the stricken expression on Griff's face when Evan publicly accused him of murder.

"I suspect he will." The butler appeared somewhat pleased. "At the very least, people will stop accusing him of murder."

"Instead he will be engulfed in a new scandal." Word of how Griff and Lady Winters spent the evening together when they were fifteen would spread quickly.

"But there is an easy way to put an end to the new scandal," he said, not unkindly.

Before she could ask the butler what he meant, the coach arrived and Hanna followed the footman out the door to be conveyed home.

"How is your mother?" Griff asked Selina when she joined him in the sitting room of her family home.

"She's resting. Once she gets over the scandal of it, she will be fine." Selina poured two drinks and handed him one. "Brandy?"

His brows went up. "You drink brandy now?"

"Scandalous, isn't it?"

"It pales in comparison to the scandal you created this evening."

She settled on the sofa next to him. "Don't look so grim."

"Your reputation—"

"Will be fine," she finished the sentence for him. "I'm a widow with three children. My eldest son is an earl. I am not without influence."

"You think your son can protect you? And how old is his lordship?"

"Robert? All of eight."

Drained of energy, he reclined against the sofa. "There is a way to fix this."

"Nothing needs to be fixed. Stop trying to save me."

"We should marry. That will quell the gossip." He tried to ignore the crushing sensation in his chest. To not think of Hanna, the woman he secretly dreamed of marrying despite the obstacles. Not that he'd given wedding Hanna serious thought. He hadn't thought about the future at all. He'd been too busy enjoying the present for the first time in more than a decade. But now his future was set whether he liked it or not. He might as well embrace the idea.

"Us, marry?" Selina narrowed her eyes. "You cannot be serious."

"Salvaging our mutual reputations is hardly something to joke about."

"You just spent the last fourteen years allowing people to call you a murderer, all in the name of protecting my virtue. Now you propose to sacrifice your entire life to protect my honor."

"You're a lovely woman, Selina." That much was true. It was also true that she didn't excite him like Hanna did. She didn't stir his blood or make him mad with the wanting of her. "Marrying you would hardly be a sacrifice. We are dear friends, after all."

She made a skeptical sound. "This evening I confessed to free you, not to entrap you."

"It is not solely your honor we are speaking of," he reminded her. "There is mine to consider as well. A gentleman cannot desert a woman after all of society knows he spent an entire night with her."

"We were fifteen. Once you have children of your own, you will understand how young that truly is. Besides, no real harm was done. I married my earl. My late husband was well pleased to have a pretty, young wife in his bed."

Lord Winters had been twenty-five years older than his bride, the daughter of landed, but untitled, gentry. Selina's beauty attracted a noble husband and elevated her family.

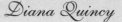

"I welcomed Albert to my bed whenever it pleased him," she added. "It was an agreeable union. I don't regret it."

"We should marry," he said tightly. "It is the right thing to do."

"I see you are still as stubborn as ever."

"Consider your children," he insisted, "and the ridicule they'll face."

"My children are just that—children. By the time they are old enough to hear of the scandal, the gossips will be focused on something else. I can shield them."

He scrubbed both hands down his face. "Do you really find the idea of marriage to me so reprehensible that you'd rather endure scandal and gossip?"

"I see you will not let this go."

"I will not. I would be a cad if I did."

"Very well." She sipped her brandy. "Here is what I propose."

HANNA PUNCHED HER pillow. It was past midnight, but she couldn't sleep. The simmering anger from earlier this evening had exploded into raging fury. After about an hour of tossing and turning, she finally gave up and slipped out of bed.

Griff and Lady Winters. Hanna had been right to suspect something between them. She couldn't stop thinking about the liberties she'd allowed Griff. The idea that he'd gone from her to Lady Winters's bed made her sick.

She crossed to the window and stared out onto the quiet street. It felt like everyone else in the city was asleep. If only she could quiet her mind long enough to rest.

Something moved across the way. Hanna strained to make out the shadowy figure. The athletic form. The dark clothing. *Griff.* Why was he outside her house in the middle of the night? He saw her and lifted a hand in greeting. She could feel his eyes staring at her. She raised her hand in return. And then hastened down the stairs to tell the *hamar* exactly what she thought of him.

She opened the front door as quietly as she could, hoping not to wake the household, to find Griff planted on her doorstep. "What are you doing here?" she hissed.

"I couldn't sleep. I need to explain." Still in his evening clothes, he'd removed his cravat, baring his throat.

"I don't want to hear it. Go away." She started to close the door.

"Please." He put his foot in the door to stop her. "Just five minutes of your time. And then I promise to leave you alone. Forever." His intense gaze locked on her face. "If that's what you want."

A tangle of emotions only he had the power to provoke wove through her. Desire. Fury. Hurt. No one drove her to the heights of pleasure or the depths of anguish like this man. He was dangerous to her. But Hanna was drawn to the danger. At least when it came to him.

Relenting, she ushered him in and closed the door as soundlessly as possible. Motioning for him to keep quiet, she led him back to Baba's office.

"Wright told me you were stranded," he said as soon as she closed the door. "I apologize. I didn't mean to desert you."

"You were busy with Lady Winters." She rested her back against the closed door, arms crossed over her chest. "Is it true?"

He nodded.

"You said you did not think of her in that way." The words trembled with anger. "You lied. Why? So I would dally with you? Were you interested in a bit of rough before you went back to your high-class lady?"

"No. Never." He came toward her. "I don't see Selina in that way. We didn't . . . we weren't intimate that night. We just wanted to have an adventure, to hike the tallest hill and watch the sun rise."

"You're saying you never touched her? That it was all completely innocent?"

"Not completely. We did kiss. There was some, mostly innocent, exploration. But just to see what it was like. She was my best friend. We were young. Our bodies were changing. We experimented."

"You kissed her."

"It felt quite wicked at the time. I never told anyone where I was that evening because people always assume the worst. Selina's reputation would have been destroyed."

"Why didn't you marry her back then?"

"I offered, but Selina was already promised to an earl. A much older man. She wanted to be a countess. I thought I could still convince her the following day, but then my parents were killed and Selina's betrothal went forward."

"Now you are both free. It isn't too late."

"Selina doesn't love me any more than I love her. She turned down my offer—"

Hanna swallowed. "Your offer?"

"Yes." He was pale. "Of marriage."

The muscles in her stomach tensed. "You proposed to her."

"How could I do otherwise? All of London will hear of her confession by morning."

"Lady Winters turned you down?" What sane woman would reject Griff's proposal?

"She tried. But I could not allow it. What we did dishonored us both. Marrying her is the only way to correct our transgression. I have no other option." Hanna registered the desperation in his eyes. "Surely you see that."

"What I think is of no matter at all." The ache in her chest made it hard to breathe. "Why are you even here? Shouldn't you be with your bride-to-be?"

"I am here because I want you to know the truth. I have not been disloyal to you."

"It doesn't matter now."

"It does to me." A fierce expression animated his angular face. "It matters to me that you know how much I care. How much I cared." He corrected himself. "There was no other woman. You were it. I'll never forget the intimacies we shared. I shall treasure them always."

She wished she didn't believe him. It would be easier

to hate Griff, to let him go, if she believed him to be a cad.

"Please tell me that you believe me," he said.

"I do." She exhaled a shaky breath and nodded. "When will you marry?"

"Selina hasn't agreed to a wedding as of yet. She insists that we take six weeks apart to consider our situation. After that, we shall meet to discuss whether to become betrothed. Affiancing myself to Selina is not what I want. But I must make the offer. Surely you understand."

She did. "Perhaps it's for the best."

"How can you say that?"

"Because we can never marry. My family would never accept the match. Besides, I am a bonesetter, and you are a viscount. Your world would never accept me. Neither of our worlds would accept our being together."

"I thought we'd have more time to discover what this is between us. To find out what might have been." He stepped closer and gently took her into his arms. His strength and warmth surrounded her, engulfed her in a blanket of security and love.

Love. She squeezed her eyes shut, a tear escaping. This desperate feeling must be love. She felt the beat of Griff's strong heart against her cheek. Relished the strength of his body. Her heart felt so full it was a wonder her chest could contain it.

"I don't regret it," she whispered. "Not any of it."

"Nor I." He found her mouth with his and gave her one last tender, almost chaste, kiss. And then he left.

Chapter Eighteen

Hanna pored over Baba's files, going through them page by page.

She was about halfway through them. The dispensary kept her busy most of the time, but she appreciated having this distraction between patients. Anything to fill the hole where Griff used to be. The ache that wouldn't go away. In the four days since the fundraiser debacle, she'd done whatever she could to keep her mind off him.

"You're still going through those old files?" Evan's tall, thin form filled the threshold. "Whatever for? I thought you were done with Griffin."

"Griff and I have concluded our association," she said coolly. "Not that that is any of your business."

"When are you going to stop punishing me? You barely speak to me unless it is about dispensary matters."

"When am I going to stop being angry at the scene you caused at the fundraiser? Probably never."

"I just said what everyone else there was thinking."

"But you were wrong, weren't you?" she said hotly. "You must be disappointed Griff isn't a killer."

"Is that what this is about? You're angry because I inadvertently exposed his dishonorable behavior with Lady Winters? I should think you'd thank me."

"And why would I do that?"

"He was toying with you. Hanging around here. Flattering you. Gifting you with flowers. We both know men and women of that class don't have honorable intentions toward people like us."

"We had mutual business, and we became friends. There was nothing between us beyond that. For you to suggest otherwise is an insult."

He held up his hands in self-defense. "It's not your motives and actions that I find suspect." He gestured to the files. "Why are those still of interest to you?"

"I need to find out where the stolen jewelry came from. Dr. Pratt is already spreading rumors that Papa was a fence. I won't allow him to destroy my father's name when he isn't here to defend himself."

"Are you certain that's all it is?"

She gave him a sharp look. "Evan, you are my business partner, not my keeper. I am not required to explain myself to you."

"I am not your keeper, but I am your friend. I hope we are still friends. I apologize for anything I've done to upset you. I had only your best interests at heart."

"I'm not a child. I don't need you to act as my guardian. I'm a woman with a brain that works quite well."

"I am aware of that. But we are friends, and friends look out for each other. That's all I was trying to do."

"I understand that, but I am still angry." She returned her attention to the ledgers. "Now go away, and let me get through a few more of these before my next patient."

He turned to go, then paused. "You do know that it is for the best? Class distinctions are there for a reason. Because toffs put them there. It's how they maintain their sense of superiority."

She kept her focus on her task. "Griff is gone. I don't want to discuss this again." She felt Evan's eyes on her before he left her alone with the files.

And recent memories she wasn't ready to let go of yet.

GRIFF STARED OUT the window. Cavendish Square was a blur in the light rain. The rivulets dotting the glass panes obscured the view.

He hadn't seen Hanna in five days. But it felt like a hundred. How was it possible to miss someone so much? Naturally, he'd pined for his parents and sisters, but that was a dull ache he'd harbored for so long that it was practically woven into his bones. Hanna was different. He missed her in such a fresh and immediate way that just drawing a breath was painful.

He'd been a loner since his parents died and his sisters vanished, but Griff had never actually felt lonely until now. Even Hunt wasn't around to distract him. He and his duchess had sailed for Greece more than a week ago. To fill the time, Griff had dined with Norman a couple of evenings ago, but there was a new uneasiness between them.

Selina was really the only other person in London with whom he was well acquainted. But she refused to see him for six weeks. Only then, she said, could they make a rational decision about their future. Not that Griff had anything to decide. He would marry his old friend, seeing through the commitment he'd made at fifteen.

The scandal sheets screamed of their story. Griff didn't care about that. Society had never held him in high regard. But it was wrong for Selina to suffer when she'd stepped forward to defend him. She might be an earl's widow, but her position in society remained precarious. Selina came from a good family, but not the best. Nor the most wealthy or powerful.

Griff's thoughts returned to Hanna, as they often did these days. In addition to missing her, he worried about her. The commission that would determine her future would convene in two days. He knew how much bonesetting meant to her, how much of a loss it would be if Hanna could no longer practice in London.

"My lord."

Griff turned, surprised to see Wright just inside the door. He hadn't heard the butler come in. "Yes?"

"There is someone here for you—"

"No." Griff turned back to the window. He didn't feel like seeing anyone. "Tell whoever it is that I am not at home to callers."

"She said it was urgent."

"She?" His heart skipped a beat. It couldn't possibly be. He faced the butler. "Who is it?"

"Miss Zaydan."

"Hanna is here?" He crossed over from the window and strode past Wright. "Where is she?"

The butler followed. "In the front hall, my lord. I can show her in if you'd like to wait here."

To hell with etiquette. "That won't be necessary."

He found her by the staircase staring up at the dancing cherubs adorning the ceiling. "Hanna?"

"Griff." She looked at him with those large dark eyes that never failed to have an impact on him. She'd been caught in the rain. Her bonnet drooped, and strands of damp hair clung to her cheeks. But even in her bedraggled state, Hanna was captivating.

"Is this about the commission?" he asked.

"What? No." Radiant, she clutched a ledger in her arms. "I found the name."

"What name?"

"The man who paid for my father's services in jewelry. I *know* his name."

Griff stilled. "Are you certain?"

She held out the ledger. "It's all in here." Her hand quivered. At first he thought it was excitement, but then he realized she was cold.

"You're trembling."

"It's nothing. It started raining, but I didn't have an umbrella."

Griff took the ledger and tucked it under his arm. "Let's get you in front of a fire."

"Oh no." Uncertainly filled her face. "I should not stay."

"It's chilly and damp outside." He didn't want her to go. "Warm up. Show me what you've discovered, and then go. I cannot have you falling ill on my account."

She hesitated. Griff held his breath, fearing she'd decline. "Very well," she finally said. "Just until I warm up."

Relief shot through him. Griff gave a crisp nod to the butler. "Please have tea sent in."

"Yes, my lord. Tea and biscuits?"

"No." Griff felt lighter than he had in days. "Bring a full tea tray."

Wright bowed. "Right away, my lord."

ENTERING HAVEN HOUSE was like being transported to another world. The study alone was larger than the entire ground floor of Hanna's terraced home.

She hugged herself as she scanned the room. An imposing carved walnut desk stood at one end. Two sofas and a pair of burgundy velvet chairs flanked the marble fireplace.

"You need to warm up," Griff said. "Come sit by the fire."

"His name is Gerard Loder," she blurted out as she took the stuffed chair closest to the hearth, welcoming its cozy heat. "The man who had your mother's jewelry came to see Papa just a few months before Papa died."

"A few months?" He settled his athletic form in the adjacent chair, the seat nearest to her. He wore no cravat. She tried not to stare at his bare throat. Just seeing him warmed her from the inside out. "When did your father die?"

"Just over three years ago. Eleven years after your parents' deaths. That is why it took so long to find the name. Because we started examining the oldest records first."

"Have you ever heard of this man?"

"No, but I will ask around to see if anyone in the neighborhood knows him."

"I'll engage a runner if necessary to find this Gerard Loder. Suppose he's the man who—" He didn't have to finish the sentence. She understood. "It's entirely possible that he knows nothing about what happened to my parents. He could have bought the pieces from someone who bought them from another person. It might be a dead end."

"At least it gives us a place to start looking."

"Us?" Tender admiration filled his steely gaze. How had she ever thought him cold? "I didn't realize you continued going through the records."

"I have my own reasons for wanting to know where the jewelry came from. It will clear my father's name."

"How so?"

"You told me yourself that that *jehish* . . . erm . . . Dr. Pratt knows my father was in possession of the stolen jewelry."

"Sorry? What did you call Dr. Pratt?"

She stared into the fire. "Never mind."

"Tell me."

"It's an Arabic word. It just slipped out of my mouth. I didn't mean to say it."

"But you did, so humor me," he urged.

"It's very rude."

"I gathered as much." She registered the amusement in his voice.

"Very well." She finally looked up at him. "If you must know, it means *mule*. As in a creature bred for work rather than intelligence."

Griff surprised her by laughing out loud. "I'm afraid to ask what you call me when you are angry at me."

She didn't dare tell him the words that came to her mind whenever she thought of him.

Hayati. My life.

Elbee. My heart.

Rohee. My soul.

In English, the words sounded far more dramatic than in Arabic. Even so, for her to have any feelings at all for Griff was ridiculous.

But there it was.

Instead she said, "You look well."

"Returning to society is quite an adjustment, but I am managing. I've been inundated with invitations. Now that I'm no longer viewed as a murderer, the ton seems quite eager to return me to the fold."

"You never deserved society's censure."

"Ah, but now that my return is at hand, do I really want it? I've been on my own, doing as I please for so long that I'm not sure I want to embrace a life that involves long and boring routs and recitals."

"You've been invited to recitals?"

"Two of them."

"Musicians of note?"

"Hardly. It seems the thing to have one's children perform for guests. No matter what the talent level of the performers."

"Oh." Her eyes twinkled. "I see."

A footman came in with the tea tray featuring an expansive spread of sandwiches, breads, cakes and biscuits. The fearsome butler oversaw everything before withdrawing.

Griff picked up a plate. "I hope you are hungry."

Hanna was amazed by the pretty array. "That's a great deal of food for two people."

"You must try one of everything," Griff instructed, his long fingers reaching for silver tongs to fill her plate. Those fingers had touched her, caressed her, brought her great pleasure. He set the plate down on the table nearest to her. "I insist."

"Thank you." Hanna nibbled on a delicious miniature cake, which distracted her from Griff's hands and what they were capable of. "How extraordinary it must be to have a cook make treats for you all day long."

"I suppose." Griff's careless tone suggested he'd never given much thought to having numerous servants catering to his every whim.

Hanna glanced at the departing footman. This was the life her cousin Delilah must live. But then Leela wasn't like Hanna and the rest of the Arab cousins. Her father had been a proper English peer, not an immigrant merchant. Leela grew up among people of her father's ilk, accustomed to having servants tend to her all day long.

Griff reached for a biscuit. "Going through my father's things has made me wonder."

"About?" She sank her teeth into an apricot marmalade, her mouth watering around the sweet, chewy concoction.

"The timing of things. My parents and I were not supposed to be in the country the weekend they died. It was June, and Parliament was in session, so naturally we were still in London."

She paused, confused. "I'm afraid I don't follow."

He smiled, the tiny lines around his steel-blue eyes deepened. "Foolish of me to make assumptions. Because Papa was in the Lords, we were always in London when Parliament met."

As she took another bite of her apricot marmalade, Hanna marveled at Griff's casual reference to his proximity to power. She knew titled men of privilege sat in Parliament. But the concept always seemed far removed from her. Like the regent. Or Japan. She knew both existed but never expected to come into actual contact with either of them.

Yet, for Griff, being part of the apparatus that ruled the most powerful country in the world was a normal part of life. Men of his class thought it was their due and didn't give it a second thought.

He drank his tea. "That weekend, Father spoke of an urgent matter that required his presence at Ashby Manor, our country estate."

"And this matter couldn't wait until Parliament was no longer in session?"

"It was early in the month. Parliament was going to stay seated until well into July. Father's plan was to go to Richmond, deal with the urgent matter and return within a day or two."

The butler reappeared, trailed by a footman. He fussed with the tea tray, handing off emptied dishes to the footman, who withdrew with them. As he re-arranged the remaining platters into a more pleasing grouping, the butler darted a quick glance at Hanna's plate, the one Griff had overfilled for her. She flushed. Ladies were supposed to eat sparingly. But then Hanna straightened in her chair and bit into a cake. She was not a lady. She was a laboring woman with a healthy appetite.

Griff set his cup down. "Father never said what the urgent matter was. Norman has his suspicions, but I don't credit them." He had a faraway look in his eyes. "I find that now, more than a dozen years later, I am most eager to know everything about the days leading up to . . . the loss."

Determined not to be intimidated by the judgmental butler, Hanna reached for a dainty sandwich. "Did you find anything among your father's papers that might explain why he went to the country that weekend?"

"Unfortunately, not. There were no papers at all."

The butler cleared his throat.

"None?" Hanna asked. "Not even in his desk?"

"I was disappointed to find the desk emptied out. This is the chamber I associate most closely with Papa, but it's as if his presence was completely expunged."

Hanna felt sad for Griff. Going through Baba's desk after his death had made her feel close to her father. She still felt his presence there. The butler cleared his throat again.

Griff looked at him. "What is it, Wright?"

"About your father's papers, my lord."

"Yes, what about them?"

"I took the liberty of sorting through the desk and putting everything away."

Irritation animated Griff's face. "Why didn't you leave Papa's papers here in his study?"

Hanna was curious to know as well. She didn't know exactly what a butler did, but scrounging through his dead master's papers didn't strike her as one of his duties.

The butler hesitated.

"Well?" Griff prompted.

The butler darted a quick gaze at Hanna.

"You may speak frankly in front of Miss Zaydan."

The butler still appeared reluctant.

Hanna scooted to the edge of her seat. "Maybe I should go."

"Nonsense. You haven't finished your tea." Griff's voice was firm. "Out with it, Wright."

The butler clasped his hands behind his back and stood up even straighter, which Hanna would not have thought possible. "Your guardian showed an interest in going through his lordship's things."

"Dr. Pratt did? Why?"

"He said that, as your guardian, it was his right to see if there were any outstanding matters that needed attending to."

"I thought my father's solicitor was in charge of those sorts of things."

The butler practically sniffed. "As did I, my lord. Therefore, I took it upon myself to box up the papers and put them away until the new Lord Griffin, *you*, came of age."

Hanna reconsidered her opinion of the butler. The man obviously disdained Dr. Pratt. He couldn't be entirely awful.

"Where are these papers?" Griff demanded.

"I will have to fetch them, my lord."

"Can you do it now? I'd like to see if my father wrote anything down in his appointment book."

"At present, the papers are not in the house, my lord."

"They're not?"

"Dr. Pratt was most determined to find the papers. He searched everywhere for them. Mrs. Tanner and I decided it would be prudent to remove them from the premises."

"To where?"

"They are in Mrs. Tanner's keeping."

"My former housekeeper has them?"

The butler nodded. "At the home of Lady Dorcas. We felt that Dr. Pratt could not impose himself there as easily as he could here at Haven House."

"Who is Lady Dorcas?" Hanna asked.

"My sister," Griff said. One of the sisters who'd deserted him.

"I shall have Felix go and retrieve them at once," Wright said. "I hope I have not overstepped, my lord. You are the viscount. Those are your papers. I felt it was my duty to safeguard them for you."

"I appreciate the sentiment," Griff said. "But I am certain Dr. Pratt was simply trying to fulfill his duty."

Hanna wasn't so certain. What had Dr. Pratt been looking for? She exchanged a glance with the butler.

Maybe it was her imagination, but a moment of understanding seemed to flash between them.

The butler picked up a plate of sandwiches. "Another sandwich, miss?"

Hanna beamed up at him. "Maybe just one more."

And, if she wasn't mistaken, the butler's lip quirked into what might, for him anyway, be accounted as a smile.

THE FOLLOWING DAY Griff pored over his father's papers. Most were ledgers, accountings from the various estates and other business matters. Others were more personal. The paperwork of lives cut short. A note from Mother reminding Father to call on someone who'd been ill. Bills from his mother's modiste. Copies of marriage agreements for his three sisters.

Griff wondered how Dorcas reacted when Felix went to retrieve Father's papers from the housekeeper she'd lured from Haven House. His sisters were in Griff's thoughts a great deal lately, even though he tried not to think of them. They had no interest in him. The retrieval of Father's papers certainly hadn't prompted Dorcas to reach out.

Griff flipped through the leather-bound appointment book, through the last few months of his father's life. Appointments with his tailor and bootmaker. Plans to meet friends at White's, the gentlemen's club. An appointment to see the dentist. A board of governors meeting at the hospital. The replacement of the garden gate.

Taking a breath, Griff turned to the second week in June, the last few days of his father's life. His gaze hitched on the final entry, from the day before they'd all left for the country house for the final time.

Norman—three o'clock.

Norman had visited Father on his last day in London? It wasn't unusual for the two men to meet. Griff wasn't completely surprised that Norman had never mentioned seeing Father on his last day in London. Norman believed talking about Griff's parents prevented their son from putting the tragedy behind him and moving forward.

Griff not only missed his parents. He'd also missed talking about them and, in doing so, solidifying and preserving his memories of them. A polite rap on the door cut into Griff's thoughts.

Wright appeared. "Dr. Pratt is calling, my lord."

"Is he?" Griff hadn't seen Norman since they'd had dinner. "Show him in."

"Shall I bring in tea?"

"Yes."

Wright remained in place with a politely expectant expression on his face.

"With a plate of biscuits," Griff added.

Wright dipped his chin. "Very good, my lord."

"Norman." Griff rose to greet his former guardian a few moments later. "Come in."

One of Norman's salt-and-pepper brows arched.

"Are you certain?" Norman paused on the threshold before advancing. "We don't seem to be on the best of terms these days."

"We would not be family if we didn't argue." He went to pour them each a drink.

"How are you doing?" Norman probed his face.

"Very well." He handed the older man a brandy. "It is good to be home."

"Take care not to move too fast. The tragedy, along with taking up all of your duties, might prove to be overwhelming if you move too quickly."

"There's little danger of my rushing things. After all, it took me fourteen years to get from your home back here to Haven House."

Norman surveyed the study. "This chamber brings back so many memories." He focused on Griff. "How have you been settling in?"

"Rather smoothly." Griff sipped his brandy. "A few of the old servants are still here."

"Like the butler, I see." Norman's mouth quirked. "Wright is not particularly fond of me. When I became your guardian, I attempted to sort through your father's things. I had the distinct impression that he was hiding papers from me."

"Wasn't the solicitor charged with resolving any existing business matters?"

"Yes, but as your father's closest friend, I thought I should see if there were any personal matters that needed to be discreetly attended to."

"What kinds of personal matters?"

Shifting in his chair, Norman stared at the book-stacks.

"Norman?" Griff pressed. "Are you referring to this alleged mistress my father supposedly kept?"

"Not in particular," he finally said. "All men have personal matters they might prefer to keep private from their families. And their solicitor."

"Were you looking for anything specific?"

"Not at all."

He posed his next question as Wright came in with the tea. "Do you recall seeing Father the day before he died?"

Norman nodded. "Yes. How did you know?"

Griff tapped on the appointment book. "It's in his calendar."

Norman sat up straighter. "You found Jeffrey's calendar?"

"I did."

"Where was it?" Amusement lit his eyes. "Wright obviously hid it. I was right to suspect him."

"Not to worry," Griff said. "I found nothing that would be a source of scandal or indiscretion."

"That's a relief."

"What did you and Father talk about on that Friday?"

Norman looked pained. "I do wish you would let this rest. Leave the past where it belongs."

"I need to know, Norman."

"You already do. Your father wanted me to tell Caroline I was meeting him in the country."

"And that was the day he asked you? The day before we left for the country?"

"Yes. Caroline suddenly decided to go with him, but he was reluctant."

Griff had badgered his mother into accompanying his father to the country because he knew Selina would be there. Guilt pressed down on him. If he hadn't pushed, at least Mother might still be alive.

Griff paused. "There is another matter I wish to discuss. It pertains to Miss Zaydan."

"What about her?"

"The commission meets in two days' time. What do you expect will happen?"

"Mansfield will be called to tell the commission what happened. The bonesetter will be invited to speak as well, if she chooses. I expect it will all be over in an hour or so."

"She doesn't have a chance against someone as powerful as Viscount Payton, does she?"

"No, especially if she is guilty of purposely putting out Mansfield's wrist."

Griff exhaled. By associating himself so closely with her at the fundraiser, he'd harmed her chances ever further. Hanna was now attached to scandal. Not just the one related to him and Selina. But there were also whispers about what had motivated Griff and Bridges to fight over her.

"I see."

"All is not lost for your friend. She is fortunate the ban on her seeing patients doesn't extend outside of London."

"She's likely to return to Manchester to work." The thought of her leaving weighed heavily on him. Even though Griff knew it was for the best. He needed to focus on a future with Selina and the family they might create.

Norman stayed for another half hour mostly discussing hospital matters. Once he departed, Griff summoned Wright. "Do you recall Dr. Pratt visiting my father on the day before we left for Ashby Manor for that last time?"

"I do remember, my lord," the butler said.

"Is there anything about that final visit that stood out to you?"

"Very little, my lord. However, I do seem to remember that it was a quick visit and unremarkable. Although both men did seem a bit tense when they parted company."

"I see." Wright's recollection fit with what Norman had told him about the two men arguing at their final meeting. But over what? Maybe Griff was naive, but he found it difficult to accept his father's supposed infidelity. "You've no idea what they talked about?"

"Regrettably not, my lord."

He paused. "Was my father known to . . . consort with other women? Did he have a mistress?"

Wright drew back. "No, my lord, not to my knowledge. He appeared quite devoted to Lady Griffin."

Griff tapped on the open appointment book. "I have to find out what Father and Norman argued about. Do you have any idea what became of my father's journal?"

"No, my lord. I never saw it after his lordship's death. Perhaps he took it with him to Ashby Manor that final weekend."

A chill went through Griff. In order to learn his father's final private thoughts, he might have no choice but to return to Ashby Manor, the scene of the most horrifying event of his life.

He drew a deep breath to steady himself. He'd managed to conquer his doubts about Haven House. He was actually happy to be home. Maybe he'd feel the same once he went to his country seat.

It was time to finally put all of the demons from his past to rest.

Chapter Nineteen

The commission met at Margate Hospital, in the same room where its board of governors convened each month. There were a dozen of them, all men, sitting around the long, rectangular table.

Hanna attended with Evan, sitting in chairs lining the chamber's walls, surrounding the table where the most important decision of Hanna's professional life was about to be made. Her nerves quivering, she scanned the faces of the commission members and recognized a few from Griff's fundraiser. Three of them even met her eyes and dipped their chins in acknowledgment. The rest avoided looking at her.

Griff was there, too, across the room from where she sat, impeccably turned out in his fine clothing. Mansfield and his father, Lord Payton, were in chairs against the wall in the middle of the room.

Dr. Pratt convened the meeting. "Good afternoon. We are here to assess the matter of whether the bonesetter known as Miss Hanna Zaydan presents a clear danger to the good people of London and therefore should be prohibited from practicing her craft in London in the interests of the health and safety of the public. We shall begin with Mr. Mansfield. Please tell us what occurred when you summoned Miss Zaydan to ask for her services."

Mansfield stood. "My friends and I were at the coffeehouse at Red Lion Square and wanted to determine whether Miss Zaydan is a fraud. I summoned her. She came and purposely put out my wrist. I was in agony for weeks." He glared at her. "She is a public menace who must be stopped."

Griff leaned forward in his chair. "Did you tell Miss Zaydan that you were testing her?"

"No," Mansfield answered.

"Why did she believe she was there?" Griff pressed.

"Pardon me," Lord Payton interjected. "You have no grounds to ask questions. You are not on the commission."

"No, but I do sit on this hospital's board of governors."

Payton scoffed. "That gives you no standing here."

"I say it does," said a commission member, a man of about thirty Hanna had never seen before. Dark-haired and wearing a stylish tailcoat, he possessed the cynical eyes one would expect of a much older man. "Let Griffin speak."

From the expression on Griff's face, he didn't know the man, either. "Erm . . . thank you."

"I agree," said another at the table, who Hanna recognized from the fundraiser.

"I agree as well. Let Griffin question the man," put in another commissioner Hanna remembered speaking with at Haven House. "The point is to get to the bottom of the matter, is it not?"

"Very well," Dr. Pratt said. "Please continue, Lord Griffin."

Griff addressed Mansfield. "Why did Miss Zaydan think you'd called her to the coffeehouse?"

"I told her that I'd put out my wrist."

"Was that the truth?"

"No, obviously not."

"In other words, you lied."

"Yes."

"So, you admit that you are a liar."

Payton jumped to his feet. "How dare you insult my son?"

Griff did not seem impressed by Payton's display. "Your son said he lied. That makes him a liar." He returned his attention to Mansfield. "Did you do anything, make any inappropriate advances toward Miss Zaydan perhaps, that might have made her feel she had to do something to defend herself?"

"Certainly not!" Mansfield had the grace to be affronted by the insinuation he might have accosted Hanna. "She attacked me for no good reason." That wasn't true, but neither was Griff's implication that Mansfield had made inappropriate sexual advances.

"This is outrageous," Lord Payton said. "Miss Zaydan is the one who needs to answer for her actions, not my son."

"We should all have to answer for our actions," said the stranger with the cynical eyes. "No matter what our rank." He observed Mansfield. "How is your wrist now? Can you move it? Or are you permanently impaired?"

"No, indeed. I am as fit as they come." Mansfield wriggled his wrist, demonstrating its mobility. "Thank goodness. I feared that charlatan had damaged it beyond all repair. But it is as good as new."

"Impressive." The stranger propped his chin on his fist. "By the way, how did your wrist get fixed?"

Mansfield maintained a mulish silence.

"I beg your pardon." The stranger cocked an ear. "We cannot hear you."

"Miss Zaydan fixed it," Mansfield said reluctantly.

"And it is as good as new, I believe you said?"

Evan leaned close to Hanna. "Who is that man?"

"I have no idea," she whispered, looking over at Griff. Was the man a friend of his? Otherwise, how would he know that Hanna had put Mansfield's wrist back in? But Griff seemed as confused as Hanna felt.

"So," the stranger continued, "you summoned Miss Zaydan and told her your wrist was out. When she left you at the coffeehouse, your wrist was still out."

"No," Mansfield insisted. "My wrist was not really out before she came to the coffeehouse."

"I see. You are telling us that you *were* lying then. But you *are not* lying now?"

"Yes, exactly!"

"It is a challenge to keep your story straight," the stranger remarked. "However, what is undisputed is that the bonesetter fixed your wrist, leaving it, in your own words, 'as good as new.' No permanent harm was done. And Miss Zaydan helped you even after you drew her to the coffeehouse after what you admit were false pretenses with nefarious intentions and she was forced to protect herself against you."

"That is not how it happened," Mansfield retorted, red-faced. "You are twisting everything."

"Who are you?" Lord Payton demanded to know. "Why are you on this panel?"

The stranger ignored him, addressing his fellow commission members instead. "We need to hear from more of Miss Zaydan's patients."

"As you wish," Dr. Pratt said.

Lord Payton shot to his feet. "Her other patients are irrelevant," he said angrily. "We're here to see that this fraudster is held to account for what she did to my son."

"I believe it is necessary." The stranger came to his feet. He was tall and had an even more powerful presence when standing. "Before I can decide whether Miss Zaydan should be banned from practicing bonesetting in London, I must hear from more of her patients." He nodded in Dr. Pratt's direction. "Please see to it."

Dr. Pratt dipped his chin respectfully. "I will do so, my lord."

The stranger departed without ever having once looked in Hanna's direction. Griff immediately rose and went over to confer with Dr. Pratt. Hanna heard him inquire about the stranger's identity.

"What was that?" Evan asked, watching the man leave.

"I have no idea." Hanna was still trying to com-

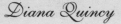

prehend what had just occurred. She'd expected to be stripped of her ability to practice bonesetting this afternoon. She'd already started considering her move to Manchester. Instead, a perfect stranger had granted her a reprieve.

Griff left Dr. Pratt and came over, prompting Hanna to turn to Evan. "I shall meet you outside."

He stiffened. "As you wish." He stepped away just as Griff reached Hanna.

"That was remarkable." He beamed. "It appears that you, unlike me, can always depend upon family to come to your aid."

Family? "Who was that man?"

"That, my dear Hanna, is the Marquess of Brandon."

"Who?" And then it hit her. *Brandon.* Leela's brother. "The cousin I've never met."

"Brandon almost never appears in society. Few would recognize him. He was a late addition to the panel. Norman says the marquess specifically asked to be placed on the commission. Norman had no choice but to grant his request. The man makes sizable donations to the hospital."

"I cannot believe he would step in on my account."

"He is brother to the Duchess of Huntington, is he not?"

She nodded, still dazed. "But he and Leela grew up quite apart from us. Their father was a marquess. The Zaydans are humble merchants. I only met Leela quite recently."

"Well, your mysterious cousin just stepped in to save the day. He's a powerful ally."

"All of the people here did seem to defer to him."

"He's a marquess. He outranks everyone in this room."

"I don't even know him," she repeated.

"But he's on your side," Griff said. "That's all that matters."

HANNA WAS ORGANIZING supplies at the commode table the following day when a well-dressed woman appeared at the dispensary with a young boy.

"May I help you?" asked Evan, who was on his way out to run some errands.

"We are here to see the bonesetter," the woman said.

Hanna closed the drawer. "I am Miss Zaydan."

"I leave you in excellent hands," Evan told the woman as he departed.

Interest swirled in the woman's blue eyes as she scrutinized Hanna. "I am Mrs. Rutland." She was a toff. Her manner of speaking and well-made gown told Hanna as much. Aside from Griff, Hanna had never treated a member of the aristocracy.

"Hello." Hanna observed the dark-haired boy with the flushed, tear-stained cheeks at Mrs. Rutland's side. "And who is this?"

"This is my son, William. He hurt his finger while playing ball."

"May I have a look?" she asked the boy.

He nodded reluctantly.

"Come on, then," she said cheerily, attempting to put the child at ease. "Can you get up on the examining table on your own?"

His chin jutted out. "Of course I can. I am ten. Not a baby."

"William," his mother warned, "mind your manners."

"It is all right," Hanna said.

Once he was seated, Hanna examined the boy's hand. His middle finger was swollen and crooked. "Ah, yes. I see what the problem is."

Mrs. Rutland edged closer. "Can you fix it? It's hurting him terribly. He is such an active boy and so competitive that he can be reckless with his body. He causes his mama a great deal of worry."

"He's in pain because the middle knuckle on his finger is put out."

"What does that mean?" William asked, his voice trembling while he clutched his mother's fingers with his other hand.

"Your bone has slipped out of its joint, and I must put it back in."

"Will that hurt?" William stiffened his spine but mostly appeared terrified.

"Not too much. We're going to ask your mother to help. If you would, Mrs. Rutland, please hold on to William firmly." Lucy came over as well. She knew what to do. She and Hanna had put many fingers back in before. Lucy held William's arm firmly for Hanna to work on.

"Have you done this before?" Mrs. Rutland asked, worry in her voice.

"Many times," she reassured her as she took hold of

the boy's finger. "It's one of the most common injuries I see, especially among the young." As she spoke, she wrenched the finger into place.

"Ooooh," the boy whimpered. "Is it going to get worse?"

"No, that's it." Hanna stepped back. "I'm all done."

He blinked. "You are?"

Mrs. Rutland stared at her. "It's repaired?"

"Yes," Hanna said as Lucy went to get additional supplies. "Now I will wrap it with the finger next to it, and in a few days William and his finger will be in fine form."

William gingerly wiggled his middle finger. "I can move it!"

"Yes, but keep it still for now. We don't want it to fall out of place again."

Mrs. Rutland watched Hanna wrap the boy's finger. "This is your dispensary?"

"Yes, mine and Dr. Bridges's. We work together." But for how long? Her cousin had bought her more time. But could Brandon save her again? "How did you find me?"

"I read about your circumstances in the newspaper."

"And you still chose to come and see me?"

"Our family doctor said to apply iodine to William's finger. But my son was in such pain that I thought it could not hurt if I visited you. I understand you cured Lord Griffin."

"Do you know Lord Griffin?"

A sad look came over her face. "I did. A very long time ago."

The bell over the door sounded. Griff came in. Hanna's skin tingled. She shouldn't be this happy to see him. But her body had a mind of its own.

"Good afternoon." He paused when he spotted her patient and his mother. "Oh, I do beg your pardon. I don't mean to interrupt, I was just—" He halted. The blood drained from his face as he stared at Mrs. Rutland.

The woman returned Griff's stare, her color high. Hanna was shocked to see tears form in Mrs. Rutland's eyes. "Tommy," she breathed.

"What are you doing here?"

Hanna's stomach knotted. Griff obviously had a history with Mrs. Rutland. How many Selinas did the man have in his past?

William tugged on his mother's sleeve. "Who is that man, Mama?"

"This is Lord Griffin." Emotion strained Mrs. Rutland's voice. "He is your uncle."

Chapter Twenty

$\mathcal{H}$anna's mouth fell open.

Mrs. Rutland was one of Griff's negligent sisters? How could an apparently devoted mother show such callous disregard for her young brother?

"How have you been?" Mrs. Rutland asked Griff.

He gave a sad smile. "Don't you think it's a little late to inquire about my welfare?"

"My name is William," the boy interjected.

Griff's face softened as he studied the child. "How do you do, William? It is a pleasure to meet you."

"Why don't you ever visit us?" the boy asked. "Mama always seems sad when she talks about you. It is because you do not come to see her."

"William." His mother warned. "It isn't polite to ask questions."

"Especially ones that are difficult to answer," Griff added.

Mrs. Rutland flushed. "I understand Lady Winters has cleared your name about Mother and Father. About that night. I'm very happy for you."

"I cannot tell you how much I appreciate your sisterly concern."

Mrs. Rutland licked her lips. "Now that you have set up residence at Haven House, I thought perhaps you would call upon me. I could give you my direction."

"I have your direction. As you have had mine all of these years."

"Then you *will* call?"

"Is it only now, after Selina cleared my name in such a spectacular, scandalously public manner, that you wish to become reacquainted?"

"No." Mrs. Rutland faltered. "That is not it at all."

"Mama, Mama." William tugged on his mother's sleeve again. He whispered something in her ear. Mrs. Rutland—Griff's sister—did not take her eyes off her brother as the boy spoke quietly into her ear.

She pressed her lips inward. "Very well." She reached into her reticule and pulled out payment for Hanna. "I must go. William has a rather urgent matter to attend to."

The boy jumped off the table. "Good-bye, Uncle Thomas."

"Good-bye William." He studied the boy with interest. "I'm very pleased I had the opportunity to meet you."

"Tommy—" Mrs. Rutland said.

"It's Griffin now."

"Griffin, I should like to speak with you again."

"Would you?"

"Hurry, Mama." William tugged his mother's hand, practically dragging her to the door.

"Perhaps, Griffin, if we could just—" She was practically pleading.

"Good day." He did not look at his sister. Did not watch her and his nephew open the door to depart. When he heard the door shut, Griff closed his eyes and exhaled a long and shaky breath. He clutched the back of a chair in the waiting area as if he needed the support to stay upright.

Hanna knew she should keep her distance. But he seemed so alone that she went to him, putting her hand on his arm. "So, that is your sister."

"Yes." He slipped into a chair.

Hanna's chest constricted at his pained expression. She sat beside him. "She seemed happy to see you."

He looked dazed. "She did, didn't she?"

"She was clearly emotional. Hers was not the behavior of a woman who does not care."

"Stop." Griff put up his hand. "I barely survived my sisters' desertion the first time. I don't think I could live through it again."

Hanna persisted. "I don't think she came to see me by chance. She was asking about you before you arrived."

"I honestly don't have it in me to discuss Dorcas any longer. I'm here about Gerard Loder."

"The man who gave your mother's jewelry to my father?" She let the issue of his sister drop. "What about him?"

"He's a fence, according to the runner I engaged. He got the necklace and ring from a man named Leonard Palk."

"And who is Leonard Palk?"

"My runner is looking into that as we speak."

"We might be getting closer."

"I hope so." He paused, his eyes darkening. "There is another matter."

"What is it?"

"My father kept a journal."

"Does it have any helpful information?"

"That's just it. I do not know. The journal is probably at Ashby Manor. The place where . . . my parents were killed." He shuddered. "I haven't been back since."

"Is there something specific you are hoping to find in the journal?" she asked gently.

"My father met with Norman the day before we left for the country. The two had words. Norman insinuated the argument had to do with my father's infidelity."

"Do you think that is true?" She didn't know the first thing about Griff's father, but she questioned the doctor's trustworthiness.

"I don't want to believe my father had a mistress. He kept a journal. Maybe that will clarify why he made an unexpected trip to the country."

"If your father was unfaithful, would he really write something like that down in his journal?"

"Probably not." He exhaled long and slow. "But Norman is withholding information. He seems to be protecting my father's memory. That leads me to wonder whether Father was mixed up in something that led to his death."

"It appears you'll have no peace until you go to Ashby Manor and find the journal."

"I'm not sure I am up to it. To be honest, I dread returning there."

"Perhaps you will find that it is like Haven House. You have a childhood's worth of good memories at Ashby. Maybe that will help balance the bad recollections. You are a grown man now. No longer a hurt and confused child."

He exhaled. "I will think on it." He looked at her. Hanna realized they were seated entirely too close together, their faces barely a foot apart. "It is good to see you. To be able to talk things through with you. There are few people with whom I can speak openly."

He seemed so alone in that moment that Hanna reached for his hand. "I will always be your friend," she promised. Griff had few true friends. She would not abandon him the way his sisters had. No matter how painful it was to be with him and know he'd soon be wed to Lady Winters.

Staring down at their hands, he interlocked his fingers with hers. "I miss touching you."

She closed her eyes for a moment, savoring the feel of his hands entwined with hers. "I miss being touched by you," she admitted, even though she shouldn't. "But we mustn't. It's dishonorable when you are bound to another."

"I am not bound to Selina yet. She said she does not consider herself bound to me and that I should feel the same." He stroked Hanna's hand. Warmth swirled along her skin. "That might change after Selina and I meet in a few weeks, but for now I am technically a free man."

She gently withdrew her fingers. "But only technically," she said softly.

"Unfortunately." He let her go, his touch lingering on her fingers as she slid them out of his hand.

The bell above the door sounded. The man who entered appeared to be in his fifties. He wore an old-fashioned plain amber tailcoat and blue trousers.

Hanna rose. The sensation of having her hand held in Griff's lingered. "Good day."

"Are you Mrs. Zaydan?"

"I am."

"I am Samuel Lockhart."

"Are you a relation to Mrs. Lockhart?"

He gave a sharp nod. "Mr. Lockhart was my uncle."

"How do you do?" she said warmly. "I am sorry for the loss of your aunt. How may I be of assistance?"

"You may assist me by shutting your doors and delivering this property back to me, the rightful owner."

Hanna blinked. "I beg your pardon?"

Griff came to his feet as well, remaining quiet, but silently bolstering her.

"The rent for this property is very valuable," Mr. Lockhart pointed out.

"I am afraid there's been a misunderstanding," she said politely. "The terms of your aunt's will allow me to operate my dispensary free of charge."

"Yes, I am aware that my uncle's wife, a woman without a drop of Lockhart blood in her, left this space for your . . . *operation*."

"Then, why are you here?" She didn't care for his tone.

"I understood you were to be stripped of your right to operate this *enterprise* of yours yesterday. That you would be forced to cease your exploits, close down and return control of this space to me."

She wondered where Mr. Lockhart had gotten his information. "You have been misinformed. The commission has made no final decision on the matter."

"I hope you will do the decent thing and move out as soon as possible. My family and I wish to sell the building."

Beside her, Hanna could sense Griff itching to intervene. "Then I suggest you sell it with the stipulation that I have the right to use this space for free."

"Now, see here." Mr. Lockhart's chin trembled. "The only reason you are in this building is because you swindled a lonely old lady with a feeble mind."

Hanna's neck heated. "I did no such thing. And I am not moving out. Good day, sir."

"Do you want me to offer you money to leave? How much will it take?"

For a moment, Hanna considered the crass proposal. In all likelihood, she was about to lose her right to practice bonesetting in London. Her cousin Brandon's intervention had likely only delayed the inevitable. Money from Mr. Lockhart could help Hanna set up a dispensary in Manchester.

But she did not care for the look in Mr. Lockhart's eyes, the surety in them that she could be bought and sold. Accepting his offer would only confirm his belief that Hanna was nothing but a greedy fraudster who'd cheated his elderly aunt.

"No amount of money is enough to compensate me for the pleasure of doing what I love," she said. "I hope to be practicing bonesetting in this space until the end of my days."

"You have no real right to be here and you know it."

She straightened. "Your aunt gave me the right, and it was hers to give. Not yours."

"I intend to see my solicitor about this matter."

"I don't see how that's any of my concern," she replied.

"You will be hearing from me," he said as he pulled the door open.

"Mr. Lockhart?"

"Yes?" He turned back to her with a smug expression on his face. "Have you decided to accept the money to vacate the premises after all?"

"No, indeed. I was wondering where Mrs. Lockhart was laid to rest. I would like to pay my respects."

"How should I know?"

"The hospital said that Mrs. Lockhart's family came for the body."

"We most certainly did not. Nor did we have any interest in doing so. As I said, Mrs. Lockhart was related to us solely by marriage. Mr. Lockhart was our family. He would have left the building to me outright." He slammed the door shut behind him as he departed.

"Charming man," Griff remarked. He noted her pensive expression. "What is it?"

"If the Lockharts didn't pick up Mrs. Lockhart's body from the hospital, who did? The matron there told me the family had come for the body. If her family doesn't have poor Mrs. Lockhart's remains, then what happened to them?"

"Perhaps someone from Mrs. Lockhart's own family, and not her husband's family, saw to the burial."

"Yes, of course." Hanna gave a swift nod. "That must be it."

"For a moment there, I thought you were going to accept his money."

"I should have. It would be the prudent thing to do. My chances of being able to continue practicing in London are slim."

"Not if I have anything to say about it."

"It's out of all of our hands."

"Not necessarily. We will assemble the people you have helped. Me. Young Annie. Who else have you successfully treated?"

"Laboring-class people, mostly. Shopkeepers, grocers, the occasional solicitor. Nobody, besides you, who might be able to influence the commission."

"You are forgetting the grandson of an earl."

"What earl?"

"Dorcas is married to the youngest son of the Earl of Tremayne."

"Truly?" Hanna marveled at Griff's revelation. Up until a few weeks ago, she'd never interacted with any of the Quality. Except for Leela, of course. Hanna had yet to even meet Leela's duke. Now she mingled with aristocrats at fundraisers and healed their children. "It was just a minor dislocation of his finger. Besides, I can hardly ask your sister, a *lady*, to intervene on my behalf."

"I can."

She stared at him. "But you want nothing to do with your sister."

"True." His expression was grim. "But if it helps you, I shall go and see Dorcas."

"I cannot ask that of you."

"You aren't asking."

"If you insist." Hanna decided not to argue. Griff *should* go and see his sister. And all the better if Hanna was the catalyst to bring them together after all these years apart. "How soon can you call on her?"

Chapter Twenty-One

Griffin. You came." Dorcas rushed into the drawing room. Her cheeks were bright, her expression expectant. "When my butler announced you, I could scarcely believe it."

Griff absorbed this new version of his sister. Before their chance encounter at Hanna's dispensary, he'd last seen Dorcas fourteen years ago, when she was nineteen and newly married, the last of his sisters to leave home. The image of her as a radiant young bride remained entrenched in Griff's mind all these years. The Dorcas before him now was a woman of thirty-three. Her face had filled out. Her figure was more rounded. But she was still the sister he once knew.

"Please sit." Dorcas settled in a French chair with rounded edges and tapestry fabric. Griff took the matching chair opposite her. They were by a large window that overlooked the back garden where Dorcas's son William rolled in the grass with a fluffy white Pomeranian.

"How is his finger?" he asked as he watched. *His nephew.* It hardly seemed real.

"It's a tad sore. But otherwise he can use it and has no real pain. Your bonesetter is remarkable."

"Yes, she is."

"I'm so pleased you've come. Tea will be along shortly."

"This is not exactly a social call." Griff struggled to keep an even tone. Seeing Dorcas in the flesh after all these years rekindled his frustration with his sisters, stoked the feelings of betrayal and abandonment embedded in the marrow of his bones. "In all honesty, if I didn't need something from you, I would have avoided this encounter."

Her face fell. He registered the hurt in her pale blue eyes. Instead of feeling triumphant, guilt panged through him.

"It was never your way to be cruel," she said softly.

"How would you know?" he said stiffly. "We never knew each other, not really."

"That's not true." She shook her head, her eyes catching the light. Like him, she had their mother's eyes. She also shared Griff's distinct nose and dark hair, a legacy from their father. An observer might say he and his sister resembled each other. Even though they'd been worlds apart for almost half his life.

"I knew you very well." Amusement lined Dorcas's forehead. "I knew all of your hiding places. I knew you used to sneak a cheroot with that footman . . . what was his name?" She considered for a moment then snapped her fingers. "Felix, that's it. And I also knew that you used to steal away to see Selina. Although I confess I had no idea that you two were—"

"I am not here to reminisce about our childhood." He couldn't bear to summon any happy memories. To share any confidences. To remember anything about the time before it all went wrong.

"Whatever your reason for coming, I cannot tell you how happy I am to see you."

The footman came in with an elaborate tea tray. They quieted while he set the plates out and Dorcas scooted forward to pour the tea.

"I seem to recall you were partial to lemon tarts," Dorcas remarked as she added them to a plate she made for him. She included his favorite sandwiches as well before setting the plate and tea before him. Griff didn't touch them. His stomach churned. He couldn't eat.

She settled back with her cup. "You were going to tell me why you've come. What can I do for you?"

"I'm here about Miss Zaydan."

Curiosity blazed in her face. "The bonesetter?"

"Miss Zaydan is to face a commission soon. If they rule against her, she will lose her right to practice bonesetting in London."

Dorcas examined him closely. Griff shifted in his chair and stared out the window. His sister always did see too much. "I gather you do not wish to see Miss Zaydan leave London? Isn't she a Levantine?"

"How does that signify?" His head snapped back to focus on his sister.

"It doesn't. I had heard she was an Arab. I thought that was curious." She sipped her tea. "I have never met an Arab person before. One conjures up all sorts of images. However, I found her to be very agreeable. And quite capable."

"She has many positive qualities," he said gruffly. "I am asking you to attend the commission hearing and give testimony in support of Miss Zaydan."

"You'd like me to tell them that a bonesetter cured William's finger when one of the ton's finest doctors could not? And an immigrant female healer, at that?" Her eyes twinkled. "Imagine the scandal. The ton's doctors will be in an uproar."

"She's not an immigrant. She was born here. Will you do it?"

William bounded in. "I heard the tea was served." He skidded to a stop by the tea table and snatched up a sandwich. The Pomeranian came in yapping behind him. "Mama, can I have some?" he asked around a bite of food.

She gazed adoringly at her son as she reached down to scratch the dog's head. "Make your hellos to your Uncle Thomas, and then you may fill your plate."

"Hullo, Uncle Thomas." His gaze dropped to Griff's untouched plate. "Why aren't you eating?"

"You may have my plate if you'd like," Griff said.

The boy looked at his mother, who dipped her chin. He reached for Griff's plate. "I have to go. I'm going to dig up worms in the garden."

Griff watched the boy leave. "He doesn't resemble you."

"He takes after his father. The Rutland blood is very strong."

"I wonder," he said.

"What do you wonder?"

"If you would desert him as readily as you deserted me."

She paled. "You didn't want to come live with me." She set her tea down with trembling hands. "What would you have me do?"

"You and my other sisters wanted nothing to do with me after the murders."

Her eyes went wide. "That's a lie," she said hotly. "I was eager to have you live with me. I hounded Cousin Norman for months."

"Norman said you were newly married and wanted to concentrate on your new family."

Dorcas's nostrils flared. "Is that what he told you? He told us that you were too vulnerable to see us. We wanted you to come with us to go through Mother's and Father's things at Haven House a few weeks after the burial. Cousin Norman said you would come. But on the day we were supposed to meet, he sent word that you'd had a very bad day and he didn't want to further upset you."

He blinked. "That cannot be true."

"It most certainly is. We all wanted to get you away from Cousin Norman. But Father appointed him guardian in the will. There was nothing we could do." Her face darkened. "I was also very young. I should have leveraged the influence of my husband's family to rescue you from that beastly man."

"I didn't know anything about meeting you, Maria

and Wini at Haven House." His breastbone ached. "Nothing would have made me happier than to be with the three of you."

"You know what this means?" Anger glinted in her gaze. "Cousin Norman lied to you. We were desperate to see you in those early days after the funeral. But Norman said you were too fragile."

"He told me that the three of you abandoned me because you believed I killed our parents."

"Never!" she said fiercely. "We never believed that. *Ever.* We told you as much in our letters. The letters to which you never replied."

"I received no letters." Griff lurched to his feet and paced away, wiping a hand down over his mouth and chin. "Is it possible? I don't know what to believe."

"Yes, you do. You are just having a difficult time acknowledging the truth. Our cousin lied to you. He's been dishonest with you since the moment he took you into his care."

"But why? What would he have to gain from keeping us apart?"

"I have no idea. You've spent all these years with him. You know him better than any of us."

"I don't know about that." His chest jerked with each harsh breath. "I might not know him at all." Could Norman have perpetuated a lie so massive, so destructive, so devastating?

"Has he spent your fortune?"

"No. He can't touch it. He never could."

"What else could it be?" she asked.

"I don't know." He strode from the room. "But there is one person who does."

"Is it true?"

"Is what true?" Norman asked.

Uncertainty flickered in the older man's face. Griff had come directly to the hospital from Dorcas's house. Registering Griff's agitated state, Norman pulled him into the nearest storeroom, where blankets, linens and other hospital supplies lined the shelves.

"Did my sisters send me letters?" Griff asked after Norman closed the door. The narrow room was dim. The scent of fresh laundry saturated the air. "Did you hide my sisters' letters from me?"

"Yes." Norman's words were calm and matter-of-fact. "I did it to protect you."

"Protect me?" Griff flattened a hand against his chest. "From what? From my own sisters? From what family I had left?"

"I am your family, too."

Griff gave an incredulous laugh. "I wonder about that. You kept me from my sisters. You destroyed what was left of my family."

"No." The older man's face firmed. "The person who killed your parents destroyed your family. I picked up the pieces and put you back together."

"By keeping me from my sisters? By letting me think that they believed I killed my parents?"

"I had a responsibility to *you*. Not to your sisters. My role as your guardian was to make certain that you grew into a strong and stable man. To prepare you for your role as viscount and to continue the family line. That was my duty to your father, and I fulfilled it. Look at you." He gestured toward Griff. "You are strong and capable. You are a worthy man. I truly believed isolating you from the tragedy was for the best."

"Shielding me from the tragedy is comprehensible, perhaps, but to cut my sisters completely out of my life?"

"The girls were a blathering mess for months after your parents' demise. Anytime I saw them, they would cry and carry on."

"They were grieving!"

"Being subjected to all of their caterwauling would have destroyed you. I needed to protect you from that." Norman adjusted his spectacles. "You were so young, so hurt, so vulnerable. I had to keep you safe. All your sisters wanted to do in the months after the burials was to talk about your parents' murders and finding their killer."

"It is natural to want to avenge our parents' deaths."

"Perhaps. But I feared you'd get it into your head that it was your duty to find the killer. What if it became an obsession that dominated, and ultimately destroyed, your life? I couldn't let that happen."

"I cannot believe this." Fists on his hips, Griff turned away. "You separated me from everything I held dear. My sisters. Haven House. They were all I had left."

"I did what I thought was right. I don't have children, and my only brother perished when I was so young that I don't remember him. Maybe I know nothing about family bonds." He paused, dismay filling his face. "Maybe I was wrong to do what I did."

"*Maybe*?" Griff raised his voice. "All you've ever done is lie to me."

"All I know is that your father entrusted you to my care." Norman removed his spectacles and pinched the bridge of his nose. "I did what I had to to keep you sound in the midst of unspeakable horror. The murders could have destroyed you. Keeping you stable and on course with your schooling was my primary focus."

"Then why didn't you tell me the truth after I was grown? Why did you let me continue to believe that my sisters wanted nothing whatsoever to do with me?"

"I tried." Norman faltered. "But I didn't know how. I feared you wouldn't understand."

"Well, you had the right of it. Because I certainly do not understand. What you did was cruel."

"But look at you now." Pride filled Norman's gaze. "You are strong and able. Your parents' killings didn't ruin you. Maybe I made mistakes, but I see the fine man you are today and know I fulfilled my duty."

"The end justifies the means? No matter what the cost? Is that really how you view the world, Norman?"

"Most people are not willing to make difficult decisions for the greater good, but I did what I had to."

Griff stared at him. "I don't even know who you are."

"Once you've had time to reflect, you will come to

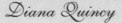

see that I honestly tried to do the right thing for every-one involved."

"Wrong. I will never accept that what you did was right." He pulled the door open, eager to escape. He was suffocating. "Never."

HANNA TURNED THE key in the lock as she and Evan closed the dispensary for the evening.

"What happened to your shadow?" Evan asked.

"Who? Lucy? She had to run an errand for *Citi*."

They turned in the direction of her house. Evan had taken to escorting her and Lucy home before walking on to his neighborhood. "Your grandmother trusts you alone with me?"

"I wouldn't go as far as to say that. She needs Lucy at home. We need to consider engaging an assistant for the dispensary."

Looking ahead, Evan's face twisted. "What's he doing here?"

Hanna followed his gaze. She caught sight of Griff up ahead and brightened. "Good afternoon," she called out. "Were you coming to the dispensary?"

"Where else?" Evan muttered. "The man seems to have a lot of time on his hands."

"Of course he does. That *is* the very definition of a gentleman. Unlike you and I, they do not engage in work for their living."

"Imagine being able to devote your days and nights solely to leisurely pursuits. And having the money to do it." He grimaced. "Life is very unfair."

"That it is," she agreed. As they drew nearer, the

expression on Griff's face made Hanna's skin prickle. Had the commission reached a decision? "What is it? What's happened?"

"Do you have a moment?" he asked, his voice raw.

"I'll be on my way." Evan moved past Griff. "I'll see you in the morning, Hanna."

"What's happened?" she asked Griff once Evan was gone.

"Can we go somewhere?"

"Of course. Come back to the clinic."

He followed her and stood by silently as she unlocked the door. They entered the dispensary. The late-afternoon shadows fell across the floor. But the space was illuminated enough that she didn't bother to light a lamp.

He sat on one of the examining tables. "Everything about my life is a lie."

"What is wrong?"

His face was stark. "All of these years I believed my sisters abandoned me because they thought I killed our parents."

"Did you visit Mrs. Rutland today?"

He nodded. "They wanted me to live with them, but Norman wouldn't allow it. He decided it was best that I didn't see my sisters."

"What? Why?" she exclaimed. *"Shu hayee!"*

He cocked his head. "Translation?"

"He's nothing but a snake. A backstabber." Anger pulsed through her veins. "Why would he keep you from your sisters? They are your blood. Family is everything. We are nothing without our family."

"Norman says my sisters suffered bouts of hysteria after my parents died. He wanted to shield me from the emotional upset."

"When you lose someone you love, of course you get emotional. When Papa died, Mama and *Citi* wailed and carried on as if the world was ending. *Citi* would have crawled into the grave with Baba if we hadn't stopped her."

"My sisters sent me letters. Norman never gave them to me."

"Oh, Griff. I am sorry."

"He apologized when I confronted him. But he *still* believes he did the right thing. That he fulfilled his duty to raise me to be a strong man who would live up to the title."

"You are a good man in spite of Dr. Pratt," she said heatedly. "Not because of him."

"Am I a good man?" He massaged his temples. "I don't know anything anymore. My sisters are strangers to me. My former guardian, a man I believed I could trust above all others, deceived me for years. Society used to think that I was a murderer. Now they believe that I despoil innocent women."

"Now that you know the truth, you have the opportunity to become reacquainted with your sisters. You can reclaim your life."

"I suppose." He rubbed the back of his neck. "Thank you for listening to me. I'm sorry to trouble you. I know I shouldn't have come."

"I am happy you did. We are friends."

He shot her a skeptical look. "Do you really believe we can be friends?"

"I am your friend for as long as you need me." Soon Griff would rekindle his relationship with his sisters. And he would have a wife and perhaps children. Her heart ached at the thought. "I shall be your friend until you return to your aristocratic world with your beautiful aristocratic wife and forget about the bonesetter on Red Lion Square."

His eyes held hers. "As if I could ever forget the incomparable woman who saved me from a life of pain and misery."

The air between them tightened. She moved closer until she stood between his legs. "I won't forget you, either."

"This is quite a mess."

She stepped even closer. "I agree."

"We should not." His voice was strained. "It isn't fair to you."

She put her hands on his strong thighs. "You said yourself that you are not officially bound to Lady Winters yet."

"No. I am not."

He pulled her into his arms. She went willingly. An intense longing propelled her forward against her better judgment. When it came to Griff, Hanna's body constantly mutinied against reason.

"Hanna." He held her so tightly as if to meld her to him. "My love."

"*Hayati.*" My life.

"What does that mean?"

She shook her head, embarrassed to tell him. "Later."

He kissed her. Deeply. Intimately. With everything in him. She put her arms around his neck and pressed herself against the hardness of his chest. His warmth and masculine scent enveloped her. The intensity of his ardor took her breath away. The kiss went on and on until the room was swirling and her legs dissolved beneath her.

"We should stop," he whispered against her lips.

"We should," she agreed before pressing her lips to his again. "I feel cheated."

He pulled back, alarm in his face. "Why?"

"Because you have seen me practically disrobed, and I have not had the same pleasure."

"What are you talking about? I took off my shirt many times when you examined me."

"That was as a healer. I could not touch you the way I wanted. Put my mouth on you as you did with me."

"Hanna." His eyes darkened.

For a moment, she pictured it. Removing their clothes and making love right there. What would the most intimate of acts be like? How would it feel to have part of Griff inside of her?

Alarm flickered in Griff's face. As if he could see her thoughts. He came up off the table. "I must go. *Now*. Before we do something that we'll regret."

"I am not so sure I would regret it," she said. "But, yes, you are right. You should go."

"I'll escort you home."

She nodded as she followed him to the door, keenly

feeling the loss of him. "At least in public we should manage to control ourselves."

"Just barely," he murmured as he shut the door behind them and waited for her to lock up.

They started in the direction of Hanna's house, walking in silence, quietly enjoying each other's company.

"I am going to Ashby Manor," Griff said abruptly.

"When did you decide to make the journey?" She knew how much he dreaded it.

"Just now. Norman has told me his version of events regarding my father's last days, but I can no longer believe anything he tells me."

"Don't go alone." She hated to imagine him confronting his past by himself. "Take someone with you."

"I wish you could be there with me."

"As do I." She released a breath. "But we both know that isn't possible."

Chapter Twenty-Two

*Y*ou didn't have to accompany me." Griff observed the woman sitting opposite him in the carriage taking them to Ashby Manor. "I could have come alone."

It wasn't a long journey. Just an hour. But it had taken him almost a lifetime to reach this point.

"But why should you have to?" Dorcas asked. She'd insisted on accompanying him. Having sisters again was going to take some getting used to. "It was once my home, too. I should like William to see where we spent our childhood."

Griff's nephew rode in the conveyance behind them with his governess and the baggage. Dorcas also had an older son who was away at Eton and three younger children in Town with their nurse and father.

Griff gazed out the window at the countryside that had once been so familiar to him. "I would avoid Ashby Manor if I could."

"Then why are you going?"

"Things eventually have to be faced. I am the lord of the manor now. I cannot neglect it forever." He decided against revealing the full truth. He would tell her of his search for their parents' killers only if the endeavor proved successful.

As they neared Ashby, Griff's stomach cramped. Memories of that terrible morning flooded back, threatening to overwhelm him. At least Griff had been spared the sight of his parents' bodies. The servants found them first, early in the morning. It was the magistrate who finally awakened Griff well past noon, hours after the rest of the household learned of the gruesome discovery.

They turned up the long drive that led to the house. The white Palladian villa soon came into view, rising up in the distance as they drew near. The household staff, about a dozen people, assembled out front to welcome them.

"It's smaller than I remember," he said. "But also more stunning."

"Do you think so?" Dorcas asked. She peered out of the window as the carriage came to a halt in front of Ashby Manor. "I almost expect Mother and Father to come out and greet us."

William was already out of the carriage behind them, loping toward the house with his white Pomeranian enthusiastically trailing him.

"We're finally here." Griff took a deep breath. "It's time to make new memories."

"THERE'S A MESSAGE for you, miss."

"Thank you, Annie." The daughter of Dr. Pratt's housekeeper was Hanna's newest assistant. Lucy had returned to her position as maid of all work at home.

"The messenger says he was told to wait for a response." Annie was still learning, but she was smart and eager. Bonesetting fascinated her. Hanna saw a smidgen of herself in the girl.

"Is that so?" She opened the note. It was on expensive paper. Was it from Griff? She quickly scanned its contents.

"What is it?" Evan asked.

"It's from Mrs. Rutland."

"The woman whose son put his finger out?"

Evan didn't know Mrs. Rutland was Griff's sister. And Hanna decided to spare herself the lecture that would inevitably follow if she enlightened him. "It seems her son fell out of an apple tree at their country estate. She wants me to come and tend to his arm. She fears it's broken."

"Where is this country estate?"

"In Richmond. If I agree, she will send a carriage for me in the morning. She asks that I plan to stay for a couple of nights so that I might see to the boy's care. She says she will pay me for my time."

"So now you are a glorified nanny for the Quality?"

"Mrs. Rutland's husband is the grandson of an earl. She could be a powerful ally before the commission."

"If she is willing to use her entitlement to assist you, it might be worthwhile."

Hanna folded the note, wondering whether Mrs. Rutland had heard from Griff. He'd left just yesterday for Ashby Manor. Had he arrived yet? She didn't know where Ashby Manor was or how long the journey might take. Although she knew Griff's home was a real place, in her mind it was some mythical grand house. She headed to the back office to pen her response at the bottom of Mrs. Rutland's note. Paper was dear. There was no need to waste a new sheet of paper when there was room at the bottom of Mrs. Rutland's missive.

"Are you going alone?" Evan asked from the doorway.

"No." She signed her name and refolded the note. "Rafi is coming with me." He was her only option. Elias had returned to Manchester, but Rafi uncharacteristically decided to spend a little more time in Town.

"He is?"

"Yes." She stood. "He just doesn't know it yet."

MRS. RUTLAND'S COUNTRY estate was something out of a fairy tale. The park surrounding the house was lush and expansive. With green grass, trees and wildflowers as far as the eye could see. Through a copse of trees, Hanna glimpsed a charming stream.

The house itself was magnificent. White and elegant and enormous. It still boggled Hanna's mind that people actually lived in such grandeur. Their house off Red Lion Square was probably one-hundredth the size of this palatial estate.

"*Yubba yay.*" Rafi stared out the window. "It's practically a castle."

"*Akeed,*" she agreed. "Imagine all of that room for one family."

"If it were for an Arab family, we'd fill it up."

She smirked. "That is true." With all of their aunts,

great-aunts, uncles, great-uncles, first and second cousins who regularly attended family gatherings, they might occupy every room.

The carriage pulled up to the manor. The footman who came for their baggage escorted Rafi to his bedchamber, while Hanna was taken directly to see her patient.

Young William was reclined on a chaise when Hanna entered what she thought must be the music room. An enormous piano had a place of pride in one corner, while a gilded harpsichord stood nearby.

"Miss Zaydan." Mrs. Rutland came toward her dressed in silk and smelling of expensive perfumes. "Thank you for coming. It hasn't been easy to make William sit still for a day."

"Hello, William." Hanna approached the boy. "What have you done to yourself?"

"Perhaps I should see about keeping you on a retainer," Mrs. Rutland remarked. "William is always flinging his body here and there. It's almost as if he doesn't realize his bones can break."

"It's nothing," William protested, squirming on the chaise. "It's just a little sore."

"Let me have a look." Hanna examined the boy's arm. She saw immediately that William's assessment was correct. Mrs. Rutland had most definitely overreacted.

"There's a slight strain and bit of bruising," she told mother and son after evaluating his forearm. "There is really no need of my services." She and Rafi could easily return to London this afternoon.

"Are you certain?" Mrs. Rutland asked.

"Yes, quite." Hanna hadn't taken Mrs. Rutland to be an overly protective mother. But clearly she'd been wrong.

"How's that arm doing?" a familiar masculine voice called out.

Hanna turned to see Griff enter the room. He stopped short when he spotted her. He was casually attired in a white, open-necked shirt that bared the strong lines of his throat.

"Hanna?" Delight filled his face. He set his hands on his narrow hips, drawing her attention to how well he looked in the formfitting breeches. "What are you doing here?"

"I asked her to come," Mrs. Rutland said. "To treat William's arm."

"Whatever for?" Griff asked. "He barely hurt himself."

"One can never be too careful." Mrs. Rutland smoothed her skirts. "But now that Miss Zaydan is here, she might as well stay for a couple of nights as she and I originally planned."

"I see." An amused expression came over Griff's face. "After all of these years, my sister is still a busybody."

And not the overprotective mother Hanna had first surmised.

"What's a *busybody*?" William asked.

"Never mind that," his mother said. "You may go and play. Miss Zaydan says you are fine."

William scampered away before his mother could change her mind.

"Well," Mrs. Rutland said cheerily, glancing from Griff to Hanna and then back again, "I have things to do. I shall see you both at supper."

She followed her son out the door, leaving Griff and Hanna staring at each other.

"You have to forgive my sister," Griff said. "She never could mind her own business."

"I had no idea this was Ashby Manor," Hanna said. "I thought this was your sister's country estate."

"Which is obviously what she wanted you to think."

"Why did she ask me here? Does she suspect there is something between us?"

"She senses, I suppose. Dorcas doesn't know for certain. I haven't told her anything." He took her in with appreciative eyes. "However it happened, I am happy you are here."

"How are you? Has returning here been as difficult as you feared?"

"Having Dorcas here helps. She insisted on accompanying me. But she doesn't know why we're here. I don't want to upset her unnecessarily."

"She seems to care a great deal about you."

"Somehow she realized that having you here is important to me. You are the only person I can confide in, completely, regarding the tragedy."

"It's a burden you shouldn't have to carry alone."

"I don't want to upset my sisters, especially if our search turns out to be fruitless."

"Have you found your father's journal?"

"We only arrived yesterday," he said. "I haven't summoned the courage to search for it yet."

"I don't mean to pry, but I can help you look. If you'd like."

"I would. Your company is always appreciated. How about if you settle in, and then we'll begin our search first thing in the morning."

"I shall be ready."

"Now that you are here, this experience isn't nearly as difficult. The moment I saw you, I thought about all of the places at Ashby that I want to show you."

"I'd love to see them."

"Thank you for coming."

"You should thank your sister."

He took her hand in his and squeezed it. "Perhaps we both should."

"I NEVER THOUGHT I'd spend the night in a house enormous enough to get lost in," Rafi remarked to Hanna. They met in the corridor outside their guest chambers to attempt to navigate their way to the dining room.

"Cleaning this house must be a nightmare." Hanna switched to Arabic so she could speak frankly without worrying about eavesdroppers. "Are you certain we're going the right way?"

"No." Rafi shifted to Arabic as well. "But at least we left our chambers early enough to give us time to get lost and still get to supper on time. How's the boy?"

"William's arm is fine." They started down a staircase with mammoth mahogany balusters topped by a wide, carved handrail. "His mother, Mrs. Rutland, is a bit overprotective."

He studied Hanna's face. "Why are we really here? The viscount just wanted an excuse to get you out here, didn't he? And I don't have to wonder for what."

"He didn't even know his sister asked us to come. Besides, you're here. You're my chaperone."

"And I will be keeping an eye on Griffin. *Aina baitha,*" he responded, the Arabic saying suggesting that Griff's eyes were so wide with interest when he gazed at Hanna that all one saw were the whites of his eyes.

"Stop it." She bumped her shoulder against her brother's. "Griff has other things to worry about. His parents were murdered here, and it's his first time back in over a dozen years."

"Splendid. Now we have to worry about ghosts, too." They paused before an ornate wooden door. "This might be the dining room."

"What if they have more than one?"

"Then, we'll have to ask for directions from one of the dozens of servants that seem to pop up out of nowhere. Did you see how they come out of the walls?"

She nodded. "I never realized that these grand houses have so many hidden doors. It's like the walls have ears."

"Here we go." Rafi switched back to English as he pushed the door open to find Griff and Mrs. Rutland standing by a shiny, oval walnut dining table that could easily seat twenty. An enormous painting of men on horses during a fox hunt dominated the room.

"There you both are," said Mrs. Rutland. "Just on time."

They took their seats, and the two footmen attending them began to serve the courses. Griff engaged Rafi in conversation, asking interested questions about the family business of cotton exports.

Hanna was hungry, so she concentrated on her food, finishing her soup and then her meat and vegetable dish. She noticed that Mrs. Rutland barely touched either course, having only a few spoonfuls of soup and two or three bites of the roast. When the third course appeared, Hanna began to understand why Griff's sister ate so sparingly. Hanna wondered how she was going to make it to the end of the meal without stuffing herself silly.

"That's a remarkable painting," Rafi said referring to the immense painting that was the room's focal point. "The horses are magnificent."

"We have a decent stable," Griff remarked. "You're welcome to take a mount out for a hack. Just ask the stablemaster. He'll set you up. What kind of mount do you prefer?"

Rafi exchanged a glance with his sister before responding. "I don't ride." Horses were a luxury laboring-class people in the city could ill afford.

"Oh?" Surprise lit Griff's face. "Why not?"

Hanna intervened. "Stabling a mount and otherwise paying for its upkeep is too great an expense." She saw no reason not to be truthful. She'd never pretended to be anything other than who she was with Griff.

"I can imagine," Mrs. Rutland said, although the expression on her face suggested such a thing had never occurred to her.

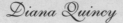

"I wish I could ride," Rafi said. "But the business keeps me busy."

"Why don't you give it a try while you are here?" Griff asked.

"Me? Ride?" Rafi asked.

"Why not?" Griff said. "I'll take you out to the stables first thing in the morning if you'd care to give it a try."

Rafi shrugged. "Why not?" he said indifferently.

But Hanna saw the gleam in her brother's eyes.

LATE THE NEXT morning, Griff watched Hanna's brother trot in a circle on a thoroughbred.

"He's handling himself well," Griff said to his stable-master. "I see you found him a suitable mount."

"We keep a small stable, my lord. But we managed." Ben, a man in his late thirties, was among the newer hires at Ashby, having joined Griff's staff at some point in the fourteen years that Griff was away.

"How long has he been out there?"

"Nearly three hours. He was at the stables at eight this morning. He caught on quickly, my lord."

Griff propped his arms on the paddock-fence rail. "One would never guess the man had never been atop a mount before."

"Aye. He can't seem to get enough."

Rafi sat the mount well with strong, still legs, and excellent shoulder and hip alignment. Had the man been born to privilege and put in the saddle as a stripling as Griff had been, he'd probably be among the finer riders of Griff's acquaintance.

A groom held on to the mount's bridle while Rafi awkwardly alighted, half sliding, half falling off the horse.

Ben chuckled. "We'll have to work on the dismount."

"Indeed." Griff said. Rafi came over, and Ben excused himself to get back to his duties.

"You're a natural," Griff said.

"I do enjoy riding," Rafi said. "I'll have to investigate renting a mount now and again to enjoy a good hack through the park."

"We keep mounts at Haven House. You are welcome to take one out for a ride in Hyde Park whenever you wish."

Rafi was silent for a moment. The contemplative look that came over the man's flushed face prompted Griff to worry if he'd overstepped.

"It's an offer I would make to any friend," he added, lest the man think Griff was offering charity. They might not be well-to-do, but Hanna's family wasn't impoverished.

"Is that what we are?" Rafi studied Griff's face in a way that made him uncomfortable.

"I beg your pardon?"

"Is that what you consider my sister? A friend?"

Rafi's expression wasn't particularly friendly. He appeared close to calling Griff out. Did the middle class engage in duels? Or would it be fisticuffs?

"I hold your sister in the highest regard." Griff chose his words carefully. "I respect her considerable skills. She cured me. I shall never be able to properly repay her."

"My sister is a good girl."

"I agree. She is one of the finest women I have had the honor of knowing."

Rafi's dark gaze drilled into Griff. "You understand what would happen to her if she is touched by scandal?"

"I don't know what you are implying but—"

"She faces banishment from the family," Rafi interrupted. "She would not be allowed to continue bonesetting. Our aunts and uncles would shun her. Our cousins would never be allowed to talk to her again."

Griff blinked. "I see."

"Do you? Do you truly comprehend my meaning? For Arabs, family is everything. Friends are nothing. Your family are your friends. If Hanna loses her family, she loses a vital part of herself. Do you want to be responsible for that?"

"Of course not. I want only the best for her."

"You are from two different worlds. Soon you will be wed to a beautiful aristocratic widow. Hanna will remain in her world, if our people still accept her. Don't take that community away from her."

"I would never do anything to hurt her."

"Good. Then when we return to London, leave her alone. There is already talk in our community about you."

"There is? What kind of talk?"

"Talk that could destroy her reputation. If you truly care about my sister, you will leave her alone."

Chapter Twenty-Three

There you are," Hanna greeted Griff in the front hallway. "Were you out with Rafi?"

"Yes." Griff seemed distracted. "In the stable yard."

Her eyes twinkled. "How many times did he fall off the horse?"

"Actually, your brother has the makings of a skilled rider."

"Really? He always wanted to learn to ride, but Papa said we couldn't afford it."

"He seems to be making up for lost time."

"Are you ready to search for your father's journal?" she asked.

"Oh." He paused. "I don't want to trouble you."

Why was he avoiding looking her in the eye? "I told you yesterday that it's no trouble at all. I want to help."

Griff shifted his weight from one boot to the other. He was incredibly dashing in his country clothes. His strong thighs encased in those buff breeches tucked into deep brown boots. "Perhaps not today."

"What is wrong?"

"You do know that I would never purposefully do anything to hurt you?"

She narrowed her eyes. "Did Rafi say something to upset you?"

He dropped his gaze. "No, of course not. Being back at Ashby is not easy. I'm still adjusting."

"What can I do to help?"

He stepped back. "Nothing. That is very kind of you. But I must become accustomed to being here on my own. If you will excuse me."

Leaving Hanna confused and alone in the front hall, Griff strode past her and trotted up the massive staircase. Rafi entered the house, crossing the front hall, heading in the direction of the stairs.

"Where are you going?" Hanna asked.

"To wash up. I smell of sweaty horses."

She followed him up the stairs. "What did you say to Griff?" she asked, switching to Arabic to avoid being overheard.

"About what?"

"I don't know about what. That's why I'm asking you. He's behaving strangely."

They reached the second floor. "All toffs are peculiar."

"What did you talk about?" she pressed. Something wasn't right.

"Riding."

"Is that all?"

"For the most part."

"What does that mean?"

"Very well." He halted and pivoted to face her. "We talked about you."

"Me? Why?"

"I told him you would lose everything, that you would be shunned by your entire family and community if you lost your reputation."

"What did you do that for?"

"Because I am your brother. It is my duty to protect you, not only from your toff but also from yourself."

"I don't need protection."

"Any *hamar* can see that something is going on between you two. And I am not a donkey."

"Nothing is going on," she half lied. "I know he is going to marry Lady Winters."

"Exactly. And yet he's always sniffing around you like a *kelb,* a dog who brought you out here on false pretenses."

"I told you that was his sister's doing."

"Why would his sister invite you here? Do you think she views you as a potential sister in marriage? You're just a plaything to her. Someone to make her brother feel better for now."

She stiffened. "That's not why she brought me here."

He gave her a look. "You're not that *jahla.*"

"I'm not naive." But what if Griff's sister really did view Hanna as a *shermoota*? A whore to warm Griff's bed until he married his aristocratic lady? Her neck burned. Was that how Mrs. Rutland viewed her? Did she assume that Griff was bedding Hanna?

"You're supposed to be the smart one," Rafi said as

they reached the bedchamber assigned to him. "So try using your brain, sister. Now, I need to wash up." He went into his chamber and closed the door behind him.

Mortified, Hanna stared at the door. She hated it when Rafi was right. But his words struck a chord. Why else would Mrs. Rutland invite her here? Members of the merchant class didn't dine with grand families, much less stay as overnight guests.

She'd been delaying the inevitable. Griff belonged to Lady Winters and fashionable society. Especially now that the ton no longer suspected him of murder. Staying here, spending any more time with Griff made Hanna appear a fool at best and a light-skirt at worst.

It was time to truly let Griff go.

"HAVE YOU BEEN hiding out here in the study all day?" Dorcas asked Griff.

Griff glanced up from his father's desk, *his desk* now. It all took so much getting used to. He'd spent most of the day working with his steward, Mr. Brown. "There are estate matters that I must acquaint myself with."

"I thought you'd spend more time with your guests."

He tipped his head toward his steward. "That will be all, Brown."

"Very good, my lord." The man tucked a ledger under his arm and quietly exited the room.

Griff leaned back in his chair. "Now what are you going on about?"

"You've left your guests unattended."

"Mr. Zaydan spends all of his time out with the horses. He's off on a hack now."

"And Miss Zaydan?"

"You invited her here."

"Because I thought Miss Zaydan would provide some . . . comfort to you here at Ashby."

He crinkled his brow. "Comfort?"

"I am a married woman. I'm not innocent to matters between men and women."

Griff stiffened. "You brought her here because you thought she'd warm my bed?"

"I thought she could provide company and warmth, yes."

"You think Miss Zaydan is my *amour*?" He lowered his chin, tucking it back toward his neck. "I assure you that she is not. She is a virtuous woman."

"I am not suggesting she's a harlot." Dorcas's tone was conciliatory. "But it isn't as if she needs to be treated with the care of a lady. You don't risk compromising her."

"I have not bedded Miss Zaydan. It is an insult to her for you to suggest otherwise."

"My husband keeps a mistress," she said. "She's the daughter of a hatmaker in Southwark. He thinks I don't know about her. I am not proposing you take advantage of Miss Zaydan. You could come to a mutually agreeable arrangement. It's clear the bonesetter finds you as appealing as you find her. She is hardly an innocent."

But Griff knew Hanna was far naiver than she appeared. She really was an innocent in so many ways, although he suspected she'd bristle if he said as much to her face.

"As I said, Miss Zaydan is a respectable woman," he repeated firmly. "You've seen her dispensary. She's nobody's whore."

Dorcas held up her hands. "I apologize if I've overstepped. I thought I sensed something between the two of you. I wanted to ease the way for you to have what you want."

"I'm not fifteen anymore, Dorcas," he said tightly. "I will thank you to stay out of my private affairs. I can manage on my own."

"I take your point. I won't interfere again. I'm just so thrilled to have you back that I want to do everything in my power to ensure your happiness."

"I shall have to create my own contentment."

She paused, studying his face. "You always were fond of Selina."

"Very," he agreed.

"You will be happy with her." It was a question as much as a statement.

"I shall be content."

"I understand Selina and her mother are back at Hall House."

"Selina is here in the country?" Her parents' home was nearby. Less than thirty minutes away on foot. Griff had often walked there as a boy.

"Shall we invite them to supper?"

"They will decline. Selina insists that we not see each other or have any communication until we meet to discuss our future in a few weeks."

Dorcas frowned. "Why? That hardly makes sense, considering that the two of you are to wed."

"Selina wants us to take this time to seriously consider our futures. She hasn't yet consented to marrying me."

"She will. Selina is very fond of you."

"I noticed you didn't mention my taking Miss Zaydan to wife."

She actually laughed. "She's a merchant's daughter. And a Levantine. Hardly viscountess material. But I imagine you'll want to say goodbye before she departs this afternoon."

He tensed. "She's leaving?"

"Yes, as soon as her brother returns from his ride. She's awaiting his return."

He forced himself to stay seated, to project a lack of interest. "Where is she now?"

"In the solarium, reading."

"I see. I'm pleased she's found something to occupy her time until her brother returns." He reached for a ledger and opened it. "It's a relief. I have much to catch up on."

He felt Dorcas's curious gaze on him. "I shall leave you to your work."

He kept his eyes on the ledger until the door closed before shooting to his feet. *Hanna was leaving.* He had to see her before she departed. He'd been cool with her yesterday after his talk with Rafi. And now, Dorcas's assumptions about Hanna proved Rafi was correct. Griff needed to let Hanna go. He couldn't leave her reputation in shambles.

But he also couldn't let her leave without saying goodbye.

HE FOUND HER in the solarium. He'd come around from the outside, not wanting Dorcas to catch him exiting his study in search of Hanna.

Hanna wore her yellow dress with a lace fichu tucked modestly into her neckline. Her hair was back in its severe bun at the nape of her neck. Her thick, dark lashes fanned out across her cheeks as she read.

"Are you reading something of interest?" he said as he came in through the door that led from the garden to the solarium.

"Not particularly. But it helps to pass the time until Rafi returns."

"I hear you are leaving."

"Yes. Your nephew is fine. There is no reason for me to be here." Her reserve was firmly in place. "We'll go as soon as Rafi returns from his ride. He was supposed to be back by now."

"Were you going to leave without saying goodbye?"

She glanced away. "You seem very busy."

"I am never too busy for you," he said softly.

She brought her gaze back to meet his. "Did you know your sister brought me here because she thought I was your strumpet?"

"No. At least, not at first. But she and your brother have enlightened me. We do need to stay away from each other."

"I agree." She closed the book. "It is for the best."

He joined her on the iron bench but took care to

keep plenty of distance between them. "Why is it that things that are supposed to be good for us make us miserable?"

"I wish I knew. I often wonder what would it be to live in a time when we can truly do as we please."

"There'd be many more happy people in the world."

The rules of society demanded that he marry Selina. The same strictures prevented him from pursuing a future with the laboring-class daughter of immigrant merchants. Even if he were free to take Hanna to wife, her family was against any match between them. Besides, the ton would never accept her. One could not be both a viscountess and a bonesetter. He'd never ask Hanna to abandon her passion for bonesetting and waste her considerable skills. And for what? In order to attend routs and recitals and make endless small talk?

They sat quietly as a wave of sadness ebbed over them.

She broke the silence. "We might as well get on with it." The words were brisk. Hanna wasn't one to wallow. "Have you had any luck finding your father's journal?"

"It's not in my father's study. The next more likely place is Father's sitting room. I haven't worked up the courage to go in there."

She paused, seeming to consider something. "I'm here until Rafi returns. I can help you look until then."

"Are you certain?" His heart lifted at the prospect of having more time with her. "Your presence would definitely make the search more bearable."

"I am positive." She stood up. "Let's go. My brother could return at any moment. He's already overdue."

He came to his feet. "I guess there's no time to waste."

Her face brightened. "Lead the way."

Taking a deep breath, Griff led Hanna to his parents' bedchamber.

HANNA WAS AMAZED by the grandeur of the family quarters at Ashby Manor.

The sitting room that linked the viscount's and viscountess's bedchambers was enormous, swathed in satins and velvets, with priceless paintings adorning almost every inch of wall space. As she searched, Hanna feared upending a vase or porcelain figure that might be worth more money than she could ever hope to repay.

Still, she was happy to help Griff. They'd begun this journey to find the truth together. It would be fitting to be able to end it together. While Hanna searched a marble-topped walnut writing table in the sitting room, Griff went into his father's bedchamber. Which was really Griff's now. But he'd been staying elsewhere in the family wing.

"Anything?" Griff asked as he emerged from the viscount's bedchamber.

"Nothing in the sitting room. I've searched everywhere."

He slumped into a seat. "Maybe it's not here at Ashby. Or if he's hidden it in one of the dozens of rooms or salons here, we'll never find it."

"Dr. Pratt wanted to go through your father's papers at Haven House. Maybe he came out here and found the journal. Have you asked him if he has it?"

He shot her a skeptical look. "What is the likelihood he'll tell the truth if he does?"

He had a point. "We haven't checked your mother's rooms. Maybe he left it in there?"

"He did spend most nights in Mother's bed." He flushed.

As did she. It did not require much imagination to understand why Griff's parents shared a bed.

Griff came to his feet. "Let's check Mother's room."

Hanna followed him into the adjoining bedchamber. She made every effort to appear nonchalant. Which was impossible considering she'd entered a bedchamber with a man to whom she was very much attracted. The mammoth canopied bed, the room's centerpiece, did not help.

She tried to distract herself by taking in the room's decoration. Bright embroidered birds and flowers against a crisp white background adorned the silk bed hangings. Birds also graced the wall tapestries and were carved into the marble mantel.

Hanna ran a hand over the bed hangings. "I gather your mother was fond of birds."

He chuckled. "Very."

"How is it for you to be in this bedchamber again?"

He surveyed the room. "To be frank, not as strange as I thought it would be."

"Where do we start?"

He walked to the far side of the bed.

"Why there?"

He flushed again. "This was Father's side."

"Oh." Being in such a private, such an intimate, space prompted Hanna's pulse to pound hard through her veins. She suddenly felt desperate. Soon Rafi would return from his ride, and she and Griff would part forever. She'd never again know his kiss or touch or be held by him. Only a fool would pass up this opportunity to be with him in the most intimate way.

"It's so unfair."

Griff looked up from the drawer he was going through. "What is?"

"That I'll never be kissed by you again."

The cords of his throat moved. "Hanna," he warned. "We should not talk of such things. We agreed."

"Not because we want to."

"No, not because we want to," he agreed softly.

"What we do is our business."

"If only that were true."

"I want you." She licked her lips. "I want you to be the one."

He stilled. "What are you saying?"

"I want to know what it is to be bedded by a man. But not just any man. *You*."

"There is nothing I want more." He swallowed. "But I cannot do that to you. It wouldn't be right."

"I am not asking for forever. I'm just asking you for this one thing. This one time. No one need ever know."

He was shaking his head. "You aren't thinking

clearly. You are moved by the moment." She sensed the tension in his athletic form. "As am I."

"You're correct, I am." She moved to him, to where he stood on his father's side of the bed. "I am moved by the urgency of our situation. Once Rafi returns, we will have forever lost our chance."

"Coming in here was a mistake."

"Was it really?" She put her arms around his waist and set her cheek against his chest. His heart beat furiously. She ran her hands up his back, feeling the tension in his muscles. He kept his hands stiffly by his side.

He groaned. "We need to stop now." The words were low, husky and utterly lacking in conviction.

"Why?" She stood on the tips of her toes to drag her lips across his closed mouth. "Consider our circumstances. I don't intend to marry. At this very moment, you remain unattached."

"Stop making this sound so reasonable." He kissed her back. But just barely. As if he couldn't let her lips touch his without responding.

"There's nothing real stopping us." She nibbled the underside of his strong jaw. "Are you truly so cruel as to deny me the chance to know what it is to lie with a man?"

"I'm being a gentleman." His voice sounded strained, as if heavy weights were pressing against his vocal cords.

"If it's not you, it will eventually be someone else. Maybe Evan would oblige me."

He stiffened. "That is not even remotely amusing."

"The problem is that the only hands I want on my body are yours." She pressed a kiss in the V of his shirt, against the warmth of his throat. His body trembled beneath her lips. "Please."

"Hanna." The way he said her name was both a warning and a prayer.

She pulled back to stare into steely-blue eyes. But what she saw in his gaze was anything but cool. "Are you going to make me beg?"

Chapter Twenty-Four

$\mathcal{H}$e groaned, his jaw stiff, tense. "You are asking me to behave in a dishonorable manner."

"Isn't it dishonorable to refuse a lady?" She nibbled on his earlobe. "Do you refuse me because I am not a lady?"

"You know that's not it. Stop twisting my words the way you manipulate people's bones."

She bit her lip, frustrated and embarrassed. She was making a fool of herself. What an amateur seductress she turned out to be.

"I'm terrible at this." Her cheeks burning, she pulled away. "I couldn't seduce you if I tried."

"Wrong." He brought her back to him and cradled her face in his large hands. "You are the most beguiling woman I've ever met."

She stared into his dazzling eyes. "And yet, here I am throwing myself at you, and you are unmoved."

Heat flared in his gaze. "I am anything but unmoved. My body is . . . very moved."

She put her hands over his as he cupped her cheeks. "Prove it."

He shook his head, his eyes bright with desire. "You make it very difficult for a man to refuse you."

She groaned. "Then don't. My body is so hungry for you that I don't know what to do with myself."

"Shhh." He kissed her gently yet thoroughly, pushing into her mouth, his tongue searching and stroking, dancing with hers. It was long, slow and deep. He tasted her as she tasted him. Without boundaries or constraint. Putting their mark on each other.

This kiss was unlike any other before. Deep, soulful, potent. Honest. An unspoken declaration of his feelings for her. Something that was best not put into words.

Breaking the kiss, he set his forehead against hers. "Are you sure?" he whispered, his breath sweetly humid. "I don't want you to regret this later."

"I've never been more certain about anything." She paused. "Except setting a bone, of course. Or putting a joint back in."

He laughed softly and kissed the tip of her nose. "I never realized how seductive a competent woman could be."

"You're about to find out. Unless you lose your nerve."

He scoffed. "Only a fool would refuse your offer. And I'm no fool." He removed her fichu, baring her décolletage, and bent to press his lips against her collarbone.

She melted into him. "Hurry. Before we lose our chance."

He pulled back. Keeping his gaze on hers, he removed his shirt, pulling the white linen up over his head and tossing it away. "You said before that you hadn't had the opportunity, back when you treated me, to touch my body as you would have liked. Show me now."

She momentarily forgot to breathe at the sight of his bare chest, the ridges and contours, the dusting of hair across his chest, down to the flat plain of his belly, disappearing into the low waist of his buff breeches. "You still have too many clothes on for me to do that."

His eyes blazed. "What a minx you are." His hands went to the buttons of his breeches. He paused as if giving her time to change her mind. As if she would ever change her mind about the opportunity to see him in all of his glory.

She licked her lips. "Keep going." Then she added, "Please."

"Are you begging?" he asked hoarsely.

"Do you want me to get down on my knees?" She would. In a minute. If it meant feasting her eyes, and her hands, on all of the private parts of him that he kept hidden from the world.

"Perhaps." He swallowed. Hard. "But not right now."

She wasn't sure what he meant by that, but she didn't care. Her eyes were glued to the movements of his long, clever fingers as he unbuttoned his breeches, one maddeningly slow button at a time.

He pushed the breeches down over his narrow hips and stepped out of one leg, flinging them off his one ankle with a few quick shakes.

She stared at him. "Oh my."

The primordial display of masculinity was almost overwhelming. Almost. Griff stood still while Hanna looked and touched her fill. She slid her hands over the broadness of his chest, roaming to feel round biceps. Heat radiated off him. He tensed and shivered as her fingers fluttered over his skin.

She circled him, her fingers feathering over his shoulder blades, down to the small of his back and over firm, round buttocks. He possessed thick thighs and prominent calves. His male member was thick, long and hard.

Coming to stand before Griff, she closed her fingers around his organ and tried to imagine such a thing inside of her. How would it feel? She couldn't wait to find out.

He grunted when she touched him so intimately. She moved her hands to cup his balls, feeling the rough-hewn, yet soft-to-the-touch skin that encapsulated them.

"Touching you as I please would start with something such as this," she said, her pulse a thumpy, whooshing sound in her ears.

He startled her by moving suddenly, swiftly. "Let's get this gown off you." He took her into his arms and gave her another long, hungry kiss. "If recent history tells us anything, it's that we risk being interrupted before we get to the main event."

"We don't want that."

He paused, eyeing her dress. "How does this come off?"

She loosened the front ribbons which tied high on her waist under her breasts. "Once I untie these, the gown goes off over my head."

He assisted her in quickly dispensing with all of her clothing and then turned to pull the counterpane off his mother's bed. Kissing her deeply he helped her recline on the bed, never taking his lips from hers.

"You do not know how much I've dreamed of this," he said as he kissed his way down her throat, continuing until his mouth closed over the tip of her breast.

"I have some idea." She arched up into his mouth. "I have fallen asleep many nights dreaming of you."

"I have no intention of putting you to sleep today." He moved down lower, over her belly. "I'm going to put my mouth on you." He touched the exquisitely sensitive place between her legs.

"You are?" She propped herself up on her elbows to better see him. "Why?"

Instead of answering, he showed her. It was a curious sensation. His tongue felt wet as it tickled her intimate folds. But then warm pressure began to build in her belly.

"Oh. *Oh!*" She fell back against the mattress. All of her nerve endings down there were coming alive. *And dancing.* His breath was hot on her as he did things with his tongue and mouth that she couldn't quite pinpoint. But it felt *wonderful.* His tongue stroked up and down. Moved in circles. He added suction. Everything inside her clenched, and she forgot how to breathe.

He moaned against her. She felt the vibrations of

that sound deep inside of her. His hands were roaming. Over her stomach, cupping and squeezing her buttocks, tugging on her intimate hair.

His fingers moved inside of her, *curled* inside of her. It was dizzying. As was Griff's single-minded devotion to seeing to her pleasure. He seemed to truly be enjoying himself. Hanna squirmed. Her body tingled all over. Tension and anticipation built to an almost unbearable point.

He moved abruptly, coming up over her. His body pressing into hers. "You're ready."

"Oh *yes*." She felt his hands between her legs and then something else. Him. She felt stretched but not in pain exactly.

He watched her. "All right?"

She kissed him eagerly in response. He pushed farther into her. There was slight pain. Some discomfort. But the overwhelming sensation was that of feeling satisfyingly full.

He began to move, stroking in and out of her.

"What do I do?" she asked, eager to get this right.

"Just do what you feel." His voice was strained as he moved inside of her. "Turn off your brain. Let your body take over."

She tried to do as he said. To stop thinking and just focus on the feel of him inside of her. On the warmth of his body pressing her into the mattress. She got caught up in the rhythmic motion and began to move her hips in a way that allowed him to find a deeper seat within her. He groaned and moved faster. Soon they were both moaning. Lost in their own needs.

And each other's. Hanna couldn't form a thought in her head if she tried.

She felt his finger down there, playing with the bundle of nerves. "Oh! That *is* nice."

He smiled and kissed her deeply, urgently. Delicious tension began to ratchet up in her body. Tighter and tighter. Like a toy being wound up. Until the tensity was almost too much to bear. Her body quivered, on the precipice of something she didn't fully understand. Until something snapped. The tension released in a cascade of sensation, waves of pleasure, that just kept coming and coming.

Griff pulled away to the bottom of the bed, spilling his seed into the bedclothes. Through her own contented daze, Hanna watched in fascination as his seed pumped out of him in milky-white spurts.

He rejoined her on her side of the massive bed, pulling her into his arms. They were quiet for a time, breathing in short heavy bursts, hearts pounding in unison.

"Well?" he asked after a little while. "Was it what you expected?"

"Are you asking for a performance assessment?" She snuggled against him, basking in the afterglow of being joined so intimately with him.

"I half expect you to jump up and write notes in that ledger of yours."

She pressed her lips against his chest. "That would be difficult."

"Why?"

"Because it would be impossible to find the words to describe how truly spectacular copulation is."

"It is." He pressed a kiss on the top of her head. "Particularly with you."

"Do you mean that it's not this way with every partner?"

"It's never been this good for me. Between lovers, the levels of attraction are different. The depths of connection vary. Sometimes two bodies fit together particularly well. As we did."

"So you are saying that I was competent?"

He ran a hand down over her curvaceous bottom. "More than competent."

Her eyes caught on the place where he'd spent himself. "What will the servants say when they find the bedclothes are a mess and find evidence of"—she gestured to the sheet—"of what went on in here?"

"I'll summon my valet. He'll clear everything away and come up with some excuse."

"Is he trustworthy?"

He nodded. "I've known Felix practically all my life. He's had a lot of practice covering up for me. I managed to get up to some mischief before my parents died."

"I wonder how many times we can do that again before my brother returns."

He chuckled, kissing her gently. "We cannot remain absent. For all we know, he is already back and turning the house upside down searching for you." He drew her closer. "Just a few more minutes and then we have to go back out there."

"Ugh," she buried her head into the crook of his arm. "I detest the real world."

Lying in bed next to Griff after being as intimate

as two people can be, Hanna felt profoundly different. Fundamentally changed in a way she couldn't quite describe. Being alive felt more precious. Sweeter. But also more bitter. Her world had changed, but the world beyond these doors had not. Everything within her was different. Yet everything outside—the rules, the expectations—remained unchanged. It didn't feel possible.

But it was.

"Come now. We have to get moving." Griff reluctantly put Hanna away from him and rolled over to the far side of the bed, putting enough distance between them so that he couldn't touch her. Otherwise, he'd be tempted to go back to bed and make love with her again. Everything in him wanted to repeat the extraordinary experience.

"I suppose you have the right of it." But she made no sign of getting up. Instead she rolled onto her stomach and slid her hands under the pillow, snuggling deeper into the mattress.

"You are not supposed to be making yourself comfortable," he admonished, his eyes nonetheless glued to her smooth, bare back.

She groaned. "Just a few more minutes."

A knock sounded at the door. Over his shoulder, Griff shot a look of alarm at Hanna. She scrambled into a seated position. Her eyes round, she snatched up the bedclothes to cover herself and scooted toward the opposite edge of the bed.

For a second, he just stared at her. She was radiant with her hair loose, her shoulders and arms bare. Anyone who caught sight of them would easily surmise what they'd been up to. The knock came again. Slightly more insistent this time.

"Who is it?" Griff barked.

"Felix, my lord."

Relief filtered through him. At least it wasn't the brother. *My valet*, he mouthed to Hanna. "Go away."

"Mr. Zaydan has been spotted returning from his ride, my lord. He should be here in about ten minutes."

Hanna's full eyebrows shot up. She bolted off the bed, still clutching the bedclothes to preserve her modesty until they got tangled and she just dropped them and hurriedly reached for her clothes. Griff could not help admiring the pretty curve of her arse, the shapely legs.

"What is your point?" he snapped at Felix while he watched Hanna.

"I thought you might want to say farewell, my lord. As Mr. Zaydan and his sister are meant to depart."

"Yes, excellent point." He and Felix played out the charade even though they both knew precisely what the point was. To warn them. To ward off catastrophe. How had his valet known where to find him? Whatever Griff paid him, it wasn't enough. "Thank you, Felix. That is all."

"Very good, my lord."

Hanna had her dress on. "At least we have a few minutes to put ourselves to rights." She tied the ribbon at her waist. "Thank goodness your valet didn't come in through one of those secret entrances. Your servants are always coming out of the walls."

He tugged on his breeches, skip-hopping as he did

so. "Grand houses do have many secret doors. The idea being that servants should vanish through them when members of the family appear."

"Why?"

He buttoned the fall front of his trousers. "To stay out of the way, I suppose."

"For a woman used to normal-size homes, it is a bit disconcerting to have people suddenly appearing out of nowhere." She paused, her gaze skimming the walls. "Are there any in here?"

"Just a priest's hole. But it leads to nowhere."

"Truly? Where is it?"

He crossed over to one of the two pilasters framing the door. "Here." He popped it open revealing a space just large enough to conceal a grown man. "I often hid in here as a boy."

She came over and peered inside. "There's something in there." She reached for the object. "It's some sort of ledger."

Griff stared at the worn brown leather book in her hands. "That's it."

"What?"

"My father's journal."

She peered down at it. "Are you certain?"

"Absolutely." His palms sweating, he took the book and returned to sit on the edge of the bed. He recognized his father's familiar writing as he turned the pages. He went directly to the last entries and read the passages. Then reread them. He felt the blood drain from his face.

"Griff." Hanna sat beside him and laid a hand on his bare shoulder. "What is it?"

"It's Norman." He stared, disbelieving, at his father's words.

"Dr. Pratt? What about him?"

"My father wanted to replace him as head physician at Margate."

"He did?" She edged closer to read over his shoulder. "Why?"

Griff read further. "Father doesn't say specifically. It somehow involves me, though. He writes that he is alarmed by what he's learned about Thomas's something or the other, and that Norman must be brought to account."

"Thomas's what?"

"I don't know. He scratched out the word after my name."

They studied the entry together.

> *I am alarmed by what I've learned about Thomas's* ~~————————~~. *Norman must be brought to account.*

"Can you think of anything of yours that Dr. Pratt accessed?"

"Nothing comes to mind." A chill skittered up his spine. "All along, Norman has acted as if Father had a secret that needed protecting from the world. But what if he was desperate to go through my father's papers because he knew they might contain damaging information that could ruin him and not Father?"

"You believe he was trying to find the journal."

"It's possible. Even if Norman managed to search these rooms in the days after the funeral, he wouldn't have known about the priest's hole."

Griff felt uprooted by yet another damning revelation about the man who'd been a surrogate father. "These disclosures about Norman upend everything that I thought was true about my life. What is real? What is a lie? If Norman is some sort of monster, what does that make me? He did raise me."

Hanna wrapped her arm around his waist. "You are a good man. A decent man." Her breath was warm on his shoulder. "Who you are is a reflection of your parents, not of Dr. Pratt. Your parents raised you for the first fifteen years of your life. Will you ask Dr. Pratt about this?"

"He will just lie again." He set the journal down. "But I will ask, just to see what he says."

"Do you think it has anything to do with why your father made the unexpected trip to Ashby Manor?"

"I've no idea." He massaged his temples. His thoughts were jumbled after uncovering yet another lie from Norman. "It's possible the two are completely unrelated."

Hanna climbed into his lap and wrapped her arms around him, hugging Griff hard. He buried his face in her hair, inhaling her sweet scent. How could he lose Hanna when he needed her most? "While I did not kill my Mother and Father," he confessed, "I do bear some responsibility for their deaths."

She made a sound of protest, but he stopped her.

"Please. I need to speak on this. Norman never allowed me to talk about my parents."

She pressed a kiss against his cheek. "I'll listen for as long as you need."

"When I slipped out to meet Selina, I left a side door unlocked so that I could get back in when I returned. I've always believed the killers got in through that unsecured door."

"Have you been carrying around this guilt all of this time?"

His throat felt jagged. "Yes."

"You don't know for certain that the killers came in through that door." She pressed her cheek against his. "Even if they did, you were a young boy getting up to mischief, which was perfectly normal."

"That's what Norman said when I confessed to him about a year after we buried my parents." But it didn't make his guilt any easier to bear. "He said it wasn't my fault even if the killers did come in through that unlocked door."

"I never thought I'd agree with Dr. Pratt, but he has the right of it."

They were interrupted by another knock on the door. "Mr. Zaydan has returned, my lord." Felix's muffled voice again. "He is in the house and asking after his sister."

"Thank you, Felix," Griff said. To his regret, Hanna shifted off his lap and came to her feet.

"I must go."

"I will send word if my runner discovers anything of interest regarding who stole my mother's jewels."

"I would also care to know how things go with Dr. Pratt. If you want to share that with me."

He wanted to share everything with her. Griff rose, his chest sore at the thought of losing her. He might very well see and speak to her again—the matter of the jewels remained unsettled—but they would not, could not, risk sharing any more intimacies.

He took Hanna into his arms and kissed her deep and slow. Until they were both out of breath again. "Good-bye, Lady Bonesetter."

"Good-bye, Mr. Thomas." She gave a sad smile, but then mischief glinted in her eye. "At least we managed to get to the good part this time."

He pressed one last kiss against her lips. "We did, indeed."

"Maybe now you will have one more fond memory of Ashby to temper the difficult ones."

He hated that she'd already relegated herself to his past. "You . . . and this"—he gestured about the room—"shall be the very best memory of all."

"Where were you all day?" Hanna asked her brother. Anything to keep her mind, and the conversation, far from Griff as they rumbled back to Town in Mrs. Rutland's carriage.

Rafi stared out the window. "I was riding."

"For six hours? You left at nine o'clock this morning and did not return until after three in the afternoon. Almost too late for us to return to Town."

"I guess I got caught up."

"You truly are the worst chaperone ever." Not that

she had any complaints. But Rafi was behaving in an odd manner. "Where did you go?"

Rafi squinted at her. "What do you mean where did I go? I just told you that I went riding." He paused. "And I stopped to take a break, and I guess I fell asleep."

"You napped for *six* hours?"

"I didn't sleep well last night."

Hanna made a skeptical sound in her throat. Her brother was hiding something. But Hanna didn't care what it was. Thanks to Rafi's absence, she'd enjoyed the most glorious afternoon of her life.

Leaning back, she closed her eyes and replayed her time with Griff. The vision of his naked body imprinted in her mind, and she enjoyed revisiting it. And coupling with him. And the clever things he'd done with his tongue—

"Stop!" Rafi rapped on the carriage roof, jolting Hanna out of her musings. "Halt!"

"Why are we stopping?" She peered out the window. A woman on horseback in a smart riding suit with military details trotted nearby. Hanna squinted for a better look as the carriage came to a stop. "Is that Lady Winters? What's she doing here?"

"She lives in the neighborhood." Rafi opened the door.

"Where are you going?"

"It would be rude not to say hello. We are acquainted with the lady."

She stared at him. "Courtesy does not require that you stop a speeding carriage just to say hello to a woman you met once. She probably won't even remember you."

But he was already out of the coach and striding in the direction of Lady Winters, who brought her mount to a stop. Rafi took hold of the horse's bridle, stroking its forehead and cheeks, as he beamed up at Lady Winters.

Hanna could not hear their conversation, but Griff's Selina smiled and chatted with Rafi. She was certainly being polite, considering that she was a countess and Rafi was a simple merchant. Not that Rafi was simple. He was smart and an excellent businessman. He practically ran the family export business. Their older uncles often deferred to Rafi when it came to making major decisions.

Rafi finally stepped away from the horse and waved Lady Winters on. He stood watching her ride away for a moment, then turned back and rejoined Hanna in the carriage.

"What was *that*?"

"What?" He responded as if waylaying a countess in the middle of the countryside was the most natural thing in the world. "I just wanted to say hello."

She laughed, realizing that her brother was completely besotted. "She's way above your touch, brother. It's time you came back to earth."

Rafi just smiled, crossed his arms over his chest and closed his eyes. Within minutes, he was snoring. Which was strange for a man who claimed to have napped all afternoon.

Chapter Twenty-Five

I must admit," Norman said, "I was surprised to receive your note asking me to call."

"Do not be," Griff said. "This is not a social visit."

They met in the study at Haven House the afternoon after Griff's return to Town. He'd stayed on at Ashby for a few days after Hanna's departure. His elder sisters, Winifred and Maria, joined him and Dorcas there. They spent the time reminiscing and becoming reacquainted.

Griff was happy to see them but also eager to return to Town. He told himself it wasn't because he needed to be in the same general vicinity as Hanna, even if he could not be with her.

"How was your visit to Ashby Manor?" Norman took a seat, even though he hadn't been invited to do so. Griff realized Norman had taken many liberties with him over the years.

"It was enlightening."

"Is that so?" Norman forced lightness into the words, even as his fingers clutched the arms of the chair. "In what way?"

"I found Father's journal."

Norman watched him carefully. "Did you?"

"Imagine my surprise to learn that Father wanted to have you removed as head physician at Margate."

"What else did you learn?"

"That he was angry with you about something involving me."

He wrote the sentence down, as it appeared in Father's journal.

Norman studied the sentence. "Thomas's what?"

"I was hoping you could tell me. Not that you can be counted upon to reveal the truth. Why did Father want you removed?"

"I did not know that he did."

"Is that so? You didn't seem surprised when I mentioned it to you a few minutes ago."

"What does it matter now? After all these years?"

"It matters to me. I'm learning all sorts of things that make me question you and your intentions. Father obviously also discovered something unsavory."

"As I have said, I am a pragmatist." He removed his spectacles and pulled a kerchief from his pocket. "Your father was a romantic, as only a man born to wealth and privilege can be. He did not appreciate the hardships, the realities, of operating a charity hospital."

"What does that have to do with him wanting to oust you, his cousin and childhood companion, his dearest adult friend?"

"The hospital's resources are limited." He buffed the glass lenses. "Jeffrey believed no expense should be spared to save every life. I believed it was better to let some patients go, for the greater good."

"You allowed people to die?"

"Only when there was little or no hope of recovery." He resettled his spectacles on the bridge of his nose. "We couldn't afford to waste medicine and other supplies on those who were unlikely to survive."

"I thought your mission in life was to save lives."

"To save the most lives possible overall. Not each individual life. Some souls had to be lost for the greater good."

Griff steepled his fingers. "Why do I get the sense that you are telling me only part of the truth?"

"I've no idea." Norman twisted in his seat, glancing toward the door. "I have not eaten anything since this morning. Is Wright coming in with the tea tray soon?"

There was a knock on the door. The butler entered.

"Ah," Norman said. "There you are at last. I am famished."

Wright directed his attention at Griff. "The visitor you were expecting has arrived, my lord."

"Very good. Dr. Pratt was just leaving."

Norman's salt-and-pepper brows drew together. "But we haven't had tea yet."

Griff stood up. "I have a very busy day. If you will excuse me, Dr. Pratt, my butler will see you out."

"Now, Griff, surely—"

"Good day, Dr. Pratt."

Wright showed Norman out and returned with the Bow Street runner Griff had engaged.

"Well?" Griff asked the small, compact man with canny eyes and a shiny pate.

"As you know, Mr. Zaydan, the late bonesetter, received your mother's jewelry from one Gerard Loder, who is a fence. Loder, the fence, got the jewels from a man, one Leonard Palk, who was eager to rid himself of the ring and necklace because he believed they were cursed."

"Why did Palk think the jewelry was cursed?"

"That, I do not know. What I do know is where to find Leonard Palk."

Griff surged to his feet. "Where?"

"Margate."

"The hospital?" Norman's hospital.

"Indeed."

"What does he do there? Is he a physician?"

"No, he is a ward clerk. To my understanding, he has worked there for many years."

"How old is he?"

"Thirty-three." Griff did a quick calculation. Palk would have been nineteen at the time of the murders. Young perhaps, but plenty old enough to take two lives.

"Have you seen Leonard Palk yourself? Are you certain he is still employed at Margate?"

"Yes, my lord. I saw him with my own eyes. He works at the hospital."

Once the runner departed, Griff took a seat at his desk to write a quick note. He then rang for Wright.

"My lord?" the butler asked upon entering.

"Please have this note delivered to Miss Zaydan's dispensary without delay."

"Very good, my lord."

"I am going out."

"YOU FAILED TO mention that Mrs. Rutland is Lord Griffin's sister," Evan said to Hanna in the dispensary's back office.

"Yes, I did." She kept her focus on recording medical notes from her last appointment.

"I don't suppose you forgot to mention it."

"It's really none of your concern."

Evan paused. "I'd like to make it my concern."

This time Hanna did look up. "I beg your pardon?"

"We should marry."

"Excuse me?"

"You and I should get married."

This time there was no misunderstanding his meaning. "But we are friends."

"That is for certain. I propose that, in addition to being good friends and business partners, that we also become man and wife."

She blinked, at first too stunned to find any words. "If this is some sort of a noble sacrifice on your part—"

"I doubt there's a man alive who'd view taking you to wife as a sacrifice."

Hanna studied Evan's face and realized he was serious. Eager even. "I am flattered, but if I marry at all, my family expects my husband to be an Arab from within the community."

Skepticism stamped Evan's face. "Your family knows me. They've always been very welcoming. Your grandmother can never give me enough food and drink when I visit."

"Arabs are hospitable. But that generosity stops short of welcoming you to the family. We've discussed this before."

"I believe we could convince them."

Hanna didn't want to. "This is all so unexpected."

"You cannot be surprised. Surely my display of jealousy at the hospital fundraiser told you all you need to know about the intensity of my feelings."

Hanna shifted in her seat. "I thought you were just being protective."

"That, too. But the truth is that I care for you a great deal. We could work together and have a family together."

"Children?" Perspiration beaded on her upper lip.

"I not only accept your bonesetting, I admire your skills. It would be criminal if you were no longer able to practice."

"Before long, I probably won't be able to be a bonesetter in London."

"You could if you worked here at the dispensary as my wife and assistant. You could continue your real work under that guise, if it comes to that. But I doubt that it will. Your cousin, the marquess, will see to it."

She inspected Evan, assessing him as a stranger might. She saw a lanky man with handsome features. Most women would find him appealing. The idea of being intimate with Evan wasn't exactly distasteful, but it did leave her feeling cold. She'd relived the memory of that afternoon with Griff over and over again in her mind every day since leaving Ashby Manor. She couldn't envision being with another man.

"Nothing would change here at the dispensary," Evan continued when she remained silent. "Except that you would have the protection of my name and would not need to have a chaperone here at all times."

"Evan," she said gently. "I am flattered, but I cannot marry you."

"Excuse me." Annie appeared on the office threshold. Hanna had never been so grateful to be interrupted. "There is a note for you, miss. The man who delivered it says it's urgent."

"What man?" Evan asked sharply. "Is he still here?"

"No, Dr. Bridges. He left."

"Thank you, Annie." Hanna took the letter and excused Annie to return to the dispensary floor. Keenly aware of Evan's eyes on her, she unfolded the message written on quality paper. Her skin tingled as she read.

I have just learned that the man who stole a certain set of jewels can be found at Margate Hospital where he works as a ward clerk. His name is Leonard Palk. I am on my way to speak with him. If you happen, by some chance, to be going to Margate this afternoon at three o'clock, you might have the opportunity to speak with him as well.

Hanna regarded the clock. It was twenty minutes to three. Folding the letter, she came to her feet. "I must go."

"What? Now?" Evan watched her with an incredulous expression. "Where are you going? We haven't finished speaking about this."

"We'll talk later," she called back over her shoulder. Although her answer would not change. "I promise."

When Hanna arrived at the hospital, she found a familiar face waiting out front for her.

"Good afternoon, Miss Zaydan."

"Hello. It's Felix, isn't it?" she asked Griff's valet.

"Yes, miss. If you will follow me." He led her through some wards and back corridors until they arrived at a set of offices. She found Griff waiting inside one of them.

"Thank you, Felix," Griff said to the valet, who bowed and quietly melted out of sight, closing the door behind him.

"Is that the footman who used to cover for you as a boy?"

"Yes."

Hanna basked in the warmth of his gaze. She'd missed him.

"As you can see, he is still covering for me. How are you?"

I miss you. "I am well. We've been busy at the dispensary." She scanned the office. There was a desk, two hardback chairs and little in the way of decoration. "Is this your office? Do governors have offices?"

"Hardly. I'm just borrowing it. Mr. Palk will join

us shortly." He paused. "I hesitated to send word to you."

"I'm pleased that you did. This is the last of our unfinished business. We are resolving the question surrounding your mother's jewels."

"It isn't exactly wise to be alone together."

"It's not like we are going to climb up on the desk and—" Her words trailed off. Her face burned when she recalled what they'd once gotten up to on her desk at the dispensary. Griff looked away. He remembered, too.

There was a knock on the door. The man who joined them was in his thirties with curling sandy hair and a plump boyish face. "My lord, I understand you wanted to see me?"

"Yes, come in, Palk. Have a seat."

Palk licked his lips. "Does the board of governors have an issue with my work?"

"No, it's nothing like that. I am not here regarding board matters."

"I see. Then, how may I be of service, my lord?"

Griff pulled his mother's necklace and ring from his pocket and set them on the desk. "You can tell me where you got these."

Palk's face lost its color. "I've never seen them before."

Griff's voice was like ice. "Why don't you save us all a great deal of time and trouble by speaking the truth rather than making false denials?"

Palk looked from Griff to Hanna and back again. "I don't know what you mean, my lord."

"You sold these pieces, my *mother's* jewelry, to a fence named Gerard Loder, who in turn gave them to a bonesetter in Red Lion Square. I know these pieces were in your possession. I will ask my question once again, and this time, I expect the truth."

Palk shifted in his chair. "I didn't know anything about them until about four years ago. They were in my father's possession." The words poured out of him. "After he suffered an apoplexy, as he lay dying, he told me about the necklace and ring. He made me promise to rid myself of them as soon as possible."

Hanna leaned forward. "Did your father tell you how he came to be in possession of the jewels?"

Palk stared at her. He had no idea who she was. Griff had not introduced her.

"Answer her," Griff barked.

"No. But he did say they had brought him nothing but misery since the day they came into his possession. He said they were cursed and that I should dispose of them as soon as possible. I did as my father asked. I sold them to a fence. I didn't know what else to do."

Griff and Hanna exchanged glances. If the elder Palk was deceased, this felt like another dead end.

"What did you father do?" Hanna asked.

"I don't know what he did to get the jewels," Palk said.

"No, I meant what sort of work did your father do?"

"Oh." Palk looked relieved. "He was employed here. His main duty was to clean the floors and tend to the hearths in the wards. You can ask anyone and they'll tell you that nobody cleaned a floor like Fred Palk. He secured this employment for me."

"And how long have you worked at the hospital?" Griff asked.

"I started here when I was nineteen," he replied, adding helpfully, "fourteen years ago."

"Do you recall the month you started here?" Griff asked, his voice strained.

"Yes, indeed. It was summertime. Late June."

GRIFF FELT NAUSEOUS. "It cannot be a coincidence," he said after Leonard Palk had returned to his duties.

"I agree," Hanna said. "Mr. Palk was hired about a fortnight after your parents were killed."

"What do you think it means?" He wrapped a hand down over his mouth and chin.

"That maybe there is some connection between your parents' deaths and this hospital. The elder Mr. Palk knew about it, and someone paid to keep him quiet."

"It cannot be Norman, can it?" The possibility that he'd resided under the same roof as his parents' killer was more than he could stomach.

"We should not assume Dr. Pratt killed your parents." She spoke firmly, grounding Griff while everything he thought he knew about his life slipped away. "As much as I would like to blame him."

"It would make sense, though, wouldn't it? They felt safe with Norman. He could have taken them both by surprise."

She considered his words. "I dislike the man intensely, but is he capable of using a knife . . . in that way?"

"Norman *is* a physician." He surged to his feet and paced away, restless energy coursing through him. "He would certainly know which cuts are the deepest and most effective."

She shivered. "Do you know where Dr. Pratt was the night your parents died?"

"He says he was somewhere here in London. That people saw him. I'll have the runner investigate."

"What is your theory?" She watched him pace back and forth. "You seem to have one."

"Either Palk's father is the killer, or he knew who killed my parents. That person, the murderer, is somehow associated with someone in a position of power in this hospital. The attacker paid the elder Palk to keep quiet by giving him my mother's jewelry. He also agreed to hire Fred Palk's son to be more than just a cleaning person."

"That theory has merit. A clerk is a step up from tending fires and sweeping floors."

Griff collapsed back into his chair. "Or I've got it all wrong. And it's all a terrible coincidence. Or I am not properly connecting the dots."

"Maybe the attacker was someone on the board of governors of this hospital who had a disagreement with your father."

"What disagreement could be great enough to drive someone to murder?"

She shrugged. "Will you tell Dr. Pratt what you've learned?"

"For what purpose? He'll only lie again."

"Still, I would be interested in his reaction."

"I'll think on it." He gave her a tired smile. "At least your father is absolved. There's no apparent connection between him and Palk or Palk's late father."

"That is a relief. But I never doubted his innocence."

They sat in silence, wondering what this latest development meant, reluctant to depart the small, windowless office because doing so would mean leaving each other's company.

Griff studied her. "The commission hearing is coming up. How are you faring?"

"I am as ready as I can be. My patients are prepared to speak on my behalf."

"I shall be the first to stand up for you."

"What about you? How have you been?"

"Racked with indecision and guilt."

"About?"

"Selina."

Her stomach clenched. "You and Lady Winters have spoken?"

"Not yet. But it won't be long now before we meet and I hear her decision."

"You are fond of her, are you not?"

"I am far fonder of you."

"You protected your Selina for fourteen years. You would have gone to your grave allowing people to assume you are a killer. All in the name of protecting her honor."

"Your point?"

"Somewhere deep down inside of you, you must

have some intense feelings for Lady Winters. You gave up so much to protect her."

"What is happening here? Why are you trying to convince me of my love for another woman?"

"She is not just any woman. She is your oldest friend. You share many experiences. You will likely marry her. And it might be easier if you could reconnect with those feelings of love you must have had for her. At least a little."

"I shall try."

"Evan asked me to marry him today."

He shot her a sour look. "Why don't you just plunge a sharp blade directly into my heart?"

"I did not accept his offer."

"But you are considering it."

"No. My family would never agree."

"And you don't love him." Bridges, or some other Arab man, might one day get the rest of Hanna: the genuine smile that made a man feel like he'd won the lottery; her relentless efficiency and competence; the stern countenance that never failed to stir Griff's blood; her warmth in his bed. A future husband might get all of that. But Griff selfishly wanted to keep Hanna's heart for himself.

She released a long breath. "Maybe I should ask my family to try and find me an Arab husband willing to accept my bonesetting."

"You haven't found such a man yet. What makes you think you will now?"

"If I were pledged to another, it might be easier for both of us to move on."

"Nothing about this is easy."

"No, but we always knew this is where matters would end up."

He studied her. "Are you always so certain about everything?"

There was a tap on the door. Palk reappeared. "I do beg your pardon. I forgot some papers." He crossed over to the desk to retrieve them.

Griff watched him. "When did your father die?"

"My father? Fortunately, he is still with us."

Griff's eyes narrowed. "I thought you said your father died."

"We almost lost him a few times, but Papa is a stubborn man. He is confined to his bed but has a strong will to live."

"THIS IS THE place." Griff helped Hanna alight from the carriage. They'd come directly from the hospital to the squalid Palk home in Wapping. The streets were crowded, and the air thick with the stench from open sewers.

Hanna stared apprehensively at the dingy home before them. "Shouldn't we have alerted them that we were coming?"

"I didn't want the younger Palk to warn his father off."

An older woman answered the door. They entered a gloomy room with few furnishings. What little the Palks did have was bundled up and stacked against one wall. The woman, Fred Palk's sister, became co-operative once Griff paid her for her trouble. "Don't stay too long," she warned. "'E sleeps most of the time."

The sickroom, humid and pungent, smelled of illness and unwashed bodies. The space was mostly bare except for wrapped bundles of clothing and other household items crowded into a corner. In the dim light, they could make out a frail figure swathed in blankets on a narrow bed. Griff stepped forward, his heart beating hard. Was he about to face his parents' killer? "Mr. Palk?"

Bleary gray eyes in a lined faced peered out from the bundle of blankets. "'Oo wants ter know?"

"I do. I am Griffin."

"The viscount?"

The lack of air, the stench, made Griff queasy. "Yes."

"It's a little late ter send me ter Newgate."

"Is that where you belong?"

"If I killt yer parents, I would not confess ter it."

Griff felt light-headed. "Why do you assume that is why I am here?"

"Because I've been waiting fer ya."

"Why is that?"

"If I'd done somefing like that, it might have weighed on me. I've had nuffing but bad luck since."

Had all these years of wondering, of not knowing, led to this moment? The cloaked confession confirmed Griff's worst suspicions. He forced himself to ask the question, even though he dreaded hearing the answer. "Did someone order you to kill my parents?"

"If I were to do somefing like that, it would be

for the jewels, the treasures. I was never a killer fer hire."

"It was just a burglary then?" He swallowed down the lump in his throat. "How did you even know about Ashby?"

"We were visiting my wife's cousin 'oo lived in the village. There was a wedding party. 'E mentioned the servants from the grand 'ouse were off to enjoy the celebration. The 'ouse was empty, 'e said. The family was supposed ter be in Town. It was going ter be an easy job. But the family was there. Fings got outta control."

Bile rose in Griff's throat. His parents were slaughtered, the family destroyed, because of a chance mention to a village visitor. "Are you saying no one engaged you to murder my parents? You acted alone?"

The old man shook his head. "I saw an opportunity, and I took it. It wernt somefing I spent a long time planning."

Hanna stepped forward. "Why are you telling us this now?"

The older man momentarily closed his eyes. "It weighs on ya. Taking a life."

"And no one asked you to harm my parents?" Griff asked again.

"No."

Relief cascaded through him, making Griff weak in the knees. Norman hadn't killed his parents. His former guardian might be arrogant, duplicitous and ruthless, but at least he wasn't a killer.

Palk coughed feebly. "I regretted it every day since.

I might be a thief, but I never saw myself as a killer. If it makes yer feel any better, I'm paying the price. I can't leave this bed. My sister 'as 'ad to take care of me since Mrs. Palk died."

"No," Griff said sharply. "It does not make me feel better. How did your son get the clerk's position at the hospital?"

Confusion lit Palk's craggy face. "'Ee's clever, I guess. I would not blame yer if yer wanted to kill me right here."

"And put you out of your misery? I think not." Griff couldn't breathe. He needed to get out of this place. He strode out of the chamber and through the front room with Hanna hurrying after him.

As he pulled the front door open to the blissful light of day, he heard Hanna speak to Palk's sister. "Are you moving?"

"Yes," the older woman replied. "Leonard insists that we move to better lodgings. They pay 'im well at the 'ospital."

They exited and climbed directly into the carriage. Griff plopped down hard on the seat and exhaled a long, shuddering breath. He dragged a hand down his face. "We have our answer. Palk killed my parents."

"Do you believe he acted alone?"

"I have no reason to doubt him."

She paused. "Maybe knowing the truth will eventually give you some peace."

He stared, unseeing, out the window. "I am relieved that Palk's story absolves Norman. He is guilty of many things, but at least murder isn't one of them."

"I am glad you can find comfort in that."

"Otherwise, I honestly don't know how I feel. Numb. Sick to my stomach."

She took his hand. "You've had quite the shock."

"It isn't every day that a man confronts his parents' murderer. And finds that he is a pathetic old man rather than the fearsome monster he'd always envisioned." He squeezed her gloved hand. "It helps that you're here."

She lifted their joined hands and pressed her lips to the back of his hand. "There's no place I would rather be."

Chapter Twenty-Six

Citi and Rafi were waiting for Hanna in the front salon when she returned home.

"*Salam*." She drew off her bonnet as she greeted them. She came to an abrupt halt, sensing a tension in the air. *Citi* was frowning more than usual. Rafi wore a grim expression.

"*Salam*?" *Citi* said. "How can we possibly have any peace around here with you bringing shame on the family?"

They couldn't know she'd been with Griff. "Whatever is the matter?"

"What is the matter?" *Citi*'s voice rose. "Why must you consort with *ajnabi* men?"

Hanna tensed. "There is nothing between us."

"Then, you ought to consider telling that to Dr. Bridges," Rafi suggested.

Her mouth fell open. "Dr. Bridges?"

Rafi cocked his head. "Who did you think *Citi* was speaking of?"

"Evan was here? What did he say?"

"He asked for permission to marry you," Rafi said.

Relief whooshed through Hanna, relaxing her muscles. But then irritation slid in. "He came here today to ask for my hand in marriage?"

Rafi nodded. "He came to seek my permission since Baba is no longer with us."

"May God have mercy on your father's soul," *Citi* intoned, speaking in Arabic. "We just threw out the viscount, and now you've taken up with another *ajnabi*?"

"I haven't taken up with anybody."

"First Blue Eyes and now the doctor." *Citi* tsked as she sucked on her hookah, engulfing herself in a smoky haze. "We should have made you close the dispensary as soon as it opened."

"Evan had no right to come here. I never agreed to marry him. And I have no intention of accepting his offer."

"I gathered as much," Rafi said. "I'd be very surprised if you did accept a proposal." Then he added, "From Dr. Bridges."

"Evan is not worth losing my family or my community over." And then, because Griff was not in contention to be her husband and never would be, she said, "No man is."

"ARE WE EVER going to finish our conversation?" Evan asked tightly. "It is not every day that a man asks a woman to be his wife."

They'd just arrived at the dispensary and were setting up for the day. Hanna bit back a sharp retort. Between Evan going to her family behind her back and the upcoming commission hearing, she'd gotten little sleep and woke with a frayed temper.

"Will you at least do me the courtesy of responding?" he asked, an edge in his voice.

"It is interesting that you would ask for courtesy, even though you did not extend the same to me."

"What do you mean?"

"I told you that my family would not accept our marrying, and yet you went to my brother, without my consent, to ask for my hand."

"Only to help ease the way. You said yourself that your family is all that is stopping us."

"I never said that. But perhaps that is what you wanted to hear." She stopped what she was doing and faced him. "I do not want to hurt you, Evan. But the truth is that I do not wish to marry you."

A vein pulsed in his forehead. "Is this about your viscount?"

White-hot anger flashed through her. "You have no right to question me about Griff or anything else that does not relate to this dispensary. I do not answer to you." She already answered to her family far more than she cared to. "We work together. That is it. If you cannot accept that, we should consider rethinking this arrangement."

His lips flattened. "I see."

She'd hurt him. But Evan had no right to question her choices. It was well past time that he stopped acting as if he did.

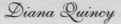

"If you will excuse me," he said stiffly, crossing to the exit. He closed the door behind him harder than necessary.

A few minutes after Evan's departure, the bell above the door sounded. Hanna did not recognize the plump, middle-aged woman dressed in country clothes who came in.

The woman scanned the dispensary, looking lost. "This used to be a grocer."

"Yes, but as you can see, it is now a dispensary."

"Yes," she answered, a troubled expression on her face. "This is a mistake. I am sorry to bother you."

"It's no bother." Hanna went toward her. "I am Miss Zaydan. Can I assist you?"

"I don't mean to intrude." One of her hands worried the fabric of her skirt, fingers clenching and releasing fists full of fabric. "I am Mrs. Florence Gould."

"How may I be of help, Mrs. Gould?"

"I am looking for my sister."

"Your sister?"

"Mrs. Lockhart. Claudia Lockhart. This used to be her grocer."

Hanna's heart contracted. "I am sorry." She paused, trying to find the appropriate words. "Your sister . . . erm . . . she became ill."

"I know Claudia is dead," the woman said with a kindly expression. "But I cannot find where she was buried. I hate the thought of her in a pauper's grave."

"The matron at the hospital where your sister died said Mrs. Lockhart's family came for the body."

"The late Mr. Lockhart's family had no interest in

seeing to my sister—in life or death. And we, Mrs. Lockhart's blood family, have asked the hospital where her remains can be found, but no one seems to know. Or if they do, they refuse to tell us." Tears filled the woman's ruddy face. "I don't know what else to do."

Hanna came to a decision. "I will try to help you."

"You are so kind." The woman's face brightened. "But what can you possibly do?"

"An acquaintance of mine sits on the hospital's board of governors." After tomorrow's commission hearing, she would approach Griff on the matter. "I believe he can be persuaded to look into it for us."

THE COMMISSION MET in the same room as before. Hanna was jittery, unable to get her nerves under control. But she managed to force herself to remain still and expressionless. Evan accompanied her as before, only this time there was a distance between them. Anger and disappointment radiated from him.

Griff, sitting across the room from them, offered an encouraging smile. He looked very dashing in a blue checked double-breasted tailcoat that brought out the color of his eyes.

As they waited for the hearing to start, she observed the others in attendance. Mansfield sauntered in behind his father. Hanna's gaze landed on a somewhat familiar face. Mr. Lockhart, the nephew of Hanna's benefactor. He inclined his chin in her direction, no doubt eager for the commission to rule unfavorably so that he could claim the dispensary space.

So many people of influence were working against her, determined to see her fail. Hanna's pulse slammed in her throat. Panic threatened. But she forced it down by reminding herself that she too had powerful forces on her side.

One of them, the Marquess of Brandon, entered once almost everyone else was seated. He wore a harsh expression and black wool perfectly tailored to his sinewy form. Brandon nodded curtly to Hanna, then did not look in her direction again. Her cousin was an enigma. A man of position and influence in the upper echelons of society. Yet also one of them. The son of an Arab-merchant mother.

Griff spoke first, describing the terrible pain he'd been in and how Hanna had alleviated his severe discomfort. He moved his arm, demonstrating the range of motion he'd regained since his treatment at the hands of the bonesetter.

Mrs. Rutland came next. William, her son, was not with her. But Griff's sister spoke in detail about how easily Hanna had put the boy's finger back in after it was dislocated.

Once she completed her testimony, a commission member asked Dr. Pratt to give his professional medical assessment of what he'd heard.

"I know Lord Griffin truly believes that Miss Zaydan cured him." He spoke in an even tone. "But my medical opinion is that the injury healed on its own, as I and other physicians told him it would. As to Mrs. Rutland, she took her son to see Miss Zaydan on the very day his finger was injured. In all likelihood, it was just bruised and would have healed on its own in a day or two. I regret to say that, on the basis of these two accounts, I am not convinced Miss Zaydan is not a danger to her patients."

"Let's have the final patient." Brandon impatiently gestured. Mrs. Peele came in.

Dr. Pratt's eyes rounded. "Mrs. Peele? This is most irregular."

"Do you know this woman?" Brandon asked.

"Indeed I do." Dr. Pratt's face flushed. "This is my housekeeper."

Brandon turned his attention to Mrs. Peele. "Please do come in, and tell us why you went to see Miss Zaydan."

Mrs. Peele cast a worried glance at her employer before she spoke. "My girl Annie had a curved spine. All of the doctors said there was nothing to be done for her. That her affliction was permanent."

"I see," Brandon said. "And was Dr. Pratt among the doctors who said there was no cure for your daughter?"

Mrs. Peele avoided looking in the doctor's direction. "Yes, sir, he was."

"Do tell us what occurred when you went to see Miss Zaydan."

"She said Annie could be healed. She massaged and pressed and pulled. She somehow managed to manipulate my Annie's spine."

"And how is Annie today?"

Mrs. Peele beamed. "See for yourself."

The door opened, and Annie marched in dressed in her Sunday best, walking straight and tall with a proud expression on her face. The room erupted. Everyone seemed to talk at once. A couple of physicians on the commission left their seats to examine Annie more closely.

"It is nothing short of a miracle," said one a few minutes later. "I have never known a curvature of the spine to be corrected."

"I have seen enough." Brandon spoke in a bored tone. "Obviously, Miss Zaydan should be allowed to continue to heal the patients that doctors cannot."

After a bit of discussion, a majority of the other commissioners concurred with Brandon's assessment. Hanna barely registered what happened next. There was a whirlwind of chatter. Lord Payton protesting. Mansfield cursing. Lockhart making an exclamation of unhappy surprise. All of her disappointed detractors made their voices heard.

Then Brandon spoke again, and before Hanna fully comprehended what was happening, the meeting adjourned. And, by some miracle, she was still a bonesetter with the ability to practice in London.

A small group crowded around her. Griff, Mrs. Rutland, Mrs. Peele and Annie all offered heartfelt congratulations.

"I can barely believe it." Hanna was stunned. "I never expected to get a fair hearing."

Mrs. Peele beamed. "Now you can continue to help people like my Annie."

Dr. Pratt approached them. Hanna tensed, but he did not even look at her. "Mrs. Peele," he said.

Mrs. Peele paled. "Yes, Doctor. I was just on my way home to see about supper."

"Don't bother. Your services are no longer needed." He walked away without sparing another glance for any of them.

Mrs. Peele appeared on the verge of tears. "I knew he'd be angry. But I had to tell the truth. He's known Annie since she was born." Her chin quivered. "I thought maybe he'd be happy she was cured."

"Mrs. Peele," Griff said. "I am in need of a house-keeper. I hope you will consider accepting a position at Haven House."

Mrs. Peele did burst into tears then. But at least they were tears of happiness. After a few minutes of chatter, they all walked out together, except for Evan. Hanna had no idea where he'd gone, but she was relieved to be free of his pouting. Mrs. Rutland, Mrs. Peele and Annie said their goodbyes.

"Congratulations," Griff said once all of the others had gone.

"This would not have happened without you." He was the one who'd brought Annie to her and convinced Mrs. Rutland to testify on Hanna's behalf.

He cast an admiring glance at her. "Your skills speak for themselves."

"Only as long as a viscount and his sister do as well."

"The world is unfair to those born to different circumstances than mine."

"Mucking around with the middle classes has afforded you some perspective, has it?"

"Serving in the army helped broaden my horizons. As have you."

She examined him. "How are you really?"

"I am coping. It's a relief to finally know what happened to my parents. But hearing Palk's confession has also made the tragedy feel fresh again." He gave a rueful look. "Consequently, I am grateful for any diversions that come my way."

She hesitated. "Well, as long as you are interested in being distracted, I happen to have one for you."

His eyes blazed. "No one can divert me as ably as you."

"It's nothing like that," she admonished. "Mrs. Lockhart's sister came to see me today."

He cocked an ear. "And who is Mrs. Lockhart?"

"The grocer who left me the space for the dispensary."

"Ah, I see."

"Mrs. Lockhart's sister cannot find where her sister is buried. The family is eager to give Mrs. Lockhart a proper burial."

"How can I help?"

"The hospital has not been forthcoming about the whereabouts of Mrs. Lockhart's remains."

"And when did Mrs. Lockhart die?"

"Several weeks ago. Do you suppose that, as a member of the board of governors, you could use your influence to learn what became of the body?"

"Certainly. I might as well do so now, as long as I am already here." He paused, casting an inquiring look at her. "I don't suppose you'd care to accompany me? Having you along could be helpful since you know more than I about this Mrs. Lockhart and her ailment."

THEIR EFFORTS SEEMED certain to prove fruitless. Each clerk, physician or ward matron gave them blank looks before referring them to someone else.

While they spoke to a ward matron, an older man cleaning the floor moved closer to them. Every step seemed like an effort as if he pulled a great weight behind him. But the man's face was alert, his expression one of interest.

After an hour of unsuccessful inquiries, Hanna and Griff gave up and departed the hospital.

"That wasn't very helpful." Griff adjusted his hat. "I suppose I could force myself to ask Norman for help."

"There must be a process the hospital follows when people die. A place where they hold the bodies."

"Pssst. Yer Grace." The summons came from a narrow lane as they passed. Hanna recognized the floor cleaner from the hospital. She stopped.

As did Griff. "You work at the hospital," he said to the man. "I saw you there."

The older man nodded. "I knows what they does wiv the bodies."

"Do tell." Griff reached into his pocket and withdrew some coins.

"Not 'ere," the man said. "Could lose me job if they see me talking ter you."

They followed him back to the narrow lane.

"What is your name?" Griff asked as he paid the man.

"I'm Bartlow."

"Very well, Mr. Bartlow. Please tell us what they do with the bodies."

"If the families don't claim 'em right away, they sell 'em ter the gravediggers."

"Good lord," Griff said.

Hanna's stomach turned. Had Mrs. Lockhart been dissected? "How do you know?"

"Cuz I 'elps carry the bodies out. If yer poor over in that 'ospital, yer ain't gettin' a burial."

"But the woman we're looking for wasn't a pauper," Hanna said.

"Don't matter. When folks ain't claimed right quick, the docs sell 'em ter the body snatchers."

"The medical colleges *are* always on the lookout for bodies to dissect," Hanna said. It was a well-known problem in the medical community.

The man nodded. "There ain't never enough bodies. Someone's always buying. The Margate bodies go ter Thomas's."

Griff's brow knit. "Thomas's?"

"St. Thomas's Medical College," the man answered.

"Who decides which corpses go to the body snatchers?" Griff asked.

"Don't know." He leaned closer, the stench of hard work, body odor and unwashed clothes assaulting them. Hanna reflexively took a tiny step back. Griff remained in place. "Rumor 'as it that it comes from the top."

"Have you ever told this to anyone else?" Griff asked.

"Once. A long time ago, I told a toff who always 'ad a kind word. 'E was good to us. Made Dr. Pratt pay us fair."

"Did this toff do anything about what you told him?" Hanna asked.

"No, 'e ended up dead not ten days after I tole 'im. 'E and 'is missus. After that, I learned ter keep my mouth shut. Until now."

Griff blanched. "Why are you telling us now?"

"Because yer that toff's boy." His rheumy gaze held Griff's. "And I reckon yer Da would want 'is son ter know the truth."

Chapter Twenty-Seven

Griff strode away, eager to put as much space as possible between him and the hospital. And Norman. And the old floor cleaner whose shared confidence had led to his parents' murders.

The sun felt hot on his face, even though it was a brisk day. His stomach gurgled and burned into his chest, threatening to regurgitate its contents. He crossed into the park, barging along the path lined with benches and flowers that taunted him with their cheeriness.

"Are you all right?" Hanna hurried to catch up. "Slow down. Where are you going?"

Griff kept up his pace. If he stopped, he might fall apart. If he acknowledged the truth, he'd be forced to face the unimaginable. That he'd been betrayed by a person he'd loved, respected and admired. A man he'd trusted. Who'd made him feel protected. The irony of it made Griff want to tear up everything in his path.

"Griff!" The words were breathless. "I cannot keep up with you. I'll trip over my skirts."

Griff stopped abruptly and bent over with his hands

on his knees. Hauling in long, deep breaths, he fought to get ahold of his emotions.

"That could not have been easy to hear." Concern filled Hanna's voice as she reached him.

"It was Norman. Norman killed my parents." The last word came out on a sob.

She guided him to a nearby bench. "Here, come sit."

Griff couldn't stop shaking. "That whoreson killed my parents."

She sank next to him. But not too close. "We don't know that. Fred Palk confessed to the crime."

"Yes, he did. Probably because Norman paid him off. Maybe that's why the Palks can afford to move away from Wapping. Perhaps Norman feared we were getting too close to the truth and made sure any evidence of his connection to the murders disappeared."

Her voice was gentle. "Can you tell me why you believe Dr. Pratt is responsible?"

"The journal."

"What about it?"

"Don't you see? We assumed the reference to Thomas's was related to me. What if it's not? What if Father was referring to St. Thomas's Medical College? The place that received the bodies from Margate."

Hanna closed her eyes and slowly repeated the words from the journal entry. "*I am alarmed by what I've learned about Thomas's* ▓▓▓▓▓▓. *Norman must be brought to account.*"

"What if the word that was scratched out held no meaning?" Griff pressed. "We attached significance to it, but maybe it was just an irrelevant mistake Father marked out while he was writing."

She paled. "But I thought Dr. Pratt was in Town when your parents were attacked."

"Norman probably did hire Fred Palk, the clerk's father, to do the job for him." He sat back against the bench and tilted his head back, staring into the cloudless sky. "Fred Palk lied. He didn't encounter my parents by accident. Norman dispatched him to Ashby to kill them."

Hanna inhaled sharply. *"Ibn al kalb."* Contempt laced her words. "What a filthy son of a dog."

"That man comforted me. Housed me. Fed me." Bile rose up into his throat. "He constantly reassured me that I was in no way responsible for my parents' deaths. I was so grateful for his complete faith in me."

"I cannot fathom it. He is truly evil."

Griff bolted to his feet.

"Griff, wait," Hanna called out. "Where are you going?"

"To finish what my father started." He stormed down the path, leaving her behind.

This was something he had to do on his own.

"NORMAN! NORMAN!" GRIFF's bellow echoed through his former guardian's house.

He came in through the unlocked front door. The house was quiet except for the tread of Griff's boots as he checked Norman's study and then the empty kitchen. Mrs. Peele wasn't here. Neither was Annie.

Had they cleared their things out of the house in just a matter of hours?

Griff had gone to Wapping to see Fred Palk again. But the Palks had already moved away. The neighbors didn't know where they'd gone. Griff then returned to the hospital only to learn Leonard Palk had recently left his position. No one at Margate knew anything about the young clerk's whereabouts. But Norman would know. Griff felt it in his bones that his former guardian arranged for the family's sudden departure.

A quick search of Norman's house revealed that no one was home. Griff resolved to wait for the doctor. It would be their last encounter. But first he needed to hear the truth from Norman's mouth. The confirmation that the man had orchestrated his parents' murders, leaving Griff an orphan, an outcast from society and his own family.

He sank into an upholstered chair in the study. The spot where he'd enjoyed countless after-supper drinks and conversations with the man responsible for the deaths of his parents. There would be no more drinks or engaging discussions.

A sense of calm settled over Griff. As awful, as incomprehensible, as the reality was, he finally had the true and full answer to the question that had plagued him for fourteen years. *Norman*.

Death was too good for the blackguard. Griff would settle for nothing less than seeing his former guardian publicly disgraced. He'd watch Norman lose everything that meant anything to him. His position at the hospital.

His reputation. His standing in the medical community. And then, once his public disgrace was assured, his reputation reduced to tatters, Griff would see him hanged.

Griff tapped his booted foot impatiently against the old carpet as he waited. It was getting dark.

Where the devil was Norman?

HANNA LIT TWO lanterns as she waited for Annie and her mother to arrive. Mrs. Peele had sent word that Annie was in terrible pain, which surprised Hanna. The girl had been doing so well.

She stayed late at the dispensary waiting for them. Afterward, hopefully Griff would come by. He might want to talk after confronting Dr. Pratt. She shivered. She'd always despised the doctor, but she never could have fathomed how truly evil he was.

She pushed thoughts of Dr. Pratt out of her mind. Drifting across the dispensary floor, she took in her surroundings: the clean floors and neatly arranged examining tables, the organized chairs in the waiting area. The ramifications of the commission's decision were sinking in. This was her clinic. No one and nothing could take it away from her now.

Annie had left a basket of freshly laundered cotton cloths to be folded and put away in the morning. Hanna started folding the linens, neatly stacking them atop the commode table, to pass the time until the girl and her mother arrived. The bell sounded over the door.

"There you are." Hanna turned to greet Mrs. Peele and Annie. Her smile slipped when she saw who her visitor was.

"I suppose you think you've won," Dr. Pratt said.

She straightened. "If you are looking for Lord Griffin, he isn't here."

"You are the person I want to see."

"I don't have time for this. I'm expecting a patient."

"Annie and Mrs. Peele? They aren't coming." His smile chilled her. "I sent the note."

"Why?" Alarm tingled down her back. "Any business between us is concluded."

"You'd like to think so, wouldn't you?" He ambled toward her. "Everything was fine before you came into Griff's life. Your sort is ruining this city. Filthy foreigners."

"I was born in England. This is my home."

"Be that as it may, you'll never truly belong here."

"What do you want?"

"You've made many enemies."

"Any woman who speaks her mind is bound to make enemies."

"The commission refused to do what needed to be done." His face gleamed. He was sweating profusely. "I am here to take care of what the commission did not."

She put her shoulders back, determined not to show any fear. "Do you intend to harm me?"

"The owner of this building wants the land back. Mansfield and his father are eager to make you pay for dislocating Mansfield's wrist." He swiped perspiration from his upper lip with the back of his hand. "They'll be so pleased by your demise they'll no doubt donate generously to the hospital."

"You would physically harm me in order to secure new benefactors?"

"For the greater good. Absolutely." He jutted his jaw. "Margate needs the funds. I pour everything I have into the hospital, into helping people."

"Except for the very poor," she pointed out. "Or people without families. Those particular patients, you help to die a little sooner so you can sell their corpses to St. Thomas's."

"Ah, you figured that out, did you?" Something akin to admiration edged the words.

"Griff did. He knows everything." She fought to keep her voice from shaking. "And if something happens to me, he'll immediately suspect you."

"Maybe. But to the rest of London, it will appear to be a tragic accident—the dispensary burning down with the bonesetter inside." Dr. Pratt gave her a mocking smile. "Even if Griff suspects, he won't be able to prove I'm responsible. Our relationship is in tatters already. Thanks to you."

"I had nothing to do with it. Murdering his parents is what destroyed your bond with Griff." Hanna forced herself to stay calm and rational. The *ibn il-haram* stood between her and the door, effectively trapping her. She might get past the bastard, but what if he had a weapon? She needed an alternative plan.

"I didn't kill Jeffrey and Caroline," Dr. Pratt informed her. "I sent Fred Palk."

Goose bumps rose on her skin. "Griff was right about you."

"But I didn't expect Caroline to be there. Nor Griff. That *was* a tragedy."

"But slaughtering Griff's father wasn't?"

He lifted a shoulder. "I replaced Jeffrey as Griff's father. But I could not take the place of a mother. Caroline's death was unfortunate. Sadly, her husband's was absolutely necessary for the greater good."

"You've taken it upon yourself to decide who lives or dies based on what you perceive is best for society?"

"Someone has to."

"And you appointed yourself." Hanna couldn't believe she was having this conversation. It was like playing a scene with a villain straight off the Covent Garden stage. "I understand some doctors like to play God. In your case, it's actually true."

"Someone told Jeffrey that I was selling bodies. He confronted me and said he'd make certain that I paid for my supposed crimes." Light from the lantern caught the sheen of perspiration on his forehead. "The man just didn't understand the realities of life. If a few people have to die for the greater good, for the advancement of medicine, so be it. Do you know how many medical advances are made because of the scientific study associated with dissecting corpses?"

"Many."

"Exactly. I begged Jeffrey to give me one more chance to explain myself. I insisted we meet at Ashby, where we could have some privacy." He removed his spectacles and reached for one of the folded cloths. "Then I sent Fred Palk to do what needed to be done.

In exchange, Palk kept the jewelry he stole. And I employed his son as a ward clerk." He dragged the cloth down over his sweat-dampened face. "I recently paid for the entire family to leave London. To get them away from Griff and his infernal questions."

"Why did Fred Palk kill Lady Griffin?" Hanna fought to keep her wits about her, to keep from giving in to the horror engulfing her. "Why didn't he at least spare *her*?"

"Caroline tried to come to her husband's defense." He tossed the cloth onto the nearest examining table and resettled the spectacles on his nose. "Palk made a mess of the entire ordeal. I never meant to completely orphan Griff. I've always been fond of the boy."

"You have a strange way of showing it." She edged back away from him. "How did Palk get into the house?"

"There was a faulty window in the music room. I told Palk where it was."

"Yet you allowed Griff to believe the killer came in through the side door he'd left unlocked." Rage knotted her throat. "How could you be so cruel?"

A wild light gleamed in the doctor's eyes. "I couldn't exactly tell him the truth, could I?"

Hanna's stomach turned. But she forced herself to remain calm. "I need a drink to steady my nerves. Can I pour you one?"

"This is not a social call, in case you have not noticed."

"I assure you that I have noticed. That is why I would like some whiskey." In reality, she did not consume spirits of any kind, but Dr. Pratt wouldn't know that. "I need to settle my nerves."

"Very well. It sounds like we could both use a drink."

Evan stowed whiskey in the bottom desk drawer in the office. The dispensary was now almost completely enveloped in darkness. Hanna reached for a lantern to illuminate the way. She contemplated throwing the lamp at him while she made her escape.

But Dr. Pratt snatched it up. "Allow me." The words were laden with contempt. The flame flickered as the lantern swayed.

He followed her back to the office. With trembling fingers, she took out the whiskey and poured them each a glass. She inched closer to Dr. Pratt and offered the drink, positioning herself so that he'd have to straighten his arm to take the whiskey.

When he did, Hanna seized her chance. She dropped the glass, letting it crash to the floor, and grabbed Dr. Pratt's forearm with both of her hands.

He stumbled backward, struggling to wrest his arm away. To shake her off. "Get away from me, you bitch."

But Hanna was strong. Thanks to years of yanking people's bones and joints into place. And, although Dr. Pratt didn't realize it yet, she already had him at a disadvantage.

Grasping his wrist in her left hand, she quickly slid her thumb under his palm and tugged his arm toward her to keep it straight.

"Unhand me," he bellowed, trying to maneuver away.

"I don't think so." Hanna stepped closer, twisting his arm until she was by his side, pushing down above his elbow, putting all of her body weight and as much strength as she could muster into the action. The awkward position of his arm and shoulder forced Dr. Pratt to bend over at the waist, his arm high up in the air. He was in pain and at Hanna's mercy.

She had none.

Using her body weight and exerting all of her strength, she pushed down on his arm above the elbow until she heard the crack.

Dr. Pratt collapsed to the floor with a scream of agony. Just as she'd expected. However, she had not accounted for the lantern, which he threw across her desk, igniting a stack of Baba's files that Hanna had yet to put away.

Fire exploded on the desk, fueled by the ledgers. The flames jumped to the woodwork. Hanna rushed to Dr. Pratt. "Get up," she said urgently. "We have to get out of here."

Pratt was still moaning. "What have you done to my shoulder?"

"I dislocated it." She tried to haul him up. "Come along!"

He grabbed onto her and yanked. She tumbled down on top of him. "You'll burn here with me, you Arab whore."

Coughing, her eyes burning, Hanna blindly tried to kick Dr. Pratt away. He held on tightly to one of her legs. The heat licked her face. An image of Griff flashed in her mind. Sorrow filled her. Would she ever see him again?

"You might as well stop fighting," Dr. Pratt yelled

as the flames raced toward them. "We're going to die together."

"Iniqbir!" she snarled, telling him to go bury himself in his grave. *"You* do not get to decide when *my* story ends." With her free leg, she kicked as hard as she could, aiming for his dislocated shoulder. He recoiled from the contact, howling in agony as he lost his grip on her.

She scrambled away on her hands and knees, the smoke blinding her. She jumped to her feet and ran straight into a wall. No, not a wall. A man.

"Hanna!" Griff yelled. "Thank God. Let's get you out of here."

"Dr. Pratt is there on the floor."

"We're getting you out first. Let's go!" The smoke searing her lungs, Hanna and Griff clung to each other as they stumbled toward the exit. They burst out onto the street, and Hanna fell to her knees, coughing and gulping in the fresh outside air.

"Mr. Rafi is still inside," a panicked female voice shrieked. It was Lucy.

Hanna regarded her in disbelief. "He's not in the dispensary."

"He *is,* miss." Desperation stamped the young woman's face. "He ran straight inside to save you."

Hanna let out a sob as she stared at the flames engulfing the dispensary. "No!" She struggled to her feet. "Rafi!" She had to get to her brother.

"Stay." Griff commanded. His eyes met hers and held for just a moment. Then he turned and ran back into the burning building.

Chapter Twenty-Eight

*H*anna watched helplessly as the blaze spread until it engulfed the entire three-story building.

The residents in the upper apartments had gotten out. But there was no sign of Griff or Rafi. Smoke billowed from the building in thick gray-black clouds. Flames shot out of the windows. Heat radiated from its walls.

Panic welled up inside Hanna, tears gathering in her eyes. How could anyone survive the inferno?

"There they are!" Lucy shouted as Griff emerged, half-dragging, half-carrying Rafi's limp body. Hanna raced over to them.

"Rafi." Hanna sank to her knees by her brother. His eyes were closed, his face covered in soot. "Can you hear me?"

Rafi's eyelids fluttered. "*Yalla*," he croaked. "Let's go home."

Her laugh came out as a sob of relief. Griff and Rafi were both safe.

"*Yalla*," she repeated, tears blurring her vision. "Let's go home."

"How is he?" Griff asked Hanna as she closed the door to her brother's bedchamber an hour later.

"The physician is examining him now." She appeared utterly exhausted. Although she'd wiped her face, black streaks smeared her chin and by her ear. She'd carelessly pulled most of her hair into a low bun, but some strands fell liberally about her cheeks. There were dark smudges under her eyes. Still, she was the most sublime sight he'd ever beheld.

Hanna gave him a grateful look. "Thank you for sending the Duke of Huntington's personal doctor."

"I could hardly send my own. Come and sit." He guided her to the narrow set of stairs that he assumed led to an attic. "You look as if you're about to fall over."

She sank onto the stairs. "It has been quite a day."

"I am sorry about the loss of the dispensary. I know how important it was to you."

"I can always return to Papa's office."

"I am rather fond of your father's office. It reminds me of the first time we met. Your fierce competence seduced me in the first five minutes."

"You didn't show it. All I saw was your disdain." She scrubbed a hand down her face. "I am disappointed about the dispensary. But we are alive. You, me and Rafi." She swiped away a tear. "When you vanished into that building, I thought you weren't coming out."

"It would take more than a fire and murderous cousin to keep me from returning your brother to you." He settled next to her. It was a tight squeeze. They were hip to hip, his body heat intermingling with hers. "Did Norman hurt you?"

"No." She managed a sly smile that flooded him with warmth. "*I* hurt *him*. I dislocated his shoulder before he could . . . do whatever it was he intended to do to me."

Griff guffawed. "Norman never did realize he was no match for you."

"He admitted it all, you know, about your parents."

Dread settled in the pit of his stomach. She took his hand. He held on to her, accepting the strength and comfort she offered, despite everything she'd been through. "Tell me."

"Your father confronted Dr. Pratt about selling corpses to St. Thomas's. Dr. Pratt begged your father to meet him at Ashby to discuss the matter. But Dr. Pratt never went. He sent Fred Palk to Ashby instead."

"So that much was true. Fred Palk did kill my parents."

"Yes. And he did not get in through the door you left unlocked. Dr. Pratt told him about a faulty window."

"Truly?"

"Yes." She squeezed his arm. "Truly."

"It wasn't my fault." All of these years, the guilt had been a vise clamped hard around his chest. At last, Griff could draw a full breath.

"Norman keeping me away from my sisters makes perfect sense now," Griff said. "They were determined to find my parents' killer, while Norman discouraged me from dwelling on the murders."

"He must have been afraid of what you would find. Dr. Pratt knew the search would lead straight back to him."

Memories of Griff's interactions with Norman came flooding back. "Norman consistently pushed for me to use laudanum to ease the pain in my shoulder. Now I wonder if he did that in hopes of rendering me insensible."

"I can certainly see Dr. Pratt wanting to keep you dependent on him."

"But why did Norman go after you this evening?"

"He felt I'd come between the two of you. He also believed he could curry favor with Mansfield and his father by doing away with me."

"Norman was truly mad." He knuckled his burning eyes. "How did I never see it?"

"Your father grew up with Dr. Pratt, and he didn't see it. He was the head physician at one of London's largest charity hospitals, and no one on the board saw through him."

"If he had hurt you, I don't know what I would have done." He stroked her hand. "Thank goodness I decided to come and see you at the dispensary. I wanted to talk after everything we learned today. I cannot even begin to contemplate a world without you in it."

Norman was gone. His sisters were back. The mystery of who killed his parents was solved. But the overwhelming emotion in Griff at the moment was profound gratitude that he hadn't lost Hanna on this night.

He could not bear the thought of ever being deprived of her company again.

"Oh, Griff." She leaned into him. He put his arm around her shoulders and drew her close. "What are we going to do?"

"We will figure it out," he said resolutely. "I promise."

"GRIFFIN." SELINA POURED her chocolate. "You are unfashionably early. What is so dire that you saw fit to interrupt my morning meal?"

Griff burst in on Selina having breakfast in her private upstairs sitting room. He couldn't wait a moment longer to put everything to rights—which started here with his old friend.

"I apologize for the intrusion but I could not rest until we settle matters between us."

Interest blazed in her clear blue eyes. "We agreed not to see each other for six weeks."

"Actually, *we* did not. *You* set those terms. But I did agree to abide by them."

"What has changed?"

"Everything." He joined her at the table.

"It is just as well that you are here." She buttered her toast. "I have made my decision. I will not marry you."

He stopped short. "Excuse me?"

"I already married one man I didn't love. I am not keen to make the same decision a second time." She sipped her chocolate. "That would be boring, don't you think? And I hate to be boring."

"Why do I get the distinct impression that you never intended to marry me?"

"You are so stubborn that I insisted on the six-week period to give you enough time to recover your senses."

"But what if I had still insisted on marrying you after the six weeks?"

"I would have turned you down flat. The first time I obeyed my parents and married to gain a title and wealth." She set her cup down. "Now that I have both, if I marry again, it will be for love."

"But you do care for me."

"Of course. But we love each other as friends. Not lovers." She picked up her toast. "Now, why don't you tell me why you are here."

"I needed to hear your decision."

"Now that you have, you can pursue your interest in the bonesetter." She took a bite of toast.

He gaped at her. "Is it that obvious?"

"Perhaps only to your oldest and dearest friends."

"There was a fire at her dispensary last night. I almost lost her."

Concern lined her delicate brow. "Is she well?"

"Yes, but her brother was hurt."

Selina stopped chewing. "Rafi? Erm . . . Mr. Zaydan? What happened?"

"He went in to save his sister but was knocked down by some falling debris. Fortunately, I managed to get him out of the building. He's going to be fine."

"That is fortunate." Selina resumed chewing.

He eased back in his seat, pleased to have Selina returned to him as a friend and confidante rather than a potential wife. "Aren't you going to tell me what a fool I am for wanting to wed a bonesetter from a family of Arab merchants?"

"Not at all." She delicately dabbed at the corner of

her bow-shaped mouth with a white linen napkin. "I can see the appeal."

"Last evening, there were a few moments there when I thought I might die. It made me realize what a fool I've been not to fight for a future with Hanna. Even though she still might not have me."

"You're a viscount. I doubt it will be much of a battle to win your beloved's favor. Especially now that I am out of the running as a potential bride."

"You would think so, wouldn't you?"

"It is not every day that a girl in her circumstances is pursued by a wealthy, young and tolerably handsome viscount."

"Her family does not approve." He toyed with the silverware on the table. "They want her to marry one of her own kind, an Arab from her community."

She laughed out loud.

"What is so amusing?"

"That a merchant family would consider *you* not good enough for their daughter. Meanwhile, fashionable society believes all of London revolves around us."

"It never occurred to me, before Hanna enlightened me, that her family would be against the match."

"It is always amusing to see a peer brought down to size. What a rarity."

He snorted. "You really are enjoying this far too much."

"Is that possible?"

"Aside from her family, Hanna herself has repeatedly said she never intends to wed. She is devoted to being a bonesetter. But I have reason to believe her position on the subject of marriage might be softening."

Selina sipped her chocolate. "Do tell, how exactly do you intend to win the woman?"

The idea had come to him that morning. "I will make her an offer that she cannot refuse."

"How intriguing."

He came to his feet. It was time to set his plan in motion. "I hope Hanna thinks so, too."

AFTER THE DOCTOR departed just before dawn, Hanna returned to her room to sleep for a few hours. When she woke, it was late morning. She dressed and went directly to check on Rafi.

She found him propped up on a pillow, bare-chested with the white bedclothes tucked neatly around his waist. Lucy had planted herself at his bedside to feed Rafi spoons full of *freekeh*, a chicken broth-based soup made with cracked green wheat that *Citi* firmly believed cured all ailments. Since *freekeh* was delicious, Hanna and her siblings embraced the remedy.

While spooning out soup, Lucy's starry-eyed gaze drifted over Rafi's bare chest. He was slender, too slender, but that didn't keep Lucy from admiring his wiry form.

"I see Lucy is taking good care of you," she remarked.

"The best." Rafi winked good-naturedly at Lucy. "That's enough soup. Thank you."

"Are you sure, sir? There's more." The girl did not

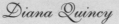

hide her disappointment at being dismissed in the midst of enjoying the view.

"I'm certain."

Lucy dawdled as she reluctantly rose and left the room, soup bowl in hand. Hanna took the chair by Rafi's bedside.

"You look good."

"That's what all the girls say." His voice was hoarse.

"I see your ego wasn't injured."

He laughed. The sound was raw. "I am sorry about your dispensary."

Hanna swallowed against the rough feeling in her throat. "I'm grateful we're all alive."

"Still, you worked so hard, and the dispensary was only open for a few weeks before it burned down."

"It does feel unfair. Especially after the commission ruled that I could keep the clinic open. But it cannot be helped." The enormity of that part of her loss was just beginning to sink in. "I can always go back to seeing patients in Baba's office." But that felt like such a setback after the heady feeling of running her own dispensary.

"Your viscount was here."

She nodded. "Yes, last evening. He sent the Duke of Huntington's doctor to tend to you."

"He was also here not long ago."

"Griff was? Here? Today?"

"He left about an hour ago."

She felt a rush of disappointment at having missed Griff's visit. "That was good of him to check up on you."

"He was obviously disappointed not to see you."

"He saved your life, you know."

"I am aware. He left a note for you."

"Griff did? Where?"

"It's on the dresser."

"I see." Hanna forced herself not to bolt across the room to read Griff's message. "How are you feeling, really?"

"I am fine. I need to rest. Now you can stop pretending you are not dying to see what's in the note."

"I'm not dying." She jumped up. "But I am eager to read it." She unfolded the paper and read Griff's note. "He wants me to meet him at the hospital in an hour."

"For what?" Rafi asked, but the knowing expression on his face suggested he knew exactly what was going on.

"You're a terrible liar."

"What did I say?"

"Nothing. But that smug expression on your face says it all."

"Go on, then. Go see your viscount."

She left him and, on her way out to meet Griff, stopped by the front salon.

"How is your brother?" *Citi* asked. The early-afternoon light filtered into the room.

"He just finished eating your *freekeh* soup, so he'll be dancing the *dabke* in no time." Hanna took the seat nearest to her grandmother. Her thoughts were all over the place. The fire had shaken up her perspective on the world. She found herself considering options she would never have entertained before the blaze. Very impractical options.

"The doctor said Rafi will recover fully," she told her grandmother. "He just needs to rest."

"Yes." *Citi* sucked on her hookah, relief etched in her face. "Thanks be to God." She peered at Hanna. "You don't look good." *Citi* was always honest.

"I only slept for a few hours. I was up all night with Rafi and the doctor."

"The *hayee* is dead?"

"The snake? Oh, you mean Dr. Pratt. Yes, I suppose."

"Your *ajnabi* saved Rafi."

Hanna nodded, her throat swelling. She'd never forget the sight of Griff pulling her brother from the building. She'd also never forget the abject fear she felt when she thought she might never see Griff again.

"About the viscount," she began. "I don't want to disappoint you, *Citi.*"

"Then don't," *Citi* said in Arabic. Having deep and meaningful talks were not *Citi*'s way. They embarrassed her. As did any show of emotion.

"I've begun to reconsider things in my life, the choices I've made. Or will make."

Citi did not ask Hanna what she meant, but Hanna saw understanding flicker in the old woman's face. She stared at her granddaughter for what seemed to be a long time.

Finally, the old woman shrugged. "*Indari, Citi.* I don't know. I am an old woman. In my time, we girls did what our family asked of us."

"Lord Griffin is the reason Rafi didn't die in that fire."

"When someone saves your loved one's life, he

becomes like family. We owe him." *Citi* took a long inhale on her hookah. "And you are very old. Much too old to marry a nice Arab boy. Or anyone else. Probably no one else will have you."

Hanna's lips quirked. "I'm sure you have the right of it."

"When I am dead, and your mother is gone, and your brothers are married with families of their own, it is better for you to have someone."

She rose and went to kiss her grandmother's cheek. "Thank you."

HANNA FOUND GRIFF'S valet waiting for her when she arrived at Margate.

"Good afternoon, miss. If you'll come this way." Felix led her to a section of the hospital on the ground floor that she'd never visited before.

"Where are we going?" she asked as they rounded a corner down a short corridor.

"His lordship is waiting for you." He stopped before a closed door and pushed it open. "Enjoy, miss," he added before walking away, leaving her standing alone.

She ventured inside to find a vast space, mostly empty except for a few scattered chairs. Like the wards she'd visited at Margate, this room possessed large windows and a hearth that was being lit by someone with a familiar face.

"Mr. Bartlow." She recognized the hospital worker who'd told them about the body snatchers and St. Thomas's. "What are you doing here?"

"G'day, miss." The older man straightened up. He wore clean clothing and had clearly bathed since she last saw him. "I'm working fer 'is lordship. That toff is like 'is Da. Looks after people who are beneath him."

"What sort of work will you be doing for him?"

He grinned, baring a smile that included several missing teeth. "I cannot say, miss. If you'll excuse me."

"Cannot say?" She watched him exit the room. "Why not?"

He smirked a little as he quietly closed the door behind him.

"Griff?" she called out, the sound echoing off the walls.

"In here." She followed his voice until she found him standing before a closed door. Her nerve endings tingled. He was freshly bathed, clad in a navy tailcoat of superfine wool with brass buttons and pale formfitting pantaloons.

"What was Mr. Bartlow doing here? He says he works for you. For that matter, why are *we* here?"

He grinned and pushed the door open. "See for yourself."

She went in. It was an office, freshly painted in the palest green, with a commanding mahogany desk and generous stone-colored window frame. A comfortable chair was by the window and a vase brimming with sunny fresh flowers adorned the side table. Hanna's gaze went to a drawing of a skeletal figure on the wall behind the desk.

Her eyes rounded. "It's the Bidloo." The one she'd

so admired in the private collection Griff had taken her to see.

She spun around to face him. "What's it doing here?"

Behind him, in the corner she spotted a familiar, life-size sculpture that took her breath away. It was the piece she'd appreciated most from the collection. The left half of the woman's body was a full-color wax skeleton, including muscles and ligaments. The other half was a living woman dressed in fine clothing.

"You remember her?" he asked. "You used her to show me the muscles and joints in my shoulder."

"Of course I remember her. She's magnificent."

He grimaced. "Beauty truly is in the eye of the beholder. In any case, I hope to have many more hands-on anatomy lessons in my future. Both pieces are yours."

Her eyes rounded. "They're for me?"

"Who else? I certainly don't want them. They'd give me nightmares if I had to stare at them all of the time."

"I cannot accept such expensive gifts from you."

"They are part of my wedding gift to you."

"Wedding gift?"

"If you agree to be my wife, of course. I've already spoken to your brother."

"Wait. What?" She struggled to keep up with the conversation. "You asked Rafi for permission to wed me?"

"Apparently my dragging him out of a burning building softened his stance on the subject. He said any man who would run into an inferno to please a woman should probably be allowed to wed her."

"Thank you for saving him."

"And then I had to face your grandmother."

She winced. "You talked to *Citi*?"

He nodded. "I believe she said something about you being far too old for any other man to want. Arab or otherwise." His steel-blue eyes sparkled. "She also intimated that I am a fool to marry a twenty-six-year-old woman when there are plenty of eighteen-year-olds to be had."

"That sounds like *Citi*." She crossed her arms over her chest. "If this is a proposal, it's not exactly the most romantic one I've ever heard."

"You are a practical woman. I thought you'd appreciate a practical proposal."

"Very well. Let's address the realities of our situation. I am a bonesetter. Even if my family will grudgingly accept you, *your* world will never accept me."

"My world didn't even accept *me* until about a week ago. I am well accustomed to being an outcast. I don't care about fashionable society. I never have."

"But I don't even know what a viscountess does. All I know is how to be a bonesetter."

"And the best one in all of London, at that."

"So where does that leave us?"

He took her hand and led her to the office door. "Right here."

She stared at the engraved nameplate affixed to the wood that she hadn't noticed at first. "What is going on? Why is my name on this door?"

Griff seemed terribly pleased with himself. "Because this is your office." He strode out to the empty larger space and spread his arms wide. "All of this is yours."

"What are you talking about? Has the smoke from the fire affected your mind?"

"The fire cleared my mind. And because of that, you are now standing in the middle of what will soon be Margate Hospital's new dispensary for the treatment of outpatients."

Her mouth fell open. "What?"

"Which will be run by you and"—he rolled his eyes—"Bridges, if you so desire. I've engaged Bartlow to help keep the place clean, run errands, that sort of thing. He's familiar with the inner workings of the hospital and could be an asset to you. However, if you'd rather choose your own staff, I'll find something for Bartlow to do at Haven House."

"No, it's fine for him to work here. But the board of governors will never allow me to open a dispensary here." It was an impossible dream.

"That's where you are wrong. I've already spoken with Brandon. With the two of us in agreement on this project, the rest of the board will go along. Naturally, we shall engage a new lead physician who agrees with our vision for Margate."

She surveyed the chamber, already imagining where the examining tables would go. "You want me to marry you and run a dispensary out of this space?"

He stepped closer, his loving gaze intent on her face. "I don't care whether you choose to call yourself

Lady Griffin or Lady Bonesetter. As long as I can call you mine, I shall be the happiest man in the world."

Tears welled in her eyes. "Oh, Griff."

"Will you make me the happiest man alive? When I thought I'd lost you, I was in anguish. But more than that, I was angry and furious at myself for wasting time. For even considering letting you go."

"I felt the same."

"You healed me. Not just my shoulder. But my heart. You were instrumental in returning me to my home, my sisters, my obligations. I was stumbling around in the dark up until that moment I first saw you in the coffeehouse."

"Do you truly think we can do this?"

"If I get out of line, you can always dislocate something on me."

"Never." She went to him. "I couldn't hurt you."

His strong arms closed around her. Their mouths met in a hungry yet tender kiss. "Say yes," he whispered in her ear. "Please. Don't ever leave me."

His humid breath tickled her ear and warmed her blood. "Yes. Oh, yes. I will stay with you. Forever."

"Thank you." His voice was full of relief. She felt his muscles relax. She tightened her arms around him, savoring his strength and warmth. Their embrace connected them from their chests, her breasts flat against his hard chest, all the way to their hips, where she could feel his erection pressing into her.

"Now, I'd like to go straight to that anatomy lesson." He kissed her as he walked her backward into the office and kicked the door shut behind them. "A very long, very slow and very leisurely anatomy lesson where we explore all of the important parts."

"Right here?" she said against his lips.

"Why not? There's the desk." He swung her up in his arms. "And we already know how to make excellent use of desks."

"We're in the middle of a hospital full of people," she said breathlessly as he laid her on the hard, cool surface. His warm hand slid under her skirts, feathering up her thigh. She shivered, goose bumps rising all over her skin. "What if someone walks in on us?"

He kissed her long and slow. "Just tell them the viscount made you do it."

Epilogue

$\mathcal{W}$here is Griff?" Hanna scanned the crowded public rooms at Ashby Manor. "I've been married less than an hour, and I've already lost my husband."

Mama stood by her side. "I still think you should have wed Nabeel. He's a good boy."

"Hanna." Her cousin Adel appeared beside her. "Or should I call you Lady Griffin now?" he asked with exaggerated loftiness.

"Feel at liberty to call me Princess," she teased back. It wasn't easy to hear above the spirited Arabic music flowing from the ballroom. "Who started playing Arabic music?"

"Khalo Adnan and Umo Sameer brought their oud and drums." Adel lifted his hands to face level and did an Arabic dance move, his pointer fingers swiping from side to side. "When the orchestra took a break, our uncles decided to fill in and provide music that really makes you move."

"I can just imagine what Griff's sisters will think." She moved through the crowd, accepting enthusiastic congratulations and kisses on both cheeks from her relatives.

"Lady Griffin." Someone came up from behind her.

It took Hanna a moment to realize that was her title now. After a pause, she pivoted. "Yes?"

Griff's sister Lady Dorcas embraced Hanna warmly. "I haven't had the chance to welcome you to the family."

"Thank you." She paused. "I realize I am not exactly the viscountess you envisioned for your brother."

"I never imagined anyone could make Griff as happy as you clearly do. And after everything he's been through, his contentment is all that matters." Her eyes twinkled. "Besides, I have four very active boys. Having a bonesetter in the family could prove useful."

"I hope your sisters will feel the same." Although Griff's older sisters had been scrupulously polite to Hanna, they were also cool and removed.

Lady Dorcas patted her shoulder. "Maria and Wini will come around once they see how happy you make Griff."

They parted, and Hanna made her way to the ball-room, where she discovered her cousins had started an energetic *dabke* dance line, the men leading at the head, women in the middle and the children still learning the steps bringing up the rear. Standing shoulder to shoulder, hands clasped with the people on either side of them, the dancers crossed the left foot over the right twice as the line moved, followed by a small hop.

Hanna's brother Elias, a skilled *dabke* dancer, headed up the line, controlling the tempo and sometimes breaking from the line to showcase more advanced moves. To her surprise, William, Griff's nephew, was at the end of the line with Hanna's youngest cousins attempting to learn the dance.

Hanna's eyes widened when she noticed another unlikely dancer in the line. Griff stood between two of her cousins near the front of the line. His eyes were fixed on other people's feet, as he awkwardly tried to copy the moves. "Griff is dancing?"

Mama, who had caught up with Hanna, tried not to look impressed. "If you had married Nabeel, you would have a husband who already knows how to *dabke*."

Hanna kissed Mama's cheek and went to join the line, cutting in so that she had Griff on one side and her cousin Amal on the other.

Griff squeezed her hand. "There you are."

"I couldn't exactly leave you on your own with my cousins. We can be a bit overwhelming to people who are unaccustomed to us."

She helped him perfect his footwork, calling out "Cross. Cross. Hop. Cross. Cross. Hop," until he got the rhythm. Soon they were both moving and laughing, perspiring and tired.

When the dance ended, he stole her away. "Let's get some air." He led her to the terrace. Hanna watched Rafi enter through another set of terrace doors farther down the ballroom. As they approached the terrace, Lady Winters slipped in from the outside.

"The bride and groom." Her eyes sparkled. "May I offer my congratulations once again?"

"You may," Griff said as they sidled past her. "We need some air. What were you doing outside, Selina?"

"Getting some air," Lady Winters said as she wandered off, "just like you."

"Come on"—Griff tugged Hanna along—"before someone stops us. We haven't been alone for a month."

Hanna craved his touch. "My family is very strict when it comes to allowing a betrothed couple to be alone together. Who knows what could happen?"

"We both know exactly what would have happened if you and I had managed to steal a moment alone together." He led her onto the terrace. It was a beautiful, clear night. The air was brisk.

"It's chilly out here."

He led her to a quiet, out-of-the-way corner and pulled her into his arms. "I'll warm you up."

She went willingly. "What if someone sees us?"

"They'll see a man desperate to kiss his wife." His mouth met hers, hungry and demanding. She molded her body to his and kissed him back with the same fervor.

"This party cannot be over soon enough," she said, pressing her lips against his jaw and nipping his ear.

"I agree." He caressed her breast, his lips at her décolletage. "How soon can we throw the guests out?"

She giggled. "We cannot."

The sound of a man clearing his throat was followed by the appearance of the butler, who kept his gaze focused on some distant point well away from Griff and Hanna.

"What is it, Wright?" Griff asked tersely.

"It is time to serve supper, my lord and my lady."

Griff groaned as his hand caressed the side of Hanna's neck, sending pleasure streaming through her. "Will this day never end?"

"The sooner we have supper, the sooner it will all be over," Hanna reminded him.

"Excellent point. We'll be in momentarily."

Wright bowed. "Very good, my lord."

"And Wright?"

"Yes, my lord."

"How many courses does Cook have planned?"

"Six, my lord."

"Serve the courses quickly. There's an extra few shillings for each member of the staff if supper is completed in under two hours."

One corner of the butler's mouth crooked upward. "I will advise them of your orders, my lord."

After the butler vanished into the shadows, Griff took Hanna back into his arms. She resisted. "We've got to get back to the guests. Or my mother will say I'm an eager bride."

"And that is a problem?"

"A bride is never supposed to appear eager for the marriage bed. People will think she's a harlot."

He released her. "I would not want to be on your mother's bad side. She might be even more formidable than your grandmother. But I have something for you before we go in." He drew something out of his pocket. A gold ring and sapphire necklace.

Hanna's breath caught. "Your mother's jewelry."

"Not anymore." He took her hand and slipped the

gold ring onto her finger. "This is inscribed to Lady Griffin, and you are the current holder of the title."

The ring was heavy on her finger. "It is beautiful."

"And this belongs to you as well." He slipped the sapphire around her neck. "It's been yours since the first time I saw you wearing it at the coffeehouse. It just took me a while to realize it."

"I shall have to think of an appropriate way to thank you."

"How about you wear nothing but the jewelry when I finally get you into bed this evening?"

She regarded him through her lashes. "I have other surprises planned for you tonight."

He stilled. "You do? Such as?"

She blushed despite herself, as she recalled sugaring her entire body. "There are certain ways an Arab bride prepares her body for her wedding night."

His eyes heated. "What ways?"

She demurred. "You will have to wait and see."

"You are going to kill me."

"We could always make supper a buffet."

"Excellent idea." He grabbed her hand. "Let's go, my love."

"What will you tell Cook when she finds out her glorious wedding supper is now a buffet?"

He grinned, slipping his arm around her waist. "I'll tell her the viscountess made me do it."

Author's Note

Bonesetters really were considered frauds in the early 1800s. People with dislocations often suffered for years because traditional medicine could not help them. The 1871 book, *On Bone-setting*, was very helpful to me in setting the scenes in which Hanna heals Griff's injuries.

Hanna's choice of a profession was inspired by Sally Mapp, a bonesetter who gained acclaim in the 1700s. Sally managed to thrive in a profession dominated by men. Her most famous case was when she fixed the spinal deformity of the niece of Sir Hans Sloane, a prominent physician and naturalist.

If you are wondering whether there actually were any Arabs in England during the Regency era, the answer is yes. Cotton goods produced in Lancashire were exported to the Arab world through Manchester. Directories show that, by 1798, there were four Arab trading houses in Manchester that were involved in cotton exports.

Special thanks go to my editor, Carrie Feron, who teaches me something about writing and storytelling every time we talk or exchange emails. I want to also express my appreciation to assistant editor Asanté Simons and everyone on the Avon team. And, I am always grateful to have my agent, Kevan Lyon, in my corner.

My friend, Megann Yaqub, reads everything I write and many of the story developments and ideas on these pages are the result of our brainstorming sessions. Joanna Shupe is a constant source of friendship and writerly support. I am overwhelmed by how generous and supportive Sarah MacLean is, not just to me, but to so many in the romance author community. And I could not have asked for a better release-day buddy than Sophie Jordan. And thanks to my friend, Faith Lapidus, for finding errors and typos that I missed.

None of these books would be possible without my husband Taoufiq's unflagging support. Thanks for having my back for all of these years.

Ultimately, it is you—the readers, bloggers, book-sellers and librarians—who make it possible for me to continue to do what I love. Thank you for taking time out of your days to spend a few hours with me via my books!